The Light of His Clan

The Light of His Clan

~

chetan raj shrestha

SPEAKING
TIGER

SPEAKING TIGER BOOKS LLP
125 A, Ground Floor, Shahpur Jat, Near Asiad Village
New Delhi–110049, India

First published in paperback by Speaking Tiger Publishing Pvt. Ltd 2016

ISBN: 978-93-85755-02-6
eISBN: 978-93-85755-03-3

10 9 8 7 6 5 4 3 2

This is a work of fiction. Names, characters, places and incidents are either the product of the author's imagination or are used fictitiously. Any resemblance to any actual persons, living or dead, is coincidental. The Chandanths are a people invented for the purposes of this novel. The names, places, customs, language, festivals and other attributes are imaginary and resemblances to any community and language are coincidental.

Typeset in Warnock Pro Light by SÜRYA, New Delhi
Printed at Sanat Printers, New Delhi

For my parents:
Chin Kazi Shrestha and Dorjee Ongmu Bhutia

In their spiritual habits and religious rituals, the people of the valley seem to have assimilated, perhaps intemperately, from the gods of the two animatedly fierce pantheons to the North and South—the Boodism of Tibet and the Hindooism of the Indian plains. These gods have co-mingled with the preexisting deities of the valley, hierarchies have been assigned and lineages constructed. The results, if one considers the statuettes being appeased at the Dhod temple, are iridescent and staggering to the inexpectant eye.

—Thomas Burney-Thrale
A Year amongst the Natives of Chyaloo, 1876
Chapter Four—Religious and Spiritual Customs

~

At Rakoo, we billeted at a hut beside the temple. When I asked the headman where its owner might be found, he pointed towards the east and said that they had chosen to have tired feet, a Chandari phrase often employed to describe those who leave the homes of their forebears. It struck me then that the owner of this house too had been part of the great movement towards Sikhim, a strategic exodus undertaken with the sanction of Calcutta.

—Thomas Burney-Thrale
A Year amongst the Natives of Chyaloo, 1876
Chapter Two—Geography and Landscape

Contents

YEAR 1

Mountain View

'Heard the latest?' Yograj stood at the door and waved a newspaper at his father.

The ex-Minister was sitting beside the window of the living room, looking out into the street. He asked, 'What now?'

Yograj handed him the newspaper and said, 'Your people.'

The ex-Minister took the copy of *Sikkim Everyday*, glanced at it, and smacked his forehead with it. 'That mule!'

The Vice President of CAS (Chandanth Action Society) had claimed that the Chandanths were the only people in Sikkim with a history of traditional shoes, the rest had all passed through history barefoot. He had challenged the other castes and communities of Sikkim to refute him on this. This was not the Vice President's first transgression. The previous year he had claimed that the Chandanths were historically responsible for bringing rice cultivation to Sikkim from Nepal, and who knew what everyone else had eaten before that. That controversy had taken some managing, especially after it was pointed out, by historians and laypeople, that one of the historical names of Sikkim—Denzong—translated into Tibetan as The Valley of Rice.

And now this. A portion of the blame would fall on the ex-Minister as well; as the President of CAS, he was the Vice President's superior. He considered his son, who looked eager to score a point. He said, 'He may have meant something else. Let me speak to him first.'

Then, before Yograj could answer, the ex-Minister asked, 'What are you doing at home? Shouldn't you be at the department?'

The ex-Minister was referring to the Department for Village Roads, where Yograj was pursuing a bill for a contract executed a year earlier. The bill had moved slowly for a year and, exhausted by the obstacles that the bureaucracy had put in its path, was now recovering on the Assistant Engineer's desk.

Yograj conceded. 'It's in the AE's office. Going there now.'

After his son's departure, the ex-Minister considered calling a meeting of his organization. There were other matters that needed discussion: Balidaan Diwas was coming up, and they needed to raise funds for their temple, under construction for eight years. The Core Committee usually met here, in the ex-Minister's living room. It was a long room, panelled with timber and with a shallow showcase at its end, which held the ex-Minister's awards, medals, certificates and citations.

The ex-Minister checked himself. The Vice President was an ally, and his remark had not yet provoked outrage. He would wait, perhaps there would not be a controversy, perhaps something more distracting would occur. Balidaan Diwas, the most important annual function for the Chandanths in Sikkim, was six months away, there was yet time to organize it.

Some tea would help, he thought, and shouted for Pemba. There was no response. He scanned Tibet Road—where his house was situated, in a fairly busy part of Gangtok—the street visible from his living-room window. He saw his servant standing beside the culvert which went past their locality. He looked abject. On the other side of the road, he saw the momo-seller who lived in a neighbouring building. Her arms were on her hips. Between them, vehicles and people passed, and children from Tiny Genius Nursery School were with their ayahs.

Pemba said, 'Return my money, Ai Doma.'

Ai Doma taunted him. 'Why should I return your money?'

Pemba sounded frantic. 'You took it from me, Ai Doma. You cheated me.'

'And Pemba, all the momos you ate from me for ten-fifteen years? Who's going to pay for that?'

The ex-Minister watched as Pemba looked into the culvert and turned towards her. 'Your momos have become shit and gone.'

The ayahs paused and giggled. Their wards copied them.

Ai Doma said, 'Ay Pemba, your money too has become shit.' She jogged to the edge of the culvert, stood next to Pemba, and pointed, 'It's in there. Look, look. There's the shit. Pick it up, that's your money.'

She walked back, affecting haughtiness. Pemba stared into the culvert, unmoved by his money's change of form. He said, 'Ai Doma. Let me feel your bum.'

Ai Doma squealed in practised outrage and broke into a run. The schoolchildren and their ayahs scattered as she advanced. She turned around and shook her posterior at him. 'Come and feel them.' Pemba moved towards her, she scampered up the stairs, shut a grilled gate and quickly locked it. Pemba considered the locked gate and shook his head in dejection. The ex-Minister shouted from the window. 'Ay Pemba! Enough. Come back inside.'

'Go Pemba go. Go to your old master,' Ai Doma said.

~

When Yograj returned home in the evening, the ex-Minister asked him, 'Any progress on the file?'

'You know what its position is,' Yograj said. 'The AE has been transferred. There's a new AE but she's on training and will join after a month. Some more waiting.'

Two years earlier, after Yograj had returned to Sikkim after his college studies in Bangalore, the ex-Minister had arranged for a contract for the construction of a village road in Tumin, an hour's drive from Gangtok. The deal was this: the ex-Minister would provide the initial investment, Yograj was to execute the project, and they would split the profits.

The work was done and the money had to be recovered. The interim payments had been exhausted and now only the final bill remained. It was for twenty-eight lakh and, allowing for the ex-Minister's outlay of eighteen lakh, still meant a profit of five lakh each.

'Don't forget that it's my money there,' the ex-Minister said.

Yograj said, 'Then tell your eldest son to help. He just sits in his office, pretending not to recognize me every time I go there.'

Pradeep DE was Yograj's half-brother and the ex-Minister's eldest child. He was also the Divisional Engineer at the Department for Village Roads, although not in the section that was appraising their bill. The ex-Minister knew of his uncooperativeness but because Pradeep DE was

Yograj's half-brother, he did not want to be seen as taking sides. Yograj continued, 'And you told him to change his nameplate a year ago. It's still the same. It still says "Pradeep Chandath" and not "Pradeep Chandanth".'

This he did not know. 'That gutless mouse!'

Chandath was the common spelling used by the Chandanths in Sikkim. It was one of their peculiarities that their names should have so many variants—Chandeth, Chandith and Chadit. To the ex-Minister there was only one standard name: the one he possessed. Everyone knew that Chandanth was derived from Chandan, after the sandalwood forests that ringed Chyalu, the valley of his ancestors' origins in north-western Nepal. And to think that his own son remained unconvinced!

Yograj started to dial Pradeep DE's number, but his father stopped him. 'No, not like that. There's another way.' He phoned Pradeep DE himself and said, 'You're coming here next week. Its Nehepau Doh on Wednesday, and Yogita is also going to be visiting.'

Nehepau Doh was a festival of the Chandanths, a day in which the rooster, sacred to them, was worshipped. It usually fell in the first week of March. Pradeep DE agreed. He had not visited Tibet Road for a while. After the call the ex-Minister told Yograj, 'Don't tell him anything. I'll fix him here.'

Three days later, Yogita arrived. It was her first visit to Sikkim in more than a year. She put her father's hands to her eyes in deference and scrutinized him for changes in his health. Then she walked through the house and proclaimed her disgust at the way the three men, Yograj, Pemba and her father, had begun to live. She showed them proof of their slovenliness: the floors were sticky, the wiping cloths stank, there were films of dust on all surfaces. She scolded Pemba and he said, 'Who told you to come back?'

She reported this to her father. He said, 'Who told you to leave?'

She spent the first day of her holiday supervising Pemba as he cleaned the house. She made him clean the kitchen, the corridors and the ex-Minister's room. She cleaned her room and the living room, where she dusted all her father's honours that filled the showcase. She decided that it needed glass panels to protect them from dust and, pleased with herself for having found a project, convinced her father that it was essential.

At Tibet Road, they observed Nehepau Doh. Yograj had sourced a rooster from a rural Chandanth family on the outskirts of Gangtok who bred the birds especially for purposes of prayer. The rooster was installed in the prayer-room overnight, worshipped by the ex-Minister in the morning, and the prayer-room sprinkled with fresh poinsettias. After the prayers, and after the morning meal was done, the bird was taken by Yograj and Pemba to Ranka, an hour away, and set free in the forest.

In the evening, Pradeep DE visited Tibet Road for a leisurely and acrimonious dinner. Yogita had cooked dishes unique to the Chandanths. She had made red rice, pork with mustard leaves, and a spicy paste of river fish. She had also taken especial care to make some mutton, a favourite of the ex-Minister. She had kept Pemba, whose cooking skills were unstable at best, out of the kitchen, and for this her family was grateful.

Pradeep DE put his father's hands to his eyes. He had come alone, his Mrs was away in Namchi, observing the festival with her family. The ex-Minister asked him, 'Why? She's too big to eat with us?'

'Nothing like that. You called me too late. She had promised her family.'

Yogita said, 'It's understandable. Next year, surely.' She served him.

Pradeep DE winced and turned to Yograj. 'How's the file moving? I spoke to the new AE. She seems smart.'

Yograj answered, 'How do you think it's moving?'

The ex-Minister said, 'If you had done your part, it would have been out by now.'

Pradeep DE raised a hand. 'Not my fault.'

The previous year had been filled with delays and disagreements. Yograj accused his elder brother of not helping enough, and was in turn accused of being tardy with paperwork. The ex-Minister sensed the start of an unresolvable discussion. 'Just help all you can.'

Yogita was used to this. She had never returned home to find amiability amongst her brothers and father. She made a valiant attempt to change the subject. 'We need a glass carpenter, for the showcase in the sitting room.'

As it turned out, a glazier had just finished working at Pradeep DE's house. 'I'll send him here tomorrow.'

The ex-Minister then undid Yogita's efforts. He pointed a finger at Pradeep DE. 'Your department is no better. Why haven't you changed your nameplate? Why does it still say Pradeep Chandath, you know it should be Chandanth. Why are you making yourself low?'

Pradeep DE explained, 'I've told them a long time ago. They said, it's just one "n". But I insisted. Still, it's the government, it'll take time. There are bigger matters besides one man's nameplate.'

'If it's there next time I come, I'll take it down myself.'

Pradeep DE remained unconcerned by the challenge. 'Please come and remove it. It's your government.'

A little later, he asked his father, 'You heard what your Vice President said? Are you doing anything about it?'

The ex-Minister's voice went low. 'What are they saying outside?'

'All sorts of things. That the Opposition may take a delegation to the Governor.'

Yograj motioned towards his father and said, 'He's waiting for it to take care of itself.'

The ex-Minister was defensive. 'It's one man's words. I'll call a meeting.'

Before he left, Pradeep DE repaid his younger brother's favour. He took his father aside and said, 'Yograj says I'm being unhelpful. Ask him what he does. Ask him who Julie Babuni is. That's why the bill is not moving. Not because of me.'

The next morning, the ex-Minister asked Yograj, 'So, not going to meet Julie Babuni today?'

Yograj was expecting this. 'Nothing happening there. She liked me more than I liked her.'

'Why?'

'She's not a Chandanth,' Yograj said.

The ex-Minister was unconvinced but pleased. 'Get the money out, then we'll find a good girl for you.'

The ex-Minister worried about the prospects of his younger children. They were motherless and young. He was eighty-two, with the soul of a father inside the skin of a grandfather. Anomalies in his life had meant that he had married Yograj and Yogita's mother late, and now, when he himself required care, he was meant to supervise their youths.

~

Shambhunath, the glazier recommended by Pradeep DE, arrived. To him the ex-Minister looked old and undistinguished but he was unsurprised. In this capital city which functioned like a large village, he had become used to the dissonances between a person's position and his appearance. Where he came from, a thakur looked like a thakur.

The ex-Minister asked, 'Are you free for the next two days?'

'Saar, what's the work?'

The ex-Minister led Shambhunath into the living room and to the showcase. Yogita had removed the honours and kept them aside. The glazier carried out his measurements.

'How many days?'

'It's just not glass. I have to make the frames as well and attach the panes. Sliding or folding?'

The ex-Minister wanted a sliding door. Yogita entered with a cup. She said, 'Appa, I've put less sugar in your tea.'

There was none for Shambhunath.

The ex-Minister sipped his tea and asked, 'So, what's your caste?'

Shambhunath said, 'Barbu caste, Saar.'

The ex-Minister had not heard of it. 'High caste or low caste?'

'Low.'

Yogita said, 'Appa! How many times have I told you that people don't ask such questions nowadays?'

The ex-Minister asked Shambhunath, 'Are you hurt?'

'No Saar.'

'See, he doesn't mind.'

The glazier finished his work in three days. At the end, the ex-Minister offered the glazier a choice. 'You want money or more work?'

Shambhunath said, 'Your wish, Saar.'

The ex-Minister explained, 'My nephew is building a hotel at Tashi Viewpoint. He needs a glass carpenter as well. If you won't take money now, I'll recommend you to him.'

Shambhunath looked unconvinced. The ex-Minister said, 'You think I'm lying? I'm going there tomorrow. I'll take you there with me.'

'Saar, there's one more thing,' Shambhunath said, 'Pradeep DE has not yet given my payment. He's your son, he'll listen to you.'

The ex-Minister said, 'He's a grown man. You're a grown man. Don't involve me in that.'

~

The trip to Tashi Viewpoint was Yogita's plan. It was her last day before she returned to Delhi to resume her work at an advertising firm, and she wanted to spend it outdoors. Nima Thendup, her cousin, had phoned her more than once to visit him before she left. They would leave after the morning meal, and while the ex-Minister readied himself, Yogita knocked, entered his room and sat on the bed. She said, 'You're not worried about my marriage?'

The ex-Minister grunted without turning. She said coyly, 'Should I start looking?'

The ex-Minister would permit no such thing. 'Don't look too hard,' the ex-Minister said. 'Unless he's a Chandanth, it's no use. You'll have to wait until I'm dead.'

And lest he be assaulted by her tears, the ex-Minister walked out of his room and made for the kitchen downstairs. He found that the glazier had arrived. Shortly before noon, they left for Tashi Viewpoint in a taxi. The settlements thinned as they gained height and reached the northern outskirts of Gangtok. It was distinctly cold; here, winter had not yet retreated.

The Hotel Mountain View Point at Tashi Viewpoint was five storeys high and located along the road to North Sikkim. It was painted yellow with monastic cornices of white, yellow and red cubes over the doors and the larger windows. The windows of the ground floor were complete with glass panes. The windows in the higher floors were timbered, but without glass, giving the building the appearance of an eyeless beauty. Shambhunath's spirits lifted.

They entered the lobby. There was some glass stacked on the side. The ex-Minister patted his shoulder. 'See, I told you! Lots of work.'

Nima Thendup, the ex-Minister's nephew, rushed out to meet them. He was the same age as Pradeep DE. He put the ex-Minister's hands to his eyes and said, 'Finally! My work is not work, I know.'

'I brought a glass carpenter for you.'

Nima Thendup inspected Shambhunath's unimpressive physique.

'Are you a Muslim?' he asked.

'No,' replied Shambhunath.

'Come from Monday and take what you earn at the end of every week.' The glazier nodded, and Nima Thendup added, 'And come barefoot. Only some people are allowed to wear shoes in Sikkim.' He looked at the ex-Minister and grinned.

So it *had* become a controversy.

The glazier left to measure the windows, and Nima Thendup gave the ex-Minister a tour of the hotel, 'Thirty rooms, all three-and-a-half star'. The ex-Minister said, 'So, people talking about the shoe business?'

Nima Thendup smirked. 'They're talking about nothing else. Everyone. Doesn't bother me, but your people should watch what they say.'

He resumed the tour of his hotel. They went upstairs, peeking into the rooms, in various stages of completion, busy with the shouts of workmen. A majority of the finishing work remained, and the opening was still a year away. The restaurant was operational though, and Nima Thendup took them to it.

The restaurant was sparsely painted and furnished but crowded with tourists. 'Didn't really want to open, but every morning people were knocking and asking for tea and momos.'

The tourist season was beginning, and Tashi Viewpoint offered a fine view of the Kanchanjunga range of mountains to its north-west. 'And something for Machi to do.' He was referring to his wife, Thinley Machi, who emerged from the kitchen. She was a plump woman, and her rotundity suggested cheerfulness. 'So busy, so busy,' she motioned to the tourists in the restaurant, 'tell them not to come and still they keep coming.'

The ex-Minister waited for her to take his hands to her eyes, but she did not. She only insisted that they stay for lunch for she was cooking beef noodles, the kind Yogita liked. Her daughter emerged from the kitchen and tugged at her bakkhu. 'The cook is eating without your permission.'

Thinley Machi mock-frowned and followed her daughter to the kitchen. Nima Thendup took them back to the lobby. He wanted to show them something.

The signboard had been delivered the previous day from Siliguri. It was large, the banner printed and pasted on a timber frame. The text was in cursive and set against a photograph of the mountains.

HOTEL MOUNTAIN VIEW POINT

GET LOST IN THE MOUNTAIN VIEW

Yogita said, 'You should just call it Hotel Mountain View. It sounds better. And write Lose Yourself in the Mountains.' Nima Thendup agreed that it sounded more amenable and said, 'So you are doing some good in the city?'

In the evening, the ex-Minister phoned members of the Core Committee of CAS, except for the Vice President. They had all heard, they were all worried. The Vice President's statement, recorded and transmitted from phone to phone, had drawn condemnation from all communities. Official delegations had visited the Hon'ble Chief Minister and there were rumours of punitive action against CAS. Everyone agreed that the situation demanded some control.

The ex-Minister told Yograj, 'The Core Committee is meeting soon. Here, in our house. You should be there.'

Yograj raised a finger and shook it. 'Leave me out of your caste politics.'

Yogita said, 'Not on my last day. Don't fight on my last day.'

~

The meeting of the Core Committee of CAS began in some agitation. The General Secretary, who was also the Secretary of the Tourism Department, said, 'I have a high-ranking job. I cannot afford all these controversies.' She had recently pacified a delegation of hoteliers who had complained against the remark, saying that it hampered the state's image as a harmonious one.

The Joint Secretary sided with the General Secretary. 'There are some things you say only at home but not in the street.'

The Vice President contemplated the floor. He was dressed, as always, in a kanchnaki, and wore a seytupi on his head. He was a politician known for his straight talk, a reputation he maintained with care. He said, 'I only repeated what all of us say here. Everyone here keeps pointing out that the Chandanths are the only people who have a traditional shoe, the gauto jutta.' He raised his foot so that they could see his shoe, made of leather and laced with a single strap.

The Joint Secretary snapped at him, 'But not in public.'

The Vice President played with the threads of his kanchnaki. He looked at the ex-Minister with repentance. The ex-Minister said, 'Enough, enough. Past is past. We should be more vigilant with our words. It was my fault. My theory.'

The Press Secretary said, 'But it is still true. No other caste has their own shoe. Everyone walked barefoot until the British came. I have explosive documents to prove it.' The Press Secretary's explosive documents were well known. He had an explosive document for everything—from the hidden aspects of Sikkim's merger with India to the last days of the previous Chief Minister—but his colleagues had never been granted the privilege of viewing them.

The Vice President murmured, 'I won't do it again.' He spoke in Chandari, in the language of their ancestors, to show the seriousness of his apology.

This pacified the committee. The Press Secretary said, 'I'll release a carefully worded statement. For the public.'

There was another, more serious matter. The Treasurer waved his hands for attention. 'They are saying this year's Balidaan Diwas won't be with CAS. That it will be organized by a Steering Committee and we have to be a part of it.'

Balidaan Diwas was the annual function commemorating the recognition of the Chandanths as a Backward Caste by the Government of India in 1997. The function, which took a full day, had been organized by CAS since the year of its inception.

The ex-Minister had heard of such rumours but was unconvinced. 'Nothing will happen. The others can't even wear their trousers straight.'

The General Secretary said, 'But still, if the HCM asks us, then we have to listen. She might ask us to be more cooperative.'

The ex-Minister said, 'We have always cooperated with those traitors. It is they who don't want to cooperate.'

A few days later, the Treasurer phoned the ex-Minister. 'President Saab. They were right. We're being asked to attend a Steering Committee meeting at DB Minister's bungalow in VIP Colony. Two weeks from today.'

DB Chandath was the Minister for the Village Roads Department, the department where their bill currently languished. Maybe some good would come of this.

The Steering Committee

On the day of the meeting of the Steering Committee, the ex-Minister predicted a hailstorm but, just like everything else in his life, no one listened to him. Yograj reminded him of it in the morning as he lay in bed, listening to the children from Tiny Genius Nursery School sing. It was a daily activity and their voices always carried to his house.

I love the pit-pit-patter of the raindrops,
I love the buj-buj-bujjing of the bees,
But the thing I love the best, the very, very best,
Is the way that God loves me.

Yograj entered his room and said, 'Make sure you talk to the minister about the bill.'

The ex-Minister looked out of the window. 'There's going to be a hailstorm. We may not be able to meet today.' He offered no evidence to back his prophecy, which he had made only to have the meeting postponed.

Yograj said, 'I'm going to the department today. I do my work, you do yours.'

The ex-Minister phoned the General Secretary but she scoffed at him. 'That is superstition. No time for it in modern life.' He phoned TB Chandath, the academic who had been appointed as the Steering Committee's Convener. Even he was uncooperative. 'It is the HCM's invitation. How can I say no? And I can give you a lift.'

The ex-Minister declined his invitation. He said, 'It's just a function.'

TB Chandath explained, 'It's not a function, Daju. It's a seminar.'

The ex-Minister terminated the call. He considered phoning Mitradas Chandith, president of CHAPS (Chandith Heritage Action Preservation Society) but a hailstorm was preferable to speaking with that traitor.

In a show of solidarity, he went with the Vice President. They discussed strategies and, at the beginning of the meeting, the Vice President stood up, adjusted his seytupi, and said, 'Sorry.'

Before he could be reprimanded, the ex-Minister said, 'I'm telling all of you there will be a hailstorm. Look outside!'

The members of the Steering Committee turned towards the window. The change in weather was alarming, they admitted, but Mitradas Chandith was not moved. 'Work is work.'

The ex-Minister snapped, 'Balidaan Diwas is months away. Why did we have to meet now?'

There were a few murmurs of assent. The meeting had been called too early. It was an inconvenience to be prepared so early. It only allowed all sorts of things to go wrong.

TB Chandath frowned. 'The HCM asked us to begin early. I only know that much.' He had prepared a list of discussion points for the day. He passed it around and it drew almost universal assent. The ex-Minister took a look and disagreed immediately. 'Why do we need so many culture dances? And who are all these speakers? Why aren't we allowed to speak?'

The ex-Minister looked around, seeking support, and found it. In previous years everyone had made speeches. For many, it was a highlight of their year. 'The HCM says we have to do things differently this time.'

The ex-Minister was not convinced. 'She says that every year.'

Mitradas Chandith rapped a side-table. 'What are you saying? Do you know whom you are insulting? She is the Chief Minister.'

The ex-Minister too rapped a side-table. 'No one is insulting anyone. All I want to know is, why hasn't the meeting started? We were called by the HCM. Why are we not in her residence or office? Why are we in her minister's house? And why isn't the minister here? And let such matters be debated by the senior organizations. This is CAS's fifteenth year.'

Mitradas shot back, 'And we all know what happened during those fifteen years.'

There was history between their organizations. Mitradas was the former General Secretary of CAS and had quit two years earlier after a tussle with the ex-Minister over the subject of lifelong presidential terms and the disappearance of funds. He had publicly called CAS, 'an organization of dacoits and bigamists' and formed CHAPS.

TB Chandath's frown slid into a sigh. In desperation, he said, 'I heard there's going to be funds for CAS and CHAPS. I heard it from the HCM's office.' The Steering Committee turned reflective.

That is, until the Minister for Village Roads arrived, a little later, followed by his Security Officer, his Personal Assistant and his Confidential Assistant. He went to those elder to him, the ex-Minister and the Vice President of CAS, and put their hands to his eyes. He accepted similar gestures from the others. He sat down heavily on a sofa kept vacant for him. He dabbed his dry face with a handkerchief, called for some water, and said, 'Public service is the hardest service.'

The ex-Minister commiserated. 'When I was a minister, it was the same. People haven't changed.'

DB Chandath gulped water. 'But people have changed, Kuldeep-jiu. They have become worse.'

Everyone laughed except for the ex-Minister, who felt the jab keenly. He was a former minister, long sterile. Balidaan Diwas, which had always been organized under his wardship, was to be taken away from him. He couldn't even get a contract bill passed through a department. He cut into their laughter. 'Let us get to the agenda. Time is being wasted.'

TB Chandath agreed. 'We should not return with empty hands.' It had darkened noticeably. The Confidential Assistant switched on the lights in the room. They were all sharply visible now, and the dissent subsided.

The Minister for Village Roads spoke, 'We had a high-level meeting regarding this. Some of us were there.' Everyone nodded. Each thought the others had been present, and each wanted to be thought of as an attendee.

Mitradas Chandith said, 'For the benefit of those who weren't there, the Hon'ble Minister should tell us what was discussed.'

DB Chandath pressed the sides of his stomach—everyone knew he had a problem with gas. 'We know the wishes of the HCM?'

They were familiar with the Hon'ble Chief Minister's wishes. A member of CHAPS spoke. 'Tribal status?'

The Confidential Assistant returned with some more water. DB Chandath accepted it and said, 'Exactly.'

He summarized recent developments for them. They knew how long the HCM had fought for her people. It was not enough to be a backward caste nowadays, not when almost everybody had been declared backward. The Minister for Village Roads said, 'Can't find anyone who is forward even if you look.'

He turned serious. 'Work is work. We represent our people here and we all know that the HCM wants to declare us as a tribal community.'

The Minister for Village Roads looked around. The members of the Steering Committee looked resolute, this was their great goal. Everyone but the ex-Minister. His objections were well known. 'But we are not a tribe.'

The Minister for Village Roads put up a hand to placate him. 'It is just a name, Kuldeep-jiu. Let's get it first. Our gods won't change.'

'How can we have gods when we don't even have a temple?'

They knew then that the discussion was lost. The temple was a concrete structure, initiated by the ex-Minister eight years earlier. It was subject to sporadic fits of construction and had stayed untouched for the past three years.

The Minister's large frame collapsed into the sofa. TB Chandath walked over to the ex-Minister and put a hand on his knee. 'Another time, Baraa. We can discuss this another time.'

Mitradas Chandith jerked up and jabbed at his watch. 'This is how we always waste time.'

The ex-Minister turned to the CAS members for support. The Treasurer, the Joint Secretary and the Press Secretary all looked away. The Vice President was dozing. The ex-Minister turned combative. 'If it hadn't been for you, we would have been offering prayers to Kumbura in our own temple today.' Kumbura was the principal deity of the Chyalu Valley, and was regarded by some as an incarnation of Vishnu. His mount was a flying rooster and he was often depicted with a cloak of feathers.

It was an old accusation, one that centered around thirty lakh rupees that had gone missing from the temple's fund two years earlier. The unresolved investigation was one of the reasons for Mitradas's departure from CAS. Mitradas leaped from his seat and shook a finger at the ex-Minister. 'Don't take advantage of your seniority.'

The ex-Minister asked, 'Or else?'

The Minister for Village Roads held out his phone. 'Speaking to the HCM.' He left the room with the phone to his ear. His Confidential Assistant remained behind and watched over them while they squabbled. The Minister returned. 'HCM is at the Secretariat. She's calling us there.'

The others looked chastened but the ex-Minister was not threatened. 'Principal calling us to her office.'

They moved out of the bungalow. The VIP colony was a settlement of identical concrete bungalows set along two roads that winded and intersected confusingly. It was an enclave built specially for ministers and had been constructed three years after the ex-Minister lost the elections. It was another perquisite that made him resent the earliness of his time in power. They had received nothing like this. Some of his colleagues had worked from rented flats. In his time as Forest Minister, he had managed to build the house on Tibet Road, a colleague had bought a bus to run a daily service between Gangtok and Siliguri, another had managed to support three mistresses for three years. That had been the laughable scale of their ambitions. What seemed like treasure back then wouldn't support a schoolteacher's wife in these times.

The colony was close to the crest of the Gangtok hill and it offered a wide view of the steep basin, a side of which was taken up by the spread of the city below them. It was an appreciable theatre but the massing of ominous clouds made them worry.

The Secretariat was ten minutes away. TB Chandath offered the ex-Minister a ride in his car and he accepted. On the ride, TB Chandath said, 'Baraa, we must work together. Our roads are different but our destination is the same.'

The ex-Minister spat, 'That snake!'

TB Chandath said, 'I understand. But past is past.'

It was one of the ex-Minister's lasting regrets that he had mistaken a baby snake for a worm. 'Mitradas used to visit me, looking like a child which has lost its way. I helped him with everything, TB Bhai, I treated him like a son. I gave him books, research papers, I took him to meet the HCM, and I made him the General Secretary of CAS. But he was not my son, he was a dog. And instead of thanking me, he bit me and left me.'

TB Chandath said, 'Looks like a storm.'

'I told all of you in the morning. But who listens to me?'

'We should listen to you.' TB Chandath reaffirmed his belief in the ex-Minister's deep experience, and the ex-Minister, who felt he had made his point, pretended to be pacified.

Then TB Chandath said. 'Lata has returned from Bangalore. She's completed her Masters in Psychology.'

The ex-Minister, who appreciated education in any Chandanth, was alert. 'You must be worried. A grown-up daughter means many responsibilities.' TB Chandath nodded and was about to speak further when the large Secretariat building came into view.

~

At the Secretariat, they were led into the Hon'ble Chief Minister's office. The visitors filed by her and put her hands to their eyes, except for the ex-Minister who was older to her by a year. They were guided to sofas arranged around her seat. TB Chandath sat next to her. The Hon'ble Chief Minister played with the rings on her fingers. 'Why is it so difficult for us to work together?'

The quarrellers had no answer to that. She held up her hands. 'Look at my hands. I am the oldest one here. In a few years, these hands won't even be on this earth.'

Instantly, she was contradicted by the Minister for Village Roads. 'Don't speak like that, Aama. You'll outlive us all.' Everyone agreed with this.

The Hon'ble Chief Minister said, 'Who put me here? Why did he put me here?'

It was a question she frequently asked of them. Yam Maya Chandath knew herself to be an unlikely chief minister. She was old, she had no public-speaking skills, and she was not from a very populous community. She had been a confidante of the previous chief minister, and had been preparing herself for a quiet retirement when his unexpected death had led to the events in which she had emerged as the compromise candidate. That was fourteen years ago and she had since held on to her office by stratagem alone.

The ex-Minister, who had known the Hon'ble Chief Minister for nearly forty years, spoke. 'We don't know. Who put you there?'

'When I find out I will let everyone know.' The room relaxed; they were not going to be harangued but won over.

Tea arrived. The Hon'ble Chief Minister's cup was placed on a side-table, its handle pointing away from her. TB Chandath leaned sideways and rotated the cup so that the handle faced her. The Hon'ble Chief Minister nodded and continued to speak. 'We need to get recognized as a Scheduled Tribe, everyone knows how important such a recognition is. Look at the Bhutias, the Lepchas, the Tibetans—life has become easier for their children. We should want this for our people, instead of fighting. There are so many things to fight against: history, poverty, illiteracy. Why should we also fight amongst ourselves?'

She spoke soothingly and outlined her vision for the year's Balidaan Diwas, which corresponded to what they had heard in VIP Colony. The murmurings from New Delhi were favourable. It was to be a two-day affair where all aspects of their tribal heritage would be showcased. The chief guest was to be the Tribal Affairs Minister of the Central government. At the end, there would be a resolution calling for Constitutional recognition of the Chandaths as a Scheduled Tribe.

The Hon'ble Chief Minister paused. 'Then one or two years for the paperwork, and we can all be proud of our work after that.'

Her persuasive powers were extraordinary and soon her audience, including the ex-Minister, found themselves regretting the pettiness of their thoughts and actions.

Mitradas Chandith was the first to admit the chastening. 'Forgive me.'

The Hon'ble Chief Minister nodded in his direction. 'Whenever DB Bhai or TB Bhai speak, they are telling you things I have asked them to. I would talk to everyone personally but I have other responsibilities.'

The members of the Steering Committee nodded. The ex-Minister said, 'You know what's best for the Chandanths.'

Mitradas corrected him. 'Chandiths.'

Someone else corrected them both. 'Chandaths.'

The Chief Minister said, 'We can't even agree on a name. And we want to change the Indian Constitution. We have so much work to do. Why can't we become one?'

The ex-Minister spoke. 'We are Chandanths. We have always been Chandanths, for our ancestors grew up in the shelter of the sandalwood trees of the Chyalu Valley.'

Mitradas countered him, 'And I got Chandith from the air? Chaandi, Kuldeep-jiu, chaandi. Meaning silver. From the silver mines of Chyalu.'

It was an unbridgeable divide, a persisting argument in which even the Hon'ble Chief Minister had declined to arbitrate. The missing funds for the temple may have been the public cause of the rupture, but this choice, between sandalwood and silver, was what had kept them apart from the beginning.

The Hon'ble Chief Minister removed her spectacles and wiped them. It was a signal for the cessation of hostilities. 'Everyone has a different theory about our origins and cultures, I know. We'll resolve it one way or another. Differences such as these are open invitations to our enemies. Look at the Rais, the Lepchas, the Pradhans, the Bhutias—they all write their names in one way. What happened at DB Bhai's house?'

The Minister for Village Roads squeaked, 'They don't listen to me at all. Kuldeep-jiu has too many questions.'

The ex-Minister said, 'I was asking why we need to do Balidaan Diwas differently this time. And why is our temple still incomplete? Are we changing our gods too? Will we no longer worship Kumbura? Will we have to eat chicken and eggs next?'

Mitradas stood up to answer, but the Hon'ble Chief Minister held up a hand and tapped the side-table. 'The temple will get done, Kuldeep-jiu. I'll see to it. CAS will do it. Put up a proposal and leave it with the Principal Secretary. And follow up on the money with DB Bhai.'

The Treasurer of CAS nodded furiously. There was a knock on the door and the General Secretary of CAS entered. She greeted the Hon'ble Chief Minister, took a seat, and said, 'So sorry. So much work at the department.'

The Hon'ble Chief Minister interrogated her on the status of some projects. She gave her an update, and the rest of them, whose only work was their organizations, feigned interest. At length, the ex-Minister earned their gratitude when he said, 'So, is our work done?'

The General Secretary ceased her update and stared at him. The Hon'ble Chief Minister said, 'TB Bhai will have to organize most of Balidaan Diwas. I request you to give him your full cooperation.' Then she turned stern and said, 'And please, no controversies. A minority should never act like a majority.'

Here the ex-Minister challenged her. 'Everyone wants to condemn an old man for saying something that he thinks. Since when have such words become so important?'

The Vice President looked chastened. 'I was speaking like always.'

The Hon'ble Chief Minister nodded. 'We all make mistakes. This age is such.'

The Vice President brightened. 'This age is such.' There were hums of agreement.

An aide entered and whispered into the Hon'ble Chief Minister's ear. She stood up and signalled the meeting's end. The members of the Steering Committee filed outside and stood around their vehicles, chatting. The ex-Minister remembered Yograj and the pending bill with alarm. He was to have brought it up with the Minister for Village Roads, instead of challenging him. He wished he had not been so involved in the discussion, that he had been more civil to the Minister. On his way out, he held the Minister's hand and said, 'Please. It's nothing personal.'

DB Chandath's smile consumed his face. 'Nothing personal.' The lack of rancour in his voice alerted the ex-Minister. He decided not to mention the bill, for that would only endanger it. It was a small bill, just twenty-eight lakh, at a time when everyone spoke in crores. It would pass on its own.

The icy wind intensified, and leaves fell and rose around them. The Vice President came close and asked, 'You think I am forgiven?'

The ex-Minister said, 'If you are guilty, then we are all guilty.'

He was about to leave with the Vice President when TB Chandath caught his arm and said, 'No, I will take him home.'

~

At Tibet Road the ex-Minister insisted that TB Chandath stay for tea. In the living room, he touched the ex-Minister's knee. 'Baraa, you should know that I'm not against you.'

'I know, I know. But everyone else…'

TB Chandath said, 'Don't worry about them. For you, I'm there.' He looked around. 'Where's your son? Isn't his name Yograj? I haven't met him.'

The ex-Minister's alertness returned. 'He's out. Works all day, chasing payments. Just finished a big contract.'

'He should meet Lata. Children nowadays. But you must be broad-minded.'

The ex-Minister assured TB Chandath that he was not broad-minded. No one was more aware how their bloodlines were withering in Sikkim. Soon there would be no pure Chandath blood left. But their children remained closed to that approaching calamity. He said, 'We cannot afford to be broad-minded. We have to make them meet.'

He paused. 'Baraa, I only want to tell you one thing. Any problem, come to me first. Even before you go to the HCM. She can say no to all of us, Baraa, but not to you. Even up there, just before I left, she said, I will make sure Kuldeep-jiu's temple gets built.'

The ex-Minister acted convinced. He held his visitor's arm. 'It's not my temple. It's our temple.'

'We know how important it is to you.'

Here the ex-Minister disagreed. 'No you don't. Follow me.' They walked towards the main door and, exiting it, he hollered at Pemba for the keys to the lowest floor of the building, below the road level. He asked for TB Chandath's assistance as he walked down the staircase. Pemba opened the door to the room.

'Come,' the ex-Minister tugged at TB Chandath. Inside, there were planed timber beams piled up in a corner. They took up most of the windowless, narrow, oblong room. He asked, 'Know what this is?' TB Chandath put a handkerchief to his nose against the smell of concentrated sweetness and nodded.

'Sandalwood. To use in the temple when it does get built. Just like the Dhod temple of Raku.'

Outside, TB Chandath said, 'I believe you now.'

'It's nothing. I've had it since my time as Forest Minister. The forest laws were not so strict then.'

It began to rain with large, heavy drops. They moved quickly towards the road level. There was just enough time to back up TB Chandath's vehicle into the garage before the hailstorm began. They heard the shattering of glass in other houses but the ex-Minister's building was sheltered by the curve of the narrow road.

After the storm, the ex-Minister picked up a hailstone as big as his fist and said, 'Never seen such a thing.' TB Chandath worried about the windows in his bungalow, but he waited until Yograj arrived. Then TB Chandath held his shoulders. 'Such a fine boy. And such wise eyes. You must come over to my house for dinner and meet Lata. She's just returned home. You young people will have a lot to talk about.'

After he left, Yograj asked, 'He has a daughter?'

The ex-Minister snorted in contempt. 'You are not to meet her. Not unless you want to get married to her.' He wished he had not been restrained by decency when TB Chandath had brought up the subject of his daughter. Did he not realize how low the Chandaths were compared to the Chandanths? Did he not know that it was the lowest of the Chyalu people who had taken up the name Chandath when they had entered Sikkim four generations ago?

The ex-Minister asked Yograj, 'So what happened at the department?'

The Concerned Citizen

The same afternoon, Yograj sat reading a novel in the office of Sumati AE, an Assistant Engineer with the Department of Village Roads. He was at Unnati Bhavan, the head office of the department, and beside him was a villager. 'Are you preparing for the Under-Secretary examination that everyone's talking about?'

Yograj shook his head and returned to his book. He did not like reading but had discovered that a book was a useful prop. It obviated unwanted conversations, and it advantaged him with an air of studious vulnerability. He had just terminated his affair with Julie Babuni, Sumati AE's stenographer, and he would have avoided the department's office altogether had it not been for the bill.

Yograj looked up. The villager took this for approachability. 'Your name?'

'Yograj.'

'Tharr?'

'Chandanth. Yograj Chandanth.'

Outside the window of Sumati AE's valley-facing office, the sky darkened and Yograj leaned over and switched on the table-lamp to read better.

The villager rubbed his hands and blew into them. 'The winter hasn't gone. I should have worn a jacket instead of this half-sweater.' He examined the paper-cutter on the absent AE's desk and scraped his callused palms with it. 'Whose son are you?'

It was the accepted way of introductions in Sikkim. Yograj said, 'My father's. And whose son are you?'

The villager was prompt with his reply. 'My name is Rann Maan. My father's name was Tanka Maan. I'm from Ramphutar. It's only the respectable who are ashamed of their fathers. It doesn't make a difference to our kind.'

Outside, a great formless cloud was descending, blanketing the upper portions of the Rumtek and Ranka hills.

A lady entered and stared at them both. She said, 'Haven't you heard? Sumati AE is not joining duty today. She has requested leave. Come tomorrow.'

Heera Babuni was Pradeep DE's stenographer, and Yograj knew that she had been delegated to deal with him, owing to the fragile condition of Julie Babuni's heart.

Rann Maan looked guilty. Yograj held her gaze. 'She was supposed to rejoin office today.'

'She should have sent a copy of the leave application to your house, no?'

Yograj spoke in English. 'It's her job to be in the office. I will leave when I am ready. And from what I understand, it is not a matter that concerns you.'

Heera Babuni glared at Yograj until her pencilled eyebrows met. She was slim, with her hair pulled back. In the indirect light of the lamp, she looked severe and matronly, but Yograj was unaffected. 'Don't let us see you talking to people you're not supposed to. Not everybody has a strong heart here. I'll tell your brother you are here.'

Rann Maan looked at Yograj with warmth and hope; he had found an ally who could speak English. 'What did she mean?'

Yograj sighed. 'It's a long story.'

Rann Maan's expression transformed with understanding. He asked, 'Your brother works here?'

'Half-brother. He's the DE.'

The Divisional Engineer's brother! Raan Maan's expression warmed further. He asked, 'What work do you have here, Bhai? Official work, I mean.'

'A road project. The contract is done, money's due.'

'I'm here for a contract payment as well. The village road they were building through Ramphutar damaged the wall above my house. I got the contract to repair it. Putkah ko maha?' he asked Yograj and reached into his bag.

Yograj shook his head. What use did he have for that strange honey? He often thought that the lower classes transformed themselves into merchants at the slightest opportunity and he felt his suspicions validated.

There were three rolls of thunder, successively louder, and after the last one, the electricity went off. The windows brought in no light; it was as if the late-evening darkness had been brought forward.

Rann Maan looked outside, worried. 'This Sumati AE. What is her caste?'

'I don't know. It doesn't matter. In the bureaucracy, everybody becomes one caste,' Yograj said. A pony-tailed man entered. He was the peon, responsible for the movement of all files in the office. He shook Yograj's hand. 'Everyone is leaving. Weather doesn't look good.'

Yograj held on to the peon's hand. 'What about the file?'

'It's there, don't worry. I have to close this office. The babunis are getting worried.' The peon winked at Yograj and calmed him with his assuredness. He had worked in the department for eleven years, ten thousand files had passed through his hands; he knew things balanced out in the end. The peon heard his name called and left.

Yograj's familiarity with the peon further impressed Rann Maan. He asked Yograj, 'Have you met her? I'm scared of lady officers. The previous AE was better, no? How is she?'

The previous AE had been a quiet, bald man who had never asked for a direct payment from Yograj, but stayed content with gifts and baubles every time he cleared a bill. Yograj had seen him leave with some regret, but his hopes had risen after he met his replacement.

'She's very forward thinking,' Yograj said.

Sumati AE had been transferred to the Village Roads Department from the Power Department a month ago, in early February. Yograj had met her twice after she had assumed her post and then she had left for her training in South India.

Rann Maan looked at his watch. 'We'll see tomorrow. I have to go, the taxi to Ramphutar leaves in half an hour.'

They said their farewells at the mouth of the long and dark internal corridor that bisected the office. It was lunch time, tiffin-boxes had been opened and the smell of lightly fried potatoes mingled uneasily with the faint smell of urine that always lingered in the lower parts of the building. It rose from the floor below, which housed the toilets and the accounts section. By the time Rann Maan turned at the stairwell, he had accosted three people with his wares, one of whom showed a genuine interest before hurrying away.

~

Yograj found Julie Babuni in the canteen, having lunch with three other clerks. Their chirpy conversation stilled when they saw him. She came over to him with solemn purpose while her colleagues watched without looking. Yograj was gentle. 'Sumati AE is returning tomorrow. We have to forget things we cannot change.'

Her answer surprised him. 'You can forget or you can remember every day. I have thrown it in the dustbin.' She spoke in a voice loud enough to be heard. Then she waddled back to her table.

Yograj then visited Pradeep DE's office even though he knew what awaited him there: a lecture for consorting with lower-division clerks. He found Pradeep DE with a file open, a pen in hand.

Pradeep DE completed the noting, rang the bell and, when the pony-tailed peon entered, hurled the file to the floor. He looked at Yograj and said. 'The babunis will get together and drag you by the hair one day.'

Yograj said, 'They are trying very hard. Your steno shouted at me in the AE's office, telling me I should not talk to Julie anymore.'

Pradeep DE leaned back on his chair. 'Leave Heera Babuni alone. She has enough problems of her own. Have you spoken to Julie Babuni?'

'That story is over. But she phoned me two weeks ago at one in the night. Said she missed me.'

Pradeep DE leaned forward. 'What did you say?'

'I said I missed her too. And we met the next day.' Yograj then described their last encounter, a tearful one, but one in which Julie Babuni had nevertheless given herself to him one last time. 'She cried and cried, but when I undressed her, she was wearing a red bra-and-panty set. My favourite. Fully transparent.'

Pradeep DE grew excited; colour coordination did that to him. But he was also sad. It was so long ago that he had been like this, or perhaps he never had been. Conversations of this kind aroused and distressed him. Yograj began to describe the encounter, Pradeep DE was saved from further torment by a visitor, a man from North Sikkim who had come to complain about his neighbour. Pradeep DE turned grave, looked at Yograj and said, 'We'll talk later.'

Yograj exited Unnati Bhavan. It was grey and windy outside. He huddled with a crowd under the porch at the entrance which had a concrete roof. A woman next to him struggled to read a governmental form in the fading light before the wind blew it away. Then it rained and, soon, individual clatters turned into an all-encompassing roar. The hailstones increased in size until they resembled riverside pebbles. Yograj put a hand out and was stung by their force. The road turned white. After the storm ceased, Yograj walked to Tibet Road. He found his house free of any damage because of the proximity of the neighbouring houses and because of the awkward angle at which it was built.

~

He visited the Department of Village Roads the following day. Sumati AE was in attendance but Julie Babuni stopped him at the door. 'Madam said not to let anyone in.'

Yograj leaned over, blew into her ear, and whispered, 'Who's there?'

Julie Babuni sniffed. Yograj said, 'You should not be rude to me here. Let's be professional.'

She blew her nose. 'What professional? My heart is not an office. Don't tell me what to do. You don't own me. You don't own my heart.' For emphasis, she jabbed a file cover with her pen. 'Sit there or I'll call Heera Babuni.'

They sat in an uneasy silence until Rann Maan emerged from Sumati AE's office. As he crossed Yograj he said, 'You were right. The AE's very forward thinking.'

Sumati AE was in her early thirties. Her hair was short and hovered around her neck. She wore spectacles and her clothes were well chosen. They had talked earlier and Yograj knew that her husband worked with the Central government; he was posted in Guwahati. She had a chronic problem with her lower back. She had told Yograj that she found him handsome. She was a great believer in systems, and disliked haphazard approaches. She had given him cause for optimism.

They talked about the hailstorm for a while. Then she said, 'Let's not waste time. I'll come to the point. Are you planning to keep something for the department?'

'Of course.'

Sumati AE drummed her painted nails on the glass top of her desk. Her fingers were long and slender, and they rose and fell in stationary gallops. 'See Bhai, it has to be done systematically. There's no point if it's ten thousand here, twenty thousand there. Who gets what, we'll never know. Things seem to be very haphazard here. I asked the Commissioner-cum-Secretary if I could work out a system.'

Yograj stared at her. 'And he said yes?'

She avoided his gaze. 'He said yes. See Bhai, suppose your payment is for one lakh, and you spend twenty thousand to get your final payment. What I'm saying is that if you make it more systematic, and we apply a percentage, say, fifteen per cent, and your file is taken care of from start to finish. It's a saving for you of five thousand rupees. It's very helpful, no? You don't waste money, you don't waste time and there is less friction between contractors and engineers. I'm surprised there isn't a system in place here; other departments have adopted it.'

'Even I am surprised. It seems like such a sensible thing,' Yograj said.

She said with some pride, 'In my previous department, I made them switch from random payments to a more systematic approach. The department got its savings but at the same time the big contractors were so happy. One of them even said, "Sister, if only more people in this office were as forward thinking as you."'

Yograj was admiring. 'You're brilliant. We wasted so much time before this.'

Sumati AE blushed. 'You're too much. We only have one month before the financial year closes. Quickly, okay? I'll work out a formula and we'll use your bill and Rann Maan's bill as pilot projects.'

Outside, Julie Babuni was not at her desk. But Rann Maan was waiting for him. He caught Yograj's arm. 'Did she talk about a system? What do you think?'

Yograj was unsure. 'Good and bad.'

Rann Maan said, 'If you look at it, in a way it's good. Better to feed one cow than a hundred dogs. You'll be there to help me? I just don't understand numbers. And I don't know English.'

~

Late in the afternoon there was a brief shower and it was followed by clarity and sunshine. This caused a stench to rise from the culvert beside the ex-Minister's house. It was a yearly phenomenon, occurring at the beginning of the rainy season. The ex-Minister ordered Pemba to close all the windows. Then he visited Yograj's room. 'Has the file progressed? Is the new AE causing you pain?'

Yograj shook his head. The ex-Minister said, 'And your elder brother? Is he helpful?'

'He'll always be useless. You said you were going to talk to the Minister.'

The ex-Minister lied. 'Talked to him. He said he'll talk to the Secretary.'

Yograj emerged from the bathroom, dressed for an evening out. The ex-Minister's tone was sharp. 'Are you going out somewhere? Why are you smelling like a prostitute?'

Yograj was meeting friends for dinner in town. As someone who had returned to Sikkim after a long spell outside, and then immediately gone into the villages to do contract work, Yograj held an attraction. 'It's perfume. And I'm going for dinner with some friends.'

'They must have names.'

'Names and castes. Some high castes, some low castes. Some Hindu and some Buddhist. Should I ask them to fill out forms?'

The ex-Minister raised his voice. 'And money? Where is the money coming from? One dinner at your hotel can feed this house for a week. One bill you have to chase and you grin at the engineers and come back home.'

Yograj adjusted his trousers around his ankles. 'I'm not paying the hotel bill with your money. You should have earned more in your time. Don't blame me,' and then immediately, lest his father hinder his plans by wailing, he said, 'we'll get it, don't worry. I'm there.'

Pemba, who had heard the raised voices, entered the room and said, 'Fighting again? Chee-chee.'

Outside, Yograj met Ai Doma, the momo-seller who was walking up the staircase to his house. She had a packet in her hands. 'Yograj Bhai, look at this. Your Pemba threw it into my house.'

He glanced into the packet of rancid vegetables and drew back. Ai Doma said, 'Is the madman home? I'm going to rub this on his face.'

Yograj went past her without replying. She walked up the stairs with the odorous bag and, before ringing the bell, paused to contemplate the putrefying package in her hands.

~

The ex-Minister visited the Department of Village Roads without informing Yograj. In the corridor he met the pony-tailed peon who said, 'There's no work happening here.'

The Commissioner-cum-Secretary's mother had undergone a hip replacement and he had taken a week's long leave. The laxity caused by his absence had rippled down like an invisible executive order. The officers were not in their offices, and the babunis and the clerks luxuriated in their freedom. It was lunch time when the ex-Minister visited and he saw them gathered around tables, surrounded by files accumulated on their desks in straggly yellow towers. The odour of urine was strong; this was the floor where the unfixable toilet was located. But they seemed inured to the stench. They shared their lunches and a clerk waved a jalebi in that piss-flavoured air, offering it to anyone who wanted it.

The ex-Minister longed to ask everyone their castes and sub-castes but controlled himself, as he had learnt to do.

The pony-tailed peon was beside him. 'Do you see? I told you.'

'Even Pradeep DE?'

The peon grinned. 'He's here all right. He won't go anywhere.'

He went to Pradeep DE's office and glanced at the plaque above the entrance to his office.

PRADEEP CHANDATH

DIVISIONAL ENGINEER

Inside, he saw his son in conversation with his stenographer. Heera Babuni sat in the visitor's chair, her elbow on the table and her chin in her hand. Peanuts were scattered in the space between them; they pecked at these languidly.

The ex-Minister said, 'Chhori, please open the window. Outside you can smell nothing but piss, inside you can smell nothing but scent.'

Heera Babuni stood up and left the room. Pradeep DE watched her leave and turned to his father. 'She was hurt, you know?'

The ex-Minister protested that his nausea was genuine; her perfume was very heavy. Pradeep DE looked pained. 'It's not easy. Everybody going on leave. It's not my fault, no? You have to learn to be patient if you're going to work with the government. You talk like I'm not helping Yograj. Peanuts?' He pushed some towards his father.

The ex-Minister waved them away and said, 'And is he still meeting that babuni?'

'Julie Babuni. I haven't heard anyone talking and he says they broke up. I send Heera Babuni to watch whenever he visits the office. Outside the office, I don't have the time to follow him around.'

The ex-Minister spoke with a resigned pride, 'We have to get him married soon.'

Pradeep DE was eager to end the meeting. He said, 'He's on the right path. Don't worry about him.'

His father stood to leave. 'And change the sign, I'm telling you for the last time.'

~

After the ex-Minister left, Pradeep DE broke open a peanut pod and thought: like father, like son. Such an unwelcome intrusion, and to think it was made just as Heera Babuni was opening up about her wayward husband. They may be in the government, but they too had lives and hearts. Her presence was like a cup of tea on a winter's morning, and it was what made the Department of Village Roads bearable, packed as it was with idiots and thieves.

Their proximity dated to the previous winter, when he had been passed up for a transfer, one that he had worked hard for, and had received a new office room as a consolation. It was a large room on the top floor, traditionally the Commissioner-cum-Secretary's room, but he had recently moved to a new office. Its only drawback was that it did not have a separate room for the stenographer but a cubicle within the large office. Pradeep DE was to work in the same space as his stenographer. Their first few days were awkward.

'Babuni, you must not talk on the phone for such long periods and so loudly. Your private life should be left outside the office,' he had said on the third day.

'You know what happens in my home. But do you know what happens inside my life?' she had answered.

From such curt exchanges they had moved towards each other gradually, like continents yearning for an eventual union, and chats had progressed to conversations. He appreciated the spatial constraints which had led to their companionship, and grew to be grateful for her hair which, when left loose, fell on the sides of her face like a partial curtain, her perfume which enveloped her like a fragrant aura. He discovered aspects of her without her sanction: her husband had left her for another woman, now she lived only for her children; when she hurt colleagues with her sharp candour, she made it a point to be kind afterwards; and her eye shadow always matched her lipstick. Then, last month, there was the letter in *Sikkim Everyday*.

> Respected Sir,
> Just yesterday I was walking back from office towards home when I saw a baby girl crying in the street because her father had beaten up her mother and then left with another loose-charactered woman. I asked myself, 'Is there no justice in the world?'
>
> In more advanced places of the world domestic violence is on its deathbed but here in Sikkim, it is alive and kicking, literally speaking. How many children are there in Sikkim who have been abandoned by their fathers? And what is the Department of Social Welfare doing? Does it have any facts and figures to show us? An iota of concern can work wonders.
>
> They must care for the children, and ensure that the fathers who indulge in these sort of 'hit-and-run' antics are made to be responsible for their children. Let us not forget that great souls have opined, 'The child is the father of man'.
>
> Lastly but not leastly, I call upon the concerned mothers to be

> more open about such abuse. Please remember that in your courage lies your beauty.
> Your's sincerely,
> A Concerned Citizen

Two days later, there was no indication yet from Heera Babuni that she had read it. He sat in his chair, hummed, and scanned the newspaper. He looked up to see her in a lemon jacket, cream bakkhu and yellow pumps, settling her work space. Above the letter, in the editorial page, was an article printed by a local botanist on the many virtues of the stinging nettle.

'Babuni, look at this. Did you know the sishnu was so useful?'

'It's good for one thing only, in my opinion. And there are many people I could use it on.' The stinging nettle, when dipped in water and applied to the flesh is uniquely painful, and has traditionally been used on thieves and errant children.

She sat down at her desk to type. He walked over and kept the newspaper on her desk. 'It's on this page.'

He went out, not trusting himself to look or be seen looking. When he returned, he found his fond hope fulfilled. She had read the letter and was weeping for the child left on the road. She made a cone from a tissue and poked the corner of her eyes, to soak up her tears, which could not be allowed to run down her cheeks, for her mascara had taken time in the morning. 'This man has written the letter with his pen dipped in my heart.'

He had rehearsed his answers. 'No woman should have to go through what you are going through.'

She held his hand. He hoped that she didn't notice his trembling. 'No man can replace a child's father. But I could try and be a good uncle.'

She let go of his hand and looked away. 'What's the use? You too will leave in some time.'

She sat down, facing her computer, and he stood beside her. She took his hand again and kissed it. He turned away lest she see the effects of her action straining against his trousers, for it would only validate her regular assertions that all men were animals whose hearts were located inside their underpants. He returned to his desk but could not work. He opened the window beside him to air the room. There was a fine mist outside and everything around, the houses and the trees close by and the landscape beyond, was shrouded in it.

Pradeep DE left for a meeting at the Commissioner-cum-Secretary's office and when he returned found the note Heera Babuni had left for him. It said: 'I know you did it for me.' She had kissed it and the lipstick marks were still fresh.

~

It was Heera Babuni who had told him the previous month about the approaching round of transfers. When the whole office was occupied with the previous AE's farewell, she had said, 'There's a letter which has come to the Secretary's office from the Department of Personnel. They want an Engineer for UID.'

Pradeep DE's heart leaped. The Urban Infrastructure Department was precisely what he yearned for, a department where cement was plentiful and contractors accommodating. He saw his house complete, his Mrs silenced, his mind closer to contentment.

'But we have to hurry,' Heera Babuni had said. 'You know who else is trying for it? Tobgay DE.'

He saw themselves apart. 'What about you? Don't you wonder who will come in my place? What if he doesn't understand you?'

She had looked out of the window at the hills of Ranka. 'It's become a habit. Seeing people I care for leaving me. I'll manage.'

And the day of the hailstorm was made doubly memorable for it announced that they had crossed a threshold. After they had shared their lunch and resumed work, Pradeep DE heard rain outside and walked towards the window, close to where Heera Babuni typed, facing away from him. Her firm, slender spine leaned towards the typewriter, her long neck continued the angle of her back, until it disappeared into the collar of her jacket, embroidered in curled lines that ended in leaf-shaped mirrors. She had chosen to bunch her hair and stray strands swayed like stalks in a breeze. Her skin was near translucent there, and her hair grew shorter along the two downy ridges where they dissolved into her skin. He let out a connoisseur's sigh.

The rain's patter built up and broke into a concatenation of knocks. Pradeep DE looked out, put his hand on Heera Babuni's shoulder, and gave it a slight turn.

'Is it hail?' he asked. She moved her head slightly, to get a better view without disturbing his resting hand. The she stood up and they took a few steps to stand against the window. The storm grew louder, the hailstones larger. She said she was scared and held his arm. It was the first time they had made physical contact and he thanked Mother Nature for bringing them closer. The angle of the hailstorm changed and a few stones clanged against the panes of the window, but the roof above shielded them.

As the hail subsided, they heard the pony-tailed peon shouting in the corridor. 'The hail has broken so many windows.'

Pradeep DE's bliss mutated into fear as he remembered his own house at Arithang and his Mrs. Heera Babuni remembered that the flowers on her terrace were about to bloom. The departmental building emptied in minutes as everyone hurried to check on their homes.

Pradeep DE's house was especially vulnerable. It jutted out on a hillside and what was earlier a spectacular advantage now showed its vulnerability. Three facades were exposed and the damage was complete. All the panes on the three sides of his incomplete building were shattered. Where the surrounding buildings seemed disfigured, his looked haunted. Inside, his Mrs sobbed. He put his arm around her, consoling because he was blameless. He remembered the glazier was still in his employment for he had not been paid. He phoned him. Shambhunath ignored his calls but phoned early the following morning.

Pradeep DE was soft and kind. 'Shambhunath Bhai, is your house all right? I was worried.'

'By your mercy, Saar, all okay. What about your house?'

'Little bit damage. Come and see for yourself. You have some payment pending. When are you coming to collect it?'

'This evening, Saar.'

Shambhunath came in the evening, collected his payment and promised to start work after two days. He even had the glass ready. When Pradeep DE phoned then, his calls were ignored. His missed calls were not returned by Shambhunath. Pradeep DE texted him in English, 'Where are you?'

There was no reply.

He texted again: 'Saala haraami'.

A reply came promptly: 'Same 2 u'.

Pradeep DE later heard his Mrs call him a holy man while in conversation with a neighbour, for having given the glazier his full payment. She made up a song and jeered him with it:

Sant Pradeep, Sant Pradeep
Open an ashram, Sant Pradeep

When their daughters came home from their boarding school for the Easter holidays, she infected them with her contempt. She kept them around her and when he tried to reach them through gifts, he found that they had turned against him. In turn he regarded them with distate, as if they were his wife's children alone. On the last day before returning to their school, his younger daughter said, 'Papa, please be more kind to Mummy,' and his elder daughter asked him if he knew what women's rights meant.

On the return journey after dropping their daughters at school, his Mrs was sullen. After he reached home, he dropped her but did not alight. He drove to Shambhunath's tenement in Deorali but the carpenter had changed his address. He tried calling but the number was unavailable. Pradeep DE did not complain to his father or to Nima Thendup, his cousin, where Shambhunath was currently employed; to do so would be to invite ridicule and lectures. Instead, he acted in the way he knew best. He wrote a letter to *Sikkim Everyday*, and it was published after four days.

> Respected Sir,
> This is to bring to your notice the rise in rowdy behaviour amongst the outsider carpenters and labourers who come in from outside and take advantage of our kind nature. We provide them with jobs and money and shelter but are they grateful? The answer is a big no. Instead they behave as if they were in their native villages and we have to bear the brunt. Their children study in the same schools as ours but do they thank us? The answer is another big no.

Do we know how many workers are there? How do we know how well their training is? Especially a profession which requires a lot of skill like a shisha mistri. In Sikkim we are still very innocent, and don't say anything even when we see others having a gala time at our expense. Sometimes I feel anybody can come to Sikkim and call himself a mistri? I strongly urge the concerned authorities to look into this matter urgently, as because I feel we are woefully underprepared in this matter.

Your's faithfully,
A Concerned Citizen

Contingency

When Yograj next visited Sumati AE, he was relieved to note Julie Babuni's absence from her desk. As he entered the office, he crossed a Marwari contractor he knew from the chases for his interim payments. The contractor shook Yograj's hand limply. 'Go in, she's in a good mood.'

Inside, Rann Maan was seated on a visitor's chair opposite Sumati AE. Between them, on the table, was a large printer. Rann Maan turned around and winked at Yograj.

Sumati AE raised her eyebrows, as if in complicity. 'Yograj Bhai, you'll wait outside for a few minutes? You can chat with Julie Babuni.'

Yograj held his heart in mock relief. 'She's not at her desk.'

He waited outside her door. Rann Maan emerged. 'She's waiting. Legs shut, mouth open for me and mouth shut, legs open for you.'

Yograj entered and opened with civility. 'You look different today.'

'You noticed my haircut!' She turned to give him a side view and, before he could offer a supplementary compliment, she said, 'Do you know anything about printers? The contractor gifted it to me. Will this work?'

Yograj examined the printer. The model had been popular a few years earlier, but was nearly obsolete now. It would soon be incompatible with most computers. 'It will work for a while but will be useless soon.'

'But it's free.'

'That it is. Any progress on the file, Ma'am?'

The AE said, 'As soon as I came. First thing I tackled. I've sent for the JE. He's coming tomorrow and I'll go through the whole file with him. Official scrutiny.'

'It's been done. See there.' Yograj pointed to the pertinent sheaf of papers.

She looked up, her hair fell in curls on her face. 'But that was the previous AE, no? If I'm signing, I ought to know what I'm signing, no? Don't get alarmed. It's just a formality.' She turned her attention to the note on her desk.

Yograj spoke, his voice thin with despair. 'Ma'am, it will be done by March end, no?'

She continued to write. 'It's your rightful payment. Who are we to stop it?'

Yograj sat down and put his hands on the table top. 'I talked with my father about the percentage system. He agrees that it will be a good idea.'

She looked up, her face bright with pleasure. 'Very sensible. I'll set up a meeting with the Secretary for tomorrow and we can all discuss this.'

Yograj acted incredulous. 'He'll grant us a meeting just like that?'

'He can't say no to me. The department is going to make more savings because of me.'

He looked out of her window and saw the sky darken. It was one of those orphan days that belonged to the winter months, gloomy and cold with the possibility of rain a constant threat. She saw him looking out. 'It's a good day to stay at home and...' She let the sentence hang.

'And?' Yograj added eagerly.

Sumati AE leaned forward on her desk and whispered, 'I've heard of your reputation, you handsome boy.'

Outside her office, Rann Maan was waiting for him. He shivered in his thin jacket and said, 'So, you settled with her?'

'No,' Yograj said, 'she didn't ask. What about you?'

There was an edge of admiration in Rann Maan's voice. 'She's asking for a percentage. She said she'll let me know after she goes through my file. She's quite up-to-date.'

~

There was a formal meeting the next day at the Commissioner-cum-Secretary's chamber. It was mid-morning and sunny outside, the chamber was filled with a warm glow and free from the odour of urine. It was an upholstered oasis compared to the shabby chaos in the rest of the building and the Commissioner-cum-Secretary occupied it with an air of efficient luxury. His spectacles were gold-rimmed. He wore a maroon shirt with cufflinks, offset by a white tie with a tiepin that matched the cufflinks. He looked like a man who never perspired.

Sumati AE was brisk. 'Sir, about the payment issue we've been having. We've talked about it, Bhai and myself. He's agreed to our proposal, Sir.'

Yograj nodded eagerly. 'Yes Sir. Much better than dealing with each official individually. Easier to give everyone at one time. Single-window system.'

'Sir, single-window system,' Sumati AE said.

The Commissioner-cum-Secretary put a finger to his cheek and tapped it, as if studiously appraising a sincere proposal. Pradeep DE looked uncomfortable discussing illicit money in the presence of his younger brother. 'Sir, should we also inform the SE and the CE?'

The Superintendent Engineer was the Divisional Engineer's immediate boss and he in turn was under the Chief Engineer. But they had reputations for recalcitrance.

The Commissioner-cum-Secretary waved a pale hand. 'No need to involve everyone. This is the first time we're doing this. Good to start small.'

Yograj said, 'Like a pilot project, Sir.'

'Sir, pilot project,' Sumati AE repeated.

Pradeep DE felt cornered and pressured to show professionalism. He asked Yograj. 'And contingency?' The contingency fund was four per cent of the project estimate, and traditionally reserved for the department.

Yograj responded to his brother's professionalism with his own. He looked at the Commissioner-cum-Secretary and said, 'Good question. Sir, the contingency will not be touched.'

Sumati AE said, 'The department's savings will be over and above the contingency.'

The Commissioner-cum-Secretary noted Yograj's enthusiasm with alarm. It was his first time seeing a contractor pledge money with such cheer. 'Bhai, you realize what you're doing, no? I hope no one is pressuring you.'

'Sir, not at all Sir. If I wanted I could have given payments to everyone, but speaking with a true heart, I'd rather give the money to the people who've worked hard for it. Sir, it is about ethics and principles.'

'Ethics and principles, Sir,' Sumati AE repeated.

The Commissioner-cum-Secretary addressed Yograj. 'So how is Kuldeep-jiu? You know I worked as a BDO in Suikeybung when he was minister? I learnt so much under him. You know what he did? There was a contract for water-supply pipes and he got the tender cancelled because proper procedures were not followed. And you know whose contract it was?'

Yograj knew the story. 'My eldest uncle's.'

'Exactly! He got his own brother's contract cancelled. Bhai, I swear on,' the Commissioner-cum-Secretary looked around for something with enough gravitas and settled on a portrait of the President of India that hung to his right. He reached out his hand and said, 'I swear on the President, I have not seen such an honest minister after that. He taught me a lot.'

Outside the Commissioner-cum-Secretary's chamber, Sumati AE waved delicately at Yograj and took her leave. Pradeep DE whined, 'You're not going to get me in trouble, no? You don't know what she's like. A minister called her stupid and she took him to the Women's Commission. She's like the dog which refuses to let go after it has bitten your leg.'

In his office they found Heera Babuni arranging his desk. She was wearing deep blue tapering jeans with matching heels and a billowing, indigo shirt. She turned towards them, her hair was arranged in a coiffure. 'You heard? Julie Babuni is getting married. Got confirmed yesterday. Engagement is next week.'

Yograj had not heard but he welcomed the news. When she went to make tea, he said, 'You have someone like her to settle your office and make you tea. Why do you complain so much?'

Pradeep DE shrugged. 'My mind is not like yours.' But after Yograj had left, Heera Babuni came with some papers for him to sign. She leaned over to point out places where his signature was required and let her fragrant hair graze his cheek. He caught her perfume and agreed with his brother.

~

Yograj reached home late and his father was asleep. In the morning, the ex-Minister's interrogation was sharp. 'So has the lady vulture asked any money from you?'

'She'll scrutinize the file. Normal procedure. We even met the Secretary.'

'Delay tactics. They are all the same. Noses like ants, eyes like vultures.' He held out his hand. Yograj assisted his father out of bed and into the bathroom. He waited outside, the door slightly ajar. The ex-Minister was sprightly for a man of eighty-two but he also feared that he would die trapped inside the toilet, his cries too feeble to be heard.

He emerged and was helped to his bed. He pulled up a sleeve. 'Look here, are these fungal growths? Am I rotting away?'

Yograj examined the discoloration on his father's forearm. He spat into his forefinger and rubbed, the discoloration came off. He tasted his finger; it was toothpaste. 'It's not so easy to rot away.'

At the Tiny Genius Nursery School, they sang the national anthem, beginning on a note which could not be sustained for the anthem climbed in pitch as it progressed. Halfway through the song, they faltered, paused, and began again, this time in a near growl.

'What does your brother say?'

'Pradeep Daju seemed happy. He's also nervous'

The ex-Minister spat. 'Coward. He won't do anything to help but he'll be the first one to ask for his cut.'

'So you don't want to give them anything? They're not asking for much.'

'Has she told you how much?' Yograj shook his head, she had not.

'Then don't speak. How long has it been?'

Fourteen months had passed since the clearance of the last interim bill. Yograj said, 'A year.'

The ex-Minister said, 'We'll go to Unnati Bhavan. If they make us go round and round, I'll complain to the HCM.'

Yograj exhaled. 'Why wait? Complain to her now. She's waiting in Mintokgang just to chase our file for us.'

They heard some shouting from downstairs. Yograj asked Pemba, 'Who is it?'

'No one. The cat scratching the door.'

Yograj went downstairs to the door. It was the momo-seller and she was in a temper. The ex-Minister heard her thudding up the stairs. She came to his room and said, 'Control your servant otherwise I'll control him. Don't think I don't know how to do it.'

The ex-Minister inquired and she explained breathlessly. Pemba had knocked on her door in the morning and, when she had opened it, she had found him with his pants around his ankles, his cock in his hand, pointed at her. 'As if it was a rifle.'

When Pemba was summoned, he did not deny it. She had taunted him yesterday. 'She said I didn't have a woman because I couldn't make it hard. So I showed her.'

Yograj patted Pemba's back. The ex-Minister held his face in his hands and made a low sound of despair. 'Day's gone now.'

But his day was not spoilt. After the momo-seller was pacified and sent away, he had a visitor, a Chandanth from Nepal. The ex-Minister had seen him in the papers the previous day. He had walked all the way from Kathmandu to Sikkim for world peace. The ex-Minister was pleased with his visit, he had always been one of the first people to call on by any visitor who had anything to do with the Chandanths. Over the years he had been visited by university students, anthropologists, researchers and politicians from as far as Dehradun and Burma.

The visitor showed the ex-Minister photographs of himself at various stages of his walk. The ex-Minister glanced at them approvingly and said, 'So how can I help you?'

'You must be knowing, Kuldeep-jiu, that I am a multiple-award winner. Here,' he showed some photographs of himself receiving various awards in Nepal, Burma, Assam and Dehradun, 'I wanted your recommendation. There will be awards given on Balidaan Diwas.'

His directness touched the ex-Minister. He spoke to the Press Secretary of CAS on the phone and asked him to prepare a recommendation letter for the Multiple Award Winner for him to sign. And then he detained his guest for most of the day, requesting and receiving updates on the Chandanths in Nepal.

~

The next day, late in the morning, the ex-Minister and his son took a taxi to Unnati Bhavan. It was raining. The office corridor was thronged with people and smelled overwhelmingly of damp clothes. Its floor had become a mosaic of uneven patches where footprints had been dissolved by water from closed umbrellas.

Yograj had coached his father. 'You act stern right now and I'll speak softly later.' They went first into Pradeep DE's office. He was alone, and he stood up and stuttered when he saw his father. 'Appa, the file hasn't come to my office. It's still with the AE.'

The ex-Minister pointed a finger at Pradeep DE. 'Isn't she your junior? Why can't you ask it from her?'

'I can't just do that. There is a protocol and a hierarchy.'

'Your father's hierarchy! Is she in her office?' the ex-Minister asked.

'She's probably not there. I heard her saying she'll be out.' Pradeep DE had his own reasons for avoiding a confrontation. Heera Babuni had just updated him on the latest developments on the transfers. Tobgay DE had recruited Sumati AE to his side, with the understanding that if he were to be transferred, she would be promoted to DE in his place. The matter needed thought and negotiation, not the reckless confrontation that his father and brother seemed intent upon.

'Let's settle this today,' the ex-Minister said and walked out, followed by his son and a sullen Pradeep DE.

With Sumati AE, the ex-Minister was at his gracious best. 'It makes my heart proud to see our children in such high places.'

Her smile was a wall they could not breach. 'The works were not done in my time. There has to be a scrutinization and I am in the process of completing it. Please wait until then. There is a notification. See.'

Pradeep DE looked towards the door, an inferior in his junior's presence. 'Bahini, it's not a very big file. I know what notification you're talking about but it's only used when a member of the public has raised an objection. It'll delay payments by a month or so; the end of the financial year is approaching.'

The ex-Minister turned pitiable. 'Chhori, I'm an old man. My house needs the passage of this bill. Take the percentage. Take five per cent, take seven per cent.'

She let out a little gust of air from her nose. 'It'll be more than that surely.'

Yograj, in a move he later recognized as reckless, said, 'You are a public servant and we are the public.'

Sumati AE looked like someone who had encountered a little-known fact. 'Just shows your family background.'

It was a mistake, one that cost them the day. The ex-Minister stood up, shook a shrivelled finger and shouted, 'You vulture! You leech! Stop the file, stop it all you want, and I'll drag you naked through the bazaar by your hair.'

There was silence. Yograj contemplated the images inspired by the threat. Sumati AE looked at the ex-Minister with a faint curve of pleasure on her mouth, as if a strategic move had been fulfilled. Pradeep DE pulled on his father's sleeve and said, 'Please, please. Not in my department.'

The ex-Minister turned to him. 'Your father's office! You wimp, you woman! If it hadn't been for me you wouldn't even be here. If you had any water in your stick, she wouldn't be acting like this today. I'll go to the Chief Minister, the Chief Minister of Sikkim.'

They could hear the murmurings of the crowd gathered outside the cabin. The ex-Minister turned towards Sumati AE and said, 'I was there when a king was overthrown, and later, when two chief ministers were chased away. You're nothing. You're just a louse from here.' The ex-Minister pointed to his crotch. 'Don't try to move here.' He pointed to his head.

Yograj was appalled. He had enjoyed it so far but the meeting was becoming unsalvageable. 'Appa, enough,' he growled. 'Appa, do you remember the Women's Commission? Even phones have cameras nowadays.'

The ex-Minister ceased his abuse and said, 'Tell your Secretary I'm coming to meet him tomorrow. And if he's not here then I'm going to bring the press and the party people.'

On his way out, the ex-Minister paused outside Pradeep DE's door. He made Yograj fetch a chair. Then he pointed at Prakash DE's nameplate and said, 'Stand on it and take out that thing.' Yograj hesitated. The ex-Minister stood on the chair himself and pushed out the metal plate that slotted into the timber frame. It came away easily. He turned to the pony-tailed peon watching him and said, 'Tell him I'll send him a proper one later.'

At Tibet Road that evening, the ex-Minister and Yograj talked with a rare companionship. A boundary had been crossed, and they found that their frustrations, which had so far trapped them in damaging battles and truces, had been purged and replaced by a new bond.

But this bond did not last long. The ex-Minister mistook it to mean that his son was now more amenable, that he would now accept what he had always hoped for: participation in the affairs of CAS. He asked, 'There is a meeting of the Core Committee in some days. You'll attend?'

Yograj's reply was swift. 'No. Keep me away from those people. I've told you.'

Incumbent and Non-incumbent

The ex-Minister expected penalties for his behaviour against Sumati AE. He considered her possible actions. A complaint to the Women's Commission would not harm him, for his age put him beyond harm, but a complaint to the Minister for Village Roads would endanger everything. He reasoned that either he had to soothe Sumati AE, that louse, or he had to meet DB Chandath, that vulture. He strategized: it was preferable to meet the Minister, repellant as the experience promised to be, for with him the ex-Minister would have additional purchase as President of CAS.

It was a distasteful appointment. How easy it would have been if the earlier Minister for Village Roads had not died the previous year. He had been close enough to ease the tendering process to favour the ex-Minister two years ago. If only he had remained! He had died returning to Gangtok from a constituency visit with some supporters when the vehicle he was in skidded around a corner, flew off the road and into a ravine. It took a day to find out that they were missing and another day to recover the bodies. They had all died from shattered spines and the detached head of a supporter was found in the minister's lap. The only survivor was a village rooster gifted by a constituent and it had survived by picking on the dead men's flesh.

He phoned the Minister's Confidential Assistant and sought an appointment. The Confidential Assistant said, 'No appointment is needed, Kuldeep-jiu, but you can come in the morning, when he meets everyone.'

~

Because the visit's outcome was uncertain, he did not inform Yograj. He took a taxi to VIP Colony. It was clearer today than the last time he had visited, on the day of the hailstorm. The sentry did not allow the taxi to enter the compound. As the ex-Minister walked in, the sentry stuck an arm out and said, 'What work do you have here?'

The ex-Minister paused and asked, 'Son, are you from South Sikkim?'

The sentry thrust a register at him. 'Write your name and purpose of visit here.'

'I was a minister before you were born.'

The sentry said, 'So what should I do?' The ex-Minister phoned the Confidential Assistant, who came out to receive him, but did not rebuke the security guard. He led him to the living room, crowded with supplicants and party workers. The ex-Minister thought he recognized one of the supplicants from a birthmark on his cheek. He sat beside the Minister for Village Roads who stood up and said, 'You should have called me. I would have come.'

'I am the only one here who believes that,' the ex-Minister said. There were titters in the room. The Minister grinned. The ex-Minister's seniority meant that it would not be seen as abuse.

'You look so healthy. Eighty-eight years, no? Just twelve away from a hundred,' the Minister asked.

'Eighty-two.'

'See,' the Minister for Village Roads proclaimed to the room, 'we should all be as healthy when we are eighty-two.'

'What is the secret?' one of those waiting asked.

The ex-Minister said, 'Don't waste time expecting appointments from ministers.'

The Minister for Village Roads pressed his stomach and said, 'You have come so far, tell me what I can do.'

'We should go inside,' the ex-Minister said.

'No. No. No. There are no secrets here. Everyone has a right to know how the state is being administered. Isn't that so, friends?'

The supplicants nodded sincerely. The ex-Minister knew he was trapped and said instinctively, 'There is no work out there. There are no contracts available to us. What will my son eat?'

The sentry's insolence, the Confidential Assistant's manner and the Minister's reception had told him that his solution did not lie in this room. But it was too late, he was here, and withdrawal was possible only after an act.

The Minister said, 'This man is like my father.' The Minister in turn was interrupted by two girls who entered the room. They were skinny, wore make-up and sequined clothes. One carried a register and the other, a bag. The supplicants stared at them with distate and longing. How had they got in so easily, the ex-Minister wondered.

'What is it, daughters?' the Minister said.

'Sir, we're doing a play at the party office. It's a play on anti-drugs. We're taking donations from everyone.'

'Not here, daughters. I'm a poor minister; it's only been three months since I received my post. Go next door, there's the Power Minister there, and the Irrigation Minister after that. They have money,' he said, and turned his attention back to the ex-Minister.

The two girls wailed, 'Sir, everyone is giving. Even the HCM will give.'

'Then ask her to give something for me as well,' he said. The girls retreated from the room. At the door, they said, 'Ashamed to call him a minister.' The Minister muttered, 'Whores,' sipped his tea and returned to his speech. 'This man here is like my father.' He was outraged. How come someone like Kuldeep Sir was without any means to support himself? Why was the administration so unkind to the state's veterans, the warriors for democracy? 'I will personally ensure that Kuldeep-jiu gets something. I wasn't made minister for nothing.'

The supplicants were roused, someone clapped. The Minister was going to look into the matter personally. The ex-Minister said, 'My tears won't let me speak.'

The Minister accompanied him outside. The rain had stopped. They sat on chairs in the lawn, the Minister stroked his moustache in pleasure. 'Kuldeep-jiu, I will do my best. And something will come soon. Believe me. The HCM's office informed me that I'll be able to sign the cheques for CAS very soon.'

The ex-Minister said, 'I wanted to speak about that as well. But inside? In front of so many people?'

The Minister commiserated. 'I know, but what to do. Public service. The money for CAS will come soon, Kuldeep-jiu. But the harvest hasn't been good this year. It would be good to see some rice come into the house.'

The sanctity of the cause made it difficult to articulate the benefits possible from it. The ex-Minister said, 'It's always raining in some field or the other. The rice will come.'

'Basmati?'

The ex-Minister said, 'Basmati. What about Mitradas, has he got his payment?'

'No no. He's in the same position as you are. But the Steering Committee, their funds have been released. TB Chandath has won a lottery.'

The ex-Minister's voice was soft with contrition. 'Is it because of what I said at the HCM's office?'

The Minister caught hold of the ex-Minister's hands. 'No! No! That was a frank discussion. How could you even think such a thing? You've hurt me; not then, but today, right now.'

This show of piety stung the ex-Minister. 'You're not hurt, DB Bhai. You're just doing your job. Just like that home-guard there was doing his job when he did not let me into your house.' He pointed to the sentry at the end of the lawn, who was eyeing them with apprehension.

The Minister shouted at the sentry, 'Ay Birkhey! Doing your job well I hear.' He put the ex-Minister's hands to his eyes, took his leave and walked back into the bungalow. The ex-Minister walked out of the compound. The sentry, rubbing tobacco in his palm, looked away when the ex-Minister said, 'I would have asked you your caste, but I know it from your behaviour.' The sentry tucked the tobacco into his lower lip and fingered his gum.

The ex-Minister stood outside the compound for a while and turned towards the valley. The landscape that had been concealed on the day of the hailstorm was now apparent. The large hill of Gangtok, pocked with buildings, was lit by the weak yellow sun of the morning. There were two great clouds. One smothered the valley and the other the summit of the Ranka hills. Clumps of fog arose from the valley and joined the ones blanketing the hilltops.

He heard voices, people emerged from the bungalow and the Minister for Village Roads was in the centre. He soaked in the thrum of people, which, in another age, had converged for him. With abrupt, important movements, the Minister entered his car and the sentry cracked a salute as the vehicle exited the compound. Their eyes met, the Minister put his hands together and bowed. And, further down, his car was swallowed up by a fog that came up from nowhere.

He saw the supplicant with the birthmark walk towards him. When he was close enough he took the ex-Minister's hand and put them to his eyes. 'I couldn't talk inside, Baraa.'

The supplicant was the ex-Minister's nephew, the son of his one living sister. She too had broken off relations with him thirty years ago, in solidarity with his other sister Kalpana, Nima Thendup's mother, whom he had exiled for marrying a Bhotey.

The ex-Minister said, 'What are you doing here?'

'This and that. We run behind the minister. Sometimes he throws something our way and we pick it up.'

'It is better than staying at home. How is your mother? And your father?'

'They are keeping well. Work every day still.'

The ex-Minister, ashamed that he had been observed, said, 'This is what I have become.' There was a light honk from behind them. It was his taxi, the driver was getting impatient. The ex-Minister wanted to send a message to his sister. But his nephew said, 'You're getting late I see,' and walked back towards the bungalow.

~

When Yograj came home, the ex-Minister said nothing of his visit. A confiding would not draw any consolation; he would only be taunted. He said, 'We'll leave the Minister out of this. The Treasurer phoned me. Money is coming for CAS as well, there'll be something for this house from there. If we go to the Minister now, that snake will bite me on both legs. Go tomorrow to the department and see. If we have to take it slow, we will do that.'

Yograj was not convinced. 'Easy for you to say. You didn't have to visit a building smelling of piss every day for two years.'

At Unnati Bhavan the next morning, Sumati AE did not look up to acknowledge Yograj when he entered. He began to apologize, she said it was not necessary. She said, 'Bhai, I was going through the file and I think the labourers' names need to be verified. You will need to provide all the labourers' identifications.'

Yograj stared at her. This was a manufactured obstacle. The names of the labourers submitted with the bills were fictitious. The work had been done entirely by workers from Bihar and Islampur but the bills had to reflect local-sounding names. The Junior Engineer had told Yograj that it was an established practice. Yograj had sat with him and written down imaginary names—it had been an amusing exercise.

Sumati AE said, 'I know what you're thinking, Bhai. That this is victimization. But we have a notification from the Chief Secretary, especially after what happened in the Water Management Department a month ago. Surely you must have heard the case.'

Yograj had heard about it. Some officials in that department had been found using labourers from their projects as servants in their homes. They were publicly reprimanded by the Chief Minister in the sternest tones and allowed to resume their work.

'It's a formality. We'll get it done shortly. Please meet the DE if you have any doubts,' the AE said.

In his office, Pradeep DE teared up when he recalled his humiliation. 'I am nothing. I have no feelings, no reputation, no seniority. My father can come and abuse everyone as he wishes.'

Yograj placated him. 'At least you don't have to live with him. He does that to me every day.'

Pradeep DE sniffed. 'No peace in the office. No peace at home. You go around from one woman to another but I have just one. She stores my faults like ammunition and, when the time comes, they come out like bullets, one after the other.'

Yograj heard him out and at an appropriate moment said, 'The AE says she's going to verify the labourers' names. No one I know has ever done that.'

Pradeep DE said, 'Our father called her a louse, from down there. Obviously she's angry. Hit in the ego. We are officers, not animals.'

Yograj said, 'Noses like ants, eyes like vultures.'

It's not just money, Pradeep DE wanted to say, there's charm as well. Charm always works better than outrage. This is what the Marwari and Bihari contractors have already realized. We are people just like you. And so what if you have to share a bit of your profits? Isn't that the basis for humanity? What you see as corruption, we only know as life. We would die if we had to live merely on our salaries. Our houses would have no windows, our cars only two wheels.

Instead he hummed and looked outside his window into the hills of Ranka. They were lit by sunlight; he soaked it in, for six months of rain now lay ahead of them. He did not turn to acknowledge his brother's departure. The weather had changed. The whole valley was in shade and in the distance to the south-east, between the Rumtek and Pakyong hills, he saw dark clouds massing for a nightly siege of Gangtok.

Pradeep DE's thoughts turned heavy. There would be a storm tonight, he knew it, if only to make his life more miserable. The window panes had remained unrepaired after the hailstorm and it shamed him that he had not been able to get hold of a single glazier. He thought of Yograj and he thought of his Mrs and he sank into a torpor of envy and regret.

The pony-tailed peon entered. 'Heera Babuni's here? The CCS wants this typed.'

'Give it here,' Pradeep DE snatched it from the peon's hand. He wished Heera Babuni were in the office, she would have surely understood the state of his life. But she was on unofficial leave today, and he had promised not to announce her absence to the office. He took the handwritten note from the peon and, after he left, sat at her desk and typed out its contents.

~

At night, as they prepared for bed, Pradeep DE's Mrs made a stern request. 'You should pray it doesn't rain.'

Pradeep DE stroked her arm. 'It's good. We'll sleep in fresh air.'

She jerked her arm away from his reach. 'If anything goes wrong, I won't let you breathe your fresh air.'

The storm broke late at night and his sleep was disrupted by a violent shake. His Mrs had dreamt of drowning and had awoken to find the bed drenched by the rain which had come in through the paneless windows. She shouted at him to move the bed and pushed him until he relented and stood up. She made him carry a mattress from another, unsoaked bed to the living room, which faced another building, and whose windows had escaped the hailstorm. He made the bed, lay down and cooed. 'Dearest,' he said, using an endearment from their early years, and caressed her.

'Your father's dearest. Don't touch me.' She shouted, 'You only act big with carpenters but lick everybody else's boots; you still have finished only one floor in the building in three years; your juniors already have five-storey buildings to their names with bank managers as tenants and you will never get a transfer to a better department but you will die twenty years later in the same office in the same department saying "Sir, Sir," to your son's classmates who would have joined the service and have been promoted above you and you'll still be showing all your teeth to the babunis from your department.'

She was sobbing now. As a calming measure, he tried to arouse her. Her stout back was turned to him. He tried to put his arm around it and despaired, he may as well attempt to embrace a water tank. He kissed her shoulder and whispered into her ear, 'Dearest.' He heard her sniffles. 'Dearest,' he said, 'this is just like camping.' He removed his wet pyjamas and underwear. His free hand caressed the upper portion of her back. He caressed her shoulders until he felt her back relax. He then won her temporary silence through seduction.

After the act, they heard the rain intensify. She left to check on other rooms. She returned from her investigations stamping in fury. There was water everywhere, some belongings were irreparably soaked. He tried to hold her, if only to win some sleep, but she sang:

Sant Pradeep, Sant Pradeep,
Open an ashram, Sant Pradeep

She sang it in the tone of a lullaby. He reached for her, she pushed his arm away.

In the morning, he woke up exhausted. He went through his house, inspecting the damage for himself. It was not as severe as he had feared. He fetched some of the tools which the glazier had ordered but not used. He attempted to cut a piece of glass. He measured out the window, went down to get a diary to write the measurements and, with a steel scale steadying and guiding the glass-cutter on the panes, made three swipes. A piece broke away easily. It was so easy; he cursed the glaziers for overcharging a naïve public. Then he found that the pane he had cut didn't fit the frame. He increased the sizes by a quarter inch on each side, and then tried to cut new pieces. His hand slipped, the cutter ran over the steel scale and cut his hand. He let go of the scale with a yelp, saw the glass fall away and, out of instinct, stuck his hand out to catch it as it fell.

It was not a wide wound but, because it had cut through the flesh of his palm, looked like a sinister mouth. His Mrs cried when she saw the wound. She kissed it, blamed herself for driving him to this and scolded him for taking her moods so seriously.

'Stay at home, Papa,' she said after she had bandaged it. She had not called him Papa in months.

'I have to go. The transfer. Our future, our daughters' future, all depends on the transfer.'

~

Pradeep DE drove through the wreckage of the previous night's storm. A large tree had fallen across Pani House Road. Workers from the Forest Department had cut through the tree and the section was littered with leaves and branches. Just like my heart, Pradeep DE thought, all ripped up and strewn about. But his mood and his thoughts would not balance for, despite the physical pain, he felt a little elated.

His decision to attend office turned to be an astute one. Heera Babuni was wearing a green salwar which seemed to have been stitched on to her as she waited. Blood had seeped through the gauze on his palm. She said, 'It's not bandaged properly.' She left and returned after a visit to a chemist's shop. She undid the bandage, her nails were buttons of pure emerald and her fragrant hair caressed his cheek. His hand grazed her ample but contained breasts, which strained against her shirt gently, like revolutionaries agitating through Constitutional means.

She exposed his wound, and he saw that the gash was deep. 'So you did this for your house?'

'For my home and for my daughters.'

He was seated on the chair. She bent over him and applied Dettol on it. He winced but did not let a sound escape his lips. She leaned over and kissed his wound. He suppressed a shudder and mocked his wound, 'It is not that serious.'

'See, the things some people do for their family. And there are other people...' She looked away, unable to complete her sentence.

His wound brought him other dividends. He was summoned to a meeting in the Commissioner-cum-Secretary's chamber, along with Sumati AE. They enquired after his hand, and he could tell them the truth. 'It was glass, from the window panes.'

'Should I send over my carpenter?' the Commissioner-cum-Secretary asked.

Pradeep DE declined the offer. 'Thank you Sir, but I have my own people.'

Sumati AE said, 'About the Tumin file. I don't think it can be processed in time for the financial year end. Too many problems—in the paperwork, in the estimates, bills. I have to sit down with their JE.'

Pradeep DE had expected this; she was too insidious for a mere complaint. He said, 'Work is work.'

The Commissioner-cum-Secretary stared at the President's portrait, as if drawing strength for a difficult conversation. 'I know they are your family, Bhai. But they shouldn't have come to us and talked like that.'

Pradeep DE rested his bandaged hand on the desk. 'Sir, even our families don't understand what kind of pressure we face. From up, the politicians. From down, the contractors and public. Plus, pressure from other officers, Sir.'

The Secretary looked at Pradeep DE. 'You have another heavy responsibility, Bhai. You have to report the news.'

Pradeep DE looked at his bandaged hand. 'I know, Sir. I'll tell them.'

Before he left the office, Heera Babuni kissed his hand again. 'May this give you strength.'

~

Pradeep DE visited Tibet Road in the morning to deliver the news. The ex-Minister looked at his son's hand and said, 'Boxing with your wife again.'

Pradeep DE retorted. 'You chose her for me.' He made Pemba fetch Yograj, who was in his room. He addressed both of them. 'It won't happen in March. That AE asked for a meeting in the morning. She wanted to go to the Women's Commission.'

Yograj jerked his head up. 'And what would she tell them? She was the one who wanted the percentage.'

Pradeep SE held up his bandaged hand. 'You have evidence, witnesses? In legal cases of man versus woman, the woman always has upper hand. Not all women are like Julie Babuni.'

The ex-Minister said, 'He's right.'

They heard Tiny Geniuses sing:

My bunny lies over the ocean
My bunny lies over the sea

My bunny lies over the ocean
Oh bring back my bunny to me, to me.
Oh bring back, Oh bring back, Oh bring back my bunny to me, to me.

It was an atonal attempt and it distracted them. Yograj shut the window and asked, 'So when?'

Pradeep DE had a ready solution. 'It's a non-lapsable fund so the money will go back to finance, and return after the vote on account and Cabinet sanction. That won't take much time, lots of pending files this year.'

The ex-Minister said, 'And it will give the vultures some time to calm down.'

Pradeep DE ignored the insult. 'Exactly. Two months. And then we can chase it again.'

Yograj looked at his father with spite. 'Louse from your balls, eh! You're only good for your communal politics.'

The accusation did not unsettle the ex-Minister, for it was a frequent one. But the mention of lapsable funds reminded him of something else. He phoned members of the Core Committee, informed them that the funds for the Steering Committee had been released, but the funds for CAS had been denied. An emergency meeting was scheduled.

~

A few days later, the core members of CAS convened at the ex-Minister's residence. The meeting began, like most high-level meetings in Sikkim, with discussions on health. They were all over sixty, and the trading of symptoms, ailments and remedies was brisk until the General Secretary, determined to be productive, asked, 'And what of the funds?'

The ex-Minister said, 'We're being lobbied against. It's not going to come. TB Chandath has received his share for the Steering Committee. Money which should have been ours.' He paused and added with finality, 'Someone from the inside told me.'

The Joint Secretary said. 'You can't build without money.' They heard him with seriousness, as they had always done. No one had shown more commitment to the Chandanth cause. The previous year, he had performed the death rites for his son who had married outside of the Chandanth clans and had since moved to Calcutta with his non-Chandanth wife. They were expecting their first child, and the CAS members waited to see if he would succumb and visit them.

The Treasurer said, 'You can't do anything without money. No money at all in the organization.' He used a wounded tone, for he dealt with money and this made him vulnerable to insinuation and blame.

The Press Secretary said, 'Not everything needs money. I can do studies, some research.' He had one unassailable advantage over his colleagues; he was the only one who could read and write in the original Chandanth script.

The ex-Minister dismissed him. 'What research? All the research you need to do is here in our heads. Ask us and we'll tell you—for free.'

The General Secretary said, 'Let's remain on the topic. We all have to go to work.' They made noises of efficiency. She continued, 'How's the money going to come? And why did TB get his funds while we were left out? The HCM must be informed of this.'

'We must form a sub-committee.' This was the Press Secretary. He had retired as an Additional Secretary of the Home Department and had retained the habits of his previous career.

The ex-Minister said, 'No need for any sub-committee. Once the money comes, everything will fall into place. We need to put pressure.' He looked around for suggestions.

The Joint Secretary said, 'Balidaan Diwas is nearing. It's in early June; that's just three months away.'

Instantly, they remembered CAS's nomination for the Steering Committee, on the day of the hailstorm. They had not been contacted since. The ex-Minister said, 'Joint Bhai is right. They chose us only to discard us.'

The Press Secretary said, 'They treat us like we haven't sacrificed.'

The ex-Minister paused, letting the idea of rebellion take root. Then he said, 'Joint Bhai here has sacrificed. But don't forget, even I have sacrificed.'

The ex-Minister was referring to the exile of Kalpana, his younger sister, almost thirty years earlier, for marrying a non-Chandanth. That scandal was well known. She had converted to Buddhism, had spent the rest of her life wearing a bakkhu and had never once tried to meet him and apologize. Though she was not ostracized by the Suikeybung family, and she kept contact with Sumitra, Yograj's mother, the ex-Minister did not visit her, even on her deathbed. That, he often asserted, that was called sacrifice.

The General Secretary said, 'We have to keep trying to talk.'

The Press Secretary wrung his hands. 'We should also increase membership, especially among the young. We need more people from other professions.'

The Joint Secretary turned sad. 'No use talking to our children. I paid for my son's education which told him that everything his father did was wrong.' And his sadness infected all of them because they were all united by a simple fact: their children, educated in schools which stressed on universal equality, despised their work.

The Press Secretary said, 'The hearts of parents rest on their children, the hearts of their children rest on stones.'

The ex-Minister was consoling. 'Bhai here is right, we need new members. Let's try and talk to our children again.' He refrained from mentioning his visit to the Minister for Village Roads, his colleagues did not need to know everything. On that hopeful note, organizational matters were dealt with, and they returned to matters of health.

Clearance

Towards the end of May, the ex-Minister received a phone call from Pradeep DE. The resources had arrived from the Finance Department. The bill could now be put up.

The ex-Minister spoke to Yograj. 'You'll go to the department? It's ready.'

Yograj shook his head. 'No. I'm not going there again. You are responsible for this.'

A low fog hung over Gangtok the next day. The ex-Minister visited

Unnati Bhavan and, at the entrance, he encountered the pony-tailed peon. 'Very inauspicious day to visit.' It was crowded inside, and the acrid smell of urine hung strongly in the damp, suffocating air. An open tender was being submitted for a large contract. The bigger contractors had brought supporters from the districts, young men who tried to appear unimpressed by the city. They were brutishly strong and, aware that they lacked wiliness, made up for it with an aggressive insolence. They smoked cigarettes in the corridor and spoke provocatively when the officials traipsed past them.

Pradeep DE's office was locked. In Sumati AE's office, the ex-Minister found Heera Babuni settling files. She encouraged him to leave. 'It's better to go home.'

The ex-Minister panted. 'I'm a tired and old man. Will the Government of Sikkim allow me to rest for a while?'

Heera Babuni shrugged and left the room. A little later Rann Maan peeped in and lightly took a seat next to him. 'They say the AE's not in? Then why did she call me today?'

They exchanged notes on the progress of their files. Rann Maan knew the ex-Minister, knew his name, and had attended a few of his rallies in his adolescence. The ex-Minister asked, 'You are from Ramphutar? Whose son are you?'

'Tanka Maan.'

The ex-Minister had known him. 'Did they call him Pharsi Maila?' They talked about Rann Maan's father, famous for a near-spherical, pumpkin-like head, and familiarity was established. The ex-Minister said, 'So you too have been dealing with her for a while.'

Rann Maan's face clouded with contempt. 'That ghichhan. Saying this is not good, that is not working. She's made me run around the whole month.'

Rann Maan shared all he had learnt about Sumati AE. Her greed was an undeclared legend. Contractors, civil suppliers and junior engineers feared her. He had met a head labourer contracted to a previous job overseen by her. When the work was on, he said, she had given him charge of the weekly procurement of meat, eggs and milk for her house. They told him that she herself took pending bills, against protocol, to the Pay and Accounts Department to get them passed. She had hidden someone's file for months because, being out of Gangtok, he had asked his mother to pursue the file. 'She's the greediest of them all. And given our officers, that is an achievement.'

He drew himself up sharply and said, 'You'll excuse me? I have a minor kidney problem.' When he returned from the toilet, he said, 'No one here from Ramphutar.' But he had done a survey of the situation. He said, 'There seem to be two contractor groups and also some small guys. Each side trying to put a lower tender.'

It was nearing two: the time for his taxi to Ramphutar. They left together. Outside the AE's door, they heard noises of aggression which grew distinct as they neared the staircase. They walked down a flight of stairs and paused at the landing, which had a window. They had a satisfying and cinematic view of the commotion in the forecourt of Unnati Bhavan. It was dense with contractors, youths, clerks and peons, who moved between the parked vehicles like water between rocks. It was a fight between the two groups of tenderers.

In the centre was a small clearing with two puddles of rainwater. This area served as a crowded arena and here the tempers were at their highest. It was impossible to distinguish sides. Men pranced around each other, waiting for the sudden movement which would prompt actions of self-defence. There was a shout, 'Son of a whore.'

'Who gave mother curses? Say it again! Say it again!' another man shouted, and slapped the person closest to him, the pony-tailed peon. This was usually accepted as the final provocation, the insulting of mothers. Movement dissolved into action. The scene erupted into a spontaneous melee of fighters, supporters, pacifiers and mediators. The water from the puddles splashed around; it added to the aura of frenzy.

The ex-Minister saw Heera Babuni in the eye of the action. Her secretarial poise had dropped. Abusing loudly, she pounced on a tenderer for slapping a peon of the department, who was a government servant. The ex-Minister saw Heera Babuni look up to where he was, her face contorted with agitation. He restrained himself from smiling.

~

When the ex-Minister next visited Unnati Bhavan, he found Rann Maan waiting in Sumati AE's office. He greeted the ex-Minister and said, 'She's just gone to the Secretary's office.'

They chatted until Sumati AE returned. She asked Rann Maan to wait outside; she was going to negotiate with each singly. There was no room for delicate phrasing. The ex-Minister said, 'Chhori, I'm an old man, I don't have time to talk in round words. What will the deal be?'

'I was just talking about that with the CCS. Twelve per cent, excluding contingency.'

Her greed was stiff and it could not be coaxed into concessions. The ex-Minister had prepared himself. 'Ten per cent, including contingency.'

They settled at twelve per cent, including contingency. She relaxed. 'It's a single-window system. It will even take care of the accounts people, the babunis and the peons. Savings for the whole department.'

'It sounds like democracy,' the ex-Minister said. He found himself admiring her tenacity and the way it made her disregard the threat of disrepute. Outside, he waited for half an hour, until Rann Maan emerged, grinning. 'The ghichhan agreed. Twelve per cent for you, twelve per cent for me.'

In the evening Pradeep DE dropped by Tibet Road to meet his father, 'Appa, you didn't come to my office. I could have helped you.'

The ex-Minister was curt. 'Your assistance is damaging. It's done now. I've settled with her.'

Pradeep DE raised an enquiring hand. The wound had nearly healed now, and the scar, slender and curved, was an attractive one. 'For how much?'

The ex-Minister told him. Pradeep DE whistled. 'And my share?'

'Single-window system. Talk to her. She said it is for all of you.'

His son was conciliatory. 'You saw my new nameplate? Says "Pradeep Chandanth" now.'

The ex-Minister had seen it and he grunted in satisfaction. 'There will be something for you. Even though you don't deserve it.'

Pradeep DE contemplated his scar. 'I don't deserve it, I know. I get tension from everywhere and I deserve none of it. Retail tension from my office and my family and wholesale tension from home.'

This confirmed what the ex-minister suspected: Pradeep DE had come to speak about something else. 'What do you want? Speak straight.'

Pradeep DE turned coy. 'There's a transfer coming up. You know the minister of my department quite well.' Then he shook his head and said, 'You have a big name. Can you can help me with the transfer?'

'Not now. I don't care about your transfer. I've helped you enough. I got you the job. You remember that, no?'

'That was a long time ago. I must get it, Appa. I must get it. My family life depends on it.'

~

Pradeep DE's Mrs had resumed her taunts after the bandages were removed. The glass panes had gone unfixed throughout April. It was only in May, after all the houses in Arithang had had their panes fixed, that his Mrs had found a glazier. She still sang occasionally:

> Sant Pradeep, Sant Pradeep,
> Open an ashram, Sant Pradeep.

He longed for the promotion which would quell her doubts and he worked tirelessly in the office towards it. He supported Heera Babuni in a discreet campaign to measure Tobgay DE's chances, and he sought an appointment directly with the Commissioner-cum-Secretary to press his case. They met in his chamber and Pradeep DE complained that he was being ostracized for his family's behaviour, even though he had apologized for their violations.

The Commissioner-cum-Secretary said, 'Bhai, I understand your state of mind. I too have suffered because of my quiet nature.' His qualifications had been overlooked by the High Command; he had specialized in finance and, instead, here he was, supervising the construction of village roads in a department with more officers than clerks. 'But I've done nothing wrong. The Constitution of India will look after me.'

'Very sad, Sir. Very sorry, Sir.'

The Commissioner-cum-Secretary nodded wearily. 'Yes, how sad it all is. But life is sad. And never apologize for your family. The government is also your family.'

Pradeep DE murmured 'Hmm,' and murmured, 'Hmm,' again, to show that the important statement had registered with him.

They talked about the burden of siblings for a while. Then Pradeep DE asked, 'Sir, about the transfer?'

The Commissioner-cum-Secretary put up his hand, like a sage weary of devotion, and said, 'I'll put up the best man's name. But I also have to do it carefully for, given my situation, recommendation might be a condemnation.'

He cackled softly, as if relishing the paradox. He looked outside, Pradeep DE followed his gaze. It was drizzling. The Secretary rang the buzzer. When the peon answered he asked for a single cup of black pepper tea. The audience had ended, and Pradeep DE thought the Commissioner-cum-Secretary was on his side.

In that hopeful mood, he opened a recent issue of *Sikkim Everyday* and turned to the editorial page. His letter had been printed and he re-read it.

> Respected Sir,
> Sikkim is a beautiful state with a rich heritage and the envy of all but it is not yet perfect and will not be so until inequality in the various levels of society are dealt with vision and understanding shown in our state only by the Chief Minister.
>
> Take for example the hot topic of people getting transferred from department to department. Some people with vested interests will say that such transfers are not good as many times officials are moved out before they have done their best but I pooh-pooh that idea and say that such rotation is necessary for the proper flow of information through all the correct channels. It is very important that especially technical officials are allowed to work in all major departments to benefit everyone with their experience.
>
> Then another point creating a buzz is who should get transferred. My opinion is that the officials who have served longest in one department should be transferred first as they have more to teach lessons to whichever departments they go to. Seniority should be respected and it must not bow before the forces of injustice which will

> not grant them it's due. It is the sincere wish of the Sikkimese people that experience should be respected and given its due.
> Your's faithfully,
> A Concerned Citizen

He sighed. It was the sigh of an artist condemned to obscurity in his lifetime. The letter had been published two days after it was sent. He had known then, as he had always known, that he could not expect any response or any criticism. Not a single public nerve would twitch in acknowledgement. Despite his detachment, he was still disappointed that there was no discussion in his office, given the especial topicality of its subject. Only Sarata Babuni said, 'I read the paper. They are talking about the transfers in other departments as well.'

~

Like all great adventures, Pradeep Chandanth's vocation had begun with an accident. This was almost fourteen years earlier; just after the ascension of YM Chandath as the Chief Minister. By then, his father had been out of power for six years. Pradeep DE was then a Junior Engineer and newly married. He was living in rented quarters in Arithang, where he had moved soon after his wedding—it had been the ex-Minister's idea to grant his son this freedom. He had also bought some land for Pradeep JE and was assisting him with the building costs. Those had been the days: he was in his own house for the first time in his life, his Mrs was still demure, her figure still shapely and her tongue not yet sharpened.

One day the ex-Minister visited him and asked, 'You've been writing lately?'

Pradeep JE bought books whenever he could and he wrote English in complete sentences. These two facts had colluded to give him a literary reputation.

'Why?'

The ex-Minister said, 'The new Chief Minister phoned me yesterday. We should begin working for the upliftment of our people, she says. She wants to do some good while she lasts. And she won't last long.'

'But I'm just an engineer.'

'Idiot!' his father had shouted and thrown a magazine at him. 'It's for all of us. You, your new wife, your children, my children. Everyone.'

After he left, Pradeep JE's Mrs asked, 'Why was he shouting?'

'Father-son business.'

His Mrs was unconvinced. 'You're married now. That's not the way to talk to a married son.'

Pradeep JE's services were simple. He had to write letters to newspapers under false names; people only wrote editorial letters under their real names to praise the Hon'ble Chief Minister, or to compare Sikkim favourably to other states. When the ex-Minister tried to dictate his first letter to him, the artist in Pradeep JE rebelled.

'Just tell me what I should write, not how I should write it,' he said.

And so, a few days later, Pradeep JE's first letter had appeared in *Sikkim Everyday*.

> Respected Sir,
> The Hon'ble Chief Minister is doing too many things for the upliftment of the Sikkimese people, so that they may awake and stake their true claim in the annals of the world. She has paid extreme attention to all the myriad castes and religions of Sikkim that have flourished since time immemorial. She has ensured that each of them gets their due representation when standing in front of the glorious constitution of India. To her efforts we say, Hats Off!
>
> But Sir, one should also not take care of the entire world and neglect one's own house. The Chandanth caste, to which the Hon'ble Chief Minister belongs, is very backward in all spheres of public life. We have suffered too long at the hands of its own fate, and it is only in recent history that the Hon'ble Chief Minister has come as a messiah for whole Sikkim. While she is leading the glorious state of Sikkim to their salvation, we also request her to make genuine efforts for the upliftment of his own people.
>
> Sir, there will not be success everytime but we must keep our spirits up even if we fail, because the whole world knows that failure is the success of pillar.
>
> Yours' sincerely,
> Homnath Chandanth, Development Area.

It was, he could now admit to himself, a callow effort. The language was not suppliant enough, and there were basic errors of language. But back then, it had not mattered. He had experienced the elation of seeing his name in print. He heard it being discussed at the wedding of a relative soon after and he realized that, like all good debuts, his letter had combined opportunity with need. And almost instantly he realized the profound disadvantage of his work: he could never take credit for any success.

Coerced by his father, Pradeep JE wrote other letters. After almost three years, during which he averaged a letter a month, he was summoned by the ex-Minister to Tibet Road. The house was crowded and he had to wade past the people who spilled over from the living room. His father saw him, called him closer to his chair, and said, 'You must have heard the news.'

He had. An organization, CAS, had just been formed with the blessings of the Hon'ble Chief Minister and his father was its first president. Once more, Pradeep JE experienced the sadness of the toiler destined to remain always unrecognized. He almost wrote a letter stating how the formation of CAS was an exemplary move, but that it still needed to be rigorously checked lest it become the fiefdom of one man. He had the letter ready in his head, waiting only for the burst of will that would make him write and post it, when he opened the newspaper one day and saw that it was too late.

> Respected Sir,
> It was with pleasure that I read yesterday of the formation of a institution which is destined to take the long-oppressed Chandanth people to their rightful place in history. Under the exemplary vision of the Hon'ble Chief Minister Smt Y M Chandath and the guidance of the movement's visionary, ex-Minister Shri Kuldeep Chandanth, it appears that the imbroglio may be at an end. The formation of the Chandanth Action Society (CAS) is the first blow that has been struck in the name of historical oppression on our kind.
>
> Sir, CAS promises to fight for the downtrodden members of the Chandanth community and get them due representation in all spheres of public life. In its first meeting yesterday, the principal founding

member and hard-core luminary Shri Kuldeep Chandanth promised that the organization must toil unceasingly until the Chandanth community will be recognized by law as amongst the Other Backward Castes (OBC) with all due privileges to be granted in lieu of centuries-old oppression and discrimination. Until then, Sir, we cannot rest.
Yours sincerely etc,
Mitradas Chandith

Pradeep DE's services had been superseded by Mitradas, but he discovered that his passion for anonymous canvassing was not easily purged. He had since written to all the Nepali and English publications in Gangtok and to some beyond, in Siliguri and Kolkata.

There was no cause too great—he wrote on the necessity of an Opposition to safeguard democracy in Sikkim—or too small—he wrote on the distressing amount of homework given to toddlers. He wrote against broken families caused by men marrying twice, he wrote on the difficulty of getting good building sites, the mental trauma suffered by the under-appreciated, the quiet heroes at the Department of Village Roads, the need for monks to be less materialistic, and the need for the quality of vegetables to be checked in the market.

He wrote as objectively as he could, examining his pulse against public opinion, as if he were merely the voice of dissent, speaking what the masses thought but dared not voice. His letters were seldom discussed in his presence but he was to blame for it. He made it a rule to never mention them unprovoked, for he believed that nothing damaged a creative artist more than solicited appreciation.

Pay and Accounts

Yograj was surprised to hear Rann Maan's voice in his house. The villager was partnering with the ex-Minister; they were going to get their payments passed together. 'Why didn't you tell me you were Kuldeep Chandanth's son? I grew up in his shade.'

Yograj saw them strategize, discussing percentages and possible approaches. He realized that they were better at this than he would have been. Rann Maan was a veteran of countless such chases, and the ex-Minister was working in a world that he had helped create. Each lifted the other, and where an uncompanioned effort might have distressed the ex-Minister, the presence of a partner turned it into a shared adventure.

A week later, Rann Maan arrived with breathless news. The Commissioner-cum-Secretary's signature, the final one, had come through. The bills, on oblong pink paper, were now in the office of the Pay and Accounts Department.

Rann Maan knew the workings of the Pay and Accounts Department. The ex-Minister could not come there. It was the one office in Sikkim where it did not pay to have a big name. The ex-Minister would inflate the cost of the whole process by his mere presence. Rann Maan offered, 'I'll say that both the files are mine, but one was done in a friend's name. If I use your name, my cost will go up as well.' It was important to Rann Maan that he was chasing an ex-Minister's bill and he asked nothing for the privilege. But there would be expenses at the office.

One irreducible law governed the whole process of payments: the accounts people had to be kept in a state of constant pleasure. They were all equal there—the boy with the twenty-thousand-rupee bill and the old-time contractor chasing a multi-crore-rupee payment. In that office, things were rational and civilized and gratitude was compulsory.

Rann Maan visited the ex-Minister every morning, to seek his guidance before he left for the Pay and Accounts Department, and he visited every evening with an update, staying over on some nights. The ex-Minister enjoyed these evenings, he sat at the dining table and Rann Maan on a stool. They would chat till late, their conversations encircling the same people and the same events, without exhaustion, without repetition.

The bills were entered into the system, five hundred rupees there; there was a peon who was useless but could do damage, two hundred rupees there; it was being processed in the large room by a good man, a thousand rupees for him, but only after it was done; the officers didn't ask him anything—Rann Maan looked too poor for that—but the

Additional Director held on to the file for two days and almost sent it back to the department with an objection, two thousand rupees upfront for him. The ex-Minister made Yograj accompany Rann Maan with this money. 'Don't leave everything to the villager. And learn what he does in the office. Your whole life will be spent there.' Then it went in to be processed for cheques, and the babuni processing it was on long leave. A clerk, who only did cheques for the Department of Urban Affairs, was persuaded to work on it. A thousand five hundred there, for there was the babuni's wrath to consider when she returned.

On the evening after the final signatures were done, and the cheques were sent back to the department, Sumati AE phoned and asked after his health; the Commissioner-cum-Secretary phoned and asked after his health; Pradeep DE brought him fruits. Rann Maan stayed over at their house and, after dinner, they polished their plans for the following day.

In the morning, the ex-Minister met Rann Maan at Unnati Bhavan. The cheques were with the accountant, who stood up when they entered. Sumati AE stood beside him like the hostess at a prize-giving ceremony. 'We're all so happy.'

The pony-tailed peon and Heera Babuni accompanied them to the State Bank of Sikkim, near the hospital. The two recipients would be paid in cash while the peon and the babuni would return to Unnati Bhavan with the department's savings. There was a drizzle and the open umbrellas slowed their movements on the pavement. Rann Maan held the umbrella and offered his arm to the ex-Minister. The pony-tailed peon followed closely behind, as were his instructions. Heera Babuni followed at a safe distance for she did not want to be seen beside any of the three. She was there to keep an eye on the peon, who had been known to stray. She wanted to blend in and not call attention to herself, so she had worn a beige shirt, baggy dark brown jeans and a pair of moccasins.

The ex-Minister moved slowly, savouring the eagerness of the peon and the babuni. At the State Archives Building, he paused, pointed to the old and gracefully proportioned structure, and said. 'We met the king here in 1972. Here we fought for democracy.'

Rann Maan's reverence returned. 'I look at you, and I look at myself. I have done nothing.'

The ex-Minister assured him that there was no such thing as a wasted life, except perhaps those of the two people following them.

A little further down, there was a fissure in the road and water emerged from it. It might have been an underground stream finding an outlet, or a water-supply pipe which had ruptured. They paused and discussed this. The peon closed in on them and said, 'Why are you walking so slow?'

Rann Maan said, 'So that the interest accumulates on our cheques.'

The ex-Minister slapped his back in appreciation. Near St Thomas's Church, the ex-Minister paused again. He pointed through the thin mist towards the SNT Bus Stop, next to which they saw a half-finished building, grey, unpainted concrete, with three floors of slabs and columns, and two incomplete brick walls in the lowest floor.

'The temple,' the ex-Minister said.

Rann Maan knew of it from his conversations with the ex-Minister. 'It will be complete soon. And you will complete it, Kuldeep-jiu. I know.'

Their umbrellas collided with those of passers-by who urged them to keep moving.

'Vultures,' Rann Maan said.

At the bank, they did not have to stand in a line. The pony-tailed peon knew the teller, and their cheques were processed immediately. Rann Maan withdrew his money first. He held his payment, two lakh twenty thousand rupees, in his hand as the ex-Minister deposited his cheque. The teller offered to give him cash, but he said, 'Son, I'm an old man. I don't want to carry so much money with me. Deposit it into my account.' He offered his account number on a piece of paper.

The teller hesitated, and looked at the pony-tailed peon behind him. 'Are you sure?'

The ex-Minister nodded. It was an old account, opened when he had been a minister. He had recently checked on its status, and was surprised to find that it was still active, with seven thousand rupees in it.

He heard the peon hiss behind him. 'But Madam said cash.'

The ex-Minister raised his voice and addressed the crowd, 'Is there a law which says I can withdraw only cash?'

There was silence. The peon played with his pony-tail. Heera Babuni approached and enquired. The ex-Minister signed the deposit slip and said, 'The money's going into my account. I am too old to carry so much. You'll have to tell your office people to wait for a few days.'

Heera Babuni was red with contempt and her complexion contrasted with her clothes. She said, 'If only you had not been so old. Men without dignity.'

The pony-tailed peon stamped his foot. 'That villager has disappeared too.'

Rann Maan had used their argument to slip away. The ex-Minister walked away from them and returned to Tibet Road in a taxi. He found Rann Maan waiting for him at home. He bowed before the ex-Minister. 'Great men have different ways of thinking. That is why they are great.'

This tickled the ex-Minister's vanity and he conceded a smile. Rann Maan said, 'If it weren't for you, they would have taken everything from me.'

The ex-Minister turned strident. 'Those vultures! They didn't deserve anything. I would have given them their share if they had shown some respect. Even this much.' He held his thumb and forefinger slightly apart. Then he felt sorry for Rann Maan and said, 'Now what will you do? The department won't give you any more work.'

Rann Maan waved away the ex-Minister's concern. 'Don't worry about me. There are more departments in Sikkim than stars in the night sky. I've already put tenders in a few other departments.'

He drew his legs in and sat cross-legged on the sofa. 'But our work with these vultures is not yet done. We still have to submit the receipts in the department. It is compulsory.'

It was Friday. They made plans to meet at Unnati Bhavan on Monday. Their faces would be something to see. Rann Maan left after a while, to celebrate in Ramphutar. Pradeep DE phoned, his voice was thin. 'The CCS heard and he shouted at me. No chance of transfer. It's gone now.'

The ex-Minister mollified him. 'Tell him not to victimize a man because of his family members. There will be something for you.'

Pradeep DE ended the call with a whine. In the evening Yograj came home in a celebratory mood. His elder brother had phoned and narrated the ex-Minister's actions. 'Appa, you did the right thing.'

The ex-Minister raised his fist. Yograj sat close. 'So the money is all in your account?'

Yograj went over their deal. The bill was for twenty-eight lakh. The ex-Minister had invested eighteen lakh and the profit was to be shared. Yograj was owed a little over five lakh from the money.

The ex-Minister patted his son's arm. 'I have asked for the cheque-book. It is almost here. And then you'll get your share. Stop worrying over money. Chandanths don't do that.'

~

At Unnati Bhavan on Monday, the pony-tailed peon—who had had time to compose a response—approached him with menace. The ex-Minister said, 'Remember the police?'

Heera Babuni walked past him and spat drily as she passed. The other babunis in the accounts room ignored him as they exchanged news. Sarata Babuni's father had been admitted to hospital in the morning with chest pains. The ex-Minister wanted to see Sumati AE's reaction but he never got to. The pony-tailed peon ran in and announced, 'Sarata Babuni's father has passed away.'

This news electrified the office; it signalled an impromptu holiday. The sombre cause prevented an outright cheer but the peons scurried, the babunis put their belongings back into their bags, and vehicles were organized. They were to go to Development Area, where Sarata Babuni lived. The engineers and undersecretaries gallantly offered lifts in their vehicles, the babunis formed pools to accompany them. The pony-tailed peon loudly offered a ride on his new bike to the babunis and settled for a male junior engineer as a pillion. The ex-Minister became insignificant, as did the few other people who had come with work.

Heera Babuni and Julie Babuni approached the ex-Minister consolingly. Heera Babuni said, 'Work won't happen today. Come tomorrow, no? But early morning because the tenderers are going to be there again. I have to deal with them and it's my hatest thing.'

Julie Babuni said, 'The tender people are harassing us so much.'

The ex-Minister felt robbed. 'At least take the receipts. I won't have to come here again.'

'But we want to see you again,' Julie Babuni chirped.

The pony-tailed peon said, 'I'm going to lock up the office.'

'No, I'll wait. If you lock up the office, I'll file a police complaint.'

The threat failed. The pony-tailed peon said, 'Okay, stay here then. Make sure no one steals anything.'

The building emptied in a series of happy clatters. At eleven-thirty on a Monday morning, the Department of Village Roads was empty. He called Pradeep DE, his phone was switched off. By twelve-thirty the ex-Minister's pride had eroded, and the urgency had gone. The receipts could be submitted later. Rann Maan appeared in the empty room and asked. 'Where have these people gone?'

The ex-Minister updated him. Rann Maan was forgiving. 'Oh! At least it's for a funeral.'

At one-thirty Rann Maan went to the toilet and returned unrelieved. The pony-tailed peon had locked the toilet before leaving. Outside, the drizzle was now a downpour. The rain's pattering aggravated Rann Maan's urgency and the smell of urine heightened his torment. He writhed for half an hour. At two the downpour had not subsided. Rann Maan grew desperate. He shouted, 'Chutiyas! Can't even leave a toilet open. These chutiyas! I need to teach them a lesson. In any case, I've got my money.'

The ex-Minister looked on with amused horror as Rann Maan seized the governmental stamps and stamp pads from the desks and the drawers and put them in his bag. His rage abated but not his urge to piss. He climbed on the desk closest to the door and, unzipping his pants, pissed as he walked. The desks were arranged in a large 'C' not very far from each other so he could walk around the room, pissing over everything: old files, new files, unfinished cups of tea, some knitting, a packet of sweetmeats. When he neared the ex-Minister, he jumped off, his cock still peeking out of the curtains of his fly. He said, 'I still have some left.'

The ex-Minister assumed Rann Maan intended to wet him next and backed up towards the door but Rann Maan walked into Sumati AE's office. The ex-Minister waited outside. Through the frosted glass he saw Rann Maan's silhouette stand on her desk, consecrate it with a few drops, and shake his cock affectionately before tucking it into his pants. Then he emerged from the office and ran away without a farewell into the rain.

The ex-Minister waited until the rain eased and the sun was out. He walked towards Tibet Road through the vapours that rose off the road, careful to avoid the slippery parts. The earth's recuperation from the dry months was complete. Every exposed patch of earth was green. There were plants sprouting in the thin strips of mud between the road and the kerb and between embedded flagstones in the shortcut to his house. There was moss on the retaining walls that lined the road. He stopped outside his house and greeted the momo-seller, who was leaving for her afternoon round at the hospital. As they talked, his gaze travelled from the symmetry of her features to his building and he noted that it needed a fresh coat of paint.

~

The relief brought by the payment was short. A few days later, as the ex-Minister and Yograj ate dinner, they heard a howl from Pemba's room. There was a great pain in his left ear. They poured a heated mixture of mustard oil and garlic into it but it worsened his pain. He would not stop howling. They drove him to the STNM Hospital. They admitted him and took some tests.

Yograj informed his father that he knew the doctor. His name, too, was Kuldeep Chandanth.

'Whose son is he?' the ex-Minister asked Yograj.

'Riwaj Chandith.'

'Mitradas' maternal cousin? Are they from Mangan?' The ex-Minister knew the family very well. Riwaj's father was a noted miser, and had once, in the old days, followed a man to Calcutta to recover fifty rupees. 'Of course, fifty rupees was a lot of money in those days.'

Yograj admonished his father. 'Don't tell him that or he'll give Pemba the wrong injection.'

The doctor arrived and put the ex-Minister's hands to his eyes. The ex-Minister was polite. 'How's your father, son? I didn't know Riwaj had a son. When did you finish your doctor studies?'

'Last year.'

'Are you married?'

Dr Kuldeep shook his head. Yograj exhaled. 'I told you to be prepared.'

Dr Kuldeep nodded in amusement. He said, 'The preliminary tests don't show anything wrong with him. Some basic medicines should help.'

'Can we keep him here for a day?' the ex-Minister asked.

Dr Kuldeep agreed. The ex-Minister asked, 'Are you going to be on duty tomorrow?

Dr Kuldeep confirmed his attendance and Pemba was admitted to the general ward. It was a crowded room, with three rows of beds. They were all occupied—some beds were shared by two patients. They settled him into half a bed, next to a boy with an eye infection, and left him to the general care of the room, and the nurses whom he outraged by attempting to caress their faces.

The ex-Minister visited Pemba in the morning. 'How's your ear? Still hurting?'

Pemba nodded. 'Yes.'

'You want to stay here for one more day? With the nurses?'

Pemba nodded vigorously. 'Yes.'

This suited the ex-Minister. Dr Kuldeep was not yet on duty and the ex-Minister, overcome by the smell of disinfectant in the general ward, ambled in the parking lot as he waited for him. The STNM Hospital dominates the intersection named after it. It is one of the hearts of Gangtok and is portioned by the National Highway 31A, with the hospital located in pieces around the intersection. The main hospital on one side, connected to the dental and orthopaedic departments by a footbridge, and the maternity and gynaecological departments further down.

The ex-Minister walked towards the footbridge, to better see the State Bank of Sikkim building, the site of his recent triumph. Beside the footbridge, he saw Ai Doma, his neighbour, selling momos. She squatted beside the entry to the footbridge, with her vessel beside her and a large umbrella to provide shelter from the continual drizzle. That was the extent of her stall. The ex-Minister winced when he considered the wet dirt around her. The ex-Minister informed her of Pemba's illness. 'Your boyfriend's very sick.'

She came in the early afternoon, as Dr Kuldeep and the ex-Minister inspected Pemba. He was asleep but he looked to be in pain. The momo-seller blew into his ear to assuage his ache, for the painkiller's effects had ebbed. She fed him some momos and told the ex-Minister, 'You go ahead with your work. I'm here throughout the day, I'll give him food. If anything happens the nurses will inform me.'

Dr Kuldeep arrived. The ex-Minister spent the morning and early afternoon in the hospital, attempting to find out as much as he could about the doctor. He was not married, that was certain.

Girlfriend? Dr Kuldeep blushed and spoke of his hospital duties and his private practice.

Did he know the ex-Minister had a daughter, Yogita? Dr Kuldeep nodded shyly. He had not met her but they had common friends.

Parents? Dr Kuldeep implied that he respected them and their wishes. If he knew of the divide between the ex-Minister and his uncle, Mitradas, he did not show it.

After the interrogation, the ex-Minister, not wishing to appear too eager, said, 'I'll go home now. I'll get sick if I stay here for too long.' The doctor agreed.

At home, Yograj asked, 'So when will I get my share? You haven't spoken about it.'

The ex-Minister looked pained. 'It's coming, it's coming. Now is not the time. Let Pemba get well first.'

In the morning when he visited, Dr Kuldeep informed him that Pemba had spent the night in a state of excitement. His deliriums had subsided but his instincts had not. He had calmly accepted the slaps delivered by two nurses for attempting to feel their bottoms. In the end, he had been given a tranquilizer for his delirium. He could now be discharged.

From the window of the doctor's office, he saw Pemba in the parking lot close to the momo-seller's spot. She had not yet arrived to set up her stall. It was sunny after a week of bad weather and the sun's sparkle reflected from all surfaces. He was surrounded by three nurses who clapped as he danced for them.

As the ex-Minister signed his discharge papers, Pemba collapsed. The pain had returned. They carried him back to the general ward, half a bed was cleared out for him again and Dr Kuldeep gave him a painkiller. Pemba slept and did not wake up. He was pronounced dead half an hour later.

'That's strange. I've never seen anything like it. I wonder what illness it was,' Dr Kuldeep said.

'A fortunate way to die,' the ex-Minister said.

The ex-Minister walked outside. The momo-seller's spot was still vacant. The sun had become stronger. He stood in the shade of an ambulance and phoned Yograj; he was not reachable. He phoned his nephew, Nima Thendup, who was in the bazaar. He arrived within a few minutes and took over the formalities while the ex-Minister signed the death certificate and envied the fool for his uncomplicated departure.

An Uncertain Ceremony

As they loaded Pemba's body into the hearse, Nima Thendup asked the ex-Minister, 'Should I call a priest or a monk? I know some monks.'

The ex-Minister had given it some thought. 'I don't know. He never told me.'

Pemba had served the ex-Minister for thirty years. He had come without any knowledge of himself, and the ex-Minister's early interrogations had yielded nothing. Nima stated, 'His name was Pemba. It's a Bhotey name. And he looked like a Bhotey.'

The ex-Minister did not want monks in his house. He spoke calmly, like a policeman analysing clues. 'His face was shaped like a Tibetan, but his complexion was like a Lepcha. His voice had a Tamang pitch. His nose was Limbu and his Adam's apple was that of a Bahun. He once brought a man home claiming he was his brother. The man was very dark and this sort of differences in brothers happens in Newaris.'

Pemba had not demonstrated a partiality for any religion—there was god and there was the devil. He had stayed away from the puja rooms of the house. The ex-Minister considered asking their regular Chandanth priest to preside over Pemba's last rites but that man was fastidious, he would surely refuse. 'A priest. But not the usual one,' he said and phoned another priest, a young man who had come seeking favours a month ago.

At Tibet Road, Pemba's body was carried over two flights of narrow stairs and laid out in the living room. Nima Thendup asked the ex-Minister to sit in the kitchen, away from the body and any possible distress. Thinley Machi arrived and took control of the kitchen. Then two youths appeared, wearing large T-shirts and trousers that hung loose on their waists. They had been summoned by Nima Thendup. They helped him clear out the living room of unnecessary clutter, anything that might hinder the movement of people. Their clothes, of a fashion beyond his understanding, fascinated the ex-Minister. 'What are they? Why do they walk like their bodies are broken in three places?'

'They are hiphops,' Nima Thendup said and sent them to fetch the priest. They discussed rations. The ex-Minister was unsure of the need to purchase much. 'There won't be many people. How many people will come to mourn a fool?'

'He was more popular than you think,' Nima Thendup said. A steady stream of people came into the house. There were the shopkeepers from the street, hotel-owners, servants from nearby houses, a few Tiny Geniuses, brought in by their ayahs who had heard on their way home. They sat around the body, laid out in the centre of the room and chatted without restraint. There were some jokes; he belonged to no one and so there was no one whose feelings had to be considered. The Tiny Geniuses began a game of hide-and-seek.

The priest arrived; young, proud and doubting. He resented this commission, paltry and demeaning, but a necessary one. He was unsure what he was supposed to do, there were few protocols for such situations and the ex-Minister could not help him. Nima Thendup offered a suggestion. 'Just do what you would do for a relative. But not a very close one.'

The ex-Minister phoned Yogita. 'Pemba's gone.'

She knew of his illness and had spoken to him in the hospital. She began to cry. The ex-Minister said, 'Come for his funeral. We'll visit the hospital where he died.'

She demurred through her sobs. 'Work is more important, Appa. I'll remember him in the way I choose to.'

Yograj entered. 'So he's really gone?' He had been at a friend's house, in a part of Gangtok where phone signals were erratic. The ex-Minister nodded and pointed at the living room.

Yograj went to the living room, returned and said, 'But he was a Bhotey. He should be with monks. Who called him?' He pointed to the priest, sipping tea. The priest put his cup down. The ex-Minister asked him to carry on. 'It doesn't matter who says the prayers. He's dead, no?'

Nima Thendup agreed. 'Even he didn't know what he believed in. And you should keep your phone switched on if you want to be consulted.'

The ex-Minister left the room and shouted at the Tiny Geniuses shrieking in the corridors. They began to leave with their ayahs. The shock wore off Yograj and he began to cry. Nima Thendup sat beside him and offered comforting words.

~

The crowd thinned towards the evening. Ai Doma visited; she had gone to her momo stall at Hospital Daraa that day and had heard after she returned home. She looked at his body from the doorway of the living room. 'So he's really gone?'

She bent over the body and said, 'Ay Pemba! You want to put your hand on my bum? I won't say anything.'

The corpse did not respond. Ai Doma wiped her eyes. 'He's really gone.'

Behind her, Nima Thendup supplied details. Ai Doma recovered quickly. She took over the kitchen work from Thinley Machi and got her to rest.

Pradeep DE arrived and sat abjectly. 'Thank you. Thank you for making me a hero in my own department. No one's talking to me now.'

The ex-Minister was unmoved. 'All vultures. They got what they deserved.'

Pradeep DE whined. 'You could have at least told me. You know my department people. Talking here, talking there.'

The ex-Minister misunderstood. 'They knew Pemba in your department?'

'Not that. The payment.'

The ex-Minister said, 'Not now.'

Nima Thendup said, 'Not now.'

Pradeep DE muttered, 'This is a family matter.'

'So is that.' Nima Thendup pointed towards the living room, where the body was kept. The ex-Minister nodded in approval. Pradeep DE was dejected, his rehearsed act had been cut short. He asked, 'Funeral?'

'We're doing it tomorrow. A simple one.'

'I'll come for his funeral. He was my childhood friend,' Pradeep DE promised and left. Inside the living room, the priest had finished reciting the prayers stipulated for a distant relative. Thinley Machi went to Yograj's room, comforted him, and brought him out.

Yogita phoned again and she spoke to everyone present there. She had known Pemba for so long; he had entered the ex-Minister's service a few years before she was born. She always associated the house with him, and it would be so much more silent when she returned for a holiday. 'He brought us up. For twenty years he looked after us.'

The ex-Minister said, 'We're cremating him tomorrow.' She protested on the phone, her reasons were the same as Yograj's. The ex-Minister overrode her concerns. 'It doesn't matter how it's done. He was a small man.'

Yogita said, 'You shouldn't call him a small man. He may have been a servant but he was part of the house.' Then she cried, scolding herself for calling him a servant.

Nima Thendup and Thinley Machi stayed over and after they had retired to their assigned room, and Ai Doma had left, Yograj recovered from his anguish. He asked. 'Cheque-book arrived? After all this is done, I want my share.'

His red eyes made him look aggrieved. The ex-Minister said, 'How much will you think only of money? There are other things.'

It was a convenient chastening, and Yograj could only answer, 'Just asking.'

~

At dawn, they woke up to the sound of rain and prepared the body for cremation. After it was done, the priest asked for his fees, saying he had work elsewhere. It was a child's naming ceremony and he needed time to purify himself. It was evident he did not want to be seen at the cremation ground performing the rites for an uncertain soul. The ex-Minister let him go.

Pradeep DE arrived and spoke again of the way he was now being treated by his colleagues. He had discovered that the department was planning to go on a picnic by a riverside and he was being excluded from their plans. Then a reluctant invitation was extended to him which he, of course, refused. They were boycotting him, and he demanded recompense from the ex-Minister for his trauma. 'Even I have suffered. Even I have sacrificed.'

The ex-Minister waved him away in irritation, 'Not now. Not now.'

Nima Thendup had arranged for a pick-up truck; it arrived with the two hiphops. The driver had a steady cough. The carrier was wide enough for the dead body and four people. Before the vehicle left, the ex-Minister gave Nima Thendup the keys to the godown on the ground floor, 'Get two of the beams from down there.'

Nima Thendup took the hiphops with him and returned with two eight-footer beams of sandalwood. 'Include it in the pyre.'

The hiphops tied some of the khadas offered to Pemba around the truck's rear-view mirrors and around its grille. The rain ceased, and the air was steamy and fresh. They decided not to take Yograj, who had cried late into the night. Pradeep DE sat in the front with Nima Thendup. The two boys stood on the carrier against traffic norms; this was an allowance made for vehicles bound for cremation grounds or cemeteries. At the Amdo Golai junction, the traffic policeman on duty saluted as the vehicle passed him.

Nima Thendup had made arrangements at the cremation grounds in Ranipool. He had found a priest, an unbiased man whom the corpse-burners knew. It was a ceremony with little fuss, for there was another large funeral due in an hour. When it was time to light the pyre, the priest handed Pradeep DE a lit flambeau and motioned towards the pyre. Pradeep DE hesitated to take it. 'Am I the only one here who can do it?'

Nima Thendup countered his hesitation. 'Give it to me. I'll light it.' The priest hesitated because he had heard Nima Thendup's name, and had slotted him to be a Buddhist. As he fumbled for an excuse, Nima Thendup snatched the flame from him and lit Pemba's pyre. The wood was wet but eventually caught. He sniffed the air; he could make out the faint, sweet smell of burning sandalwood. He instructed the hiphops to take care of the priest's requirements.

'What do I do with the ashes?' the caretaker asked. It was customary for the ashes of the Chandanths to be dispersed in the forest on the day after cremation.

Nima Thendup had not received any specific instruction from his uncle. He pointed to the swift, narrow river. 'There.'

On the journey back, Pradeep DE said, 'I would have lit the fire. I was just asking.'

Nima Thendup said, 'It's just a fire. Who knows what happens to us when it all ends?'

Pradeep DE shared this view with him. He too thought all men were equal and that the politics of communalism was played by men with no work. 'Silver, sandalwood—what is the difference?'

'I know, I know. He's one communal man. But he's old.'

Pradeep DE turned to his cousin. 'You don't mind his speeches?'

Nima Thendup said, 'You know me. Half here, half there. I don't mind.'

'People who belong to both sides sometimes don't belong anywhere.'

Nima Thendup had a quick sense of injury. 'What are you trying to say? Be open.'

Pradeep DE was silent and looked at the road ahead. Nima Thendup's temper rose. 'Just because you earn more than me? Just because my mother married a poor Bhotey and your father drove her out? Just because I studied in a local school?'

'I didn't say all that.'

'You don't have to say everything. I can understand.'

The driver sensed the argument was likely to deepen. He coughed and accelerated. Nima Thendup said, 'Stop the vehicle! Stop it right here.'

The pick-up stalled. It was raining hard. Nima Thendup leaped out and, through the window, put a finger close to Pradeep DE's face. 'Watch your mouth. If it wasn't for your father I would have fixed you right here.'

A vehicle honked impatiently from the rear. Nima Thendup said, 'Take Engineer Saab home. I'll return in a taxi.'

Two days after the funeral, there was a notice in *Sikkim Everyday*:

> FAREWELL MY PEMBA DAJU
> You shared our lives for twenty years and you had the good fortune to leave with smiles on your face. Even when I was not at home I thought of you often. Your oceanic concern, your near-absent culinary skills, and your enthusiasm towards the fairer sex. You made us laugh everyday and with each laughter we learned to celebrate life. You will be remembered always, by me, by my family and by all who will pass through the doors of our happy home.
> Your chhuchi kanchi,
> Yogita Chandanth

She had emailed a journalist friend at the newspaper. The notice was accompanied by a photograph of Pemba. He was grinning in it, a wide and typical grin which the ex-Minister had often taken as a sign of clinical idiocy but it abstracted well in the photograph, and suggested gentle humour and boundless compassion.

~

The ex-Minister began a search for a new servant the following day but it was not like the old days. Helpless people no longer showed up looking for shelter and support, as Pemba had done, and, even if they did, the city's possibilities made their sincerities suspect.

Pradeep DE, still attempting to inveigle money out of his father, promised to help, but did not offer any of the three servants that his Mrs needed to run the house. Yograj's numerous friends were of no help. Servants were an uncomfortable topic with them since their conversations often touched upon independence and self-sufficiency. The ex-Minister would not phone his colleagues from the Core Committee; it would be an admittance of weakness and would also create the encumbrance of a favour due.

The responsibilities for the search fell on Nima Thendup. 'As usual.' He asked Pamphaa, a labourer on his construction site, who had experience as a cook. He brought her to the ex-Minister's house, and she sat on the lowest stool in the kitchen. The ex-Minister scrutinized the prominent bones on her face. 'What did you do before this?'

Nima Thendup said, 'It's better to talk straight. They say she stole in her last job.'

She was shrill. 'I didn't steal. The wife was jealous. She said I wanted to steal her husband. Then a necklace got lost and she blamed me for it. But I know she hid it herself.'

The ex-Minister knew that times were such that people no longer had the luxury of choosing their servants. He was only relieved that she seemed sensible, for his time with Pemba had led him to think that all servants were damaged in some way. He said, 'I don't have much to steal from.'

Nima Thendup told Pamphaa, 'Don't believe him. He is a big man.'

When Yograj returned home, Pamphaa was introduced to him and he helped her settle in. She was given Pemba's room near the kitchen. She had never had a room to herself before, she said. At the end of the day, she cooked her first meal, which the ex-Minister and Yograj enjoyed, but did not praise out of respect for Pemba.

Some Company

On the second day, as the new servant swept the living room, the ex-Minister stood behind her. 'How old are you?'

'Forty-five, forty-six.'

The ex-Minister thought she resembled Sumitra, Yograj's mother, who had died at forty-six. Her appearance had been unremarkable and over the years he had found many who resembled her. Still, the resemblance comforted him, for it gave credence to his self-deception. The ex-Minister had held off asking for her caste until now. He surrendered to his curiosity, 'What are you?'

Pamphaa shrugged, 'I don't know. Sometimes my father told me he was Rai, sometimes he was a Gurung. My mother said she was a Chettri, but she never showed me any of her Chettri relatives. One day I met a man who said he was my uncle. He said he was a Newar.'

Her answer alarmed the ex-Minister. It confirmed what he had long suspected, the lower orders were causing chaos with unsubstantiated claims. Who was going to enforce the purity of each person's blood, so carefully preserved through the centuries, and why was the modern world stirring this blood into an irreversible dilution? He had caught himself expressing doubts more than once to himself, on seeing someone claim that he was a Chandath, with a nose too flat, or an Adam's apple too pronounced. He blamed this on migrations from Nepal. People changed their castes mid-journey, everyone had become a high caste by the time they reached Sikkim: the further the stream was from the mountains, the more contaminated it was. How pure things still were in Nepal! There, ancestry had value, and castes and tribes were the inescapable compartments they were always meant to be.

The servant said, 'Some say that I look like a Chandath.'

Alarmed, he responded, 'It's not easy being a Chandanth.'

'It's what other people said. Who said I wanted to become a Chandath?'

'Do your housework,' he said.

'I was doing it. *You* came here asking me about jaat-paat.'

~

The ex-Minister blamed himself for the graceless beginning. He re-evaluated the distance between them. He would watch her from his position as her master. She would not be indulged too much, neither would she be kept too distant; that was the modern way.

As she adjusted to his house, he felt her authority assert itself in degrees but did not resent it. Her work showed experience. She had an innate sense of cleanliness, and a housewife's rhythm with chores. She was talkative and this challenged him, for he had only known Pemba's inarticulate outbursts.

'Why do you rich men have small wood pieces on floors? Why not big planks? It would make my job much easier,' she asked as she polished the parquet floors, greasy with neglect. The floors, installed in all the bedrooms and the living room, dated to his time as the Minister for Forests. It was one of the earliest such floors in Gangtok, an innovation for its time, and the ex-Minister thought of himself as a pioneer of parquet flooring in Sikkim. How many men had come, seen his floors, and copied the style? But it had all ended in futility. What was the use? he thought, and stayed silent.

'Old man can't hear anything,' she said.

She complained about the oppressive smell of mould that ran through the house. The ex-Minister and Yograj were used to it, it had become a characteristic of the house. She identified the source, it came from the countless cupboards. Sumitra had liked them and he had shared her enthusiasm. In this they were like those who grow up without possessions and find affluence in their later years.

She declared that they needed to be emptied. He protested. Then she found an ally in Yograj whose earlier pleas for cleanliness had been blocked by the alliance of sloth that had existed between his father and Pemba.

'Just do your work,' Yograj said.

The servant emptied the cupboards stuffed with damp, rat-eaten quilts and sheets, with clothes from another age, their fashions distant and absurd. She separated the usable ones from those that were irreparable, which she kept in a heap. The ex-Minister surveyed the bundles, and the formless assault of memories besieged him. There were women's clothes in bright colours, shades which he knew had been Sumitra's favourite, and children's clothes, which he remembered buying from Darjeeling when Yograj and Yogita were infants.

It was an act of intrusion for a servant to be so forceful so early, but she seemed without any apparent motive. He saw that she was merely restless, a wondrous attribute in a servant. She washed the usable ones over two days, and the ex-Minister could hear the thumps of her steps as she commuted between the terrace and the kitchen, two floors apart. The drying, hampered by intermittent rain, took longer than usual. When it was done, she showed him a pressed and folded set of clothes and linen.

'What should I do with these now?' she said.

She said this to elicit some praise from him, for she had made a tremendous effort. He looked over her and walked away.

'Old man can't hear anything,' she said.

One day, he sat at the living-room window and looked out on to Tibet Road. The servant entered and took to dusting the tables and chairs. She went to the showcase of his honours, and dusted the honours and glass panels, installed a few months earlier. He turned away from the street and looked at her. She picked up a piece, sculpted in glass, which he had received from the Vice President of India in 2002.

'What did you get this for?' she asked.

He returned his gaze to the street.

'Old man can't hear anything.'

'Old man can hear everything,' he said. 'Old man got it from the Vice President of India in 2002, for being useful to his country.'

'For what did old man get it?' she asked, bringing it to him.

'What does it matter?' He had forgotten what he had received it for. He took it from her and inspected it closely. It was for attending a conference in Delhi on 'Ethnic Harmony amidst Regional Diversity'. He looked up and said, 'It was for helping people live without biting each other.'

'Agya Nima was right. You are a big man,' she said.

'It is not a man who achieves greatness, it is his people who rise with him.' This had been the standard answer of his youth and middle age, whenever someone had called him great.

'Big man, big words.'

It returned smoothly. The trophies and photographs, and the events behind them. He explained things. She knew of the Chandanths as just another tribe, she did not know how great they actually were.

She paused, as if in reflection, and pointed to a framed photograph, 'What are you doing with the Chief Minister?' It was of the ex-Minister and the Chief Minister, just after he had joined her party. He was wearing a kanchnaki and a seytupi, she wore a phupopo, the embroidered dress of the Chandanths. They were standing, their clasped hands held high above their heads.

He ignored her question and said, 'Look at this.' He opened a locked cabinet beside the showcase and extracted a folder. She went through its contents, and he could see that she was moved. It contained photographs and press cuttings of the first Balidaan Diwas held in July 1997, just after the Chandanths had been declared a backward caste by an Act of Parliament.

~

The day his people were officially declared backward had been the happiest day of the ex-Minister's life. So many events had come together at a propitious time: the ascension of a clanswoman as the Hon'ble Chief Minister, the formation of CAS, the fruition of years of sacrifices, and the ex-Minister's own availability to take charge of his people's destiny.

She went through the photographs. There the ex-Minister was, at the head of a celebratory rally—it had since come to be known as the largest-ever gathering of Chandanths. He had walked arm in arm with the Hon'ble Chief Minister at its head. Chandanths from all over Sikkim and from places as distant as Nepal, Assam, Dehradun and Burma had taken part in it. There were poets and filmmakers, artists and singers. The rally had begun at Baluwakhani, outside the Vajra Cinema Hall, and taken the route via Mintokgang, the Hon'ble Chief Minister's residence, where everyone had paused for a moment to pay obeisance to one of their kind who had made it. They had also paused for a moment before the Palace gates which the ex-Minister had not seen since the last days of the monarchy that he had helped overthrow nearly twenty-five years earlier. The rally had passed through the bazaar—flowers had been showered on them from the tops of the buildings—and it had culminated at the Sikkim Conference Centre for a day-long function. They sang and hooted, for never had a people been happier to be called backward.

Then some photographs of the function. On stage, the ex-Minister and the Chief Minister, wearing their distinctive attires; the ex-Minister receiving the award from the ambassador of Thailand for working towards the upliftment of the community; the food festival just outside Sikkim Conference Centre showcasing the rich culinary heritage of the

Chandanths; and the arts and culture programme inside. There were photographs of the renowned orator, Late Yagung Chandeth, who had taken the pen-name Bishwa-Gyaan. With a raised clenched fist, he had recited an ancient poem, which had revealed to his people their eventual destiny as world rulers and had ended with the observation that a Constitutional acknowledgement of their backwardness would be the first essential step in that direction.

'What about you? You didn't give a speech?' she asked.

He was waiting for this. He cleared his throat and showed her a faded foolscap sheet. It was the transcript of his speech, delivered in English. She asked him to read and he accepted.

It began: 'We have gathered here to commemorate one of the greatest days in the history of our illustrious people. A moment comes, which comes but rarely in history, when we step out from the old to the new, when an age ends, and when the soul of a people, long suppressed, finds utterance.'

It was a long speech, it had taken the ex-Minister and Mitradas three days to write it. The ex-Minister read it with a voice that tried to summon the fervour of that day. It was the best effort yet made to encapsulate the mythical origins of the Chandanths and their struggles through history, first at the hands of the Tibetans, just across the Chyalu Valley, who had persecuted them for attempting commerce; then at the hands of the Mallas of the Kathmandu Valley, who had lured away all their artisans; then the depradations at the hands of the Shah kings, and the forced migrations from west Nepal to east Nepal at the hands of the British who ran their tea plantations with whips; and when they had come into Sikkim, oppression by the royalty and the aristocrats; and finally even after the dream of democracy was achieved with the merger into India, at the hands of the dominating castes, who thought they could continue in Sikkim what they had perfected in Nepal.

It ended: 'Ask not what your ancestors can do for you, ask what you can do for your ancestors.'

She was silent as it ended, and he could not tell how much she understood. She asked, 'And then what happened?'

The ex-Minister had thought of it as the beginning of a revolution.

The recognition of the Chandari-speaking peoples as a backward caste was an instrument to correct the great historical wrongs done to them, despite his reservations about them being labelled as a caste. But his hopes of exclusivity for the Chandanths were gradually undone. For out of expediency or large-heartedness, no one could say, the Hon'ble Chief Minister had ensured that almost everyone else was since declared backward. These days everyone had glorious histories and everyone had been oppressed by history. The speeches were identical, appeals to pride and hurt, and the speechmakers were the same, rivals in self-degradation and arguing at once for glory and squalor.

He said, 'We are all the same again.'

~

That evening, she made nettle soup with rice. There were ferns and buffalo meat cooked with glass noodles. The food was light and its tastes subtle. The ex-Minister was pleased that his bowels would not suffer, as they had done under Pemba. 'The house was like a desert. Now a woman's touch has come like rain.'

The expansive statement embarrassed Yograj. 'Are you talking about the servant?'

'Don't call her "servant". Her name is Pamphaa. Use her name.'

Yograj stared into his food. 'I'll call her whatever you want me to after you give me my share.'

The ex-Minister was calm. 'Soon. Let the cheque-book come.'

This did little to convince Yograj. 'And you are giving everything to CAS? I met the Treasurer in the bazaar. He says you're planning to give them money.'

The ex-Minister put up a hand. 'From my share.' He became mollifying. 'They were asking about you. You should attend our next meeting. All we are doing, we're doing for you people.'

'You're doing it for yourselves. Because you could not make friends outside your kind.'

Boycott

Pradeep DE visited Tibet Road with his daughters, who were on their summer vacation. He guided them towards the ex-Minister. 'Go to him, he's your grandfather.'

The girls approached the ex-Minister reluctantly. He saw himself through their eyes, old and remote, and he shared their hesitation. They took his hands, put them to their eyes, and withdrew. He said, 'Now what?'

Pradeep DE sniffed. 'I don't have a face in the department.'

The ex-Minister grew alert from experience. 'Your department doesn't deserve a face.'

Pradeep DE pointed at his daughters. 'Look at them! Look!'

The girls held hands and stared at the ex-Minister. He already knew that they had been brought as support but he was impressed that they had rehearsed. Pradeep DE removed his spectacles. 'You don't know how it feels. Tyau-tyau here, tyau-tyau there. It stops as soon as I enter. Who else can they be talking about?'

It was theatre, and the ex-Minister succumbed and participated. He brought his granddaughters closer to him and tousled their hair. Without any felt affection, for they seldom visited and when they did, he saw them as creatures of their mother's making. He gave them some money. They brightened and kissed him on his cheeks. He called in Pamphaa and told her to take them out to the shops.

'More than you gave me,' Prakash DE said after they left.

He was still being ostracized. From the Commissioner-cum-Secretary downwards, they were sidelining him. Pradeep DE had proof. When they made groups to visit Sarata Babuni's house on a condolence visit, he was not informed. Then there was Tobgay DE's birthday; he later found out that everyone but he had tasted the cake. He wasn't even sure if Heera Babuni was still on his side.

The only affection he received, and it was of such dubious origin that it did nothing to comfort him, came from Sumati AE. He had expected surliness from her; instead she dropped by his office and said, 'There are other projects. Life must go on. Work must go on.'

Her grace alarmed him. He knew it had something to do with the transfer question but developments were kept from him. His only ally was the pony-tailed peon, a recent adversary of Sumati AE's, whose enmity had formed on the day in which all the governmental seals had disappeared from the common room.

'The seals disappeared, eh?' the ex-Minister asked. 'Are you sure your department people didn't hide it themselves?'

The accusation surprised Pradeep DE. 'Why would we try to cut off our own legs?' His sobs ceased, and his face coloured as he described all that had occurred in the office after that day, the description that he would have given a few days ago, had it not been for the fool's death.

It was the worst day of his career. He had not known or else he would not have gone, he suspected he had not been warned deliberately. As soon as he reached, he was severely admonished by the Commissioner-cum-Secretary. The day would have become worse for him but he was saved, strangely, by a fight in the accounts section.

The ex-Minister probed. 'Why? What happened there?'

It was the day of the re-tender and there were no seals. The paperwork stalled and the tenderers saw it as a retribution for the fracas in the department a few weeks earlier. There were abuses, and Pradeep DE had spent the whole day negotiating in that accounts room, which had reeked more of piss on that day than usual. It was only Heera Babuni's reputation and the threat of police action that had prevented another incident. Sumati AE publicly blamed the pony-tailed peon for negligence. He fought back, she complained to the Commissioner-cum-Secretary about his insubordination, and the peon was scolded in public. Pradeep DE was the only one who had supported the pony-tailed peon.

'You were in the office on that day. You didn't see anything?' Pradeep DE asked.

'Nothing,' the ex-Minister replied.

Pradeep DE said, 'Hell to work, that place.' His voice lost its whine and his narration continued.

Now it was the pony-tailed peon who updated him on the intrigues behind the transfer selection. Tobgay DE had the upper hand because his father was not an ex-Minister who had disrupted a smoothly running system and his brother was not a contractor who fiddled around with babunis.

But Pradeep DE was not his father's son for nothing. His initial reasons for the transfer were still intact, now there was an additional one: the recovery of pride. The pony-tailed peon was recruited as an ally, and a competitive campaign was currently in progress.

Tobgay DE had put together a report with all his projects and the timeframe for completion of each. Pradeep DE compiled a similar document and had it book-bound.

Tobgay DE bought lunch for the entire office from Porky's because his son got ninety-two per cent in his ICSE examinations. Pradeep DE's eldest daughter was in Class Eight, too young for examination glory. He excused himself from the lunch.

The Commissioner-cum-Secretary's vehicle was out of order—a faulty suspension was suspected. Pradeep DE moved immediately. He offered his vehicle, a new Bolero issued to him the previous month, and which was newer than Tobgay DE's vehicle.

Tobgay DE was planning to buy a sofa set for the Commissioner-cum-Secretary. The pony-tailed peon saw him leave a brochure in his chamber. The brochure disappeared.

At home, Pradeep DE had told his Mrs that the transfer was a distinct possibility. Things were looking up for them, and their two children.

'What transfer?' she said. Her voice was plump with scorn. 'You could not even get the window panes fixed, Sant Pradeep.'

Sant Pradeep, Sant Pradeep,
Open an ashram, Sant Pradeep

The ex-Minister slapped his thigh. 'Sant Pradeep, Messiah of Light. It sounds nice.'

Pradeep DE whined, 'Don't give me anything. At least send some money to the department. Only then will the back-biting stop. My transfer will become easier. Don't give me, give them.'

The ex-Minister grew weary. 'All right, I will.'

Pamphaa returned with the girls. Pradeep DE removed his spectacles; they had misted over and he wiped them. 'What if you don't?'

'I'll send it. Every time I see you like this my years reduce,' the ex-Minister said.

Pradeep DE's elder daughter said, 'Mummy said not to stay for more than an hour.'

The ex-Minister glanced at his son, who averted his eyes.

~

The cheque-book arrived in the post. The ex-Minister looked at it without joy. He spoke to Yograj. 'We'll have to give some money to the department people. Your elder brother will not let us rest otherwise.'

Yograj's reply was sharp. 'He's not my brother. Give me my share before you start distributing.'

'You'll get it. Why will I not give you anything?'

Yograj said, 'What if he takes from us and doesn't give the department?'

It was a distinct possibility. The ex-Minister had considered it. 'Take it yourself to the department.'

Yograj thought about Julie Babuni, Pradeep DE, Rann Maan, and the bill. He said, 'I'm not going to the department anymore. '

They compromised. Yograj would visit Sarata Babuni's house to offer condolences. He would also inform them that some savings would be sent through Pradeep DE. There would be some people from the department but, being a sombre occasion, he would escape any cutting behaviour.

Sarata Babuni lived in Development Area, in a housing colony, on the third floor. Yograj met Julie Babuni on the steps; she was leaving with Heera Babuni. There was a moment of awkwardness which Yograj graciously broke. 'I've come to offer condolences.'

Heera Babuni looked at a point above and behind Yograj's head. 'If only this was not a house of mourning.'

Julie Babuni was chirpy. 'Come for my wedding, okay? I'll send you a card.'

Yograj said, 'I spoke with my father. He did not do the right thing. I'll make sure he sends some money through Pradeep DE.'

The two babunis paused at the landing. Heera Babuni's expression softened and she said, 'Speak with the peon. He's in there.'

Upstairs, Sarata Babuni looked surprised as he deposited the requisite envelope. She said, 'I'm alone, Bhai. Please help yourself.' There were visitors and Yograj recognized the pony-tailed peon. He sat near him and said, 'I've come to offer condolences.'

The peon stood up. Yograj held his arm and tugged at him. He sat down and Yograj said coaxingly. 'Father will send some money through Pradeep DE sometime next week. Please distribute it in the office.'

The peon swung his pony-tail to demonstrate his indifference. Yograj said, 'He doesn't want to victimize the people who really worked for the bill. But the people at the top...'

The peon paused and agreed. 'Someone cooks the food, someone licks their fingers.'

Before leaving, Yograj met Sarata Babuni again. She bore him no ill will. She was excluded from the list of those expecting any savings from the bill. She said, 'Such a big man's son. I didn't know you were going to come.'

After Yograj returned home with a report, the ex-Minister made out two cheques. The first was for forty thousand rupees, Yograj was to deliver it to Pradeep DE. The second was for twenty thousand rupees and it was for Yograj. 'Only? What happened to fifty-fifty?'

The ex-Minister spoke tenderly. 'What will you do with everything at once? Everything will come to you the day I die.'

'Waiting.'

~

Buoyed by the payment, the ex-Minister called for a meeting of the Core Committee. They were only two months away from Balidaan Diwas and CAS was yet to be invited to any of the Steering Committee's meetings. He was suspicious that it was a conscious snub. He spoke to the Press Secretary on the phone. The man said, 'Wait till the meeting, President Saab. I'm getting an explosive document.'

At the meeting, the Press Secretary waved his document. It was an invitation card he had inveigled from a contact at the printing press.

> The Steering Committee of Balidaan Diwas requests your gracious presence on the auspicious occasion commemoration of the crystal

> anniversary of the Victorious Occasion of July 2002. The Honourable Chief Minister Smt Y M Chandath has kindly consented to be the Chief Guest, and Pitu Kej Chandeth, esteemed Poet Laurate of Chyalu, has consented to be the Guest of Honour.

The ex-Minister banged on the side-table, a tea-cup jumped. He shouted, 'This is an injustice.'

The Joint Secretary asked. 'Who is Pitu Kej Chandeth?'

The Press Secretary knew him. 'He's a writer. Number-one poet after the death of Yagung Chandeth. HCM has given him a house in Kathmandu to sit and compose the long-lost epic of our people.'

The General Secretary snorted, 'This is deliberate.'

The Vice President nodded and said, 'What can we do? They've done this because they know we can't do anything.'

The ex-Minister said, 'Boycott!'

The General Secretary queried, 'Boycott?'

The ex-Minister affirmed, 'Boycott.'

They stared at him, for it was an extreme step. The Joint Secretary said, 'Is it sensible?'

The Press Secretary, whose militancy occasionally asserted itself, said, 'It's the only way to fight domination.'

The room was divided. The Treasurer said, 'But we have only twelve thousand rupees.'

The Press Secretary was contemptuous. 'Money is not everything.'

'We should at least attend it,' the Treasurer squeaked, 'we may get some money from them.'

The General Secretary sniffed the mutinous air and edged away from it. 'I have to leave. Late for office. But I am with whatever the committee proposes.'

After she left, the Vice President rubbed his hands together. 'Ran away so she can tell she was not present when the decision was made.'

The ex-Minister was seized by a surge of passion. He stood up. 'We have to show Mitradas and TB what we can do. Lie down once and we'll never stand up again.'

They debated amongst themselves for an hour but could reach no decision on the course of action. Ultimately, they resolved to convene after three days to take a final decision. As the President of CAS, it was the ex-Minister's task to phone DB Chandath, who had the Chief Minister's ear, and inform him about the possibility of revolt.

The ex-Minister took up the task with visible willingness. As the committee watched him, he dialled the Confidential Assistant's number and said, 'Tell the Minister to ring me. We are about to make a press release.'

They did not have to wait long. The Minister for Village Roads phoned immediately. He picked it up and, after updates and explanations, said, 'DB Bhai, there's only so much torture we can take. CAS has decided to boycott the Balidaan Diwas seminar. Core Committee is meeting after three days, then we give a press release.'

He terminated the call. The Press Secretary said, 'So the agitation starts.' On that note of cautious cheer, the meeting broke up.

~

The ex-Minister's chosen stance was further validated when Pamphaa said, 'I went out to buy vegetables today. The shopkeeper said he was a Chandath but changed his name to Chandanth because of you. And his son got a job in the Forest Department because of you. So you were telling the truth.'

'No I wasn't lying,' the ex-Minister said. 'But that was a while ago and the war has changed.'

She cooked mutton with turnips. It was a dish from his childhood and he ate it with relish.

After dinner, as he watched television, she completed her chores and sat on the floor beside him. She rested her hand on his knee. He looked at it and summoned some desire into himself but it would not come.

There had been only two women since the mother of his children had died. They had both been Chandanths; it was a source of some pride for him that he had never been with a woman who was not a Chandanth. The last affair had been nearly fifteen years earlier, with the woman who was the current General Secretary of CAS. Even then it had been an effort of will, a stand against the passage of middle age. And now Pamphaa's hand, of unknown caste and thirty-five years younger than his, was on his knee. He could be mistaken that, for her, it was a harmless gesture on a harmless man.

He placed his right hand on her shoulder, to feel the strap of her brassiere. It was a texture which ought to have aroused him, but his hand was numb.

'Not so old also,' Pamphaa said without turning around, and without moving away.

He felt tired and demanded to be taken to bed. She caught his arm and helped him upstairs. The rain's steady prattle was clearer on this floor. The heavy dampness in his room reassured him and helped him sleep. He woke up at night, and the rain was heavier and a fever had come upon him. His body hurt but the pain could not be confined to or pointed to any specific part. He felt himself wet, but did not know whether it was sweat, or if the moisture in the air had condensed on his body. The necessity for sleep won over the location-less ache at dawn.

Call the Doctor

It was Pamphaa who found him. She brought him his tea in the morning but he did not stir. She felt his body, he was still breathing and she touched him: perspiration had soaked his body. She moved her hand lower, he had soiled himself.

She went to Yograj in the next room and shook him. 'Your father has the fever of a child.'

They moved him downstairs, to the spare windowless room next to the kitchen. It would be easier to care for him there, and it had an adjacent toilet. The room was infrequently used. It had almost become a dining room when Sumitra had been alive. She had wanted to put in a window, to brighten and air it a bit, and, just when work was scheduled to begin, she had caught her fatal fever.

They settled him into the room. When Yograj resisted cleaning his father, Pamphaa did it without revulsion and put fresh clothes on him.

His body was limp in her hands and he made no attempt to assist her or to cover himself. She then prepared the windowless room and, after it was done, they carried him down and settled him into the freshly made bed. The ex-Minister lifted his head and asked for some water. Yograj reached for his phone, intending to call Nima Thendup, but she said, 'It's bad luck calling someone over for a small sickness.'

She fed him soup and spoke to him through the day, babbling and cooing to him, and he responded to being treated like an infant. The room helped. It was panelled with wood and, being windowless, was shielded from the dampness of the air outside. He revived towards the evening and lifted his head to say, 'If I haven't recovered by the morning, call Yogita.'

He felt his body stiffen in degrees until he had no control over his movements, but his mind would not stay still. He thought that if he died, heaven would be denied to him because of his failure to build the temple. He prayed for his health's restitution, if only partially, just for enough strength to complete the temple with its sandalwood-lined sanctum.

His fever returned in the night and Pamphaa sat on the floor beside the bed and spoke of trivialities. His fever increased and he became delirious. He called her Sumitra. He referred to their marriage, of all the things that had happened in their ten-year union. He insisted that she lie next to him. She obeyed him and he slept with his hand on her shoulder.

His breath remained heavy through the next day. In the night, he made Pamphaa lie next to him. He spoke of a woman called Sopu Kin, and referred to their meetings in the maize fields, and Pamphaa sensed it was a youthful affair, a root exposed by a storm. Towards midnight, he slept, oppressed only by the weightless density of his dreams.

~

He awoke the next morning to the singing of the Tiny Geniuses. Their song, clearer on this floor, carried through the kitchen window.

> Stomach paining. Stomach paining. Stomach paining just now.
> Stomach paining. Stomach paining. Stomach paining just now.

Call the doctor, call the doctor, call the doctor just now.
Call the doctor, call the doctor, call the doctor just now.

He heard them through his stupor and felt them to be taunting him. He tried to shout but his throat was dry. He felt his forehead, his fever had not abated. He picked up his walking stick, kept beside the bed, and hit the door thrice.

Operation, operation, operation just now.
Operation, operation, operation just now.
I am alright, I am alright, I am alright just now.
I am alright, I am alright, I am alright just now.

Pamphaa looked in and he held his hand out, demanding to be taken to the toilet. She helped him to the seat. Yograj said from outside the door, 'I've called Dr Kuldeep. The same one who looked after Pemba.'

It did not sound like a recommendation. The ex-Minister's voice was weak but combative. 'There's nothing wrong with me.'

Pamphaa, still holding the ex-Minister in position, said, 'Let the doctor say that. I'm not going to stay awake every night listening to your life story.'

Thank you doctor, thank you doctor, thank you doctor just now.
Thank you doctor, thank you doctor, thank you doctor just now.

Dr Kuldeep arrived in an hour and put the ex-Minister's hands to his eyes. His diagnosis was reassuring. It looked like a fever that came from indigestion. The ex-Minister was to stay away from meat and oily food. 'Soon, you can walk every evening in the bazaar.'

The ex-Minister was not convinced. 'Call Yogita,' he instructed his son, 'and let me speak to her.'

Yograj phoned her; she was at home. She did not know her father was ill. 'Nothing serious,' he said, 'but I don't want to die without seeing you.'

She began to cry. The ex-Minister said, 'But nothing serious. Here, ask the doctor.'

Dr Kuldeep demurred, but the phone was already in his hands. He spoke to Yogita, sensed the impotent panic of a distant child, and sought to reassure her. It was a minor fever and he would recover quickly.

The ex-Minister was not so sure. When the phone returned to him he coughed into it. Dr Kuldeep recognized it as harmless and forced. He said, 'No need to come,' and coughed again. Yogita sniffed. 'I'm applying for leave tomorrow.'

The ex-Minister's conversation with his daughter lifted him. He held the doctor's hand. 'You must come here every day.'

~

Nima Thendup visited his uncle in the evening and found him at the dining table in the kitchen. 'Machi was about to send pork momos for you but I said no.'

The ex-Minister acknowledged this greeting with a scowl. 'Where were you yesterday? Waiting for me to die?'

'Problems everywhere.' Nima Thendup was anxious. The deadline for his hotel had shifted. The rains had disproved his estimates and he was not going to make the October-November season.

The ex-Minister was wary. 'No money here.'

Nima Thendup hastened to reassure him. 'No Appa, no. Applying for a loan. But it will take time. I'll do it slowly. Aiming for the May season next year.'

The ex-Minister grunted that it was a sensible move. And to block any lengthening of that conversation, he said, 'Get the TV downstairs.' Nima Thendup carried the television downstairs from the ex-Minister's earlier room to his current one. He rerouted the wires into the windowless room; it involved much stretching and shouting. He complained about Yograj's absence. 'It's your son's work. Where is he?'

The ex-Minister said, 'Leave it if you don't want to do it.'

After the television was fixed, Pamphaa announced dinner. She had made a tasteless but nutritious gruel for the ex-Minister and beef curry for Nima Thendup.

Nima Thendup said, 'If I knew you could cook so well, I would have kept you for myself.'

Pamphaa said, 'Now, no chance.'

'How's she doing?' he asked the ex-Minister.

'Better than the last one,' Pamphaa answered.

'Talks too much,' the ex-Minister said.

After dinner, Nima Thendup watched as Pamphaa took the ex-Minister to his bed, and gave him his medicines with warm water. The rain was heavier, and there was a heavy wind, it sounded like a squall. Nima Thendup decided to leave after it abated. He talked with Pamphaa, so far he had only seen her as a worker, soiled through the day. In his uncle's kitchen, removed from the site, she looked respectably domestic. She was of a piece with the kitchen; a stranger would have identified it as her domain. Still irritated at being ordered to do work which was not his, he asked her, 'Where's the prince?'

'Disappeared as soon as his father recovered.'

'The boy needs to get married.'

Pamphaa pointed towards the ex-Minister's room. 'Look at the man who's supposed to be responsible for him.'

Nima Thendup put up a hand. 'Nothing there for me to say.'

The next day, as Pamphaa fed the ex-Minister some gruel, she asked him, 'Nima Thendup is a Bhotey? Why does he call you Baraa?'

The ex-Minister was lifted by her question. The past was all that he had seen in the lucid hallucinations of recent days. This, combined with the fear of a sudden end, made him eager and confiding.

'All that I have done, I have done for my people,' he said, and looked at Pamphaa assessingly. She looked eager, and he added to all that he had told her since her arrival.

Contrary to what everyone assumed, he had not exiled Kalpana, Nima Thendup's mother, because she had married a Bhotey. She had done worse: she had fought for the king between 1973 and 1975, while he, Kuldeep Chandanth, had joined everyone in fighting for democracy. Kalpana was twenty years younger than him, the youngest child of his father's second wife. There were three brothers and two sisters between them, and, when she was born, he was living with Sopu Kin in a house beside his father's. She was his first wife, whom he had married when he was seventeen years old, in 1949, the year India got its independence, and when he had just been enrolled in Class Three in the local high school, on the insistence of the headmaster who had found him intelligent.

Kalpana was two years old when Sopu Kin had run away with a man who had come from Nepal, selling transistor radios. He had never forgotten his brothers' laughter. Around the same time Kalpana's own mother had died and he looked after her for five years, become as much a father as a brother to her, until he left for Darjeeling to study in a college, for he had to an extent fulfilled the headmaster's foresight. He received his Bachelor's degree at the age of twenty-nine, the first person in Suikeybung to get a degree, and returned home. The shame of his first wife's elopement was behind him, and he married another woman, Sopu Ban, whom he considered to be his first wife, for it was she who had given him a son. Their first and only child was Pradeep, and in the same year Kalpana too had her first child, Nima Thendup.

He was in Gangtok when he found out that Kalpana had married the Bhotey. She was eighteen years old and, contrary to what they later said in Suikeybung, he had allowed the marriage to occur despite the opposition of his father and brothers. It had seemed a trivial matter then for he was busy with his work as a revenue officer, and then later, as the movement against the king gathered momentum, busy with the revolution.

The man she married, Nima Thendup's father, was not a kazi or a yabla but was employed by the king, and it had broken him completely when he found that Kalpana was working in the palace. They were on opposing sides, and it affected his standing within the circle of revolutionaries to have a sister working with the enemy. By now, he was spending all his time in Gangtok and its surrounding hills, and it was here that he met Sumitra, a lady who did not have the manners of the village.

And even after the referendum and the merger, when all the people in Sikkim called themselves Indian, when he should have had the victor's magnanimity, he could not bring himself to forgive her. In the first years of Sikkim's existence as an Indian state, he found that Kalpana was living in Phagcha with her husband and child, and though it may seem like he had exiled her, the truth was that she did not want to return.

She didn't come to seek forgiveness, or meet him when he married Sumitra and began building the house in Tibet Road for her, for the lands in the village had gone to Sopu Ban, whom he had left by now. She had taken his second marriage with equanimity and only requested that Pradeep be provided for, and that he had ensured, first through Sumitra and then by himself. He had paid for his studies and, when the time came, purchased land in Arithang where he could build a house.

Kalpana did not come to help when Sumitra was with child and Yograj and Yogita were born, three years apart. She did not come when Sopu Ban died in Suikeybung and Pradeep entered the house under Sumitra's care. She did not congratulate him when he was given the ticket for Suikeybung in the 1985 elections, nor did she come to mourn when Sumitra died a few months after the election, leaving him three children to look after. He did not hear from her in 1994 when he lost the elections after ten years as a minister, and she certainly had nothing to say when he formed CAS for the protection of the Chandanths. By then she was a widow herself, and had adopted the customs and rituals of the Bhoteys. He did not go when she died, for she chose to be cremated at the top of the hill, in the Buddhist way, rather than at the river and the foothills, with the ashes scattered in the forest, in the Chandanth way. The only good thing was that Nima Thendup had a larger heart than anyone in the family, and he did not bear any ill will towards anyone.

Pamphaa heard him out and said, 'Rest now or you'll fall sick again.'

~

As the ex-Minister recovered, he had a surprise visitor. The General Secretary arrived with a furrowed expression, squinted to adapt to the lights in his new room, sat beside him, and felt his pulse.

He jerked his hand away. 'Forgive me for not being dead.'

Her look of concentration faded, and her face compressed in apparent pain. 'Say whatever you want. The Steering Committee for the Balidaan Diwas met yesterday. They can't do it without you. Mitradas asked me to tell you.'

'And he can't call me himself? *You* are their postman now?'

She reached for his hand and felt his pulse again. 'No one has to send me anywhere. They have heard about your boycott. It's not enough that you make trouble, you have to get everyone involved.'

The ex-Minister stared at the lit bulb on the opposite wall. 'I'm old. What does it matter where I go and what I say?'

'You never wanted me to succeed. You always blamed me for leaving you. Just because I married Papa.'

Papa referred to her husband, now an Additional Secretary in the Food Department. A decade earlier, when the ex-Minister was in power, he had been embittered enough to influence a transfer for her husband. Her husband had spent some years posted to the Fisheries Department, which has the reputation of being a bureaucratic gulag, for Sikkim's rivers are swift and its fishes small and lean.

The ex-Minister spoke dreamily. 'Ah! Your husband. Where is he these days?'

'Wherever he is, he got there without your help. At least he is of some use. You spend all your time shouting, "Chandith this, Chandath that."'

'Chandanth!'

'Chandanth, Chandith, who cares? It is just a name. Now when the time comes to do something, you still want to fight everyone.'

He was quiet. She shut the door and put her hand on his brow. 'Even if someone is feeding you, you won't open your mouth. The HCM told me she wants to unite all Chandiths, Chandanths, Chandaths, Chadits under one organization. Everybody is saying that you may be named President of the new organization. Why boycott all that?'

'I'm all alone. Everyone cares only about themselves.'

'You sent me away, Kuldeep-jiu. You wouldn't have been like this. I would have taken care of you.'

The ex-Minister arranged his pillows and coughed loudly. It was a signal. Pamphaa entered and said, 'He needs to sleep.'

The General Secretary stood up and smoothened down her sari. 'So will you come, Kuldeep-jiu?'

'No!'

~

Yogita arrived and, when she embraced her father, her arms went around him easily. His skin seemed to hang on his bones without the intervening support of flesh. She began to cry and he said, 'It's the illness. The meat will return soon.'

She insisted he had to have exercise and brought him out to the kitchen. She told him, in effervescent words, about her journey to Gangtok, her work in Delhi, her promotion which was inevitable because the president of the company had himself acknowledged her efforts, the open-hearted kindness of Punjabi families. She was appreciative of Pamphaa whose food was superb, almost professional. It was a welcome departure from Pemba who had never made the same-tasting tea twice.

She was sad. 'How was Pemba in the end?'

'He got away easily. Dancing one minute and dead the next. Not like this.'

She scolded her father for being so negative. They talked until Pamphaa interrupted them. 'Enough. Time for medicine and sleep.'

Yogita felt the discomfort of an intruder. After her father was asleep, she took in the changed environment of her house. It was cleaner, the displays in the living room looked rearranged. It seemed airier, she didn't know why. She went to her room and found it prepared for her arrival. The photo-frames and the school trophies had been dusted and kept where they belonged. She thought of her previous visits, when her first quarrel with Pemba was always about her room's neglected state. She felt the absence of her mother anew, for this was how it should have always been.

She went to the terrace. It was getting dark. There was some residual daylight and a fog which was steadily punctured by orange and yellow patches, as lights were switched on in neighbouring buildings. She smoked a cigarette and took care to spend some time chewing a mint before returning downstairs.

Yograj arrived at night. She was in her room when he came by and said, 'Good to have you back. Old man almost took a holiday.' She giggled and then admonished him for speaking so casually. Yograj was affronted. 'Don't lecture me. I was the one who had to look after him.'

She did not rise to her brother's taunts. She was tired; she turned away to sleep and heard him withdraw from her room.

The next day Yograj left early: a friend was getting married in South Sikkim. Yogita went to the bazaar and had a photograph of Pemba enlarged and framed. It was the same one that she had sent her friend in *Sikkim Everyday*. She returned home and hung the photograph in the living room and garlanded it with a khada.

~

Pradeep DE took his time to visit but the ex-Minister was not offended. 'You would have made me more sick.'

Pradeep DE felt his father's throat and, feeling it to be normal, said, 'You didn't trust me. You had to tell everyone in the department that you were sending money through me.'

'I thought it would help you.'

Pradeep DE stood up and paced the room. 'What help? Three babunis came to my office and took twenty thousand from the envelope. When I tried to stop them, they said, "Women's rights." Then everyone else asked for their share, like I had opened a dharamshala. By the time everyone was happy, I had spent forty thousand of my own money.'

Pradeep DE did not let his moroseness slip, and tell his father how pleased he really was. The disappointments of the previous month were behind him. People had forgotten so quickly. They had lined up when word went around that he was distributing money. The Commissioner-cum-Secretary had even congratulated him for retrieving some of the department's pride, so greatly wounded by the ex-Minister's actions. Sumati AE had walked into his office and said, 'Even I worked hard for that boy and his father.' She had gone away with five thousand rupees. It wasn't quite twelve per cent of twenty-eight lakh, but she didn't seem disappointed.

And as for the money which the babunis had taken, Pradeep DE was secretly unaffected. It had given him a reputation for large-heartedness and he knew Heera Babuni would have received the largest share.

The central preoccupation of Pradeep DE's recent days had not been the equitable distribution of the department's savings but something more ambitious. Heera Babuni, wearing a yellow sari with a saffron border, had told him a few days earlier, 'Just yesterday, the CCS told AE Ma'am to start taking interest in all the projects that you are working on.'

He had looked away. 'I don't want to leave.'

Heera Babuni reminded him of his responsibilities. 'Think of your family, your children.'

'They can't force me to leave,' he asserted, and then asked, 'what else did he say?'

'I'll find out but we have to start preparing our goodbyes.' She swung her head away; he caught a flash of a lemon-shaped hair clip.

'I hope we never have to,' Pradeep DE had said.

And now, with his father, he asked, 'You always tell me, the Chief Minister this, the Chief Minister that. Why don't you speak to her?'

Pradeep DE continued to make his case until Yogita returned from a short visit to the bazaar. She entered the room and acknowledged Pradeep DE but did not, as he had expected, take his hands to her eyes. She said, 'There are some mutton momos. Should I heat some for you?'

The ex-Minister nodded. She went out and Pradeep DE said, 'You saw her? Didn't offer me any respect.'

The ex-Minister shrugged.'Women's rights.'

Yogita returned, sat beside the ex-Minister's pillow and fed him some momos. Pradeep DE's presence made her feed him with extra care.

Pradeep DE said, 'It's time for you to leave us. Appa and I have been looking around for someone for you.'

Yogita turned sharply towards him. 'Worry about your daughters. I can take care of myself.'

Pradeep DE simpered. He had succeeded in pinching her where it hurt the most. 'It's for your good.'

'I should get married, I know. So I can dominate my husband just like your Mrs. And make him come to my house for Dasain.'

They snapped at each other until the ex-Minister belched twice. He asked to be taken to the toilet, where he vomited into the basin. As he returned to his bed, he vomited again. Then his fever returned. Before losing consciousness, he looked at his children and said, 'If I die, the two of you have to complete the temple.'

Pradeep DE wagged a finger at Yogita and said, 'Mutton momos.'

~

Yograj was in the bazaar when he received a phone call from Pradeep DE. Yograj asked, 'He's not acting, no? He wants Dr Kuldeep and Yogita to meet.'

Pradeep DE described the ex-Minister's condition. Yograj phoned Dr Kuldeep, picked him up from his house and rushed to Tibet Road. They found the ex-Minister in bed, eyes closed and breathing faintly. Pamphaa was massaging his feet. Dr Kuldeep asked her to massage his chest instead and give him sips of water. The ex-Minister's breathing slowed and he said, 'It must have been the momos.'

This triggered a fresh burst of tears from Yogita. The ex-Minister turned to her. 'Stop crying. You're just like your mother.' This observation lightened her. She saw Yograj and said, 'Outside food. But nobody told me.'

Yograj looked around with impatience. He had been summoned for this? 'Should we take him to the hospital?'

Dr Kuldeep looked worried. 'I know I'm probably overreacting but I don't want to take any chances. Not at his age.'

Then the ex-Minister went still. They prodded him but he did not respond. Yogita cried and Pamphaa took her out of the room. They carried him down to the road and put his warm but lifeless body into Pradeep DE's vehicle. At the hospital, Dr Kuldeep took over. The ex-Minister had a faint pulse and heartbeat. The hospital was crowded, and there had been a scandal the previous week when a corpse had been laid out in the corridor for want of space and had remained there for two days.

But the ex-Minister was a politician aligned to the ruling party, and Dr Kuldeep's intervention helped. The Intensive Care Unit was full but a room in the VIP ward had just been evacuated. They admitted him there, in a separate room with its own toilet. The ex-Minister opened his eyes briefly but was too febrile to speak. His heartbeat ceased at least four times, causing alarm. He stabilized and was kept under sedation. He remained unconscious through the night, while Yogita stayed awake to watch him. Dr Kuldeep stayed back at the hospital, even though he had just worked two consecutive shifts.

The ex-Minister was stable in the morning but remained too weak to speak. Dr Kuldeep recommended another day's stay before leaving for home. Nima Thendup arrived with some food, and acted aggrieved. 'I know, I know. I'm not important.' The momo-seller visited. She abandoned her shift for the day and chose to stay at the hospital, taking it upon herself to feed the visitors. She held Yogita and said, 'He's old. These things happen to old people.'

The ex-Minister stayed in the hospital for a second night, attended by Yogita. In the morning Yograj entered holding a copy of *Sikkim Everyday*. He waved it and said, 'Thieves! Can't even wait for him to die.'

She glanced at the newspaper: 'Leading Light of Chandanth Community Passes Away. Kuldeep Chandith Dies at the Age of 81'.

Over the previous evening, through channels that were never properly established, word had gone around that the ex-Minister had died. Yograj checked his phone, condolences were coming in. A friend called offering help, any help that he needed. Yograj swore at him and turned off his phone.

Nima Thendup was upbeat. 'First time I'm hearing of such a thing. Very auspicious.'

A little later, the ex-Minister asked for Pamphaa to massage his feet. They had to fetch her from the house and she massaged his feet, speaking to him with an intimacy that his children found discomfiting. But it helped and by afternoon, they had removed the intravenous feed. They did not tell him about his obituary.

Dr Kuldeep came to check on him. 'He's breathing normally now. All signs are normal as well. He should be able to go home tomorrow. No point keeping him here, he'll become more sick.'

Yogita held up the newspaper. 'Maybe this cured him. He never agrees with anything in the newspapers.'

Pradeep DE rushed in weeping, he had heard. Nima Thendup said, 'He's not dead. He'll outlive all of us.'

Yogita said, 'That's what happens when the newspaper has to give you news about your own father.'

Pradeep DE resolved to write a stern letter to the newspaper.

The Core Committee visited later in the day. They denied that they had received the news from the newspaper. But they were not allowed to meet him. Nima Thendup, in particular, derived pleasure in telling them that any shock could be fatal to the old man, and that if they truly cared for him, they should visit him the day after the following day at home.

May Such News Be False for All of Us

The next morning, they told him about the report. He did not believe them and they had to show him a copy of the paper. He read, the encomiums gave him pleasure, but he looked stern as he said, 'Vultures.' His wheelchair left thin tyre-tracks on the half-wet floor of the corridor of the VIP wing and, returning for a forgotten thermos flask, Yogita saw that the family of the next patient were settling the bed and cleaning up the toilet.

At home, the stream of visitors remained steady. The crush of vehicles caused traffic jams on the road outside, and a traffic policeman had to be posted for the day. Pamphaa made a gesture of mock exhaustion. 'So many people to make tea for? Who told you to become so famous?'

The ex-Minister snorted. 'All vultures. Came only when they heard of my death.'

In the evening, the members of CAS converged on his house. The Vice President, the Press Secretary and the Treasurer sat formally in the living room and when the crowd, mostly people from neighbouring buildings, thinned, the ex-Minister joined them. He had received calls from the General Secretary and the Joint Secretary, and they were relieved to hear his voice. The Vice President said, 'I always said you'll live longer than me. Just came to check.'

The Press Secretary said, 'I know Mitradas was behind the rumour. I'll give him such a counter in the press.'

'What do we do?' asked the Vice President, 'are we still boycotting?'

'We'll wait for their move,' said the ex-Minister.

'He who has no money, has nothing to do but wait,' said the Treasurer.

'It's only money,' the ex-Minister said, lifted by his recovery and the recent payment from the Department of Village Roads.

'It's working,' the Press Secretary said, 'Mitradas is worried. TB is worried. DB Minister is also worried. His Confidential Assistant has been calling me non-stop.'

Yogita entered the room, put their hands on her eyes and said, 'He needs to rest. No politics.'

The Treasurer said, 'Ah Chhori! You're too strict on us.' He held her shoulder and stood up to announce, 'If that's what the Core Committee wants, then I shall follow it.'

'You'll have to lead us, Baraa,' the Press Secretary said.

'If I'm alive,' the ex-Minister said at the door. His visitors laughed in encouragement as they claimed their identical umbrellas from each other.

~

Dr Kuldeep arrived to check on him in the evening. They were all attentive as he checked the ex-Minister's temperature, pulse and blood pressure. 'Healthier than most people ten years younger.'

Nima Thendup said, 'As long as he doesn't eat mutton.'

The ex-Minister looked at Dr Kuldeep and said, 'Why aren't you married?'

Yogita admonished him, 'Appa! Behave yourself.'

'The only job of men nowadays is to tell women when to get married.' This came from Pamphaa.

The ex-Minister snorted. 'Nobody's going to marry you, that's for sure.'

'Why? What do you know?' Yogita said, and the two women giggled, embarrassing the men.

The ex-Minister asked, 'Have there been any calls from Suikeybung? Did they even find out?'

Yograj shook his head. There had not been any calls from the ex-Minister's brothers and sister in the village. Perhaps they had not heard. Nima Thendup, who still maintained relations with them, said, 'I'll send them a message tomorrow.'

Dr Kuldeep wanted to leave. The ex-Minister threatened to fall sick again, if that was what it took to make him stay for dinner. Yogita was unexpectedly shy. The conversation over dinner was civil, and it remained focused on the ex-Minister and his achievements. Dr Kuldeep promised to come by every evening for a week to check on the ex-Minister's health. After he left, Pamphaa took Yogita aside and said, 'For you. He's coming for you.' Yogita waved her away.

Yograj stayed up late to care for his father. 'You want water?' Without waiting for an answer, Yograj fetched a glass of water, then, finding it to be cold, took it back to the kitchen and returned with a glass of hot water. The ex-Minister, though feeble, was suspicious. 'What do you want?'

'Nothing.' Yograj smoothened the bedcovers at the corners where they had crinkled. He then felt his father's pulse.

The ex-Minister, wary of a private conversation with a son to whom money was due, pretended to sleep.

Sarata Babuni visited him the next day. She had read about his supposed passing away at Unnati Bhavan—she was usually the first person to read the newspaper. She had told everyone and they had offered their condolences to Pradeep DE, and Heera Babuni had held him as he wept openly before leaving for the hospital. Even after it had been exposed as a rumour, they had spent much of the day discussing the ex-Minister and his achievements, but most of all, for the way in which he had put Sumati AE in her place. Sarata Babuni too was a Chandanth and she knew how much he had done for the furtherance of his people.

Her face was narrow and pallid. Her appearance was neat, but to the ex-Minister, she looked older than Yograj. 'Your husband didn't come?'

'He passed away three years ago,' she said. She adjusted her spectacles and continued, 'When Yograj Bhai came to offer condolences after my father passed away, I was very touched. And I thought, So what if the rumour is false, the ex-Minister must still be sick. That is why I came to see you.'

He asked her about Pradeep DE. 'Everybody likes him but we feel that he's too romantic.' The ex-Minister pried further but she was circumspect. 'We are all hoping he gets the transfer. He deserves it.'

When the time came for her to leave, it was raining. Yograj offered to drop her home. In the car, they rolled up the windows to avoid the rain. The windscreen misted over; she leaned over and wiped it with her handkerchief. She said, 'Are you still in touch with Julie Babuni?'

'Not anymore. It wasn't anything serious.'

'I don't like her. Her perfume's too strong. And she never gets lunch but always wants to eat ours.'

This revelation tallied with Yograj's experience; she had never cooked anything for him. Sarata Babuni waited for a reciprocal indiscretion from him. He said, 'She's lazy.'

'Exactly.' Sarata Babuni then narrated a series of incidents, all centered around Julie Babuni's laziness and each hurting her in the end. They reached her house and Yograj asked for her phone number, just in case he needed something from the department. It was always good to have a sympathetic hand. When she alighted from the car, she said, 'Come by sometime. I'll cook you a nice meal.'

When Yograj returned home, his father wagged a finger at him. 'The HCM's Principal Secretary phoned. The HCM wants to know if I am well or not.'

Yogita looked at her father and pouted. 'None of the medicines have any effect on him, but one call from the Chief Minister and he recovers.'

The ex-Minister warned them not to inform Pradeep DE. 'He won't let me rest or sleep if he hears.'

~

The Principal Secretary phoned again the next day, to inform the ex-Minister that the Hon'ble Chief Minister would visit in two days' time. Then the ex-Minister had two visitors. The first was Mitradas Chandith. As if it were the old days, he tried to enter the ex-Minister's room, to announce his familiarity by sitting at the foot of the bed. But things had changed. 'Take him to the sitting room.'

So Mitradas sat in the more formal surroundings, his body small against the sofa, reprimanded without even having been spoken to. The ex-Minister was helped in by Pamphaa and Yogita and chose the sofa furthest from his visitor. Mitradas played with the teacup but drank little of the tea. 'I cried when I heard.'

The ex-Minister said, 'Tears of happiness?'

Mitradas looked reproached. He shifted in his seat, and played with the tassels of a cushion.

The ex-Minister said, 'You're only here because the HCM is coming to see me, and she will ask me the names of my visitors.'

Mitradas deflected this. 'The HCM called me personally to make sure you will be there. She said she'll cancel the whole Balidaan Diwas if you don't come.'

The ex-Minister had expected this appeal to his vanity, and had prepared himself to be unmoved. 'Then cancel it. I'm sick here. I need rest.' To stress his point, he coughed. 'You are the intellectual. Go, have an intellectual seminar.'

Mitradas remained impervious to offence. The tea had cooled, he finished it in a succession of measured sips. 'You helped me. Wherever I am, I am there because of you. Kick me if you want, kill me if you want, but don't boycott. Please don't boycott.'

He did something unexpected. He removed a small white packet from his pocket and presented it to the ex-Minister with folded hands. 'A small gift for you. We had gone to Europe for a conference through the government.'

It was a souvenir, a replica of the Eiffel Tower as tall as his hand. The ex-Minister examined it. 'What was the conference for?'

'Water sanitation.'

'And who went?'

'Two engineers from the Water Sanitation Department and the central body of CHAPS. The department organized everything.'

The ex-Minister fondled the souvenir and placed it on the table. The arched legs of the tower were uneven and the souvenir wobbled lightly on the glass surface. The ex-Minister, acting unsurprised, said, 'Even we'll be going. The HCM said so. But we don't know where yet.'

'Talk to the Home Department. They let you choose from a list of conferences all over the world.'

The ex-Minister raised his eyebrow; this was progress. Then he remembered his position as Mitradas's former mentor and present adversary. 'I remember the first time you sat here, in that same sofa, wanting to do your PhD.' His voice choked. 'Why did I trust you so much?'

'I'm still here, Kuldeep-jiu, I'm still here. The past does no one any good. Let's look ahead.'

Events of the previous week had made the ex-Minister generous. They reconciled, the ex-Minister promised never to bring up the matter of the missing funds; the matter was closed. Yet, still focused on money, they talked about the funds due to their organizations. Mitradas revealed that CHAPS's payments too were being held up by the Minister for Village Roads.

As he departed, Mitradas lifted the ex-Minister's hands to his eyes and asked him to reconsider his boycott. The ex-Minister promised to do so but made no assurances.

~

The second visitor arrived the next day. TB Chandath did not ask to visit the ex-Minister in his bedroom. He waited in the living room. He was dressed in a dark suit with a tie held by a tie-pin, and sitting close to him, the ex-Minister felt slovenly in his loose, convalescent clothes.

'We will not allow you to leave us,' TB Chandath declared.

'Not going anywhere.'

TB Chandath grinned and put one leg over another, exposing his monogrammed socks. 'But you will come to Balidaan Diwas, haina Baraa?'

The ex-Minister had no history of animosity with this man, and had nothing against him, except the way he obscured his real name. He checked his tongue and said, 'Now I didn't say that.'

TB Chandath was too civil to be insistent and he did not push his persuasions. When Yogita entered to greet him, he asked her pointed questions about her post-graduate course, which she had completed two years earlier. He knew some of her professors, and the discussion moved beyond the ex-Minister's control. TB Chandath declared himself impressed with the way the ex-Minister had brought up his children, and told Yogita, 'You must come for this year's Balidaan Diwas Seminar.'

Yogita said, 'But I won't be here. I'll have to leave in a week.'

'Then you must send your father to represent you.'

The ex-Minister found himself charmed. But he held himself when TB Chandath, finding themselves alone, asked after Yograj.

'Boy's out. Busy all day running around. Not easy these days.'

'Have you thought about it, Kuldeep-jiu? Does Yograj know? Lata's waiting for her interview results. Should be appointed an Undersecretary if all goes well.'

The ex-Minister was temporarily seduced by the idea of a bureaucrat as a daughter-in-law, a prize in Sikkim, but he recovered in time. 'I told him. But he's just not interested in girls or marriage. Too busy with his career.'

TB Chandath betrayed no disappointment. He stood up and put the ex-Minister's hands to his eyes. 'I'll see you at Balidaan Diwas. I know I will.'

After he left, Yogita said, 'I heard him asking about Yograj. Does he have a daughter? You want me to find out about her?'

The ex-Minister dismissed her offer. 'Let TB find out about his own family. Trying to rise up just because everyone is supposed to be equal.'

They had an argument about equality which Yogita, aware of her father's condition, took care to concede.

~

The next morning, the ex-Minister made them move him to his actual room on the upper floor. It was larger and better lit. He stayed in bed and on the side table he placed the Eiffel Tower. He informed the Press Secretary and word quickly spread amongst the Core Committee. They converged at Tibet Road after their morning meals and awaited the Hon'ble Chief Minister.

Early in the afternoon, they heard the siren from her cavalcade. From upstairs, he heard her say, 'Where is Kuldeep-jiu? I'll meet him where he is.' Then, a little later, 'Stay here. I'll have to talk to him first.'

The Hon'ble Chief Minister entered his room alone, took the ex-Minister's hand and touched it to her eyes. 'We were all glad the news was false.'

He looked away. 'I wish it was true.'

Her voice was soft and aggrieved. 'If you had gone without meeting me… How would I have carried on?'

This broke his resolve. He blurted, 'It's only the dead and the almost dead who are allowed to meet you. You have no time for the living.'

The ex-Minister narrated all he had endured in the recent months. The humiliation of CAS, the humiliation at the Minister's bungalow, his son's humiliation by his department, his humiliation by Sumati AE. He paused as she repeated the name to herself. He said, 'It was all that tension which almost killed me. The food poisoning was just an excuse.'

Then he realized he had forgotten another issue and said hurriedly, 'What about our names? They tell me we all have to write our names in one way.'

The Hon'ble Chief Minister played with the folds of her sari. 'It's better, no? We need a common name. The "n" in our names is no good. They say it's the tone of the elite in Kathmandu. It won't get us anywhere.'

The ex-Minister looked away, unconvinced. She leaned forward and held his hand. 'I look older than you. I'm going to give it all up soon; I'm looking for a successor.'

The ex-Minister said, 'What will happen to us? So many things are still incomplete.' Instantly, he realized he was trapped.

She continued, 'That is why this year's Balidaan Diwas and next year's is important. Tribal, non-tribal are not important. It is we who have to stick together. You have to come and you have to bring CAS. Whatever you have on your mind, say it on the stage. We'll listen and we'll all make a common decision.'

She took his hand in hers. 'We fought together and our times are almost up. You're eighty-two, I'm eighty-one. This is not the age to be fighting. Tell me, what do you want me to do? Resign?'

The ex-Minister withdrew his hand and shook his head guiltily, thinking hard for other demands to make. He said, 'This is the only time I'm going to ask you. What do you think of the temple? You made me get the sandalwood, and it has been in my godown for ten years. Please see if you don't believe me.'

The sandalwood had been purchased and smuggled into Sikkim in a time of laxity, in the early days of the Hon'ble Chief Minister's rule, when she believed that her fortune was a result of the intercession of his gods, who needed to be felicitated. It was his idea, but it had been endorsed by her. Then, construction had stalled as she moved her attention to other projects, and the ex-Minister was left with 130 cubic feet of sandalwood, whose combined aroma threatened to expose him at any time, and which was subdued only by the stench of the culvert that went past his building.

'Let me use it or let me burn it.'

The Hon'ble Chief Minister said, 'Wait, Kuldeep-jiu, wait. The money has been sanctioned. The file is with DB Bhai. It will come to CAS.'

The ex-Minister scoffed, 'You gave the file to DB Minister? You asked the fox to deliver the rooster?'

She said, 'I always trust the wrong people.'

Her face fell but the ex-Minister wasn't done. He reached for the Eiffel Tower, placed on the side table. 'Here, this is for you. Mitradas left it here. He got it from his Europe tour.'

She returned the souvenir to its position and patted the ex-Minister's arm to calm his petulance. 'I can't send everyone at once. What will they say? I'll talk to the Principal Secretary. I'll send CAS to Europe and America.'

The ex-Minister permitted himself a slight nod. She stood up and said, 'Let us go downstairs. They must be wondering what we two old people are up to.'

They walked down, each supporting the other. In the living room, the Core Committee rose in unison. The Hon'ble Chief Minister proclaimed, 'May such news be false for all of us.'

They hustled around, trying to find the best seat for her. After it was found and the Hon'ble Chief Minister was seated, she said, 'I have talked to Kuldeep Daju about attending Balidaan Diwas. If CAS doesn't come, we will not celebrate it this year.'

The ex-Minister spoke on behalf of CAS. 'We didn't ask to be on the Steering Committee. We were pulled in and then without any reason we were pushed out.'

The Core Committee agreed with this. The Hon'ble Chief Minister removed her spectacles and wiped them. They turned silent and she said, 'CAS will get the money. My word has been given in this gathering. But I want to place a deep request before everyone here, please attend Balidaan Diwas. After that, the State government will send the Core Committee of CAS abroad for a research holiday.' The Core Committee members accepted this honour gravely.

'Europe and America,' the ex-Minister said, to show that he was responsible.

~

In the late afternoon, after all had left, he had his bed moved downstairs to the room beside the kitchen. Pradeep DE phoned, 'I know, I know. I am nobody.'

The ex-Minister said, 'She was supposed to come tomorrow, I would have called you in the evening, but she arrived suddenly. What was I to do? Tell the Chief Minister to go back?'

Pradeep DE enquired, 'You talked about me?'

'Yes, even though you don't deserve it.' The ex-Minister ended the call, it was time for evening medicines. As Pamphaa put them in his hand, she said, 'The Chief Minister, in this house, who would have thought.'

The ex-Minister grunted. 'Make sure you tell the doctor when he comes.'

Yogita was at home when Dr Kuldeep visited. He pronounced the ex-Minister stable but some tests were still needed.

The ex-Minister agreed readily. 'Can you call your parents to the hospital? The HCM told me to meet as many Chandanth families as I can before Balidaan Diwas.'

Yogita was appalled by his brazenness. 'Appa, we all know what you are doing. No, he will not bring his parents.'

The ex-Minister rubbed his hands and changed the subject. 'Yogita is leaving tomorrow. Getting phone calls all the time from her office.'

The ex-Minister studied the doctor's face and was pleased to see his smile disappear. 'I didn't know that.'

Yogita was shy. 'I have to go. If I don't want to get fired.'

Dr Kuldeep was persuaded to stay for dinner. The ex-Minister noted the ease of his table manners and after he left, told Yogita in a tone of genuine wonder, 'Who knew such a grandson could come from such a grandfather?'

~

At the hospital the following day, the test results were normal. A few medicines were prescribed and they waited in Dr Kuldeep's office, while a peon was sent to purchase the medicines. Outside, a woman from the North district waited with a child who had a pus-distended eye. The child's wailing defeated the ex-Minister's questions. They heard a nurse arrive, the mother petitioned her, and the nurse scolded the mother for leaving it so late. 'You should have taken your child to the witch-doctor. Why did you bring him here?'

Dr Kuldeep closed the door to his office, the clamour dimmed. 'The other day, a person needed oxygen, so the nurse took it from the person on the next bed and that person died.'

The peon returned. All the medicines were available, except one. Dr Kuldeep said, 'I'll get it to Tibet Road in the evening on my way home. My shift ends at four.'

The ex-Minister stood up and rubbed his hands. 'No. Absolutely not. You've troubled yourself enough. Yogita will come and pick up the medicine when your shift is done.'

He picked up the medicines from Dr Kuldeep's desk and hurried out. In the car, she scolded her father, 'Why are you so shameless?'

'He doesn't know anything. I know how to handle such situations.'

Yogita dropped by when Dr Kuldeep was about to finish his shift. He gave her a packet and said, 'The medicines. I hope you don't think I staged all this.'

She shook her head. 'Fathers!'

Outside, he asked her if she would accompany him to the bazaar. He had to buy some air-tight containers for his house. They walked to the bazaar and he made his purchases. Soon they were in a coffee shop, one of many that had opened since the stretch had been pedestrianized a few years earlier.

He spoke of his family, and encouraged her to speak about hers. He knew Yograj; they were acquaintances bound by a common network of Chandanths. But they did not meet often. Dr Kuldeep said, 'My circle is more studious.'

Yogita blew into her coffee. 'You will take care of my father?'

'Of course. But he's old, and nature will take its course.'

Yogita nodded. 'You must be wondering, no, why my father is so old and we are so young?'

'Second wife?'

Yogita looked at the table. 'Not very difficult, no?

He opened his palm upwards. 'Not difficult at all but that was the way they lived.' She asked for his number so she could check on her father's health and he gave it to her.

Dr Kuldeep knew most of the people who visited the café. To some a smile and a wave sufficed, some walked up to their table and chatted with him. Yogita, despite her resolve, enjoyed the studied indifference with which they appraised her. He was of a piece with Gangtok, its concerns were his. He would become respectable. He would be consulted and his opinions would carry weight.

Yogita had very few friends here, she had been educated in a convent in Kurseong. Then she had moved to Bangalore for her Bachelor's degree, to Delhi for her Master's and then the job. Delhi was someone else's city but she tolerated it for its freedoms.

Outside, it was going dark. A cold wind blew into the café, even though it was June. They were seated at a window and ahead of them were the green roofs of the lower buildings which occupied most of their view. Far away, against the opposing hills, dark and light clouds tussled. Nothing like Delhi, where every surface radiated heat.

When they were alone, she said, 'You don't seem very affected by my father's attempts. Girlfriend?'

He frowned into his coffee. 'Yes. From Orissa. I met her during my internship. Let's see where it ends up.'

She commiserated with a platitude. 'Long distances are always difficult.'

'And you?'

'I'm alone,' Yogita said, 'Delhi doesn't give you time for boyfriends.

Everyone is so rude there.' Then she asked him, 'So are you a Chandanth or a Chandith? Everyone seems to be in camps here.'

Dr Kuldeep waved at somebody at the counter. 'That was the first thing your father asked me. We have been writing Chandanth for a long time but one thing is just as good as another. It's just a name.'

'I find it all so silly, as if the world has run out of problems that we should create ones like these. But it's his passion, it drives and challenges him and in a way, keeps him young. My angry young father.'

They heard clangs. He explained, 'Hailstorm. But it'll be brief at this time of the year.'

She put her hand out to feel some of it, but the roof's overhang denied her. They waited out the hail. Outside, the bazaar felt clean and cold. It was the clarity of winter in the heart of the monsoon. 'I need to have a cigarette. Anywhere I can smoke around here?'

He didn't smoke, and there was no place he knew where she could. She took him down one of the wide and steep public staircases that connected the bazaar to the highway below. There was a shallow cove beside a cluster of electricity-distribution boxes. She took out her cigarettes and saw that they were spotted with mould, even though she had bought them only the day before. The enveloping humidity had made them useless. Dr Kuldeep went up to the nearest shop and returned with cigarettes. She smoked while he nervously kept watch for acquaintances, more for himself than for her.

At home, the ex-Minister waited until after dinner. It gave him enough time for him to appear casual. 'So, how did it go?'

Yogita clapped, and giggled. 'He kissed me on the lips when he dropped me home.'

The ex-Minister grunted, not because he believed her but because it showed how little control he had over his children's manners and talk. Yogita left the following morning after extracting a solemn oath from her father that he would look after his health, and left a list of instructions for Pamphaa on his care.

Her anxieties were wasted. The Hon'ble Chief Minister's visit and CAS's renewed involvement in the upcoming Balidaan Diwas had given him strength. Then Nima Thendup visited with news. He had visited

Suikeybung for some work. 'Our relatives are also strange. They all heard of your illness but they don't want to come.'

The ex-Minister waved away the information. It didn't matter now, the apathy of his brothers and sister. He saw them now as petty villagers, determined to nurse their inconsequential grudges. He could live without them for he was one of the leading lights of his community and the brightest lights glowed alone.

A few days later, Pamphaa said, 'Some hard paper for you.' A bundle of cards had arrived. He opened one; CAS had been added as a constituent of the Steering Committee, its name on the list preceded CHAPS. The ex-Minister was named as one of the speakers. He began to prepare his speech.

Officially Backward 1: Balidaan Diwas

This year, like all other years, they assembled early in the forecourt of Vajra Cinema. There was an easy drizzle but the sky was light beyond the film of immediate rain and they knew the day would improve. The Hon'ble Chief Minister singled the ex-Minister out for greetings and clasped his hand in gratitude for attending. 'I knew you would not let your people down, Kuldeep-jiu.'

The members of CAS huddled, uncomfortable in their new role as participants when they had always been organizers. They watched the members of CHAPS, under Mitradas Chandith, distributing packed breakfasts in paper bags, distributing placards and organizing the walkers. The ex-Minister spat, 'Vultures!'

Like all other dignitaries, the ex-Minister had come dressed in a kanchnaki and worn a seytupi on his head. The kanchnaki was new, stitched in a hurry because the others hung loose on him after his illness. Pamphaa had chosen the fabric for him and she had brought it from the tailor the previous evening. It was stiff and he felt the cloth bite or constrain him in various places. At least the gotay jutta was comfortable, though its open-laced structure meant his feet would be wet.

He took care not to stand next to the Vice President who, because everyone was dressed traditionally, had chosen to stand out with a silolo, a black shawl with gold embroidery.

The General Secretary had chosen to wear a sari instead of a phupopo. He approached her and wagged a finger. 'Not a tribal dress. Will the HCM like it?'

She seemed happy to see his cheer but her reply was sharp. 'A woman should not do what is expected of her. All expectations have been imposed by men and for men.'

The drizzle turned into rain. The rally was abandoned, to his relief. They were to congregate at Sikkim Conference Centre instead. The ex-Minister was offered a lift by the Vice President who asked him, 'So how do you think it will be?'

The ex-Minister reassured him, 'All things happen for a reason.'

At the Centre, the ex-Minister was guided to the second row, with the Press Secretary to his left and the Vice President to his right. His exclusion from the first row bit him, but he pacified himself by noting that it was reserved for international guests, with the dispiriting exception of DB Chandath, the Minister for Village Roads. It pleased him to see Mitradas Chandith and TB Chandath both seated in the second row.

The theme of the day's seminar—they had themes now—was 'The Confluence of Tradition and Modernity'. They observed a minute's silence for Yagung Chandeth and then the lamp was lit by the guest of honour, Pitu Kej Chandeth. The day's proceedings were initiated. After the lighting of the lamp, a magazine called *Chyalu Sikuradaa—The Ancestral Songs of Chyalu* was released and copies were distributed. It was edited by Mitradas Chandith and was to be an exclusive quarterly summary of the movements and achievements of the diaspora.

The ex-Minister held the magazine—he would not stoop to peruse it—and leaned towards the Vice President. 'The pages must be made of silver.'

The seminar began with a traditional rice-sowing dance. The ex-Minister was dismayed to find that the dhaanpu, the women's dress for the dance, was incorrect. The real dress, the dress he remembered from his Suikeybung childhood as worn by his mother and aunts on the first day of sowing, was flared and had its hemline just below the knee, to assist with the sowing which took place during the summer rains. This version was far too high above the knee and far too tight. 'Only good for sowing one thing.' Even the male dress, the dhaanla, looked suspicious. The trousers were not loose and they tapered in a modern cut.

The ex-Minister leaned towards the Vice President. 'Jokers. It is better if tradition disappears than to be remembered like this.'

The Vice President leaned towards the ex-Minister. 'Jokers.'

After the dance, the Master of Ceremonies spoke. The history of Chyalu, as everyone knew, was one of bravery in the face of oppression. The inhabitants of Chyalu had long been oppressed by the Shah royalty and the upper castes. The list of their injustices would take a year to recite but he would not, for this was not a time for grudges. The banner of revolt against their oppression in the modern era had been raised by the Late Yagung Chandeth, as everyone knew. His second-in-command, the heroic poet, Pitu Kej Chandeth, also known as Chyalupath—The Voice of Chyalu—was present with them and he would give the keynote address.

The poet was old, his movements slow and his voice heavy with accumulated honours. His accent was tinted with the inflections common to Nepal, and the audience tittered at the peculiar pronunciation of certain common words. He read his poetry in Chandari and the audience feigned raptness, betraying themselves only once—when they applauded, assuming he had finished a poem, and it turned out he had merely paused to sip some water.

The Press Secretary leaned in from the left. 'Have you read his poetry, Kuldeep-jiu? We only get the Nepali version in Sikkim but the poems are beautiful in Chandari. '

The ex-Minister said, 'Son, first I was busy for Sikkim, then for Chandanths, and then for CAS. No time for poems.'

The Press Secretary, undaunted, repeated some lines, absorbed by their effect on him. The ex-Minister leaned away.

On stage, the poet announced that the struggles of his people had crystallized in him. The King of Nepal had banned his books, the

Maoists had threatened to assassinate him, and the Democrats had tried to exile him. He spoke for a long time and, being distinguished, could not be nudged to cease. He announced that he was proposing a new title for the Hon'ble Chief Minister of Sikkim—she was to be known as Hijeru Dan this day, the mother of her people. It was the only tribute for a woman whose virtues were as rare as fragrant gold.

The applause ceased only after the Master of Ceremonies pleaded from the stage for some quiet. The poet had consumed an extra half-hour from the day's programmeme. The ex-Minister leaned towards the Vice President. 'No value for time in Nepal.'

The Vice President agreed. 'He's not getting invited again.'

His speech was followed by the rice-harvest dance. Again the ex-Minister was dismayed. They were using the common scythe. The Chandanth scythe was different—its curve was less pronounced and its blade wider. Every year, after the functions ended, he informed the dancers but they had never changed it. And these were the custodians of their culture!

The next speaker was TB Chandath, in his capacity as the Convener of the Steering Committee, and an alumnus of the London School of Economics. He described his tears of relief and disappointment on that fateful day in 1997 when the Parliament of India recognized the Chandaths as a backward caste. In that phrase were two words, backward and caste. One of them was right—backward. The other one was wrong—caste. The Chandaths were backward, no doubt about that. How backward were they? Everyone in the hall knew how backward they were, an itemized list would only be a waste of time. But he would point out one, just one. His father was once denied rice by a shopkeeper—he would not mention the shopkeeper's caste for this was not a time for grudges.

The ex-Minister leaned towards the Vice President. 'I knew his father. Had a tongue like a knife. I don't blame the shopkeeper.'

The oppression, TB Chandath said, was still continuing. In some corner of Sikkim, India or Nepal there was still a Chandath man who was being denied rice for who he was. There was only one way this continual error could be rectified. They would have to deny the caste system altogether. The Chandaths would have to be declared a tribe. TB Chandath read out an internationally accepted list of the defining features of tribes and announced that Chandaths fulfilled all the criteria.

The ex-Minister leaned towards the Press Secretary. 'All nonsense.'

The Press Secretary leaned away. 'It's a matter of opinion.'

The ex-Minister longed to oppose the mistaken man. The Chandanths were a caste; he had a lifetime's worth of experience and research to prove it. One of their major gods was Kumbura, the feathered incarnation of Vishnu. He tried to summon the courage to ask a question but failed, because he did not trust the stability of his voice.

The last speaker before lunch was the General Secretary of CAS and she had chosen a subject which was no longer fashionable to ignore. She spoke on 'The Role of Women in Traditional Chandanth Society'. Over the course of her talk, she proved that traditional Chandath society was egalitarian enough to have impressed visiting officers from the British Empire in 1862.

The ex-Minister leaned towards the Vice President. 'What about all our second wives?'

The Vice President giggled. 'I'm on my third.'

~

Lunch was announced. The ex-Minister avoided the mutton. He conceded that the food was better this year. He sat down with a plate and the Vice President sat next to him. He looked around for the Hon'ble Chief Minister but she was in an inner chamber, eating with Pitu Kej Chandeth. A bit further off, the Joint Secretary was adjusting his seytupi. He felt a nudge. It was the Treasurer. 'Have you heard anything about the oxygen?'

The ex-Minister extracted a sinew of pork from his teeth and said, 'The pocket may open today.'

This excited the Treasurer. 'Who did you hear it from?'

The ex-Minister concentrated on his food. 'No one. Just my feeling.'

The Treasurer, hurt by the absence of leadership, sniffed. 'I heard DB Minister will announce it later.'

The ex-Minister continued to chew. 'He'll eat the banana and throw us the peel.'

The ex-Minister went to the dessert counter and selected a chocolate brownie covered in chocolate sauce. There he met the Multiple Award Winner. 'I wanted to thank you, Daju. Because of your recommendation, I am getting an award today.'

The ex-Minister accepted his gratitude, and was surprised when the Multiple Award Winner embraced him. He said, 'I was only doing my duty.'

He returned to his seat, followed by the Multiple Award Winner, and they conversed. The Vice President was close by, struggling with a piece of mutton. The General Secretary was talking closely with the Joint Secretary. Mitradas could not be seen and this worried the ex-Minister. He though he ought to walk around to see what that traitor Mitradas was up to but a functionary announced the end of the lunch break.

~

The ex-Minister was the first speaker after lunch. He had prepared his speech, and stayed within the traditional template. He began by promising to provide an honest and thorough appraisal of the Hon'ble Chief Minister, her achievements and failures. He warned the audience that he would be critical; at his age there was no one left to fear. Many people did not like him, Kuldeep Chandanth, and many of them were here, but he would not name them, for this was not a time for grudges. He was going to say what he thought of the Hon'ble Chief Minister, whatever the consequences.

The Hon'ble Chief Minister, for him, was a female incarnation of the god Vishnu, the preserver. Sikkim had not been created by the Hon'ble Chief Minister, but she had done everything to preserve the fragile cultural threads of the smallest state in India.

The applause was not as substantial as he hoped.

He moved to his criticisms of the Hon'ble Chief Minister. She worked too hard, even at the cost of her own health, and she did not consider what would become of the Chandanths of Sikkim should anything happen to her. Also, her heart was too large, she gave too much, and she spoiled those who harboured evil designs. These were faults he hoped she would address. He saw the Hon'ble Chief Minister lean towards the person on her right, her Principal Secretary, who stood up, walked up to the stage and disappeared behind the curtains.

The ex-Minister had begun the final section of his speech. He spoke of the qualities of sandalwood—unyielding yet possessed of a sensual fragrance that would captivate the hardest heart. That was how the Chandanths were. He paused to sip some water and heard a hiss from his left. It was the Principal Secretary; he was gesturing with urgency. 'Stop. They are asking you to stop.' He pointed at the front row, where the Hon'ble Chief Minister was seated. The ex-Minister continued.

He spoke of Mon Gyal, the last great historical king of the Chandanth, finally defeated by a combined alliance of Mughals, Rajputs, Tibetans, Chinese and the British. As the great temple of Dhod was being destroyed at Raku, had he not asked to be burnt along with it? Everyone knew the legend. Had he not said, 'Wherever the fragrance goes, let my people thrive there, and I will be reborn in the east. This temple will be reborn in the east?' The fragrance had travelled as far as Sikkim, and they now knew whom the king had alluded to. It was only fitting that it was from here that the push for a new category should begin.

He ended by putting two proposals before the gathering. The first was the completion of the temple, for it had stood incomplete for so long that the locals had begun to wonder if Kumbura, the incarnation of Vishnu, had abandoned his favourite children. The second was the adoption of Chandanth as the official way to spell and pronounce their fragrant name. How India's Parliament and Constitution chose to classify him was immaterial, as long as the memories of his origin were preserved.

He thanked everyone and stopped. They were a few stray claps which picked up when the Hon'ble Chief Minister applauded.

~

The ex-Minister took his seat and asked the Vice President, 'Saw how I gave it to them?' There was no answer. He turned and saw the Vice President dab at his eyes. 'Too good. Too good. Just too good.'

But the reaction was not unanimous. When he turned to his left to elicit praise from the Press Secretary, he was told, 'Let us see what happens.'

On the stage the seminar had moved on. Awards were being given by the Steering Committee to those who had contributed to the cause and to the name of the Chandari-speaking peoples. Amongst the awardees was the Multiple Award Winner, his award given for increasing awareness through his solo walk for Chandath unity.

Mitradas Chandith was introduced. He said he didn't want to argue about theories but it was well known that the word Chandith came from chaandi, the word for silver. There were also historical records of there being extensive silver mines in the Chyalu Valley; in fact, Chyalu silver was so untarnished that it was used as currency in Tibet. But those were discussions for other times.

He did not mean to offend those who had spoken before him and those who would speak after him. He was simply going to state his views. How fortunate the Chandiths in Sikkim were to have someone like the Hon'ble Chief Minister. Someone who had rebelled—peacefully, of course—against the historical oppressors of Sikkim; everyone in the hall knew who they were, but this was not a time for grudges. It was for these efforts that he, Mitradas Chandith, was proud to be an emissary of a noble distinction. The Mankind Buddhist University of Bangkok had conferred an honorary doctorate on the Hon'ble Chief Minister who, after the investiture ceremony, would be known as Dr YM Chandath. It was the least the world could do to acknowledge the great lady.

The applause seemed, to the ex-Minister, undeserved and unending. He turned to the Vice President and said, 'Spoonholder!'

The Vice President nodded his sleepy head. 'I've said that before.'

Tea was announced. The ex-Minister sat alone with his tea and biscuits, avoided by all. He felt a pat on his arm. It was the Hon'ble Chief Minister's Principal Secretary, the man who had pleaded with him to stop. The ex-Minister said, 'You should have let me speak.'

The Principal Secretary said emotionlessly, 'You can speak again. There will be a private meeting chaired by the CM after her main speech in the meeting hall. She wants you to be there.'

The Principal Secretary left and his place was immediately taken by the Treasurer. He asked, 'What did he say?'

'The HCM has called me for a private meeting.'

The Treasurer's expression crumpled in anxiety. 'About your speech? You think she's hurt? Will she scold?'

The ex-Minister tried to reassure him. 'I'll take whatever she says for CAS. One has to bear the kicks of the milk-giving cow.'

The Treasurer said, 'What a great President we have,' and moved away.

The ex-Minister was then approached by the Minister for Village Roads, who caught his hands and took them to his eyes, but the ex-Minister yanked them away. The Minister spoke with distress. 'I hear you're hurt. You should have spoken to me before going to the HCM.'

The ex-Minister had imagined this encounter many times and now he did what he had promised himself he would do. He turned around and walked away.

~

The Hon'ble Chief Minister was the last speaker of the day. She thanked everyone for their contributions and remarked that the slight drizzle outside was the tears of their ancestors as they watched the best and the purest among their descendants gathered under one roof. There was much she had learnt through the day, and much of it was in concordance with her beliefs. She knew today what she had long suspected, the hearts of the Chandiths were still with nature. There would be different interpretations for sure, but they were all deduced with sincere hearts: sandalwood or silver, it didn't matter, it was enough to know that the children of Chyalu were made of precious stuff.

'We shouldn't change our names yet. Imagine the headaches for our poor bureaucracy, already so overburdened. The number of affidavits that will have to be filed…' she said. The Vice President leaned towards the ex-Minister and said, 'She doesn't mean you.'

The Hon'ble Chief Minister also said that she could not accept honours, for she was one amongst many Chandiths fighting for their people. She would appreciate it if she was not called Hijeru Dan, the mother of her people. All she had done, she had done as a servant of her destiny. She could also not accept a doctorate from the distinguished university which had offered it, not while there were people such as TB

Chandath who had earned their doctorates through years of fruitful labour.

She ended by thanking everyone, and blessed them so that they would continue working for the furtherance of their legacies. 'We must do justice to our ancestors. We have our differences, we fight, we quarrel, but why am I here? Because of our common ancestors.'

~

In the meeting hall, the ex-Minister looked around with disappointment. It was not a gathering of the select few. There were around twenty people and they all seemed similarly disappointed. But it gave him some satisfaction to see that he was the only member of CAS, aside from the General Secretary. Mitradas Chandith was there, as was TB Chandath. The Hon'ble Chief Minister entered and sat down on a large sofa that had been kept vacant. The Minister for Village Roads followed her and sat on her right.

The Hon'ble Chief Minister thanked everyone for the day's events which had progressed seamlessly. 'This was only a dress rehearsal. In next year's seminar we will make a united petition for recognition as a Scheduled Tribe. It will not be easy and I will not be able to do it without you.'

She outlined her plan. The seminar was a primer for an international Chandith festival, for which people would come from Nepal, Bhutan and Burma. Then they would make a grand request to the Indian government to recognize the Chandiths as a Scheduled Tribe and provide all the benefits that such a recognition guaranteed.

The ex-Minister, wishing for some attention even if it was a rebuke, said, 'I didn't mean to offend. I only said what I feel.'

The Hon'ble Chief Minister said, 'No no. Anyone can speak. That's why we have mouths.' Then she turned grave. She looked at her wrinkled hands and then up at them. 'I am old, probably only three people here are older than me. My bones are asking for rest. Once our people become recognized as a Scheduled Tribe, my life's work will be done. I can then retire, and the next Hon'ble Chief Minister will be from another community. Until then, there will be no fighting in public.'

Those present knew this was an announcement, and they were expected to spread it. And they conversed in soft tones, for the Hon'ble Chief Minister's presence civilized all discourse. Towards the end, she coughed lightly. 'I almost forgot to talk about the money.'

They laughed to cover their embarrassment. CAS and CHAPS were both to receive eighty lakh rupees each, to be used as the organizations saw fit. 'DB Bhai will be in charge of the money's disbursement.'

The Minister for Village Roads looked profound and impassive, as if it were a grave responsibility. The faces of the beneficiaries darkened. The ex-Minister took a sip of his tea. 'Better that the cheques come from your Principal Secretary.'

The reaction was surprisingly positive, all the beneficiaries nodded vigorously. The ex-Minister had touched upon a common fear. The Minister for Village Roads adjusted his body on the sofa, as if in anticipation of a fight. 'Are you saying something?'

The ex-Minister placed his cup on the side-table. 'Money is a heavy thing, and the burden will be too much for you.'

A few uncultivated people in the room could not contain their sniffles, but, otherwise, the moment passed calmly. The Minister for Village Roads patted his stomach. The Hon'ble Chief Minister sipped some tea and requested everyone to have theirs as well.

Consolations

Early in July, Yograj had his third lunch at Sarata Babuni's flat. 'You shouldn't have taken so much effort. Three labourers couldn't finish all this in a week.'

She had prepared pork trotters, chicken legs, three varieties of vegetables, rice and an assortment of pickles. She watched him struggle with a chicken thighbone. 'Your father won't mind you eating chicken?'

'Only if he finds out.'

She had texted him the day after she had visited his father: 'Thanx so much 4 droping meh'. He had replied, a correspondence had ensued, and it had led to lunch invitations, made illicit by the promise of forbidden meats.

She wiped some perspiration from her forehead with the back of her hand, leaving an arc of gravy. 'It's all I know. My father always made me cook heavy meals. He grew up poor, and believed that to die eating was the greatest luck for an old man.'

Two months had passed since her father passed away, and she had redecorated. The walls had been repainted in lighter shades, the chairs had cushion covers with abstract patterns and there were real flowers in vases. The flat now looked spacious.

At the first lunch, he had asked, 'Your family doesn't stay with you?' It was his first move beyond conversational formalities.

His plate was empty. She offered him some extra rice, gave her hands a quick wash, and served him. 'Three brothers but they are all married outside Gangtok. They were here for the funeral and left after the rites.'

At the second lunch, he had asked, 'Boyfriend? All the smart women in Gangtok have boyfriends.'

She sniffed. 'Bua's care took up so much time.' She was divorced. They had met when he had come working for a vacuum cleaner company setting up in Sikkim. The company had not done well and when it had retreated from Sikkim, he had chosen the company over his wife.

'That's why I tell everyone, "Never trust a man from Darjeeling. They only know how to break hearts."'

Now he admired her clothes, a beige T-shirt that fell loosely over her wide-hipped jeans. 'You dress stylishly even when you're at home.'

She was pleased. 'Now you're making fun of me.'

She insisted he stay in the living room while she cleaned up the kitchen. He listened to the noises from the street below. There was a frantic honking of car horns. He looked outside; a driver had parked beside an electric pole braided by creepers and clumps of bluebells, a result of the rains. The driver had entered a medicine shop to make a purchase. The electric pole and his stationary car narrowed the road. Vehicles stalled on either side, the honking increased. The driver emerged from the medicine shop and admonished the honkers by holding up the packet of medicines. 'It's for my daughter. You don't have any daughters?' He moved his car, the street returned to normal. It drizzled. Yograj thought about the car he was going to buy, now that he had his share of the contract's profits. He picked up a magazine but felt listless. The meal had made him heavy, he drowsed.

She came in and put her hand on his head. 'Lie down in the bedroom. You can sleep properly there.'

She took him to a bed in a room with a window. The next building loomed close, and the room was one into which daylight seldom reached. He heard woman's voice yell at someone, a servant perhaps, to pick up the washing before the rain worsened. Sarata Babuni entered the room and closed the window. The room turned dark. She sat on the edge of the bed, close to his recumbent body, and after a moment of indecision, pressed on him. Their mouths collided, there was some grating of teeth. The remnants of the meal were still in her mouth, and Yograj wondered if the taste came from her's or his. Some spit dribbled and she withdrew from the kiss, ashamed. 'I don't have much experience. Even though I look so mature.'

She removed her clothes. He handled her large, deflated breasts and caressed her blanched skin. His sleep had vanished but his arousal was marred by the thought that her father had probably died on the same bed. Her hand travelling downwards banished the thought from his mind.

She looked up at him and said, 'You'll have to teach me everything.' Yograj removed her spectacles and kissed her eyes. He was going to enjoy this one.

After they were done, she brought him some tea and biscuits. 'Tell me, who's better? Julie Babuni or me?'

He dipped a biscuit in his tea. 'No comparison.'

He began to see her every day. One day he had her apply for casual leave so that they could spend the whole day together. She agreed readily, for her life had been without mischief so far. He did not let her cook; the food made them heavy, and there was less time for other things.

She had bought some red lingerie, and seeing her pale, tubular body unaccommodated by the garment designed for curves, he felt sad for her. 'Put on some music, your favourite, and take them off slowly.'

He discovered that her eagerness to learn was an abstract wish. She wanted to learn but was an unenthusiastic student, whose morals often hindered the attainment of knowledge.

It was a challenge to get her to do something as simple as sucking him off, and she had promised to do it that day.

She did it clumsily and, when he tried to tutor her movements, she demanded to know the names of all those who had done this to him before. Was it Julie Babuni? What else had Julie Babuni agreed to do?

This led to an argument. In the end, to appease him, she tried it but it gave him no pleasure. She apologized but the mood of tawdriness remained. He dreaded the evening, for he had promised her the entire day. He was relieved by persistent calls from his father. He avoided them, and when they would not abate, he answered. The ex-Minister said, 'Come home immediately.'

Yograj showed Sarata Babuni the missed calls. She whimpered, 'Go. Family is more important.'

~

As Yograj entered the kitchen, the ex-Minister threw a cup at him. 'You thief! You thief!' He tried to charge at his son, and was restrained by Pamphaa.

The ex-Minister waved a cheque-book at his son. Yograj had expected his theft to be discovered at some point. A few weeks earlier, he had taken the cheque-book, forged his father's signature, and withdrawn his share from the bank. He nodded his head. 'I took what was mine. If that is stealing, report me to the police.'

The ex-Minister broke down and each heaving of the chest felt like a physical blow. 'My son, my own son, stealing from me, stealing from his own father. Thuiyaa!' The ex-Minister spat, but he had no strength left and the spit dribbled feebly on to his chin.

Yograj leaned against the doorframe. 'You steal from me, I steal from you. Same to same.' He asked Pamphaa, 'What do you think?'

The ex-Minister sobbed against her chest, raging against the theft, against his son's physical power over him. Pamphaa held his head and said, 'Come back after a while.'

Yograj left the house. Outside he saw Shambhunath emerge from the mist. 'I heard about your father. He was a good man.' A vehicle drove through a puddle and the glazier jumped aside to avoid being splashed.

He was amongst the final victims of the rumour of the ex-Minister's death. Yograj held his shoulders and giggled. 'Yes, yes. A very good man. Go in and pay your respects.'

Shambhunath hurried ahead, pitying the man maddened by his father's death. The main door of the house was open. He entered and saw the ghost of the ex-Minister sobbing in the kitchen. Shambhunath hid his alarm for he knew, from the truths of his village, that fear was useless, even harmful, in such situations. It was best to talk sensibly, at least in the beginning, and remind the ghost of its irrelevance to the world. He wagged a finger at the ex-Minister and asked, 'You know what has happened to you? You are dead.'

The ex-Minister hurled a steel glass at him. Pamphaa rushed to tear out his hair. As he fled, Shambhunath heard the ex-Minister shout, 'You'll go before me. Your son will go before me.'

In the street, Yograj was waiting for him. He held Shambhunath's arm and said, 'Give another try.'

Yograj did not come home that night and the ex-Minister forbade Pamphaa from enquiring. The next day was lightened by Pradeep DE's visit. He came and touched his father's hands to his eyes three times. It was his first such gesture in many years. He had not received his transfer. He had received something better, a promotion. He was now Pradeep SE, a Superintendent Engineer. And he had heard that it was the result of his father's lobbying with the Hon'ble Chief Minister. He said, 'I am sorry for having such a small mind.'

The ex-Minister did not speak of Yograj's theft; to do so would have exposed his own weakness. He blessed his elder son, weak and sly but at least grateful. He asked, 'What did you tell the Chief Minister?'

The ex-Minister was suitably enigmatic. 'You wouldn't understand even if I told you.'

Pradeep SE sat stiffly on the chair. One of the first things he had vowed to correct as a SE was his posture. 'Of course.'

~

Tobgay DE got the coveted transfer to the Urban Infrastructure Department. Sumati AE was to be transferred to the Fisheries Department. The present SE was transferred to the Cottage Industries Department and Pradeep DE was promoted to replace him.

'Pradeep SE,' he said to himself, and decided that he liked the way it sounded. There was a new deference shown to him. Sumati AE's transfer further sweetened the mood; by now she had offended everyone in one way or the other. He made it a point to be there on her last day and felt robbed when she sent her driver with her handover letter. The Commissioner-cum-Secretary was vocal about his relief. 'Bhai, just like a woman can make or break a home, same with departments.'

The pony-tailed peon was enthusiastic. 'Let her torture the fish now.'

Heera Babuni played with his sleeve. 'Say what you want. But I liked her. That doesn't mean I'm not happy for you.' She blew away a stray eyelash from his face.

His Mrs agreed and she demonstrated her pleasure by purchasing a silk nightie. She called him Papa, deviating from her previous taunts. She told him, 'At last your father has come of some use, instead of just sitting there with a heavy name.'

On the day he assumed his post, the other engineers, administrative officials, clerks, babunis, drivers and peons offered him khadas, and in turn he distributed sweets. A JE said he looked forward to working under him. No engineer would work under him, Pradeep SE said, they would all work together.

Julie Babuni handed him an invitation to her marriage. 'You look so fresh and handsome. Sitting in an SE's office and looking like a JE. So unfair!'

Pradeep SE was going to be immune to flattery. People always wanted something from big men. 'Responsibility makes me feel older.'

Sarata Babuni said, 'I'm happy it was you who stayed.' Pradeep SE only gave her a brief smile. He had heard things were happening between his brother and the babuni. It was one of his recent worries, the cloud in his sky. He had not informed his father, for the old man would insist that he manoeuvre to terminate it. Pradeep SE was not going to waste his time on such small things.

Heera Babuni was the proudest, though she kept her emotions in check, for this department, above all other departments, was famous for gossip. She wore the dress that he liked most. A crimson sari, maroon pumps, mauve eye-shadow and lipstick. Her colours had never matched so radiantly. 'Just sweets won't do for me. It has to be a treat.'

She had brought him a gift, a pen which felt heavy in his hands. She giggled. 'So big, and so heavy.'

Pradeep SE wondered how one man could handle so much good fortune.

He soon found out.

The impersonal matrix of transfers and postings which had brought him and Heera Babuni together worked to part them. Within a month, he received orders to take up duties as the Superintendent Engineer of the Small Industries Department; it was in accordance with an established policy to transfer out promoted officials.

Pradeep SE rejoiced. The distance would bring him and Heera Babuni closer. Liberated from the constrictions of a shared office, their romance would achieve its due maturity. His disappointment was gradual. He paid for not one but three lunches, in grand and discreet hotels. On all three occasions, Heera Babuni declined to inspect the fabulous interiors of the rooms of the hotels, tours he had arranged at much expense. 'I have to be home. The children are waiting.' And when he dropped her home, she did not invite him upstairs, preferring to show her gratitude by squeezing his arm. 'There are children in the house.' His suggestions for out-of-town trips to Darjeeling or Siliguri went unheeded for the same reason; the children could not be left behind.

He realized that she would let him into her heart, but other, equally vital parts were to be kept out of his reach. With a stone over his heart, he smiled and made up his mind to withdraw, and lest it appear obvious, he did it in stages, so slowly that Heera Babuni would not sense his withdrawal. And so, like diverging glaciers, they moved apart over the course of the year, and he knew how well his strategy had succeeded when she phoned him in November and said, 'There will never be another one like you in our department.'

There were consolations. His family had no contracts or pending transfers with his new department, and he could work undisturbed, without the fear of unrecoverable embarrassments. The change in his situation also purchased him peace with his Mrs. She was less combative with him, scolding him only when she felt he was damaging his health by working too hard. She went on a diet and took morning walks. She lost weight, and he could discern her neck as separate from her body but, while her efforts touched him, they also made him more wistful, for he now remembered Heera Babuni's neck, so slender that swans would have wept in envy.

~

The remainder of the year was disappointingly uneventful for the ex-Minister. Pamphaa effected a settlement between him and Yograj after a week of estrangement. She sided with his son. 'Who told you to keep his share from him?'

The world tour was not realized and neither did CAS's fortunes rise, for the money promised so convincingly by the Hon'ble Chief Minister did not appear. Discreet queries sent out to CHAPS revealed that they were in a similar situation: they, too, were without funds. And because the absence of funds was bound to embitter any gathering of the Core Committee, he did not call for any meetings of CAS and none was requested by any member. Only the Treasurer phoned occasionally with sour updates. 'President Saab, nothing has come as yet. Do you know why? Have you heard anything?'

The ex-Minister said, 'Who knows? Perhaps there's a shortage of pearls in the queen's house?' But he rationed his outrage, for the money would come when it was needed. Now he was buoyed by the payment from the Department of Village Roads.

The only Chandanth of stature to visit him over the next year was the Multiple Award Winner. He arrived to thank him and to seek his blessings for his next venture, which was to walk from Dehradun to Manipur, visiting all the places with sizeable Chandath populations on the way. He would return to Sikkim just in time for next year's Balidaan Diwas.

'Chandanth,' the ex-Minister corrected him.

'Of course,' the Multiple Award Winner said, and did not repeat the mistake.

The ex-Minister's health remained fragile and stable. He accepted it, for he was at an age when a complete recovery was impossible. And Pamphaa injected a routine into his diet whose benefits he felt. Her claims over him advanced: she took care of his food, checked his bones for signs of reduced strength, and moderated the few appointments he made outside of the house—he surrendered completely to her care.

It was Pamphaa who averted another disagreement between Yograj and his father when Yograj sold the family car and bought another one just after the Dasain festival, which went unobserved. He bought it, he said, from his share of the money and he was going to drive it wherever he pleased. The ex-Minister wished his son were more frugal, and in Pamphaa's company he wailed against Yograj. 'He doesn't know what hardship is. Hasn't been hungry even for one day in his life.'

Pamphaa sought to calm him down. 'Let him find his own way.'

She counselled him similarly with Yogita. The ex-Minister had taken to feigning illnesses only to have Dr Kuldeep attend to him. These sessions were marked with hints by the ex-Minister and, on the part of the doctor, increased shyness. 'What is he so shy about? Doesn't he have a stick? Doesn't he want a woman?'

Pamphaa said, 'Let them meet again. He looks like the kind who has to be led. Yogita will do that.'

The ex-Minister began to canvass actively for Yogita's return. But she resisted his pleas and his threats. 'I have work here, Appa. It's not like working for the Sikkim Government where you can take off whenever you want.'

'Come for my funeral then.'

'Appa, Appa, Appa, don't speak like that.'

She visited during Tihar. Once again the ex-Minister had a mild fever which needed Dr Kuldeep's attention. He came by and the ex-Minister and Pamphaa watched with satisfaction as Yogita and Dr Kuldeep conversed more comfortably than they had done earlier in the year. Surely they were communicating with each other. At one point, he saw them compare their phone screens and took that to be another sign of their closeness.

YEAR 2

Oxygen

Sometime in June of the following year, the Treasurer phoned the ex-Minister. 'Daju, the oxygen has come through.'

'How much?'

'Eighty lakh, as told.'

A meeting was announced and everyone had time to spare. After a year spent in sequestered resentment, they were appreciative of each other's company. At the meeting, they appraised each other on their ailments.

The General Secretary fingered the folds of her sari. 'We should all get something for our hard work. Personally, I don't want anything. No salary from CAS.'

The Treasurer corrected her. 'Not salary, honorarium.'

The General Secretary dissented. She could not accept the honorarium. The other members of the committee, alarmed that they would have to emulate her, said it was for her services to CAS, and if she didn't take the money, then they wouldn't either. The General Secretary sighed and signalled her agreement. The Treasurer announced, 'We can spare two lakh for everyone.'

They discussed and discarded various ways to utilize the money. The Joint Secretary suggested a study tour to Nepal to re-establish connections with the Chandanths there. The Vice President said, 'The President can't travel. And if he can't go, nobody should go.'

The Press Secretary suggested the publication of some volumes of Chandanth epics. The ex-Minister shot this one down. 'Let the epics be written first.'

The General Secretary said, 'That's TB's department.' TB Chandath had published much of all there was to publish on the Chandari-speaking peoples.

'World tour? We could go on a world tour.' The Vice President offered. Because they were all complicit, they laughed at their earlier innocence. Then, the ex-Minister rapped the table with his palm. 'Does anyone remember what we got the money for?'

The Treasurer was sullen. 'Temple.'

Pamphaa entered with tea and biscuits; she had put on weight over the previous year and her form had filled out. When she approached the Treasurer, he asked about the cups and saucers; they looked attractive. Pamphaa explained that they were from a new set, she had purchased it the previous month. The ex-Minister coughed, Pamphaa turned towards him, he broke a biscuit and it came away easily. The season's humidity had made them soggy. She nodded and left the living room.

The General Secretary looked at the ex-Minister. 'We also need an office building.'

The ex-Minister said, 'The office building can wait. We can always meet here. There are some rooms lying empty in the lower floor. We could make an office for CAS there.'

The Treasurer moved quickly to forestall any talk of rent. 'No no. Your house is fine. So much light here.'

The Joint Secretary said, 'Balidaan Diwas is coming up. Perhaps we should keep some aside, as CAS's contribution.'

The ex-Minister had spent the past few months waiting to be contacted by either Mitradas Chandith or TB Chandath. He showed everyone his palm. 'No. They don't want CAS's help. The Steering Committee has not contacted me.'

The Joint Secretary said, 'The Chief Minister has not yet asked the Steering Committee to meet. I don't know if anyone here knows anything more.'

They looked at one another. The Treasurer coughed slightly and said, 'This weather,' and turned to the General Secretary.

The General Secretary said, 'We received a letter. They want me and him,' she motioned towards the Treasurer, 'to participate. And it's not called Balidaan Diwas anymore. They are calling it Libhanaya Bhod. It will be in September and not in July.'

'It means Awakening Day in Chandari,' the Treasurer explained.

'We know what it means!' the ex-Minister shrieked. The smaller discussions ceased. Pamphaa entered with some crisp biscuits, her presence a warning against undue exertions. She began to distribute them in smaller plates.

The General Secretary put both palms on the low table before her, to show it was a considered decision. 'We told them that we would not cooperate without the involvement of the President and our other members.'

It was the first validation of an old and persistent doubt. The General Secretary would be the first to betray him, and the Treasurer would follow her. The ex-Minister said, 'We'll see. So when do we restart the temple? The half-naked building is there, looking at anyone who can see it. And the sandalwood below in my godown, rotting away.'

The Press Secretary said, 'There is time.'

The ex-Minister looked around for support. 'Then tell me if I've said anything wrong.'

The General Secretary tapped her watch. 'It's time for office. But we don't have to decide right away.'

The ex-Minister felt fatigue rise in him. 'Another way in which the money can be spent. Youth programme. We should do a youth programme, get our children and their friends into CAS.'

It was a lonely but inextinguishable hope that his sons, despite previous evidence, would begin to show an interest in CAS and affairs pertinent to the Chandanths of Sikkim. There were reasons to be optimistic. Pradeep, he knew, would be pulled into it by eminence alone. As a senior technocrat, he would soon receive representations for influence from the Core Committee, even if the ex-Minister forbade it. As for Yograj, money attracted him and would lure him into the organization.

The Press Secretary, still offended by the dismissal of his literary proposal, said, 'Let's discuss that some other time.'

The Joint Secretary spoke in his martyred way. 'I have no son to offer for the youth programme. There's no need for me to stay.' He looked at his watch and stood up. 'I'm getting late.'

His son and non-Chandanth wife had a child now, and the grandchild was the Joint Secretary's first. There had been overtures and emissaries from his son, and his daughter-in-law's family in Calcutta, but the Joint Secretary had spurned them all, conceding only to allow his wife a single visit. He had risen above his colleagues at CAS by his peerless sacrifice.

The ex-Minister rose to the challenge. 'You all know about my sister.' He wanted them to recollect his estrangement with his sister, more than thirty years ago.

It was one sacrifice against another, an old wound against a fresh one. The Joint Secretary twitched. 'Maybe my half-blood grandson can join.' Then he trembled and, with slow shakes of his body, began to wail. For such a large man, he was surprisingly shrill. The Treasurer rushed to hug him, and turned disapprovingly towards the ex-Minister. The Vice President consoled from his seat. 'Don't cry, Joint Bhai. We all have the same problem.'

The ex-Minister had lost, the Joint Secretary's sacrifice would be seen as being greater. The loss of a son was greater than the exile of a sister. The son's marriage was still fresh, Kalpana's story, though well-known, was ancient. Reluctantly, he stood up to hold the Joint Secretary's convulsing shoulders.

After the scene had passed, the Vice President arced his hand around the room, to show universal concordance. 'Daju, you must talk to Yograj. We should find him a good Chandanth girl. Not someone else's wife.'

The ex-Minister knew then that Yograj's affair with the divorced babuni was common knowledge. He had no refutations. It had tormented him too, the possibility of relations with that bloodless clerk, and he feared that when that happened, he would not have the Joint Secretary's strength. A vision of the woman in his house came to him, cooking, cleaning and caring for him, and it repulsed him. He saw the years of contempt that lay before eventual conciliation, the mockery of his relatives in Suikeybung. He wished he had taken up TB Chandath on his offer. If it had to be a low Chandanth, at least it could have been a useful match.

'Sensitive topic, I see. Some other time then,' he said. The topic was not abandoned completely, as they spent the remainder of the meeting discussing the uselessness of the present generation of Chandanths when it came to their own kind.

~

Had the ex-Minister known about the status of Yograj's affair, it would have reassured him. Yograj had first experienced fear when, after a particularly enjoyable afternoon session at her house, Sarata Babuni had offered herself to him for eternity. Everything—her life, her body, her cooking skills—was his. To prevent a quarrel, he had accepted her offering, and so bound himself to a promise he had not made. Early in the year, she had insisted on being seen in public together. He had relented, and had taken to meeting outdoors. He was aided by the predictable early monsoon: a shower in the morning, cloudy through the day and another shower in the evening, during which he drove her around.

Then she demanded that he walk with her in the bazaar. He had done this a few times, in stressed alertness, given the range of acquaintances who could mock him later.

On the day of the CAS meeting, Yograj was at Sarata Babuni's house. She had said, 'I feel so sad for the two of you. Father and son all alone.'

Yograj's voice tightened. 'We're doing fine. And the servant is there, almost like a step-mother now.'

'Don't talk like that. It's not good. A servant will always be a servant. You need something more, no?'

She had made such leading statements lately. The hints that she kept house very well, the assurances that his life wouldn't change. He had sensed it apprehensively for a while, and now that its blunt exposition was done, he felt relieved. He was evasive. 'I would be nothing without you.'

But this no longer meant anything to her. 'Talk to your old man. If you don't, then I will. I know he likes me.'

Yograj said in a tired, distracted tone. 'Yes he likes you. And you'll meet him soon.'

But his day was not done. At home, he found his father waiting for him in the kitchen, sipping tea with sullen purpose. Yograj asked Pamphaa for food, and the ex-Minister said, 'So that widow's not feeding you?'

Yograj looked at him, more amused than scared. 'She's not feeling well today.'

The ex-Minister threw the cup at his son and shrieked, 'Running around with whores.'

Yograj dodged the cup, strode up to his father, caught him by the collar of his pullover and shook him. 'Save your energy. You don't have much left.'

The ex-Minister felt his son's grip rattle him. He wished he were younger, he wished this child had never been born. 'You have no shame. You care nothing about my name. Roaming around with that barren woman.'

Yograj felt Pamphaa tug at his shirt. He let go of his father and Pamphaa arranged the ex-Minister's clothes. 'Enough.'

Yograj withdrew and picked up pieces of the broken cup. 'She's not barren. And it's my life.'

The ex-Minister trembled against Pamphaa. 'You care nothing about my name.'

Yograj placed the broken pieces on the table. 'You have no name left. Your dead wives and your dead sister took it with them.'

The ex-Minister whimpered and looked at his hands, unwilling to admit he knew nothing of the world outside his house. 'Your elder brother says they talk about you and that widow all over town. He says it affects his work.'

'That eunuch! I'll handle his work for him.'

Pamphaa smoothened the ex-Minister's hair. 'Enough now. Let him rest.' She took him to his room, arranged his bed, and emerged to serve Yograj his dinner.

~

He phoned Yogita to complain. 'Tell your brother to stop visiting that woman.'

Yogita's reply was sharp. 'You live with him, you tell him.' Then, regretting her sharpness, she said, 'What's happened now?'

The ex-Minister whined, 'Everyone knows about him and that babuni.'

Yogita mollified him: it was no more than a passing affair, Yograj was not ready to settle down. The ex-Minister then asked her, 'And what about you? Waiting for me to die?'

'Why do you speak like that? Let Yograj get settled first, and then we'll worry about me.'

The ex-Minister was not convinced. 'Has that doctor come to visit you in Delhi? If he hasn't then I'll send him.'

This frightened Yogita; he had sent suitors to Delhi before, and she ended the call with an excuse. The ex-Minister was left with a sense of dread; his lineage would terminate with him. Yograj would be with that low Chandath, and Yogita with whoever she had in Delhi. Only Pradeep had married well, if a little unhappily.

~

The ex-Minister phoned Pradeep SE the following morning and warned him. 'Be careful. Your younger brother says you've been spreading lies about him.'

Pradeep SE spent the day nervous. He did not fear a scene as much as the simple possibility of Yograj appearing at his office. He dreaded the repetition of all that had passed at the Department of Village Roads: the affairs, the tawdry involvements in petty disputes, the file chasing. He feared even more because the Department for Urban Infrastructure was efficient, its babunis possessed swank. The building was a new and recent one, a sleek structure of glass and dressed stone, and their poise was not threatened by the stench of urine. Heera Babuni would have flourished here, he often thought. In such moments, he admitted that he still had not recovered, even though he kept in touch with her through occasional phone calls, in a civil tone that carried no hint of former tumult.

He wished Yograj would take some lessons from his career and his life. He was one of the youngest Superintendent Engineers in the Service. He had just been selected for an itinerary of tours in different parts of India, and a possible one in Malaysia. The bounties that came with his promotion followed him even outside his office; in the bazaar and in gatherings people greeted him with a greater enthusiasm, his counsel was sought by strangers, supplicants visited him at home with gifts and promises of largesse if only he would consider their files.

And his house! The completion of his house had required no effort from him. Two contractors had competed for the honour and had nearly come to blows in his office. He had graciously divided tasks amongst them and the materials had appeared at his house, as had labourers and overseers. He had moved into the upper floor just in time for Dasain the previous October, and overheard his Mrs tell their daughters, on holiday from their boarding school, 'All done by your Papa, and your Papa's Papa'.

All this was endangered by an idiotic brother who didn't know what was good for him. Pradeep SE shook his head at the iniquities of this world. He phoned Yograj, who snarled at him. 'So you've been telling the old man all sorts of things. It's your fault if anything happens to him.'

Pradeep SE was genuinely hurt. 'Only because I am your elder brother,' and to prevent Yograj visiting him in his office, he said, 'we'll talk when I visit tonight.'

~

When he reached Tibet Road in the evening, Pradeep SE found his father in bed in the windowless room beside the kitchen. Even though it was summer, he wore a muffler and a woolen cap. He scanned him for signs of decay, as he did on every visit. The ex-Minister said, 'They're keeping me out of Balidaan Diwas this year. I know the General Secretary and the Treasurer are behind it. Vultures!'

Pradeep SE eased; if his father was well enough for intrigue, there was no cause for worry. 'Not their fault. After all the commotion you caused last year.'

The ex-Minister played with the ends of his muffler. 'But I only said what I believed in.'

Pradeep SE said, 'Different people believe in different things.'

Pamphaa entered with some tea. She set it down and settled some pillows behind the ex-Minister. She touched him freely and Pradeep SE looked away. The ex-Minister drew a long breath. 'The CM wants us to worship stones and trees. Forget the gods—forget Vishnu, forget Kumbura, they haven't done anything for us.'

Pradeep SE put his cup down. 'Sandalwood, silver.'

The ex-Minister ignored the barb and spoke of the temple, which was constantly on his mind, 'The money has come, you know, for the temple. Almost sixty lakh.'

Pradeep SE was instantly on his guard. He knew he would be asked to contribute his services as an engineer. 'It's against public servant regulations to be involved in such matters.'

'You'll need to handle the estimates.'

Pradeep SE was unmoved by the mention of sixty lakh. He oversaw much larger projects in his office. 'Net amount is too less.'

The ex-Minister struggled, and sat upright on his bed. 'You think I don't know? There'll be more. It won't be enough to finish the temple.'

Pradeep SE's interest quickened and he hummed softly. Pamphaa was called in and was asked to prepare food for Pradeep SE as well. His Mrs phoned and the ex-Minister could hear the harsh cackle of her voice as she instructed a pliant Pradeep SE on a domestic matter. After he had disconnected the ex-Minister said, 'I should have chosen somebody else for you.'

Pradeep SE said, 'Too late now.'

Then Yograj put his head in through the door, stared at his brother, and left. Pradeep SE followed him to his room, saying, 'You haven't understood me. I didn't say anything.' They compared versions and decided quickly enough that it was mischief caused by their father. He had done it before.

Pradeep SE said, 'This I'm not lying. Your Sarata Babuni's been talking of marriage in the Department of Village Roads.' It was true; he had heard it from Heera Babuni on one of their recent phone conversations.

Yograj was not surprised. 'That's how women talk. She's been talking like that since the first time I did her.'

Pradeep SE squirmed. 'What all did you do? How was she?'

Yograj recalled. 'Very hard-working. Very good at sucking. Sucked me all over the place.'

'She looks like she couldn't even suck her thumb properly.'

'She couldn't. I had to train her.' Yograj then described the places and occasions Sarata Babuni had sucked him off. 'Once, as she sucked me, she started crying.'

'And what did you do.'

'I wiped away her tears with this,' Yograj said, and pointed at his crotch.

Pradeep SE whistled and said, 'Who would have thought? And she never even looks anyone in the eye in the office.' He grew alarmed. 'Not in my office! You didn't do anything in my office.'

Yograj winked at him. 'But you attend office every day.'

Pradeep SE's voice turned into a sedate wail. 'Only when you're young you can do all this.' He looked with sad eyes at the door. 'My youth, our father took my youth. You get to do whatever you want. Yogita gets to do whatever she wants. Only me!'

'Don't start crying.'

Over dinner, Pradeep SE expressed concern about Yogita, so far away, unmarried and unsupervised. 'Kalpana has a cousin whose son is working in Delhi. He's unmarried. She just found out. Yogita should meet him.'

The ex-Minister paused his chewing. 'She's another one. You ask her to meet him. There was that good doctor last year. He still calls me every week to find out if I'm okay.'

Yograj said, 'Dr Kuldeep? He has a girlfriend. Someone from Orissa. Everybody knows that.'

The ex-Minister glared at him. 'Why didn't you tell us? Wasting everyone's time.'

Yograj called for some more rice. 'Because it would have been like printing a poster. You would have told everyone.'

The ex-Minister was philosophical. He licked his fingers. 'There's still time.'

Pamphaa said, 'Not much time if you think. She's pretty and lives alone in a far-away place.'

The ex-Minister snapped at her. 'Quiet. Tyau-tyau the whole day.' He had arranged so many marriages in his time, and almost everyone had had boyfriends and girlfriends from other castes, tribes and religions. In his experience, it was a serious factor but never an insurmountable one. He would reach out to the doctor's parents through a series of complex manoeuvres for, being an ex-Minister, he could not afford to appear too keen.

Yograj asked, 'So CAS got money I heard?'

The ex-Minister had not forgotten his son's transgressions from the previous year. 'You won't even get to smell it. It's going into the temple.'

They discussed the temple, and each was enthusiastic in his own way. The ex-Minister saw the fruition of a project which had long stalled and was, in an obvious way, his legacy. Yograj saw the opportunity for a contract, his money had depleted considerably after the purchase of the new car. Pradeep SE saw himself guiding his people through a grand building project.

The ex-Minister spoke of the opposition to the temple. 'Vultures want to build an office.'

At once, Pradeep SE saw the merits in that project. 'Sensible thought, an office is more practical.'

The ex-Minister hacked, bits of food flew out of his mouth, 'What office? It will be a temple. If you want an office building, go and eat at the Treasurer's house.'

Yograj said, 'Either way is good. But what guarantee is there?'

The ex-Minister was confident. 'My signature is my guarantee. This is my organization.' They made plans to visit the half-finished building the next day.

~

The temple was located near the Motor Vehicle Department. It was large; a landmark which had reneged on its promise of a future magnificence. But the unfinished frame, now eight years old, looked derelict; rows of reinforcement rods sprung out from the sides, tendrils with heart-shaped leaves twined through them, moss covered one entire side of the structure. Inside, a part of the concrete had been eaten away, exposing the aggregate within. The floor was slippery with algae. They walked through the large frame, the ex-Minister pointing out the locations of different areas—a kitchen, a small apartment each for the resident priest and hajuju, a central hall for large gatherings and, finally, the sanctum sanctorum on the uppermost floor. Here, the column, slab and beam frame that rose up four levels were modified, the central slab was missing, a separate and higher roof was meant to arise over Kumbura's idol, and it was here that the sandalwood so diligently preserved by the ex-Minister would be used.

Yograj was skeptical. In a contractor's tone he said, 'Eighty lakh won't be enough. Carriage and head-load will be the main difficulties. Needs two-and-a-half crores at least.'

The ex-Minister was reassuring. 'All we have to do is start. Nobody likes seeing a half-finished temple. The money will come after we begin. So?' He looked towards Pradeep SE, who nodded neutrally. 'Lots of potential. What if everyone wants to make an office, and only you want to make the temple?'

'Let them try.' The ex-Minister could afford to be stubborn. The land deeds were in his name, for it had been purchased when his power in CAS was absolute and no one had then questioned his methods.

The New Window

A few evenings later, as the ex-Minister scanned through an album of photographs of temples in Nepal for designs to emulate, he heard a clang from the kitchen, and assumed a vessel had slipped from Pamphaa's hands. Then some quick rustling, more clangs and a thud—together, they signalled trouble. He hobbled to the kitchen and saw Pamphaa on the floor; her eyes were open and she was trying to strangle herself. He leaned against the doorframe, looked away, and called out to Yograj, upstairs in his room.

Yograj ran down and froze at the door. The ex-Minister had witnessed several such possessions by spirits in Suikeybung but this was Yograj's first. He looked at Pamphaa on the floor, her hands around her neck, and her eyes only visible as white. 'Is she dying?'

'No.' The ex-Minister considered praying, but he recalled that the possessing spirit was not to be treated with reverence. Then he gave in to instinct and ordered Yograj. 'Get some incense from the prayer-room.'

Yograj ran out. The ex-Minister knelt beside Pamphaa, feeling a keen strain on his knees and legs. He slapped her thrice, and tried to pull her hands away from her neck. He failed, her grip was too strong. Then she opened her eyelids and her stare screamed at him. Yograj rushed in with some lit incense, bent and circled it around her. She snatched the incense sticks from his hand and put them in her mouth.

The ex-Minister instructed Yograj. 'Kick her lightly on the side.'

Yograj kicked her side, she spat out the incense, jerked and went still. He took out his phone to record the scene but stopped when his father shouted at him. She was still sprawled on the floor, the hem of her nightie around her thighs. She spoke in a voice that was not hers. She spoke as Sumitra, the ex-minister's third wife, now dead for twenty years. 'Appa, why haven't you looked after our son and daughter?'

Her spasms resumed. They caught her arms and legs and pinned her to the floor until she stopped resisting. Then Sumitra spoke again, of events and details, people they had met, the hardships they had endured. She caressed Yograj's face. He had lost his fear and his expressions only reflected the conflict between his skepticism and his willingness to believe. When she grew quiet, Yograj carried her to her bed and the ex-Minister trailed them.

~

Pamphaa did not bring the ex-Minister his tea in the morning. He knocked on her door and opened it when there was no reply. She was not in her bed. He shouted out to Yograj. He ran down and looked into Pamphaa's room. 'Don't worry. Her clothes are still here. She has not run away.'

The ex-Minister's voice was soft and kind. 'You know how to make tea? I need to have my medicines.'

This request alarmed Yograj. It brought back memories of the dark days after Pemba's death, when the kitchen had become his responsibility. 'We should wait.'

Yograj made some tea and brought it to his father. 'I got very little sleep. Is it true what she's been saying? Do you think it was our mother's spirit?'

The ex-Minister looked at his son. 'Believe if you want to. It's up to you. It doesn't matter at my age. I will be seeing her soon anyway, and I'd rather meet her then.'

Pamphaa returned. She had visited the temple at Paani House. She wore a white salwar which, allied with the experiences of the previous night, made her appear pure. 'What happened yesterday shouldn't have happened.'

The ex-Minister had prepared himself to be stern. 'Has this happened to you before?'

'In my childhood.'

'You should have told us.'

'Would you have let me stay here if I did?'

Yograj asked, 'How did it feel?'

She looked at her feet. 'I don't remember. I woke up at night, my hands and legs felt cold, and I knew that someone's spirit had come over me again.'

'Do you remember anything?'

She shook her head. 'I remember nothing. I don't even want to.'

They had finished their tea. She approached the table to clear it but Yograj took the cups to the sink and washed them. 'You need rest.'

The next few days were quiet; the constant carping in the house was replaced by deference. Yograj stayed at home, domiciled by the possession, the rain and a shrinkage in funds. Every evening, he watched Pamphaa with an edgy expectation. The ex-Minister requested Pamphaa, 'Maybe you should have a fit just for him.'

Pradeep SE heard and he took to visiting them every evening. He mistook Pamphaa's gifts for that of clairvoyance and asked her how long he would have to wait to be promoted to a Chief Engineer, and became a doubter when she declined to answer him.

Then Yogita phoned her father. 'Yograj told me about what happened. Is it true?'

'What do you think?'

Her voice was doubtful. 'I don't know. These things seem to happen only in Sikkim.'

'Stay in Delhi then.'

~

The possession occurred again on the fifth day, when Pradeep SE was at Tibet Road. It was Yograj who found her in the prayer-room, where she had gone to light the evening lamps. There, surrounded by idols, posters and brass objects of worship, she sat, cross-legged and taut, on a bed of poinsettias. Her face glowed in the light of the prayer lamps she had just lit and her posture was heightened by the slight tremors of her body. She called to him in his mother's voice. Yograj fetched his father and brother.

Sumitra scolded the ex-Minister for ignoring his children's health. Did he know where they were, what they were doing? Why had he sent Yogita so far away? And why had he not yet found a husband for her, a wife for his son? He should have remarried, and found someone who could have looked after the house and their children. But that time had passed.

Pradeep SE's voice quivered and neared breaking. 'And what about my mother?'

'I know Sopu Ban. We meet quite often, and she often has maize in her hands. We are not angry with each other.'

His voice broke. 'Does she know me?'

'She says, "He is not happy. But he will become a big man, and then he'll be happy." We wish we were with our children.'

Yograj phoned Yogita, who listened to her mother's voice over the phone. In her flat in Lajpat Nagar, she bit her lip as she heard the voice—absent since she was eight years old—scold her for living so far away from home, when her father needed her in his final years.

'What made you come to us now?' Yogita asked.

'I found a vehicle to bring me home.'

The possession differed from the earlier one, and from all those that the ex-Minister had experienced. There were no fits, no foaming at the mouth, no abuses. Sumitra scolded him, and her admonitions were those that he gave himself in moments of self-doubt. He looked at Yograj, a phone in one hand and the other supporting Pamphaa's back, and he felt a wash of pity for the boy, without a mother and without any near sibling, with only a decaying man for a father. Sumitra said, 'I will be happier on the other side if you help our children with their lives.' The possession ended, and Yograj and Pradeep SE carried Pamphaa to her room.

~

The ex-Minister felt differently the morning after the possession. He was too old to reacquire such beliefs. He knew of them for he had grown up in a village where discontented spirits outnumbered the living population. He was reminded of an incident during his tenure as the elected representative of Suikeybung. Three piglets went missing in the village and a hajuju, a nephew of the ex-Minister, was consulted. The hajuju went into a trance to recover them after which he took one of the retrieved piglets as his fee. The ex-Minister uncovered his trick and beat him in public. The beating, which passed into local legend, gave him a reputation for impartiality and forward thinking, someone from whose house the spirits had been phased out by televisions, refrigerators and magazines. But the same incident had put further divisions between him and his family in Suikeybung, and had become one of many accreting frictions until, finally, relations had ceased and the ex-Minister's life was reduced to his building in Gangtok.

He phoned Nima Thendup and shouted at him for delivering such a servant. Nima Thendup said, 'Nobody said any such thing about her.'

'Did you ask the whole village, you fool?'

Nima Thendup sought to calm his uncle. 'These things happen. I am modern but my driver just told me about his uncle's ghost who returned, seven years after the man died.'

'Don't come here and tell us that story.'

Nima Thendup offered help. 'I'll bring a hajuju if you want.' Then he giggled and added, 'In the meantime treat her well, like a goddess.'

'No need,' the ex-Minister grunted. Pamphaa was encouraged to rest as much as she could, and when the ex-Minister visited her room, he received a turn to find that it had become a shrine, with incense and posters of deities.

'Who did this?'

'Doma Momo-seller.'

It was common knowledge in the locality, and the ex-Minister feared what would come next. Pamphaa would be elevated, and he would have to feed her devotees. He locked the main door and, when the bell rang, with strangers asking to be let in to meet Pamphaa, he shouted at them until they gave up and left.

Nima Thendup visited and listened with fascination but in the end was convinced that it wasn't serious. 'Everyone has a fit once in a while. It's part of life. But tell me if you need a hajuju.'

'Contact one, just in case we need him,' the ex-Minister said. Then he turned mellow. He spoke of his sister and said, 'I shouldn't have.' Nima Thendup, who always grew emotional when his deceased mother was mentioned, stopped him. 'Past is past.'

The ex-Minister, trying to make amends for an event beyond recovery, said, 'I feel even she has returned to this house.'

~

The possessions had other benefits: they gave the ex-Minister currency with his colleagues in CAS, for they allowed him to lay claim to some aspects of their tribal heritage. It was a welcome development, something which could soften his querulous reputation and grant him an advantage in the fractious times ahead. He phoned all the members of the Core Committee and, under the guise of alarm, invited them to come and see for themselves. 'Little bit of tribal in all of us.'

He was visited by the Vice President, the Treasurer and the Press Secretary. They were accompanied by a foreigner, a professor from England, Robert Black. The Professor put the ex-Minister's hands to his eyes and greeted him in Chandari. The ex-Minister replied in Nepali, 'We should think of others around us.'

The Press Secretary said, 'I can translate.'

Professor Robert Black looked ashamed and answered in Nepali, 'I didn't mean to.' He then said, 'I've always been interested in the shamanic practices of the Chandiths.'

'Chandanths,' the ex-Minister corrected him.

'Chandanths,' the Professor corrected himself and asked, 'Is she a Chandanth?'

The ex-Minister looked outraged. 'Of course she is a Chandanth. Ask her.'

The Professor stood up. The ex-Minister put up a hand, in a gesture of patience. 'She is resting right now.' Yograj entered with some tea and biscuits and passed them around reluctantly. The Vice President said, 'Son, that is not a man's job. You need someone to help you with that.'

The ex-Minister saw Yograj prepare a retort and, to deny him, he said, 'Take the Professor to meet her.' The Professor held out a hand for Yograj to shake and they left the room.

The members of CAS sat stiffly—the President, the Vice President, the Treasurer and the Press Secretary. The money had been transferred recently, two lakh for each member of the Core Committee. They showed little interest in Pamphaa's possession and their visit soon assumed the proportions of a formal meeting.

The ex-Minister, eager to bait the Treasurer, said, 'How strange it is...? The first time in ten years that July has passed without Balidaan Diwas.'

The Vice President picked up a biscuit. 'On that day I thought about the food. Only the food. Aah!'

The Treasurer stayed unprovoked. 'It's just postponed by two months, and good weather is guaranteed. They'll send us invitation cards soon and,' here he looked at the Vice President, 'I'll make sure they consult us on the menu.'

The ex-Minister turned to the Vice President and the Press Secretary with an expression of scorn. 'Make sure no one accepts the invitation cards, even if that traitor Mitradas and that snake TB deliver it personally.'

The Press Secretary looked at the floor and shook his head. The Treasurer was unaffected. 'The report is almost ready. The report on spending the money.'

The ex-Minister looked surprised. 'All goes to the temple. Just like we decided.'

The Press Secretary pleaded. 'But some for research. On tribal practices. On language.'

The ex-Minister turned magnanimous. 'Some funds will be kept aside for that.'

The Treasurer spoke in a low tone. 'But what about CAS House? General Secretary says that will be more useful. Joint Secretary is with her.'

So their office building already had a name. The ex-Minister said, 'How is that a new thing?'

Pradeep SE entered the living room and was greeted. His promotion had invested him with a new gravitas; he was one of only two Chandanth Superintendent Engineers in Sikkim. The Treasurer turned towards him. 'So SE Saab, what do you think? Should CAS construct an organization office building or temple?'

Pradeep SE raised both hands. 'I can't say. I'm not a formal member of CAS. And I'm here as a son, not as a Superintendent Engineer.'

Pradeep SE's ambivalence was noted. The Treasurer raised his hands. 'Of course, of course.'

The discussion ended here, for Professor Robert Black had returned from his interview. 'She's not talking right now. Will you call me if it happens again?' he asked the ex-Minister.

Pradeep SE agreed vigorously. 'Most definitely, without question.'

The ex-Minister turned towards the Professor. 'Mr Robert, you know the famous Dhod temple at Raku in Chyalu?'

'Of course, yes. Though it is in ruins now.'

'And why was the temple famous?'

'The temple was dedicated to Kumbura and it was reputed to have been built entirely of sandalwood. There are reports which say that the final battle against the Shah kings took place in the temple complex. Mon Gyal died in that battle, and his followers burnt him on a pyre of sandalwood.'

The ex-Minister smacked his hands in a triumphant clap. 'See,' Robert Black continued, 'it is an intriguing theory and the relationship between Chandanths and sandalwood should be studied in depth.'

The ex-Minister turned towards the Press Secretary and the Treasurer. 'See! It is only here in Sikkim that I have no value.'

The Press Secretary hastened to reassure him. 'Of course you have value.'

The Treasurer appeared chastised. 'You're priceless.'

Pradeep SE turned to Professor Robert Black. 'I am proud to have him as my father.'

When the time came for them to leave, the ex-Minister, supported by Yograj, walked down with them. On the road, he insisted that they follow him to the floor below the level of the road. Professor Robert Black walked behind the ex-Minister. The Treasurer and the Press Secretary followed them uneasily. The ex-Minister flung open the store-room's door, caught the Professor's arm and said, 'There! Look! This will be Sikkim's Dhod Temple.'

The Professor disengaged his arm from the ex-Minister's grasp. He stared at the wood stacked neatly and occupying the whole room. 'So much sandalwood. Is it allowed by law?'

The ex-Minister had perfected his answer a long time ago. 'If this is illegal, then God is illegal.'

~

The next day Nima Thendup arrived with a hajuju, a young man who dressed like a clerk. He lived in a village near Mountain View Resort, where he had just completed an exorcism. He began with a professional announcement. 'Keep me away from the spirit's vessel.'

The ex-Minister, unimpressed, said, 'You won't meet her. Are you qualified?'

The hajuju's reply won him over. 'Agya told me this is a Chandanth house. I only perform these ceremonies for Chandanth houses.'

The hajuju was installed in the ex-Minister's former room on the first floor. Pamphaa took his arrival with an effete calmness. 'I heard my doctor has come.'

In the late afternoon, the hajuju entered the ex-Minister's room and squatted beside his bed. 'Whisky?'

'After the work.'

'We need liquor for our work, you know that.'

'Then let her start shaking. Whisky after that.'

The hajuju sulked but there was little he could do. He needed a room close to Pamphaa's for the exorcism. The ex-Minister gave up his windowless room, the hajuju proclaimed it to be ideal, and the ex-Minister moved to the living room. The single bed was removed from the windowless room, the television relocated to the kitchen, and the hajuju prepared a design on the floor using a paste of rice, vermilion, curd and maize seeds. In its centre he made a minute pyre of sandalwood shavings.

He made a list of items he would need and Yograj found most of them in Laal Bazaar. The feathers he had got were white, from a broiler chicken, while the hajuju insisted that only a village rooster's feathers would work. He had asked for goat's blood, but the mutton shop was closed, and Yograj had returned with bull's blood. Also, Yograj could not find banana leaves, and he suggested the hajuju work with leaves from a rubber plant that grew beside the culvert. He complained that this was the case with all the practices in the city. He compromised reluctantly. 'I'm like any worker. I can't work without my tools.'

The ex-Minister shared his distress. He felt it as a constant twinge, the distance of his city life from the practices of his ancestors. Rituals were diluted for lack of constituent ingredients, prayers were expedited for lack of time. Everything was severed, and the youngsters, supposedly the custodians, were the ones initiating these truncations. What was it about the city's soil that made it incapable of nutrition? How would it be for those who came after him, how faceless would they grow up to be?

He worked with the hajuju in setting up the room, returning the hajuju's grumblings with grimmer grumblings of his own, until the hajuju gave up grumbling altogether. Nima Thendup visited every evening to check on the hajuju and to deliver the food which Thinley Machi had prepared. On the third evening, as they talked in the kitchen, Yograj rushed in. 'It's happening.'

Yograj remembered Professor Robert Black. 'Should we call the foreigner?'

The ex-Minister had considered this. These possessions, with their strong biographical bent, were different from others. They had the potential to expose family affairs. 'No need. Leave him out of it. The way she goes, he'll find out our whole family history. Don't call Pradeep. And don't phone Yogita.'

They alerted the hajuju who leapt up and ran towards Pamphaa's room. Whether it was professional competence or the promise of alcohol, the ex-Minister could not say. She was on her bed, motionless but foaming at the mouth. Sumitra asked, 'Where did you bring this man from? Do you think I can be scared?'

The hajuju held out his hand for drink. Yograj handed him a glass of whisky without any water. The hajuju gulped it down. She bared her teeth and spat at him.

There was a gasp from the door. It was Nima Thendup, who had so far remained unbelieving. 'Do you meet my mother, Kalpana, your sister-in-law?'

He never found out. The hajuju stood up and jiggled. 'Enough. Get out of her body, you whore!' He dragged her towards the windowless room.

Yograj lunged at the hajuju to defend his mother from the slur but Nima Thendup restrained him. The hajuju turned around and put a finger to his lips. He held Pamphaa's head and slapped her. The ex-Minister told Yograj, 'Stay if you want, but be quiet. This is not your mother, this is not my wife.'

They stood against the wall as the hajuju dragged Pamphaa by her hair through the kitchen and to the windowless room. He shut the door after him. The ex-Minister, Yograj and Nima Thendup listened from the outside to a fight filled with abuses. They cursed each other inventively. Now they sparred like friendly rivals, now they switched to an implacable enmity.

When they were let in, Pamphaa was on her bed bathed in sweat. The sandalwood shavings were nearly burned through, their aroma filled the room. The hajuju sat on the side of the bed, shaking feebly. 'She's free.' The ex-Minister was relieved.

Yograj was in tears because he had lost his mother again. The following morning, the hajuju said, 'You won't be troubled any more by your wife. But you will have to make the carrier of her spirit happy with a few things that belonged to her. It'll help if they are valuable. You'll have to open the wall in your bedroom by making a window on the western side. The spirit is still in the room and it needs to escape.'

The ex-Minister went to Pamphaa. She had woken up without any signs of fatigue. He asked her, 'How do you feel?'

'As if I have woken up after a three-day sleep.'

The hajuju received his payment and a bottle of whisky as a bonus. After he left, the ex-Minister called Pamphaa in. He had a jewellery box open. It consisted of the remnants of a collection Sumitra had purchased for Yogita at her naming ceremony, in keeping with the Chandanth custom of deciding dowries for daughters soon after their birth. The collection had depleted over the years for he had often dipped into it. The only items that remained were a large necklace, two pairs of earrings and four gold bangles. He gave Pamphaa a gold bangle and a pair of gold earrings. She took the ornaments without any show of surprise or gratitude and resumed work in the kitchen.

~

The ex-Minister moved back to the windowless room. He ignored the hajuju's advice and did not build a new window. He was deterred by the inconvenience, the expense, and a reluctance to source and supervise carpenters. There was no need, he told himself. Pamphaa had recovered and he had not been affected adversely. Memories, whose resurgence had discomfited him during the possessions, abated, and life in the house resumed its former pace.

Then he woke up one morning with a fever, and though it was not as severe as the last time, the pain in his bones was acute. He heard the Tiny Geniuses sing:

> I love the pit-pit-patter of the raindrops,
> I love the buj-buj-bujjing of the bees,
> But the thing I love the best, the very, very best,
> Is the way that God loves me.

Pamphaa found him in bed motionless, his expression frozen as if he had died witnessing a calamity. She massaged his face and he recovered. She gave him his phone and asked him to call Dr Kuldeep.

'Later,' he said, 'he's a future son-in-law. He should not see me like this.'

Pamphaa thought that eating would benefit him. She made a gruel of rice, daal and potatoes but his body seemed to be a channel free of constrictions, without the ability to digest or absorb, and the food was expelled from his body almost as soon as it was ingested. Pamphaa insisted on the doctor and wanted to wake Yograj. The ex-Minister stopped her. He phoned Nima Thendup, and asked him to send a carpenter and a labourer immediately. He was going to build the window.

The workers arrived late in the afternoon. Pamphaa let them in.

'Namaste, Saar.' It was Shambhunath, the glazier, accompanied by a young, skinny helper.

'You! What have you come for? I asked for a timber carpenter.'

'Now I work with wood, Saar. Not much work in glass left.'

The ex-Minister reached for his phone. Shambhunath pleaded. 'Agya Nima sent me, Saar. At least see my work, Saar. Don't pay if you don't like it.'

The ex-Minister hesitated, dissuaded by his weakness and the prospect of seeing the carpenter grovel, something he did not have the strength to endure. Shambhunath seized on this hesitation. 'Saar, sorry, saar.' He apologized for his last visit, when he had mistaken the ex-Minister for a ghost. However, he was neither hurt nor fearful, for in his village this meant that a long life was due.

The ex-Minister was pacified. 'This life is long enough. Where did you get your helper? He looks just like you.' Shambhunath shoved his son forward, who joined his hands in a namaste.

'He's my son, Saar. Instead of sitting at home getting into trouble with local boys, I told him to learn the trade.'

The ex-Minister showed them the spot where the wall was to be punctured. They had to move a cupboard. The ex-Minister relocated to the living room again.

Shambhunath proposed a single window, two feet by five feet, with a panel that could be opened. The ex-Minister made him forage in the storeroom on the terrace and the carpenter found some suitable timber beams. Though it was nearing dusk, the ex-Minister made him set up his working space.

Yograj, returning home, saw the labourers and said, 'So... believing after all.'

'Better than dying.'

Shambhunath and son worked for two days to the accompaniment of shrill songs played on his mobile phone. When it was done, the ex-Minister inspected the work. The sill was sloping, the frames were uneven and the hinges were not securely fixed. But the carpenter made a pitiable face, and the ex-Minister, fearing a round of depressive whining, gave him his full payment.

The new window offered no view. All he saw through it was the building next door, with squash vines that climbed on the service pipes, the ripe fruit smudged with slime. Nevertheless, the window made a difference, the room was brighter and airier than before. It aligned with the flat where the momo-seller stayed. She came to her window and said, 'After so many years, you decide to talk to me.'

In the evening, he asked Pamphaa to massage his upper body. She agreed and when he removed his shirt, she said, 'So weak you've become.'

He had thought of the end again during his illness. Yogita, he was sure, would take care of herself. But Yograj worried him. 'What sort of a woman will he bring home?'

Pamphaa allayed his fears as she massaged him. She sensed, without being told, that Yograj's affair with Sarata Babuni was ending. She had overheard arguments on the phone, and he spent more evenings at home. The ex-Minister was not soothed by this knowledge. True, the possibility of shame had receded, but the relief was accompanied by dread, for he knew Yograj would do something similar again, and that the great blackening of his name had not been eliminated but only deferred.

His body absorbed the heated oil and he felt vitalized. He asked her to stay beside him while he slept holding her hand. She was not there when he woke up at dawn. Through the new window, he could see into the momo-seller's house. He sat in a chair a sufficient distance from the window and turned off his lights. The lights in her flat switched on. He had a clear view of the windows in her kitchen and in her bathroom. She went into the toilet first. He saw her squat over the pan and then clean herself with water. Then she entered the kitchen, rolled up the sleeves of her light sweater and kneaded dough on the counter. When she laid the momos to steam, she took off her sweater and worked in a cotton shirt, chanting prayers as she did.

He heard the cooing of birds, another unexpected benefit of the window. It was time for tea. He went to wake Pamphaa up, but her room was empty and her clothes were missing. He dragged himself from room to room shouting for her but she had left.

Outing

The ex-Minister paled and moved beyond approach. He stayed in his bed throughout the day, unspeaking and incapable of effort. Nima Thendup visited. He felt responsible, for he had sourced Pamphaa. He could not persuade his uncle to sit and watch television, or in the living room, from where he could look out to the street. There were no visitors. The Core Committee of CAS stayed away and the ex-Minister, without the strength to defend his temple against the practical merits of an office building, did not regret their absence.

Yogita phoned but provided little comfort. She wanted to come desperately, she said, but she had only just been promoted at work. She had been made Assistant Creative Director, the youngest ever in the firm's history. She could not take leave, lest she send a negative signal to her colleagues and juniors.

The ex-minister, enfeebled and bitter, said. 'Stay there then. Stay there and die there.'

Later she called up weeping, wanting to know why he could not understand. The ex-Minister said, 'Don't worry about me. I'll be fine. Concentrate on your career.' He instructed Yograj, 'Don't tell her anything. Whenever she calls tell her I'm getting better.'

Yograj ran the house now and he did it without cheer or rancour. They fell into a pattern, the father and son. Yograj cleaned the house as best as he could, cooked with limited interest, and kept the time for his father's medicines, and the ex-Minister accepted his efforts without complaints. Then, one morning, the ex-Minister asked to be taken to the sitting-room window, signalling his recovery. He told Yograj, 'Get her, get that babuni if you want to.'

Yograj said, 'You recover first.'

Recent events had given Yograj a cover for ignoring Sarata Babuni, but her phone calls had resumed, and in them she displayed aggressive concern. She phoned him one morning. 'I wish I could come there and help.'

Yograj made a kissing sound. 'I wish it too.'

'Ask your father, no?'

From the street, Yograj heard the tolling of a familiar bell. 'The garbage truck has come. I'll call you in five minutes.'

She phoned again an hour later, asking why he had not called back, why things had changed. She arrived without notice at his house in the evening. Yograj let her in. 'See for yourself.'

He took her to the room with the new window. The ex-Minister was sleeping, his breaths were shallow and abrupt. There was a little light in the room and his shrivelled frame occupied less than half of the narrow bed. He was not wearing his cap, the few companionless white hairs which twirled on his scalp like frozen smoke made him appear abject and in need of consoling. Sarata Babuni sniffled. Yograj guided her outside and took her upstairs to his room. It was the first time she had entered his room and the event, which ought to have been special, had come without any excitement.

She sat on his bed and played with the ends of her dupatta. 'I want to help but there's nothing you let me do.'

Yograj explained that his life had changed. All considerations of romance paled beside it. 'He's very weak right now but still as stubborn. Said he'll commit suicide if I do not marry someone he chooses.'

She looked up. 'He said that?' Her voice was raised and Yograj sensed an oncoming fit. He drew on experience to combat her hysteria and narrated the effect of the appearance of his mother's spirit on him, the mother he had hardly ever known. He buried his face in his hands.

His feint softened her. 'There's always someone who doesn't want to see two people happy.'

She held him close and said that she would make the sacrifice, but she was sure Yograj would return to her. He agreed, what they had was stronger than all the rules the world had made. She did not resist when he undid the hooks of her salwar. She stood up, her clothes fell to the ground and she stood before him. Her skin was bright in the darkening room, her breasts drooped and there were creases of fat on her stomach and thighs. She reached to remove her spectacles but he stopped her. 'No, leave them on.'

After the act, she offered to make dinner for them. The ex-Minister, exhausted by his day-long watch at the sitting-room window, was asleep in his room. There was some pork and some vegetables. She cooked as Yograj watched television, unaffected by the scene of domestic simulation. She felt drawn to the house and repulsed by it: the dying man inside, his caring but stony son outside. She scolded herself for wanting a husband so badly as to want to trap this young man near her, led only by his flesh. He had made her do things which she had never done and which she did not enjoy. The world was large and she did not have to return to this house; but while she was here, she would cook them a good meal.

~

The next morning, as Yograj heated the leftovers from the dinner Sarata Babuni had cooked them, he heard a moan from his father's room. He rushed in and the ex-Minister had his head in his hands. In front of him was the jewellery box from which he had given Pamphaa the gold bangle and earrings. The box was empty. He looked at his son through his tears. 'The servant is not going to return.' He would not refer to her by name anymore.

Yograj filed a report of theft at the Sadar Police Station and then phoned Nima Thendup to apprise him. Nima Thendup said, 'Tension upon tension. And just when the season starts.' Though his hotel was barely functional, he had adopted the hotel-owner's poses. 'Come to the resort tomorrow, we'll work out something.' Mountain View was no longer a hotel, it was a resort. Yograj and Nima Thendup could go to the servant's village in Pangthang, and the ex-Minister could rest in one of the rooms, from where Pangthang was visible. 'Maybe that will clear his head a little.'

The ex-Minister, taking strength from a retributive energy, agreed to visit Nima Thendup.

~

They travelled the next day. It was a clear morning, with the road still wet from the previous night's rain. At Tashi Viewpoint, they saw the new banner that Nima Thendup had installed.

MOUNTAIN VIEW RESORT

LOOSE YOURSELF IN THE MOUNTAIN VIEW

Mountain View Resort was almost complete. The facade was crossed by scaffolding bamboos and painters were at work, applying the primer coat. The windows were half-complete, and the ones on the highest two floors were yet to be installed. Nima Thendup met them at the door and showed them in with proprietorial pride. The lobby was in a state of rough completion, and littered with furniture whose packing plastic had not been unwrapped. The walls were painted, as were the doors and windows which had intricate Buddhist motifs on them. The floor was freshly tiled. From the upper floors they could hear the sharp, repetitive clacks of carpenters at work. 'Making all the room furniture now.'

He wanted it functional a month later, by late September, when the first wave of tourists would arrive in Gangtok. Four rooms were complete, and they had begun letting them out. Not because he wanted to, but it was the only hotel at Tashi Viewpoint, and there were many tourists who came in the evenings, lost and demanding shelter. 'Idiots. Coming with torchlights to look at the mountains.'

The ex-Minister sat down on a sofa, still in its wrapping sheets, and seemed to shrink further within it. 'Why are we here? She's not going to come back.'

Yograj said, 'We don't want her back. But thieves need to be caught and whipped.'

Nima Thendup agreed, 'That's what. We should at least recover something.' He then saw Shambhunath's son loitering in the corridor and yelled at him. 'Ay Badri, am I paying you to walk around like the Chief Minister's son-in-law?'

The two hiphops, whom the ex-Minister and Yograj remembered from Pemba's funeral, passed them, carrying beams of timber. Their trousers still hung loosely around their buttocks. They looked at the ex-Minister and dipped their heads in acknowledgement.

The clacks from the upper floors ceased and, over the sudden silence, some chanting came through from the lower floors. Nima Thendup explained. 'Getting the shyabdo done; one Head Lama and six monks. Want the blessings before we start.' He looked at the ex-Minister inquiringly. 'You also want to get blessed?'

The ex-Minister glared at him. 'Not letting a Bhotey touch me.'

Nima Thendup laughed and called out to his wife from the counter. The receptionist said, 'She's in the kitchen. We have a guest. Indian from America.' She pointed to a tall, dark man in a window-facing corner, on another sofa whose wrapping had not yet been removed. 'She's making food for the Indian foreigner.'

Nima Thendup admonished her. 'Don't say foreigner, say guest.'

The receptionist looked up and raised an eyebrow in defiance. She had a red vermilion streak in the parting of her hair and a mole between her eyes. Yograj defended her. 'You can say foreigner. That's a fact only.'

Thinley Machi emerged from the kitchen with her daughter walking behind her; a stately procession of two. She took the ex-Minister's hands and touched it to her eyes. It was the first time she had offered this salutation and he recognized it as a gesture of pity. She scolded her husband for not offering him anything to eat or drink. She sent the receptionist into the kitchen. 'Tell them to get some food ready.'

She ushered the ex-Minister and Yograj into the restaurant. It was the only space in the hotel untouched by construction work, and it had to stay that way to cater to the daily groups of tourists who came in for a snack. After a meal of rice and beef curry, they moved back into the lobby. The ex-Minister sat on the sofa, and Yograj leaned against the reception desk.

Nima Thendup looked out of the window and then at his watch. 'We have to leave now. The road only goes till Pangthang and we have to walk down after that.'

Yograj gestured at his stomach. 'A little later.' He looked with concern at his father. 'He needs rest.'

Thinley Machi said, 'Go quickly. And don't worry about Appa, I'll make sure he gets rest.'

She knew exactly what was going on. Yograj wanted time with the receptionist. Agya Nima had told her all about that boy and his affairs. The receptionist was married, but Thinley Machi knew that was rarely a serious obstacle. And there was her character, which Thinley Machi knew, through instinct rather than evidence, to be dubious. She was sure that even the receptionist's sindoor, which she wore so prominently, was to taunt Thinley Machi's sensibilities as a Buddhist. Of course she could not tell this to her husband. Agya Nima's mother had been a Nepali and Thinley Machi knew how seriously he took his mixed parentage.

The ex-Minister said, 'I need to lie down.' A simple vehicle ride had taken so much out of him. Despite his hopes, he did not feel any nearer to Pamphaa, even though he was close to her village, where she had grown up and lived.

Thinley Machi assumed an expression of tenderness. 'Rest in our room downstairs. You won't hear the carpenters. But some monks are praying in the lakhang.'

Nima Thendup and Yograj assisted the ex-Minister down the staircase. Yograj returned quickly. He said, 'Appa wants to say something to Agya Nima.' Nima Thendup said, 'Tension upon tension,' and walked downstairs.

Thinley Machi watched as Yograj leaned against the reception counter and whispered to the receptionist, who suppressed a laugh. Thinley Machi prepared to insert herself between them, but a large group of tourists entered the restaurant. She looked at her daughter, who was awaiting her command, and made the briefest of motions with her eye. The child walked over, let herself into the reception area, and sat next to the receptionist. Thinley Machi went into the kitchen.

Yograj offered the child a sweet but it remained untaken. Her vigilance was unfailing and her loyalty incorruptible. She played with a glass paperweight. Her role was to keep her mouth shut and her ears open for all that her uncle and the receptionist said to each other. The meanings were not important, it was enough that her mother would understand.

The receptionist leaned over to fill in a voucher.

'Busy?' Yograj asked.

'Too busy,' she said. 'One guest.' She pointed with a pout at the tourist at the far end of the lobby.

'Is he handsome? Your guest?'

The receptionist sniffed with disinterest. 'You tell me. I don't see such things. But he talks only in English. Says he was born in America.'

The clacking from the carpenters upstairs increased. The tourist folded his book, walked up to the counter and rested an arm on it. He was in a vest, and a curtain of stiff hair spanned the curve of his armpit. 'Do you have any guidebooks? Anything on Boodism.'

The receptionist looked at him severely. 'No. Nothing here.'

The tourist walked away without disappointment, his slippers slapping on the marbled floor. Yograj said, 'He likes you.'

The receptionist said. 'He's asked me for Buddhist books for three days now. When I am at work, I only do work.'

The child rotated the paperweight on the table. It whirred and growled to a stop.

Nima Thendup returned to the lobby and said to Yograj, 'Get ready.' He went into the kitchen and told his wife, 'Go down when you can. The old man is crying.'

Thinley Machi looked up, her face powdered with flour. 'Let him cry. We didn't hurt him.'

'Now, now! You told me last night you would control yourself. I'll go down to Pangthang to look for the servant.'

Thinley Machi took a ladleful of soup, blew on it and tasted it for salt. She turned to her husband. 'La, la. Just take his son away from that receptionist. Tension upon tension.'

~

A little later, after Nima Thendup and Yograj, accompanied by the hiphops, had left for the servant's village, Thinley Machi's daughter entered the kitchen and recited all that had transpired under her watch. She spoke in a monotone, unconcerned by the meaning of what she had heard, loyal only to her task. Her mother patted her and sent her upstairs. 'Watch over the carpenters. Make sure they work.'

A couple entered the restaurant. Thinley Machi gave them a copy of the menu and went downstairs for a quick check, curious because she had never seen the ex-Minister crying. She found him sitting upright in bed and he turned towards her as she entered the room. His eyes were red and dry. 'I'm dying.'

'Please don't die here.'

He coughed and she regretted her archness. There was a metal roof outside the room and they heard the patter of raindrops on it. The monks in the lakhang raised their chants in competition. She hoped Agya Nima and Yograj had taken umbrellas. She sat down at the other end of the bed. 'She took a lot?'

'There wasn't much left. A few bangles, a few rings. Should have gone to Yogita but she will take care of herself. Earns two lakh a month.'

'Agya told me about what happened. So you believed that the spirit had come?'

'I can't say. But she knew a lot.'

'Like what.'

'She knew about Nima Thendup's mother. And what I did to her.'

Thinley Machi took a deep breath. It had happened long before she met Agya Nima: the exile of Kalpana Chandanth, the ex-Minister's only sister and the mother-in-law she had never met. No family interaction, not a word exchanged after that, all for marrying a Bhotey? Are we so unfit for them, she had asked Agya Nima when he first told her the story. It was one of the reasons she had begun to dislike the Nepalis, a people whose fortunes had not concerned her in Phagcha, her village in North Sikkim. She had since been careful not to get too close to the ex-Minister, despite her husband's gruff gratitude towards him.

She smoothened the bed around him. 'Is that why you were crying?'

He nodded. She propped him up with pillows behind his back, to make it easier for him to watch television. She reassured him, 'It doesn't matter now. No person is completely good.'

'Is Nima still hurt? What else does he say?' The patter of rain on the roof outside subsided. He looked out the window, so much larger than the one in his room. The air had cleared, and beyond the near clouds, he saw sunlight on a hill in the distance. Beside it another hill, spotted with houses, was darkened by locally falling rain. He wondered if that was the servant's village.

Thinley Machi followed his gaze and said, 'She died when Agya was a child, he doesn't remember much of her. Now he says all men are equal and all religions are useless. That fool, he still respects you.'

As the patter of the raindrops on the metal increased in volume, the monks in the next room raised their chanting again. It was time for their lunch. She said, 'I have to get their food ready. Here,' she put the remote control in the ex-Minister's hand, 'watch TV.'

She peeped into the lakhang next door. The prayer-room was long, and painted in a multiplicity of colours; one end was taken up by a three-segmented altar facing east. There were three large idols. The central one was Guru Rinpoche, and flanking it were statues of Manjushri and the Buddha. The altar was intricate, its ledges were lined with lit butter lamps and offerings of khabseys, biscuits, fruits and a packet of potato chips.

Two rows of monks, seated on cushions and leaning against the walls, looked at her and nodded, their expressions pleasant with expectation. She looked at Karma, a young monk who ran errands for the elder monks. He followed her out and they returned with trays of food: rice, beef with gravy and fried potatoes. The monks ceased their chanting and, in the presence of the deities they had just appeased, began their lunch.

~

Late in the afternoon, Thinley Machi sent the receptionist to check if the ex-Minister wanted lunch. She found him dozing, lulled by the pattering, which had resumed. She said, 'Thinley Machi asks if you're hungry.'

The ex-Minister shook himself awake and, evaluating her prettiness, asked, 'A little later. What's your name, chhori?'

'Binita,' she said.

'If only I could get a daughter-in-law like you. Are you a Chandanth?'

'I'm a Scheduled Caste,' she said and giggled in anticipation of his embarrassment.

It was too late to retract, and the ex-Minister's curiosity demanded precision. 'All castes are equal but there are so many types of Scheduled Castes. Which one are you?'

She scowled and snapped. 'What does it matter? Do you want food or not?' She looked at him for an answer and then left, leaving the door open behind her.

The ex-Minister did not mind her rudeness. He mourned the death of individuality in castes. Everyone wanted to be part of something larger. They preferred big rivers to smaller streams and this meant that the subtleties of clan lines were disappearing. His own people were no better. There had been so many kinds of Chandanths in the past, they had had a complete and self-sufficient system of sub-castes to themselves. And now? Now they only fought for the right to spell their names differently, like priests fighting over ash. Meanwhile, he thought, looking around the room he found himself in, strewn with the evidences of another way of life—bakkhus, chimmis, khabseys and thangkas—meanwhile they were being smothered by foreign faiths. He thought of Kalpana—who had abandoned the gods of her childhood and had chosen to end her days as a Buddhist—and a wave of revulsion come over him. He closed his eyes.

Outside, the rain gained in strength, it now sounded like a stampede. His thoughts on castes and religions had given him strength, as they had always done, and with strength came hunger. Then he became aware of the throaty chants from the next room. He wished he could join his troubles with those prayers, foreign as they were. He wished for the souls of his dead wives to be left in peace, and for the servant to be caught and punished, not for the sake of the jewellery, but for the way in which she had exposed the wretched state of his old and decaying heart.

When he saw Karma walk down the corridor, he motioned to him and said, 'Tell the plump lady upstairs that I am hungry.'

The monk ran upstairs and saw Thinley Machi in the lobby, beside the reception table. As he informed her, a commotion diverted everyone. It came from the stairwell. It was the shirtless Indian tourist, clutching Shambhunath by one hand and Badri by the other.

The receptionist sighed. Thinley Machi wiped her hands on her bakkhu and steadied herself. The guest said, 'I've had it with this joint. I'm trying to *meditate* here. Either give me my money back or I'm going to lodge a complaint.'

Thinley Machi shrugged and asked, 'Why complain?'

The tourist shook Shambhunath and Badri said, 'I'm a Boodist. I came here to be closer to the mountains, to meditate. But you lied to me. That's what the two of you did, you lied to me, you and your husband. Your hotel is incomplete and there are carpenters working all through the livelong day. That's grand larceny, do you know what larceny means?'

The receptionist said, 'What you will complain?'

'For underage labour.' He shook Badri. Thinley Machi noticed that Shambhunath's helper did look very young.

The tourist's anger was justified. He had come to Gangtok hoping to channelize his inner peace. He had found Mountain View Resort by accident and, thrilled with an undiscovered hotel, paid for ten days' stay. Neither the receptionist nor the proprietor's wife had told him about the construction work. The first few days had been tolerable, for he had the city to explore. But these were precious days, earmarked in his itinerary for a realignment of his chakras. Instead, he had been tormented by the hammering, the clacking, the day-long arguments between workers, and the shrill orders of their employers. It was an invasion of his innermost sanctuaries and it was cushioned only by the monks who chanted downstairs and with whom he spent as much time as possible, and who gently denied him every time he tried to join in their prayers.

The tourist noticed Thinley Machi's apprehension and pressed his advantage. 'Complain. That's what I'm going to do. Complain.'

A voice came from behind them. 'Ay you!' It was Pradeep SE who had just entered through the main door. He removed his sunglasses and walked towards the reception desk. Thinley Machi, grateful for his arrival, hurried to meet him. She said, 'He's a dark foreigner. He speaks only English.'

Pradeep SE absorbed this challenge. 'Mind your language. This is a four-star hotel.'

The tourist turned and yelled. 'It will be, when it's *finished* with the help of this underage worker. And who are you?'

Pradeep SE retreated. 'I am a Superintendent Engineer.'

'So, you're in charge of building this joke that you guys call a hotel? Should I mention you in the complaint as well?'

Pradeep SE looked around, unsure of support. 'This is racism.'

These fresh charges made the tourist pause. He let go of Shambhunath and his helper. Pradeep SE shrugged his shoulders at the easy victory and then he noticed the glazier. Instantly, he remembered the hailstorm of the previous year, the shattered panes of his building, the glazier's promise to fix them, the abuse he had sent via texts and the song of derision his Mrs had composed and sung. Shambhunath's face crinkled with recognition, he offered an appeasing smile and backed up against a large unwrapped dining table close to him.

Pradeep SE approached the narrow end of the table and said, 'Saala chutiya! Don't show me your teeth. Where have you been?'

'Home, Saar,' Shambhunath moved deftly to the other side of the table. They faced each other like table-tennis players.

'Before that? Why didn't you answer my calls? Cutting my phone calls like a bloody minister.' Pradeep SE moved to his right.

'No network, Saar.' Shambhunath moved to his left.

'I'll network your face right now. When he came,' Pradeep SE addressed the puzzled gathering, 'when he came, he looked like a skeleton. All bones everywhere. Wanted advance because he hadn't eaten. And now look at him, look at his stomach.'

They looked at Shambhunath's stomach, which pushed his shirt out discreetly, like a nascent pregnancy. Shambhunath sucked it in and put on a haggard expression.

'What's going on?' the tourist said. 'Can somebody tell me what's going on? Who is this man?'

Pradeep SE recalled that he was now a Superintendent Engineer. He looked at Thinley Machi and asked, 'Where's my father?' In silent fury, she pointed at the staircase. Pradeep SE walked slowly towards the stairs, Shambhunath relaxed and took a few steps towards the reception counter, towards the tourist who now seemed like a sanctuary. Pradeep SE spun around, rushed back, gave the glazier a swift kick and walked away whistling.

Thinley Machi pushed Shambhunath and Badri towards the staircase. 'Go, go and work.' The other workers were crowded at the stairwell and they scrambled up when she shouted at them. The tourist said, 'I don't understand. What just happened?'

Thinley Machi approached the tourist and asked, 'Pray to Buddha?' with her folded hands near her forehead. It worked, the tourist followed her to the prayer room below. She entered, nodded at the Head Lama and said, 'Tourist.' The Head Lama nodded in return. The shirtless tourist entered and took a seat beside the Head Lama. The chanting resumed and the tourist sat erect, motionless. It was his first invitation to the prayer room. Within a minute his eyes were closed, his breathing controlled, and his focus complete. He travelled for moments such as these.

In the next room the ex-Minister was shaken awake by Pradeep SE. He groaned at his son's inescapable persistence. 'When did you come?'

'I called up Yograj and he said you were here. I heard about the jewellery. I wanted to help.' Pradeep SE assessed the room. 'Such a big hotel. Such a small room.'

'You should have stayed away.'

Pradeep SE ignored this. He spoke in a considerate tone. 'I have begun looking for someone for you. A good servant.'

The ex-Minister stared outside. The rain had eased and a darkly silver fog enveloped the hill. Evening was setting in. He wondered whether Nima Thendup and Yograj had found the servant. The chants from the next room continued. Pradeep SE moved closer to be better heard. 'I met the Treasurer yesterday. He said time is running out. We have to prepare the paperwork.'

~

It was true. The previous day, Pradeep SE had visited the bazaar with his Mrs to purchase more powerful eye-glasses. She had sniffled in the spectacle shop and made noises against his superiors who were making him work like a servant. They walked through the bazaar. It was warm and slightly humid; the rains were retreating, and the sun was more assertive. They met the Treasurer of CAS, who held Pradeep SE's hand in both of his and shook his head in admiration. 'Not many Chandanths have reached such positions. We plan to felicitate you soon.'

Pradeep SE was instantly shy. 'A man shouldn't be honoured for just doing his duty.'

The Treasurer's head shook some more. 'That is exactly why they should be honoured. We need a technical member in CAS, and we want you to become the Technical Secretary. It's a new post. And we heard you write too.'

Pradeep SE's shyness continued. 'Now and then. Only on social issues.'

They exchanged phone numbers. The Treasurer said, 'You understand, SE Saab, an office is more important than a temple.' Pradeep SE assured him that he was on the side of progress. The Treasurer turned to his Mrs and said, 'He's going to become a great man. And then you'll tell me how true I was.'

As Pradeep SE and his Mrs strolled through the bazaar, they met some more people he knew; a subordinate, two contractors and the pony-tailed peon who tried to hide behind a woman who did not look like his wife. They all greeted him with warm and effusive respect. His Mrs then broke from protocol and held his arm for the remainder of their walk.

~

Pradeep SE pressed his father. 'What do you think?' But the ex-Minister was removed from any concern for CAS. His son's pleas felt distant to him. He pointed to the wall, towards the praying monks in the next room and said, 'I don't like their chanting.'

Pradeep SE sniffed. 'You don't even want to discuss it.'

Nima Thendup and Yograj entered the room, barefoot and wet. They had returned from the villages below Pangthang. The ex-Minister asked, 'So?'

They were unsuccessful, and Nima Thendup acknowledged it had been foolish to assume the servant would have returned home after the theft.

The ex-Minister said, 'I want to leave. Let her keep what she stole.'

Nima Thendup had received an update from Thinley Machi about the incident in the lobby. He turned to Pradeep SE. 'I heard you were making trouble with the tourist.'

Pradeep SE raised his hand. 'I did it for you. He said you were using underage labour.'

The ex-Minister hobbled towards the door on Nima Thendup's arm. Nima Thendup spoke without looking up. 'Because it is my hotel. When you have your hotel, you do whatever you want. But stay like a guest in mine. If he wasn't there,' he pointed to the ex-Minister, feeble against his arms, 'I would have showed you. Engineer from nowhere.'

Pradeep SE almost protested but his position was weak and Nima Thendup was larger than him. He followed them to the lobby. Yograj was missing; he had taken the car and left, nobody knew where. Pradeep SE, eager to leave the premises, declared that he would drop the ex-Minister home. He got the driver to move to the passenger seat in the rear, installed his father in the front, and hurriedly drove away.

Yograj reappeared after his father and brother had left, still wearing his wet clothes. As it turned out, the receptionist was just leaving and he offered her a lift home. Nima Thendup was inside, inspecting the day's work. Thinley Machi threw Yograj a stern and disapproving look. She knew he had disappeared on purpose but she could not be explicit without proof.

Yograj drove home with the receptionist. The day was nearly done. The weather was overcast but the clouds were a thin film through which rays penetrated and stayed trapped, enveloping Gangtok and its neighbouring hills in a glow. She lived near the District Court at Sichey, and he said it was perfect for him; he had some work near the District Court. Just after Mountain View Resort had passed from the rear-view mirror, Yograj put on some music. The receptionist was still sour. 'Your grandfather asked me for my caste. I told him to shut up.'

Yograj did not correct her. 'What to do? They are all like that, that generation. I always say everyone is equal, except for the pretty ladies. They are a bit above.'

The receptionist's mood improved. 'You're quite wet,' she said, and dabbed at his neck and shirt with her scarf.

Yograj said, 'It's nothing. You know how to drive?'

The receptionist rolled down the window to feel the wind in her hair. 'Not yet. But I want my own car some day. To go wherever I feel like, whenever I feel like.'

'Good time to start. Here, come a bit towards this side and hold the steering. This is the best time to learn driving. The road's quite empty at this time.'

Birds without a Nest

Respected Sir,

I wish to bring to your notice the sheer number of hotels which seem to be running, nay thriving, without proper licences. Most of them are fly-by-night operators who have made a beeline to our beautiful state to cheat and thug our simplistic brethren and it makes me see red. So many hotels are languishing in a state of utter incompletion and still they are opening their doors to innocent guests. It seems to be a maxim in our new hotels that good service is a rarity while bad service is aplenty. Indeed, Sikkim may soon have to change its slogan from Come Get Blessed to Come Get Harassed!

Just a few days ago I visited one hotel and was utterly shocked by the miserable conditions in which the poor tourists were staying. I asked them why they had not complained to the right authorities and they said it was because the hotel-owner had threatened them with dire consequences.

This is exactly what gives our pristine state a bad name in the national and international press. This will not do if we want to increase our tourism revenue and make Sikkim the number one destination in South East Asia in accordance with the vision of our beloved Chief Minister. The cat, as they say, is now out of the bag. Our vigilance must be unflagging and hence I am crying myself hoarse urging the Tourism Department and the Police Department to watch out with an eagle eye for offenders.

Yours sincerely,

A Concerned Citizen

Inspiration had returned to Pradeep SE but did not find a welcome home. After his letter was published in *Sikkim Everyday*, he briefly considered writing to the newspaper on the need for the Chandanth people in Sikkim to have a proper office, a building that could reflect their illustrious heritage. But, he told himself, he was now a Superintendent Engineer, and such activities were not compatible with the stature of his new position. He could effect change publicly, he did not need to be silently concerned. Anonymous letter-writing, for whatever social good, was beneath him. With sad resolve, for he was a sensible man abandoning an inconvenient passion, he decided that the letter on unscrupulous hotel-owners would be his final one.

There were other ways of effecting positive change. Some days later, the Treasurer visited Pradeep SE at home and was received in his new living room. The curtains had embroidered valances. The sofas, over-upholstered to indicate opulence, were plush and enveloping. The walls had been painted in a combination of green and pink, to complement the pink and green flowers on the floor tiles. There was a large porcelain tiger in a corner and a standalone bar in mahogany finish at one end. The Treasurer petted the tiger and looked around with approval. 'You can always tell when it's an engineer's house.'

Again, Pradeep SE was shy. 'We are technical people. We can't help it.'

'The Core Committee thinks you should become the Technical Secretary of CAS.'

Pradeep SE glanced at him. 'Even my father?'

The Treasurer looked at his hands. 'We have been meeting without him because of his health. And he'll understand when we tell him.'

Pradeep SE had expected this. Who had asked the old man to be so stubborn? He said, 'I told him that the temple will take care of itself. We carry our gods inside us. More important to have an administrative centre. You know I visited the site? Only the posts, beams and slabs are done. It can easily be converted to an office.'

The Treasurer slapped his thigh. 'Exactly. Meeting here and there like refugees without a home. We should make the estimate for CAS House.

Pradeep SE probed. 'Even if he doesn't change his mind?'

The Treasurer slapped his thigh. 'He will change his mind. And when he does, we'll have everything ready. No time wasted.'

A servant girl came in with some tea and biscuits. The Treasurer held her arm and helped her guide tea into the cup. Pradeep SE asked, 'Is there a design? Have the drawings been done?'

The Treasurer waved an unconcerned hand. 'All that can come later. The estimate is most important.'

Pradeep SE corrected this. 'This is a big misunderstanding amongst laypeople. Design comes before estimate and not the other way around.'

Open admiration settled on the Treasurer's face. 'See? That's why we need a Technical Secretary. So who does the drawings? It will have to be you. You'll make the design for us. Just looking at your house is enough to know your talents.'

Pradeep SE's voice softened with embarrassment. He had never thought of himself as someone with a trend-setting sense of taste. But the Treasurer's endorsement, and his sitting-room's luxuriance, convinced him that he had always been a designer. He said, 'Design is just my hobby. But I am ready to help.'

After the Treasurer's departure, Pradeep SE felt trapped by his own offer. Half-afraid, he informed his Mrs, expecting her to taunt him for his social service and sing the Sant Pradeep song again. She only asked, 'Will the Chief Minister be there at the opening?'

Pradeep SE assured her that she would, and she recommended his social spirit.

~

Word travelled. The General Secretary summoned Pradeep SE to her office at the Tourism Department. She wore a sari with a half-blouse and Pradeep SE watched her fleshy arms ripple as she wrote a note. He was always vaguely discomfited by her. He alone, of the three children, remembered the time when, so many years ago, she had almost married his father.

She finished, looked up, and gave no hint of any inner turbulence on seeing him. She adjusted her spectacles. 'I'll come to the point straight away. We are concerned about your father's health. He should stay away from this year's seminar. Balidaan Diwas. Sorry, Libhanaya Bhod.' The Chandari phrase, from a language none of them spoke, did not come easily. She practised it again as he watched. 'Libhanaya Bhod. Yes, as I was saying. The President should rest. The Steering Committee has been given orders from above. Will you talk to him? Some things are best done by family members.'

Pradeep SE nodded vigorously and said, 'He's not well, Madam. I don't think he even wants to come,' and then he added, 'and he's only occupied with the temple.'

'Ah yes, the temple. The High Command is not encouraging it. The whole world is moving away from temples. The CM has approved an Animist Park for the Chandaths. We have to shift our focus there.'

Pradeep SE continued to nod. 'That's what, Madam. An administration building is more important. Right now we are like birds without a nest.'

The analogy made her look up. 'Your younger brother is a contractor, no? He can do the contract.' The General Secretary pressed the bell on the side of her table. A peon popped his head in. 'Send in the others.'

Pradeep SE left, irate at the brisk manner in which he, a Superintendent Engineer, had been dismissed. If only he had not been constrained by professional dignity, he thought, the things he could tell her. Pradeep SE told himself that when he became a Secretary, he would not treat his juniors like this.

~

Strategically, Pradeep SE invited Yograj for lunch on the weekend. 'You haven't seen the new flat upstairs.' His sister-in-law gave him a tour of the house and told him the price of most acquisitions. In the living room, Pradeep SE asked, 'So what do you think?'

Yograj looked around at the spectrum of colours in the room. 'You should give visitors sunglasses at the entry.'

Pradeep SE winced. 'All your sister-in-law's choice.' Then, in a pained voice, he spoke of the generation gap, as he often did when he had to complain against their father.

Yograj asked, 'What do you want?'

'You'll have to talk to the old man. It's better to build an office than a temple.' Pradeep SE enumerated reasons why an office building was better than a temple. A temple was much more laborious, following no fixed template, and with innumerable carvings and decorations. An office building by contrast was simpler to design, easy to build, the rewards apparent within a year or two. Not so with temples, never in history had a temple been finished on time and that was because everyone was an expert on temple design, they would be endlessly criticized no matter what they did. There would be no savings—could he imagine the scandal if the accounts for the temple didn't match up? Hell on earth. And there was all that sandalwood their father would insist on installing. 'His life's over, no one will come to get him. But you and me, we'll be the ones in police custody.'

Yograj agreed. 'He's become awkward after the servant ran away. He told me he wants to build the temple before he dies because it'll get him into heaven.'

Pradeep SE slapped his thigh. 'See! Find a way to talk to him. The General Secretary said you'll get the contract but he has to agree. I heard they won't call him for this year's Chandanth celebration.'

They heard Pradeep SE's Mrs yell for them to come for their meal. At the dining table, also new, she said, 'Heard good news about you.' She caught his perplexed expression. 'Your father called me yesterday. He says I must look out for a good Chandanth girl for you.'

Yograj sighed. 'Our father. No physical energy, no mental energy.'

Pradeep SE's Mrs packed some rice, fried potatoes and a dish of pork with spinach for the ex-Minister. At home, Yograj served his father in his bed and said, 'Why are you announcing my marriage to everyone? Why didn't you tell me first? Why do I have to hear it from Bhauju?'

The ex-Minister, undisturbed at being found out, continued to chew. 'It's only natural. She called me up. Said she has a girl in mind for you. Her brother's wife's sister.'

'That fat liar!'

'Exactly! Talk to her first. I only said I would like to see you married. Is that wrong of me? To want to see my children settled before I die?'

Yograj offered his father some water. 'Supposed I do agree to marriage. What will I need?'

'To that babuni?' the ex-Minister asked. He accepted the water, gulped, gargled and spat into the plate. 'Only after I die.'

'No no,' Yograj said, quietly, 'you choose for me.'

The ex-Minister handed Yograj the plate and said, 'What more do you need? You have everything. A house, a car, money—that.' He pointed to Yograj's crotch.

'Income is more important than money.'

'So get a job. Why bother me?'

Yograj let the discussion end there.

After a few days, he took care to cook some beef and cabbage, the ex-Minister's favourite, and said, 'Pradeep Daju was saying that I could get the building contract for the CAS House. There will be good money there. Almost two years' worth of government salary.'

'So take it. Go to them. Lick their shoes.'

'Your signature is necessary, no?'

The ex-Minister motioned to Yograj; he had finished eating. Yograj picked up the tray. 'Let me think about it.'

When Yograj updated Pradeep SE, he asked, 'He didn't curse me for putting that idea in your head?' His voice was taut with compressed excitement.

'No. But he warned me to beware of you.'

The caution meant progress. 'Good good. We must do it fast. Talk to him about it, but not so often that he gets angry. Did you tell him about Libhanaya Bhod?'

'No. It's your job to inform him, if you can pronounce it. But I don't think he cares for all that anymore.'

~

The absence of a servant was more important to the ex-Minister. Sometimes, stung by his own deterioration, he summoned the energy to move around the house. He felt the accumulation of mould on things and in rooms, for outside, the monsoon was still displaying its final reserves of strength. He felt the withdrawal of order from the house as keenly as he was feeling the withdrawal of health from his body. It was this that made him long for company: a servant, or even better, a daughter-in-law. The most assured way to do it, given how fickle servants could be, was to get Yograj married before he abandoned his newly acquired maturity.

He regretted snubbing TB Chandath the previous year. Now, that man's lower stature did not seem prohibitive; instead, compared to the pale babuni, it seemed desirable. He phoned TB Chandath and his call was not, as he feared, ignored.

After pleasantries, the ex-Minister said, 'Yograj has been asking about your family a lot. Says he wants to come, but I told him you'd be busy with the Steering Committee work.'

TB Chandath, unfailingly polite, said that he was indeed busy. 'But not so busy to have no time for your family.'

'And your daughter?' The name escaped the ex-Minister.

'Lata is here, helping me with the preparations for Libhanaya Bhod.'

The ex-Minister was won over. 'Our younger generation is responsible, good to hear.'

'She's very responsible. Asked her mother and me to decide what would be best for her future. A family is coming to visit her soon from Kathmandu. The boy and girl have already spoken. So forward, this generation.'

The ex-Minister offered his congratulations. 'Which family in Kathmandu, TB Bhai?'

The ex-Minister never found out. TB Chandath replied, 'Yograj is helping out a lot. The younger generation is always welcome. I met him the other day.' He was called away and, requesting the ex-Minister's leave, he ended the call.

The ex-Minister was stung by this double revelation. TB Chandath's daughter had always been a distant probability. But to hear that Yograj was a volunteer for the Libhanaya Bhod preparations, only a month away. How close had the snakes built their nests, that his children were poisoned?

He resolved to act and, immediately, the resolve drained away when he saw himself as others saw him. Emaciated and alone, without friends, without influence and now without even a family to demonstrate control over. It caused him pain, but he could not remember a time without pain. His sensorial memory could not see beyond the immediate; it hurt now, and it had always hurt, contentment existed only as an obtainable illusion.

When Yograj returned home, he said, 'I spoke to TB Chandath. Had asked him some days back to put you in as a volunteer. What is happening with the seminar plans?'

Yograj sat beside him. 'All sorts of things, in all sorts of places.' To assuage his father, he held his hands. 'It's small work. Buy this, buy that. Deliver this package to this minister.'

'How's the General Secretary?'

'She's very helpful. Keeps telling me I'm the future.'

'Her father's future. Beware of that woman—snake in the grass.'

Yograj nodded in apparent understanding, but offered no details from the preparations. He went to cook dinner. Later, as they ate, the ex-Minister asked, 'Have they handed out the invitation cards as yet?'

Yograj shook his head as he ate. The ex-Minister said, 'Tell them to be careful and to print more cards. There's always a shortage of cards in the end and that's when the trouble starts.'

Yograj nodded. 'I will inform everyone.'

'And bring and show me one of the cards. There is bound to be an error, there always is.'

Greatness

One morning, the ex-Minister sat on a chair beside the window and watched Ai Doma make momos in her kitchen. She looked up at him and greeted him with a namaste.

The ex-Minister, keen for conversation, asked her for beef momos. His voice did not carry through. Ai Doma made a gesture with her hands—'Wait!'

A few minutes later, she entered the ex-Minister's house and surveyed the kitchen. 'Amamama! That Pamphaa was no good, but at least she would have kept the house clean. Where's your son?'

The ex-Minister looked ashamed as he admitted, 'He's in the bazaar, preparing for the function. Quite active now.'

Outside, the Tiny Geniuses sang:

This is the way we brush our teeth, brush our teeth, brush our teeth
This is the way we brush our teeth, early in the morning.

She glanced at the ex-Minister. 'Hungry?'

He shook his head. 'Hungry or not, you need to eat.'

She left his house and returned with momos and soup, and served him on crockery from his kitchen. 'You need a good person to stay here. I'll talk to my family in the village. They told me there was this woman looking for work.'

The ex-Minister groaned. 'No. Not another woman. Somebody just like Pemba.'

This is the way we say thank you, say thank you, say thank you
This is the way we say thank you, early in the morning.

Ai Doma watched him eat. 'That idiot, always smiling. Very difficult to find people like him.'

They reminisced about Pemba. Ai Doma pointed at her behind. 'He was always trying to touch me here.'

The ex-Minister was curious. 'Did he ever touch it?'

'No,' she said, 'maybe that's what killed him.' She picked up his plate and bowl and walked to the scullery.

He asked, 'And you? Not marrying again?'

She set some tea on the gas stove. 'Dead so many years ago. We were married for five years and no children. And even though I was still young, I didn't marry. What if the man expected children? What to give him then?'

Then, as if moving to a more pressing matter, she said, 'I'll make some momos here today for you. Keep them in the fridge, heat and have them when you want to. Will you do that?'

The ex-Minister nodded weakly. She looked around and found a moktu—the circular, storeyed vessel used for steaming momos. She washed it and oiled its inner surfaces. She brought fresh vegetables, some kneaded dough and marinated beef-mince mixture from her kitchen. She chatted with manufactured gaiety as she made the momos. She flattened small chunks of dough with a rolling pin into circular skins. She wet the edge of a skin, scooped some minced mixture into it and, moulding with quick movements of her fingers, soon had a dumpling ready. She laid them out concentrically inside the moktu. From time to time, she watched the ex-Minister as he alternately talked and dozed. So old, she thought, and dying alone.

A little later, she prodded him. 'The momos must be done now.' The water boiling in the moktu gurgled and wisps of steam escaped from it. She lifted the lid. A puff of vapour rose; some of it condensed on the lid and dripped off the rim. She plucked two momos from the vessel and gave them to him on a plate. 'Here, taste this.'

The momos bulged with steam and stuffing. He blew on one, bit into it, and sucked on its juices before chewing. He ate the two momos and said, 'I'm done. Enough for me.'

She helped him to his room. She looked into his toilet and the accumulated filth almost made her retch. 'Big in name only,' she muttered. She would have cleaned the bathroom and the house as well, but that was a day-long task and she had no time for social service. Then, she relented, and cleaned the toilet quickly. She had never been too fond of the ex-Minister and his family but who knew how these accumulated merits would choose to repay themselves.

She waited for a little longer; she wanted to see the son's face when she told him how his father had almost starved. But when Yograj did not appear even by late morning, she left. She made calls to people she knew in her village. As it turned out, there was a boy who could be spared.

~

A few days later, it rained heavily in the afternoon. Ai Doma could not go to Hospital Daraa to set up her stall. She chose to visit the ex-Minister with some noodles in pork-bone soup. She found him reading the day's edition of *Sikkim Everyday* in his bed. Yograj had purchased it in the morning in the hope that it would occupy his father for the rest of the day, and then, in keeping with his recent routine, he had left for the Sikkim Conference Centre.

'Ah!' he said encouragingly. There was an article about the Multiple Award Winner—'Walking for Ancestors'. He had completed the western leg of his walking tour. He had begun in Delhi, walked to Dehradun, and entered Chyalu through the Garhwal hills. From Chyalu he had walked to Kathmandu and then to Sikkim. He had come, he said, to take renewed inspiration. He was due to embark on the eastern leg of his tour, on which he would walk from the Burmese border towards Sikkim. The ex-Minister said, 'See. This man took my blessings last year. And look where he is now.'

Then something else in the newspaper caught his eye and he shouted, 'That vulture!' He waved the newspaper. 'Look here! Look what this man is saying.'

She kept the casserole beside his bed. 'Who?'

'This vulture, this traitor, Mitradas. He says he has studied Chandanth history. Says the Chandanths had no contact with Hinduism until 1900.'

She said. 'It may be so. They say God is everywhere and nowhere. Who knows?'

'I know,' he cried, 'that's why I'm telling you. I know.' Phlegm rose up his throat and he choked. She rushed in with water. After he had recovered, she patted his hand and said, 'Don't shout, it's not good for you. Why do you want to die shouting about someone you don't like?'

He stared at the newspaper, tearful. 'But he's lying. This man is lying.'

'Let him lie. Who doesn't lie? What difference will it make even if he is lying?'

'The truth should prevail.' He held his hand out to be assisted out of bed. She helped him towards the toilet. He entered the toilet but left the door partially open.

She waited outside the door. 'Then you write to the paper. Tell them what you think.'

His voice came from the toilet. 'No time to write for newspapers.'

She looked around the room and said, 'That's what. Too busy

keeping the house clean.' Then, in a louder voice, she said, 'Tell the Chief Minister. She's your caste-sister, no?'

He emerged from the toilet, hobbled to his bed, pulled the quilt over him and turned towards the wall. 'Who will buy my words now? In which shop will my words sell?'

To avoid his self-pity, she said, 'You should eat something.' She went into the kitchen and returned with the noodles. He turned, propped himself up and ate. As he finished, she said, 'You need to walk about or you'll rot in bed.'

He wanted to be taken to the living room. She supported his weight easily, but his bony elbow hurt as it pressed against her shoulder. She installed him in the chair beside the window. He watched the rain and she wanted to give him some strength. 'I keep hearing about you. They tell me you're a big man. And I say, "I find him ordinary."'

He looked her in the eye. 'I'm not a big man. I just want justice for my people.'

He said this with a reluctant defiance. Ai Doma was a Bhotey and in his mind, she belonged to the side of historical oppressors, even if he currently depended on her assistance.

She said, 'We have to fight for our people. Too much mixing happening. You're Nepali, I'm a Bhotey, we're different, and we should stay different. Fight, I say. If I knew who to fight, even I would fight.'

He was surprised by her agreement and appraised her in a new light. Her views gave him an unexpected strength and, bolstered by it, he spoke to her of the children of Chyalu.

~

If only the common destiny of the Chandanths had reached its natural conclusion, they might have ruled over an empire as large as that of the Mughals and maybe even the British. Of all the people and races which had had the fortune of being rooted in Nepal, none were as exemplary as the Chandanths. They lived in and around the Chyalu Valley, four days walk north-west of Kathmandu. But in reality, their origins were far more extensive, and intricately tied with the history of India. They were originally from Karnataka, in the belt where sandalwood was abundant, and where they derived their names from. In these times, it might be difficult to imagine the origins of his people as being so far away, but it was not unusual. The priests of Pashupatinath temple in Kathmandu, among the holiest shrines for all Hindus, come from Udipi, also in Karnataka.

The lineages of the Chandanths went back thousands of years, into those ages of antiquity which even legends couldn't reach. A small example to show how ancient their history was: there was proof that in all the battles of the *Ramayan* and the *Mahabharat*, it was the Chandanths who offered sandalwood for the funeral pyres of the slain demi-gods and princes.

At some point—no one knew why and brilliant men were still trying to find out—the Chandanths moved towards Nepal. It was his measured opinion, which had evolved after years of analysis, that it was because the Chandanths were always mountain people, and there was geological evidence that some of the valleys of Nepal were once very warm and could have supported sandalwood plantations. So they were only going back to their roots.

'The Chandanths are that old?' Ai Doma asked.

'That old,' the ex-Minister replied.

In Chyalu, the biggest city was Raku, where the Chandanths had their capital, and even if you went today you could still see the palaces of the old Chandanth kings, beside which the Newari palaces from Kathmandu were nothing. They had trade links with Tibet and China in the north and with all of India in the south. It would have been the most prosperous kingdom in Nepal, if only the Newars from Kathmandu had not monopolized trade. Not that money mattered, for the Chandanth kings realized that the culture of a people was often its greatest strength. They patronized all the arts, their music was far better than those of the Tamangs, their handlooms and embroidery left the people of Tibet speechless. They were warriors; beside them, the greatest warriors of Manang and Gorkha were nothing. And the food, there were stories of the Thakalis putting away their utensils once they had tasted Chandanth delicacies. And literature: patronized by their benevolent kings and inspired by their incomparable histories, the Chandanth poets composed dramas and epics in their unique script which put the literature by the Bahun poets to shame.

'If things were so good there, then why did you come to Sikkim? There's nothing here but hills,' she asked.

'It was a difficult decision,' he said.

Nearly four hundred years earlier, around the time Akbar built the Taj Mahal, there was a famine in and around the Chyalu Valley. That famine led to a war with all the petty kingdoms that surrounded the Chyalu Valley. The Chandanths would have won, had it not been for the cunning Britishers who arrived with guns. The Chandanths were a brave people, and they had never seen guns, and even if they had seen, they would not have used a weapon which killed people from such a distance. In the battle the Chandanth warriors discovered that while their race was immortal, its constituents were not. It was a massacre, and Mon Gyal, the great Chyalu king, rather than surrender, killed himself and his pregnant wife in the temple of Dhod at Raku, ending the great dynasty. The Chandanth people were forced to disperse after that. They moved eastwards and entered Sikkim after they heard that the Chogyal of Sikkim had invited anyone who believed in the Buddha to his land. And it was a well-known fact that the Chandanths worshipped many things: deers, trees and rivers, but they also worshipped Guru Padmasambhava who, as everyone knew, was an incarnation of Kumbura, who in turn was an incarnation of Vishnu. And this was why it was so easy for them to settle in Sikkim, unlike the rest of the stragglers from Nepal.

Somehow, along the way, after they had come to Sikkim, they had abandoned their common name. For twenty years, the ex-Minister had singlehandedly been championing the cause of that true name. And now, under the influence of that traitorous vulture, Mitradas, they were claiming their names were actually taken from silver, from the silver mines found in the Chyalu Valley. Who names themselves after things found around their homes? If there are a lot of pigs in the forest, people are not going to call themselves Sungureys, no? But the ex-Minister had made steady progress. So many people of his tribe had changed their name to Chandanth after listening to him. He was trying to get the

Chief Minister to do the same. The day he managed to convince the Chief Minister to change her name from Chandath to Chandanth, he would begin to wait for death with a patient heart.

'They are right,' Ai Doma said, 'you are a big man.'

The ex-Minister was breathing heavily now, exhausted by the narration. 'I have become small. They are not even inviting me for the seminar.'

'Why do you need an invitation? Just go if you have to. No point sitting at home looking like a lost cow.'

She helped him back to his bed. She made him some tea and as she served it, she remembered the purpose of her visit. 'There is a boy in my village. They can send him in a few days to look after your house, cook and clean. You want him? Four thousand rupees a month.'

He replied, his voice lifting a little, 'Send him.'

She made a call to the boy's family in her village. 'They'll send him day after tomorrow.'

She said, 'You're spending too much time thinking. It's not good at your age. You should be thinking about your children's marriages. Then grandchildren will come and you'll be young again.'

His eyelids lifted, his melancholy dissipated by the thought of company. He sat up in bed and coughed. They spoke of Yogita first.

'What does that doctor say? The one you were running after for your daughter.'

The topic revitalized the ex-Minister. 'He's another idiot. He likes her, but is scared, I think.'

'That's exactly what you want, a quiet husband. She'll make sure he always looks after you. And he's a doctor. He'll make sure you live to be a hundred years.'

'He's not shown up here for almost six months.'

Ai Doma made susurrant sounds. 'Poor boy. Call him here and give him some encouragement.'

Encouragement was just what the ex-Minister needed. He reached for his mobile phone and phoned Dr Kuldeep to tell him he was feeling unwell. 'There's a shooting pain in my lower abdomen.'

Dr Kuldeep promised to visit the following day. After the call, the ex-Minister waved his phone, pleased with himself. They moved on to

Yograj. Ai Doma had some advice. 'You have to be more careful there. She is going to live here and look after you. You have to choose carefully.'

The ex-Minister's voice carried some pride. 'The boy has said yes.'

Ai Doma heard him out. These plans had their use. They were lifting the fog which had settled on him over the last month.

~

The next day he was visited by the Multiple Award Winner, who rushed in and put the ex-Minister's hands to his eyes. 'All because of you. All because of you.'

He stayed for the afternoon, and when he found that the ex-Minister was alone, he took it upon himself to make tea for both of them. To the ex-Minister, who had never visited Chyalu, the Multiple Award Winner's achievement appeared doubly glamorous. He had made the Chandanth's proud, and he had made the ex-Minister especially proud. He said, 'I wish my sons had your dedication.'

The Multiple Award Winner took the compliment humbly. He had visited Sikkim to collect the funds due to him. The minister, DB Chandanth, was to be the disburser and the Multiple Award Winner had heeded the ex-Minister's warnings of the previous year. DB Chandanth had given him the payment that morning, after he threatened to publicly abandon the walk. 'I told him I'm from Nepal and I speak to the point.'

This pleased the ex-Minister. 'I wish I could have seen his face.' He then interrogated the Multiple Award Winner about Chyalu.

Had he walked around Chyalu? He had, and it had taken him an entire month.

How was it? The Multiple Award Winner answered, 'Mostly hills, but not as steep as Sikkim.'

How were the people? 'Poor. Very poor. They followed me around thinking I was from the government who had come to distribute money.'

Was there a lot of sandalwood? 'You know me, Daju, can't tell bamboo from teak. But the forests were fragrant, very fragrant.'

Did he visit Raku? How was the palace? 'Not much to see there. Old houses. The palace is as big as this building. Nobody lives there anymore. The temple is a heap of stones, full of grass with leeches.'

The ex-Minister said, 'There were many capitals of Chyalu,' and withdrew from his questioning.

The Multiple Award Winner lifted the ex-Minister's spirits. He would be returning just in time for Libhanaya Bhod and the ex-Minister would see him on stage, receiving another award. The ex-Minister assured him that nothing would keep him away from the seminar.

~

Dr Kuldeep was his next visitor. He pronounced the ex-Minister to be weak but stable. The abdominal pains were because of his old age. He just needed to take his meals regularly. The ex-Minister agreed. 'But no one to cook. Look around, son. This is what a house without a wife or a mother looks like.' He let the thought sink in and then asked, 'Have you spoken to Yogita recently?'

'Not speaking. But we have been exchanging messages on the phone.'

'On the Internet?' the ex-Minister asked.

Dr Kuldeep looked at his watch. 'On the Internet also.'

'Are you going to Delhi anytime soon? I need to send her something.'

As it turned out, he was. 'A friend is getting married in Delhi next week. I'll leave on Thursday; his marriage is on Saturday.'

Before Dr Kuldeep left, the ex-Minister put his hand on the doctor's. 'Son, we have the same name. Kuldeep. It means that we are the lights of our clan. We have to keep our names alive. Once it becomes dust then we won't be able to retrieve it. Are you understanding?'

Dr Kuldeep looked away and nodded. 'Good,' the ex-Minister said, impressed by his shyness, 'I would have told you to stay for dinner but I can only offer you air.'

Three days later, the ex-Minister received a combative call from his daughter. 'Dr Kuldeep called. He says you're sending me a parcel? Your parcels are always dangerous.'

'Why? I can't send you anything? He had come to do a check-up, and said he was going to Delhi. He offered to take something for you and I said yes. Is that a crime? Should I surrender at the police station?'

She yielded to his exaggerations. 'Okay. I'll take it from him. Make sure you send the dalley-and-bamboo shoot pickle. The one from Darjeeling, not from Sikkim.'

'Ungrateful children,' he said. To underscore his annoyance, he ended the call without any farewell. Life was improving.

Ai Doma brought a servant. He was a bald, snot-faced, genial boy with a nonsensical name—Toksing—given to him by people in his village. The ex-Minister renamed him Pemba. He could not cook but the momo-seller would give him lessons in her house. He would keep the house clean, as long as the ex-Minister followed him from room to room, prodding him with his walking stick. That, too, the ex-Minister did not mind, for it was a form of exercise.

When Dr Kuldeep came by to pick up the parcel, the ex-Minister said, 'Give it to her as soon as you reach. I've sent fresh dalleys, the kind she likes. They rot very quickly.'

Dr Kuldeep agreed to do that. The ex-Minister let him go with some advice. 'Remember, don't be shy. Shy people only get to eat after everyone else has eaten.'

The fresh chillies were a ruse suggested by the momo-seller to the ex-Minister. They would ensure that the doctor would have to meet Yogita early in his trip. It might lead to more meetings during the doctor's stay and, in concordance with the ex-Minister's hopes, some romance would occur. This was the way things were done nowadays, and he was willing to accept it, as long as it concluded in a marriage.

At Panchsheel Marg

When Dr Kuldeep reached Delhi, it was seasonably hot and sticky. It was the month now, the taxi-driver told Dr Kuldeep, of sudden storms. They were making their way from the airport to New Sikkim House in Chanakyapuri. They talked like friends. Dr Kuldeep learnt that the driver had three children, two of whom were in college. He knew the value of education and was proud of himself for having educated them despite his circumstances. Two hands and one brain were all a man needed. For his part, Dr Kuldeep confessed that he was unmarried but was seeking to change that. That was why he was here in Delhi. The driver offered his best wishes, Kuldeep accepted them.

They reached Chanakyapuri and Dr Kuldeep repeated New Sikkim House's address for him. It was on Panchsheel Marg, opposite the American Embassy.

The American Embassy has a large estate. It occupies two blocks of Chanakyapuri and the road between these blocks is barred. Dr Kuldeep looked to the right, where New Sikkim House ought to have been. Instead of its reassuring pink facade, there was only a white wall.

'Where is this?'

'Amreeki Embassy.'

Dr Kuldeep informed the driver that he was wrong. Ruptures appeared in their friendship. 'Now I have to go around. So much time wasted.'

The taxi skirted the Embassy complex in a long detour and Kuldeep saw New Sikkim House behind some trees. They stopped at the driveway. 'One-fifty extra.'

Dr Kuldeep had readied himself. 'This is a prepaid taxi. I already paid at the airport.'

Here they argued, and their friendship suffered further. The taxi-driver was stocky and moustachioed. He threatened at points to come out of his taxi and settle it like a man. Dr Kuldeep drew his strength from the presence of New Sikkim House behind him. 'Come out.'

The driver modified his challenge. 'One hundred.'

Dr Kuldeep placed fifty rupees on the passenger seat. The driver got into his taxi and, without reaching for the money, started his vehicle and sped off. Further away, near the roundabout, the taxi paused and Dr Kuldeep saw the driver twist his body around and reach behind.

New Sikkim House is a large four-storeyed building with each floor receding from the one below. The building is clad in pink stone and this reflected the evening sun, each softening the other's harshness.

~

From his room, Dr Kuldeep phoned Yogita but she did not respond. He hesitated briefly before texting her: 'Hi! Reached your city. Free to catch up?'

He then phoned Harish Dane, his friend whose wedding he had

come to attend. Harish was pleasantly surprised. Where was he staying? He should have informed before coming, he could have been put up with the rest of the gang. Not everyone had come but there were enough of them for a good time. The actual reception was in three days but they were all meeting up tomorrow evening, when most of the gang would arrive. He gave Dr Kuldeep the address before being called away.

After dinner, Dr Kuldeep received a text from Yogita: 'Sorry was at work...shitty day. I need a new job!! Awesome you're here. When do we meet?'

'You want your parcel or not?'

She did not reply. Eventually he texted her again: 'Was a joke... ☺'

'Of course... Got busy, sorry. Want to meet but not sure how the work scene will play out...though badly need a break... Will confirm tomorrow?'

'Sure. Call when you can.'

His last text went unanswered. The next morning he was woken up at 6:30 by a call. It was the ex-Minister. There were no greetings. His voice sounded strained. 'Have you called her?'

'I called her. She didn't answer.'

'SMS?'

'I sent her an SMS and then she sent me an SMS.'

'Son, remind her that I've sent her fresh dalley chillies.'

Dr Kuldeep agreed that the chillies were a priority. After the call, he thought of his parents, who were unaware that he was being wooed by Kuldeep Chandanth for his daughter. If they knew, their pressures would be greater than those exerted by the ex-Minister. He wanted to surprise them and he knew it would be a pleasant one. For three years now, he had endured their entreaties and arguments, all of them reasonable. They had brought up Yogita's name on a number of occasions, they knew she worked in Delhi and was an exceptional match. And, half-dreaming of the ex-Minister, he returned to his sleep.

Later, he texted Yogita again. 'Your dad has sent fresh dalleys for you...they'll bigreyko if we don't meet soon...not joking ☹'

'Uff...why does he have to do so much drama'.

And then, later: 'Sorry ya... I should be happy he sent it...I haven't tasted fresh dalley for years...you're staying at Sikkim House no? Can we meet tmrw evening? A campaign has to leave the office by tmrw afternoon and we're all working our asses off... Oops'.

'Of course, we'll have momos and dalleys'.

'Yay...'

~

Dr Kuldeep prepared to meet Yogita the next day. He still had the evening at hand. He phoned Harish and asked for directions to the hotel. There, the conviviality of the reunion eased his anxieties. A number of friends had come, and time was spent in the polishing of reminiscences, for it had been six years since they had graduated. Many had married, some of them had completed their MDs, others were planning to. They called him Sikkim, his nickname in college. They talked about a classmate, who had interacted with no one, and who had died recently. Then they compared salaries and professional environments. They had all heard that it had not worked out between him and the doctor from Bhubaneshwar he had met during his internship. Where was she now? Dr Kuldeep updated them: Debashree was working in Bangalore and had emailed a few months ago to say that she had met someone. He accepted their condolences with grace.

Harish's father, flushed with satisfaction, joined them. He had located and chosen the bride. She was a Maharashtrian working in Delhi and he had found her through a network of clansmen. 'Say what you want, but I am a traditional person at heart.' He asked Dr Kuldeep about his 'situation'.

'There is someone.'

They congratulated him. Was it arranged?

'She has the same surname, but I met her on my own.'

Harish's father was impressed with his understanding. 'Caste is not a bad thing. The world is so large, and sometimes family is not enough to find one's way in it. That is when your caste, your gotra can help.'

There were a few nods in the group, and Dr Kuldeep was among the nodders. They asked him her name and he didn't tell them, preferring to wait until the subject had changed. The groom came and slapped his back. 'Guess who's coming tomorrow? Bhavna.'

They teased Dr Kuldeep. Bhavna was a senior who had followed Kuldeep for weeks until his classmates pointed out her intentions to him. They had lived together for two years until she graduated. 'But watch out. She's now married to a boxer.'

On the way back to New Sikkim House, Dr Kuldeep asked the driver of the auto-rickshaw, 'Are you married?'

'Yes Saar. Three children.'

'Same caste?'

'Yes Saar. Caste is very important. A name without caste is like a body without hands.'

Dr Kuldeep asked him to repeat the saying and tipped him when they reached New Sikkim House. In his room, he received a call from the ex-Minister. He spoke in a voice soaked in pain. 'Son, are you meeting her soon? I don't want the chillies to go bad.'

Dr Kuldeep said. 'Not yet. But we may meet tomorrow. People are busy in the cities.'

~

To the ex-Minister's credit, he resisted the urge to phone Dr Kuldeep and demand an update through the day. As part of his effort to distract himself from events in Delhi, the ex-Minister focused on Libhanaya Bhod and Yograj's involvement in the preparations. The ex-Minister now welcomed his involvement. Who knew, maybe he would meet a girl volunteer? If only, he thought, if only Pradeep and Yograj confided in him. He had so much experience in dealing with the snakes and sheep in the three organizations, he could have helped them navigate. But they had shut him out. He was in one room, everyone else was in the other room, he could hear them talk but the words remained indistinct.

When Yograj arrived for his morning meal, he found the ex-Minister waiting at the dining table, in an expectant posture. 'So preparations going well?'

'Well enough.'

'Let me know if you need any help. Talk to the Joint Secretary, he's the only one reliable. The rest are all crooks or fools.'

Yograj shot him a look. 'And who are you to say all this?'

This wounded the ex-Minister. He shouted, 'I am the President! If I want I can dissolve the whole organization. You, your half-brother and your new fathers will all have to start from the bottom.'

Yograj said nothing. He waited until Pemba had served him his food—underdone rice and a watery daal with over-salted potatoes. He walked out of the kitchen, towards his room. 'Do that then. Nobody's stopping you.'

The ex-Minister wanted to shout, but he was aware of his depleting reserves of strength. Calming himself down, he told himself he was still needed. He phoned the General Secretary. He was almost ambushed by the warmth of her tone. 'Daju! You're keeping well, I hope. Yograj and Pradeep Bhai keep us updated about your health.'

She had always addressed him as 'Sir'. To now call him a brother meant a levelling of deference, and a claim to equality. He said, 'I wanted to know if you needed any help. I have been so aloof. This is CAS's show, I say to myself.'

'We've told ourselves that the seniors will not be disturbed at all. This is a job for us, the next generation.' The ex-Minister drew in his breath. This from a woman who was to have retired five years earlier and was on her third service extension. But she was not completely to blame for, in Sikkim, the next generation included anyone who was younger than the Hon'ble Chief Minister.

He made a tactical change. 'I've been thinking about CAS House.'

There was a pause, and then he heard the rise in her voice, signalling interest. 'Yes?'

'Let the next generation build it. The real next generation. I will be sending out a tender call for the temple next week. I have discussed this with the Vice President.'

'After Libhanaya Bhod, let's speak after the seminar,' she said and ended the call abruptly. This satisfied the ex-Minister. She would call Pradeep SE and he would call Yograj.

In the evening, he knew his ploy had worked when Yograj entered the house, looking harassed. 'You don't want to see me succeed, no?'

The ex-Minister raised his palms to the ceiling. 'Where have I stopped you?'

'The GS says that you are not in favour of CAS House.'

'Ask her to repeat what I said. I said the younger generation must do it. And who does the younger generation refer to?'

Yograj said, 'They also asked me to find out if you are going to come.'

The ex-Minister said, 'I'll think about it.' The General Secretary phoned him sometime later to apologize. 'Yograj says you may not make it. We'll all be very sad.'

'Then cry. Who's stopping you?' She gasped and her response lifted the ex-Minister. In that mood of elation he phoned Dr Kuldeep, late at night. 'Son, if my daughter's doing too much drama, forget her. You don't have to meet her.'

Dr Kuldeep's answer soothed him instantly. 'We met today.'

The ex-Minister's voice peaked. 'And?'

'It went well.'

~

Yogita chose to meet Dr Kuldeep at New Sikkim House; the momos in its restaurant were her favourite. When they embraced, she apologized for being so oily from the day's work and the traffic; she teased him for his deodorized freshness. The restaurant at New Sikkim House is small and its food's consistency depends on the management, which changes contractually. Until recently, its food had enjoyed local renown and in the afternoon, employees from the diplomatic enclave could be seen eating there, congratulating themselves for having discovered it. In the evenings, families and couples from across Delhi would arrive and the air would thrum with conversations in many languages. Until, that is, a senior bureaucrat complained to the Home Department in Sikkim that the waiters were paying far more attention to these guests than to the ones in the rooms waiting for room service. The restaurant was then closed to outside guests, its menu abridged and a governmental indifference settled in the waiters' eyes.

In the restaurant, he gave her the parcel. She opened it, broke open a dalley chilli and inhaled its aromatic and precise pungency. A waiter asked, 'What will you have?'

'Chicken momos,' she said, and grinned at Dr Kuldeep.

He asked, 'So your father knows you eat chicken?'

'Of course not. And don't you dare tell him. How's he?'

He apprised her. The ex-Minister's health was steady, but there were reverses, caused mostly by loneliness and age. She looked at the table. 'What do you think of him?'

'Very blunt, but we expect that in old people. He's very stubborn.'

'I've inherited that quality from him.'

He asked the waiter for two steel glasses and when they came, poured some beer from a bottle he had concealed. The momos arrived and they were just as she remembered. 'My father is the one thing in my life I feel guilty about. I live for marketing, advertising, all that. What will I do back home? It's easy for you, no. You're a doctor, wherever you go there'll be work for you.'

He did not take her side. 'We are all responsible for ourselves.'

'Are you sure my father hasn't sent you?'

He denied it. She asked him to describe the marriage he had come for, and the conversation progressed to marriages in general. He replenished her beer.

She played with a momo and said, 'I have to tell you something.'

He had guessed. 'You already have someone?'

She nodded. 'He's a Punjabi Hindu. We've been together for almost ten years. His name is Vinay.'

'What does he do?'

'Teaches sociology. And I'm in advertising. The fights we have!'

'Does Kuldeep Baraa know?' he asked.

She balled her hands into fists. 'He knows but he doesn't want to know. He doesn't ask me a single question about my life in Delhi because of what I might tell him.'

'And Yograj?'

She said. 'We have a non-interference treaty. He doesn't ask me about my life and I don't ask about his. We'll fight like cats and dogs otherwise. But he's tried to talk to Appa, who just doesn't want to listen.'

Dr Kuldeep concealed his trembling hands. 'I don't blame him. It's what all parents ask of children.'

Yogita picked up a momo. 'You don't know half the story.' The momo's skin burst, she had squeezed it too hard.

Dr Kuldeep offered her a napkin. 'Calm down. It's not the momo's fault.'

She put the momo down. 'You haven't given me details about Debashree.'

They had tried really hard. Debashree had visited Sikkim a number of times and stayed at Dr Kuldeep's house. It looked like his parents were accepting her. She had visited this January, to finalize dates. Then something had turned; after a number of incidents—long stories, all of them—his parents had gone against the match. Dr Kuldeep blamed a poisonous uncle. Debashree tried hard to please them but nothing worked. It had ended for sure when she told Dr Kuldeep's parents to 'go fuck themselves'.

She giggled into her beer. 'I like the girl already.' He conceded a smile, as if the humour of the incident was only now apparent to him.

'You'll find someone. Sexy single doctor and all that. I hope Yograj marries a Chandanth.'

'I hope so too. Most of your father's problems come from loneliness.'

Yogita's voice was low. 'I know, which is why he got so attached to the damn servant,' here she corrected herself and said, 'maid'.

They discussed Pamphaa's possession and exorcism. Dr Kuldeep had not been a witness but he had heard of it. There had been instances in his family too. Yogita said, 'She was giving him such good company. I was so happy for him. And then she runs away with a few bangles.'

Dr Kuldeep said, 'What's done is done. He's still alone.'

'You don't know half the story,' she said.

'What will you tell me? That he's married twice?'

They were on opposing sides, and Dr Kuldeep was defending the father from his daughter.

'Thrice. He took his first wife when he was very young. She ran away with someone. Then he married Pradeep Daju's mother. Then after he became a politician, he left her because she was a tribal Chandanth and not a Hindu Chandanth, whatever that means. And she was from the villages. Then he married my mother; she was his city wife.'

Dr Kuldeep stared at his plate. Yogita said, 'No one seems to mind that the whole damn state is crowded with bigamists. You must have wondered why Nima Thendup, a Bhotey, is our cousin?'

'No. But it does seem strange, no?'

'He asked for his loneliness. Nima's mother, Kalpana Kaki, was my father's sister. She married Nima's father, a Bhotey. And just like that, my father kicked her out of the family. He never met her again, just like how he never met his first wife after leaving her. His brothers and sisters in the villages were far more open. They stopped speaking to my father because of that, but he just did not give in. He would have more company now if he had been flexible in his early years. Pradeep Daju still has issues against my father.'

She slumped in her chair. 'He has a lot of things to answer for. And he's still trying to manipulate us into doing what he wants. Just because he's a leader. I'm sorry I'm telling you all this. Too much information for a second meeting, no?'

They agreed to meet again before he left. 'I want to send him a few things. Parcel politics.' They set up a lunch meeting at Khan Market, halfway between her flat and New Sikkim House.

She had consumed three plates of momos. 'I told you I was serious about momos. A last favour? Can I take some home? I won't have to cook for Vinay. He's coming to pick me up in some time,' she said.

Dr Kuldeep requested the waiter to pack two plates. After dinner, she wanted to smoke. 'Can I have a ciggie in your room?'

The balcony of his room gave them a view of the wire-topped walls of the American Embassy, rendered orange by the street lamps. Halfway along the wall's stretch, two sentries sat languidly on the sandbags meant to provide them cover.

Her talk had not lightened. 'Is caste that important?'

Dr Kuldeep gave her a practised answer. 'Not to me. But it's important to the people who are important to me. I won't force it upon my children.'

She expected him to elaborate but he stayed quiet. She had finished her cigarette. Her phone beeped and she glanced at it. 'He'll be here shortly. I'll wait downstairs for him.'

She stubbed out her cigarette and prepared to leave. He stretched out his hand to shake hers, but she came close and hugged him. The embrace continued into a kiss. She relented enough to let their tongues meet and he got a strong taste of onions mixed with nicotine. She pushed him away, picked up her parcel and the packed momos, and was out of the room.

Dr Kuldeep did not tell the ex-Minister all this. When he phoned in the evening, eager for details, the doctor parried. 'Baraa, how can I tell you what all we spoke about? It would not be good.'

'And today? Are you two meeting today?'

'We're both busy. My friend's marriage reception is today.'

The ex-Minister improvised. 'Ask her if she wants to go as well. Take her with you.'

'I'll ask her,' Dr Kuldeep said. He went alone and early to the marriage reception and kept his phone turned off. There, amongst friends he had not seen for four years, time passed more easily than it had the previous night and this morning. Bhavna arrived without her husband. Though they were shy with each other, they ended the evening dancing to a remixed version of 'Koi roko na dewaane ko', a favourite from their college days. She asked him if he was married, he said no and accepted her admonitions. They parted, promising to keep in touch.

He was to leave for Sikkim the day after, on Monday. At night he saw that Yogita had tried to get in touch with him. He called back and she said, 'I'll take you out tomorrow.'

~

They met at Khan Market the next afternoon. She was not alone: Vinay, tall and bearded, accompanied her. They allowed Dr Kuldeep, in his privilege as a visitor from the provinces, to choose where they would eat. It was a warm day, he thought it good for beer, and he chose a restaurant done in the style of an English alehouse with the timber in its interiors treated and marked to look old. They ordered beer and pork ribs. The beers arrived. To make Vinay comfortable, Yogita said, 'We were talking about castes and communities, and all those sort of problems in Sikkim. Your favourite subject.'

At once, Vinay became comfortable. He said, 'It's there everywhere in India. And you know where it comes from? From the imposition of political boundaries over cultural boundaries.'

Dr Kuldeep stayed neutral. 'Could be.'

Yogita sipped her beer. 'I don't mind caste, tribes and all that. It is how we lived. But I do hate this association business. Each one shouting, and my father is amongst them, that their caste or tribe is the best. Who wore shoes first, who came to Sikkim as labourers, whose ancestors had the hardest life.' Then she checked herself, 'I must sound like someone who has forgotten her roots.'

Dr Kuldeep conceded. 'They do talk about those things a lot.'

Yogita continued, 'And why is everyone obsessed about the Chief Minister? Is she dying, is she alive, when will she give up the chair, who will she give it to? You're the first one I know who hasn't yet talked about the Chief Minister.'

Vinay added, 'And oppression. Have you heard their stories about oppression?' He turned to Yogita, 'Who is that man who tries to feel your back whenever he can.'

'The Treasurer of CAS,' Yogita said, and mock-shuddered.

The pork chops arrived. Vinay picked up a knife and fork and sliced the meat. 'The Treasurer of CAS. The organization seems like such a wonderful case study, it almost makes me want to visit Sikkim. Apparently, the Treasurer told my darling here that he could never trust a Newar—am I pronouncing it correctly?—because a Newar cheated his father of some land beside a river. But that is not oppression, it's only the story of a swindler and an idiot.'

Dr Kuldeep's eyes widened. 'My family is full of such stories. You should come and meet them.'

Vinay waved a rib with bits of attached flesh. 'They have no idea what caste and religious violence is. Where I come from the whole village is divided into two camps, and each camp claims the other is lower. Last year, a boy strayed into the wrong part of the village. They tied his hands together, and then his legs together. They taped his mouth shut, and watched as he crawled, if that is the word, to the other side. And imagine, it used to be worse. You must have heard them, the shit-eating stories. Those are the kind of injustices for which reservations were designed.'

'Vinay!' Yogita exclaimed and slapped his arm.

Dr Kuldeep said, 'Sikkim is milder than that.'

Vinay gulped his beer and jabbed a sauce-stained knife into the air. 'Precisely. My people have a saying, "The elephant's medicines will kill the deer".'

Yogita was annoyed now. She said, 'You'll get along so well with my father. Talking about nothing but caste and using animals to describe everything and everyone.'

She then asked Dr Kuldeep about the wedding. He had enjoyed it but found it loud and garish but they gave him examples to prove that, by Delhi's standards, he had witnessed a sober demonstration. She made him promise that he would take care of her father's health. Once married, she and Vinay planned to come to Sikkim and spend time with him, but, until then, all she could do was hope from a distance.

Dr Kuldeep asked them, 'So what do I tell Baraa, I mean Yogita's dad?'

Vinay shrugged, 'That's her territory.'

Yogita handed him a small parcel. 'Say what you think is best. I'm sending some wheat biscuits and some dry fruits for him. You'll give it to him, no?'

After Dr Kuldeep reached Gangtok, he had the parcel delivered to the ex-Minister, but he avoided visiting him or taking his calls, which increased in frequency before they ceased altogether. There was nothing to say and the old man needed to understand that.

Waiting for an Invitation

The ex-Minister abandoned his pursuit of Dr Kuldeep. When Ai Doma visited repeatedly to inquire for updates from Delhi, he scolded her for having a long nose. She left in anger. 'Don't call me when your daughter falls pregnant.'

Yogita phoned a week later. 'Has Dr Kuldeep come by to check on you?'

'He's disappeared.'

'I think he was interested in me.'

'He has not told me anything.'

The ex-Minister knew he was being probed but did not yield. To admit complicity was to further expose himself to scorn and ridicule for the innocence of his intentions.

Nima Thendup visited with news. 'The servant has not been seen in her village, but one of the workers building the retaining walls at the resort says he met the hajuju some days earlier in Laal Bazaar. Says the hajuju tried to sell him some gold. We can get her.'

The ex-Minister waved a feeble hand. 'Let them be. Someone else will punish them.'

Pemba entered with some tea. Nima Thendup scrutinized him and said, 'Good you got a boy. There'll always be talk with women servants, even if they have wrinkles.'

The ex-Minister said, 'What will happen to the two of them if I die?'

Nima Thendup waved his hands in front of his face. 'No. No. No. Don't speak like that. Yograj and Yogita have more than what I started out with.'

The subject of Nima Thendup's parents threatened to change the course of the ex-Minister's crafted talk. He sought to pacify his nephew. 'You have a bigger heart.'

This soothed Nima Thendup and he agreed to stay for dinner. He phoned Thinley Machi and, braving her irritation, said, 'He needs someone to talk to.'

Nima Thendup insisted that the ex-Minister eat at the table and not in bed. Dinner was bland. Nima Thendup declared it fit only for unreformable prisoners, but the ex-Minister appeared indifferent to the quality of the food. Pemba sat on a stool and accepted this criticism of his work with equanimity. The ex-Minister leaned on Nima Thendup and hobbled towards his room. 'I'm all alone, Nima, all alone.'

'Where's Yograj? Where's Pradeep?'

The ex-Minister reached his bed and said again, 'I'm all alone. They don't talk to me anymore. I phone Pradeep every day but he doesn't answer. Yograj treats this house like a hotel, only comes in to eat, sleep and check if I'm still alive. Busy with the function, they say, and they spend whole days with my enemies.'

Nima Thendup patted his arm. 'Enough. Enough. Calm down.'

The ex-Minister did not calm down. He spoke of CAS, the gathering rebellion in which his sons were active accessories, his exclusion from a tradition that he had birthed, the isolation of his days and the sleepless turmoil of his nights, Yogita's sharp selfishness and his wish to be released from all of it. 'I have no power left. Spit at the sky and you'll only wet your own face.'

Nima Thendup offered, 'Come and stay with me then.'

The ex-Minister considered Nima Thendup's house, with its Buddhist decorations and objects of worship. He shook his head. After his nephew left, he realized he had not really been heard. Nima Thendup's views were impersonal and moulded by common ideals; they reduced everything to consoling generalities.

He could not change, not so late in his life. All through his career he had found no Chandanth who disagreed with his principles and his methods, and now he could not find one who agreed. Especially now, when appreciation was a near-tangible nutrient for his body. He had never felt so feeble as he did now, even a lessening of air seemed enough to cause suffocation. He had seen the induced strength that came from the assumption of power: the Hon'ble Chief Minister was healthier now than she had been fourteen years earlier. And that strength was to be denied to him. He was condemned to disappear in the manner of small men, mourned only for the prescribed period.

Work remained. His fears for the Chandanth name, always strong, now became pitched. He knew its limitations, for as an idea, the sandalwood hypothesis had never caught. He had heard it in his youth and, attracted by its symbolic appeal, adopted and championed it. There were many who had adopted the name under his influence, or as a submission to a fad, but they done it without self-belief. They would just as easily take another name. And without him at the front, he knew the Chandanth numbers would dwindle. He needed the strength to preserve their fragrant name.

Then again, he was stung by the futility of his task. The Chandari-speaking peoples in Sikkim would be content to be scattered, refusing to be united even by a common name. He knew his ideas were too forward, and that they would die with him, but he steeled himself against bitterness. Bitterness was a trophy for the vanquished, and he would not exhibit it.

~

His resolve eroded as Libhanaya Bhod approached. Each day he waited for the formal invitation and each evening found him disappointed. *Sikkim Everyday* covered the preparations—'Mammoth Event Planned'. It was to be a two-day spectacle and there were indications that it would be memorable. The newspaper ran features on the various scholars and members of the community who were going to be present. The Multiple Award Winner was prominent; by now he had walked for a year. He was in Assam, returning from the Burmese border, and they showed photographs in which he walked at the head of a swelling mass of people. Another feature was on Professor Robert Black, who had researched in the Chyalu Valley for eighteen years.

He phoned the Vice President first. His wife answered the phone in a young, sharp voice that stirred the ex-Minister. The Vice President could not speak to him. He was in bed, recovering from a fall. Yes, the invitation card had come last week, but the doctor had ordered him rest for a month. He wanted to attend, but she would not let him. The ex-Minister blessed her before ending the call.

He phoned the Treasurer next. He answered in an eager, transparent voice, 'Is this about CAS House? Has Yograj spoken to you?'

'I was just thinking about that. Temple or office, I still can't decide. We should call a meeting, no? Tomorrow? You have time tomorrow?'

'Not for a few days, Kuldeep-jiu. Let this drama get over.' Then the Treasurer clicked his tongue and said, 'Did I tell you, they made me Treasurer for the Steering Committee as well. What a headache!'

They joked about the possibilities of embezzlement and towards the end of the call, the Treasurer sounded concerned. 'Daju, please take care of your health. We all wish you were here, taking charge of all that's happening. Instead we have to listen to fools. If only your health were better.'

'I am better than you think. You'll see on that day.'

The Treasurer's voice lost its gaiety. 'Nothing better than to see you attend, Daju. Have you received the invitation card? Even we haven't received it.'

The ex-Minister had prepared his answer. 'Yes. It came a few days ago. Will be so good to see you there.'

Let the foxes fight each other, the ex-Minister thought. He waited for the General Secretary's call. It did not take long. 'We're so relieved you received the invitation. Who delivered it?'

The ex-Minister said, 'I didn't see the messenger. Should I have noted?'

She turned abrupt. 'No no. Nothing like that.' She enquired after his health, suggested some poultices, and said, 'I still need to discuss CAS House with you.'

'Nothing to discuss. We're building the temple.'

She exhaled and said, 'For your children at least.'

'My children can take care of themselves.'

He phoned the Joint Secretary but his call went unanswered. The General Secretary must have warned him, he thought.

He overcame his dislike for the Press Secretary and reached out to him. He was surprised when his call was received. The ex-Minister said, 'The HCM's office called and asked me to get involved with the Steering Committee's work. But I said no. All that is the younger generation's work.'

The Press Secretary said, 'If only all of them thought like you. Mitradas Sir spoke to me the other day. He thinks it is all a big drama and I agree with him.'

'I agree too. Please tell him that.' The ex-Minister controlled his pleasure. So Mitradas too was encircled. Their positions had at last converged, the traitor and the betrayed.

He phoned Mitradas and was civil. 'I'll be seeing you at the seminar, Bhai.'

Mitradas returned his civility, 'Yes Daju. Of course. Incomplete without you.'

'I heard many things are happening?'

This query broke Mitradas's reserve. 'Too many Daju, too many.

You would weep if you knew what TB is doing. Please allow me to visit you.' The ex-Minister granted him an invitation and settled down to wait. There was another issue that needed to be discussed with Mitradas.

He phoned TB Chandath and asked, 'All going well, Bhai? How's the seminar coming up?'

TB Chandath was aloof. 'It's not a seminar. It's a conclave.'

The ex-Minister ignored this and said, 'Mitradas says you're handling the situation very well. Let me know if you need any help.'

TB Chandath assured him that all was well. He said, 'So you won't be coming, Daju. I felt sad when I heard that.'

Vulture! The ex-Minister said, 'Too old for it all, TB Bhai. I'll send my sons. Let them take over.'

'Very modern of you, President Saab.'

Snake! The ex-Minister said, 'The HCM herself says that tradition is the elder brother of modernity.'

~

He schemed for attention from his colleagues and his family. He thought of eating mutton, to make himself sick, but it involved genuine risks. Then he discovered the advantages of his age. He had shrunk so much that all he had to do was withdraw any cheer from his face and replace it with an expression of gloom. He looked sick and, because he looked sick, he became sick.

His children responded to this illness. Yograj turned attentive. He would spend a few moments in the morning and evening administering him but would not discuss the conclave. He also did not, as the ex-Minister hoped, call Dr Kuldeep. Instead, he brought home another doctor, a bespectacled, middle-aged man who pronounced the ex-Minister's case to be a 'classic case of old age'.

'His father's old age,' the ex-Minister snarled after the doctor left.

Pradeep SE sent him home-cooked meals but did not visit. The ex-Minister phoned him and said, 'I'll come whether I am invited or not. Even on a wheelchair.'

Pradeep SE immediately visited the ex-Minister to dissuade him. 'Why do you want to bring us all down?' And the ex-Minister appeared to be conciliated at the end but he had sown alarm in his sons, and this contented him.

Yograj, pretending to be absorbed in the preparations, attended to him tenderly and avoided any talk. He made Yogita speak for him. She phoned the ex-Minister and sniffed. 'Yograj says that you may go to that conclave. Don't go Appa, why do you want to be around people who do not value you?'

'Why should I not go? I am a Chandanth. I have every right.'

'You just want to shame everyone around you.'

'No one seems to have any shame. *You* don't have any shame. Why should I be the only one with shame?'

He slept through three days of a mock fever, the Eiffel Tower by his bedside, in case anybody visited. He persisted in his charade of illness and it lured the momo-seller. Ai Doma visited him every day. She shouted at Pemba for dawdling. 'Not your father's house. Work quicker!' Then she wagged a finger at the ex-Minister. 'Be more strict with him. He thinks it's the village where you walk around with a goat all day and call it work.'

One evening, she stayed back and supervised the preparation of dinner. The ex-Minister heard her tell Pemba, 'Take good care of the old man. He's dying and if he dies when you are around then it'll be jail for you.'

Pemba was not scared. 'I'll run away.'

The ex-Minister heard a low thwack; she must have knuckled his scalp. 'Where will you run? The police can catch anyone anywhere. Have you seen the bikes they have?'

Pemba acknowledged that the police bikes were indeed very swift. Ai Doma said, 'What do you want later in life?'

'A bike.'

'Very well. If you look after him, Buddha Bhagwaan will make sure you get a bike. But only if you look after him well.'

~

The ex-Minister set his sights higher. He phoned the Hon'ble Chief Minister's Principal Secretary. 'Bhai, I wanted an appointment with the

HCM. To discuss the Steering Committee for Libhanaya Bhod. So much work, so little time.'

The nasal voice came over the phone. 'She's in Delhi, Kuldeep-jiu. Gone there for the Budget. She'll return the day after tomorrow.' This was not a lie, the newspapers stated that the Chief Minister was indeed in Delhi.

When the ex-Minister phoned in two days, he said, 'She's still in Delhi, Kuldeep-jiu.'

'Is she the Chief Minister of Sikkim or of Delhi?' The Principal Secretary tried to soothe him. 'As soon as she comes, Kuldeep-jiu, as soon as she comes. She always scolds us if senior party members don't have access to her.'

The ex-Minister said, 'So let me meet you and explain everything. And you can explain everything to her. Just like talking to Ganesh was the same as talking to Parvati.'

The Principal Secretary was unmoved. 'Ah Kuldeep-jiu, we can't meet. Even I am in Delhi.' He would not commit on the Hon'ble Chief Minister's return date, and hinted that even after her return, she would be preoccupied with matters of state until the Dasain break.

The ex-Minister waited for a call from her. When it did not come, he phoned the Principal Secretary again but his call was not answered. So he had been put aside by the Hon'ble Chief Minister. He had fulfilled his usefulness, he knew, and he was now an irritant, part of the public's clamour that needed to be shut out.

He turned charitable, his vision drifted and he held imaginary conversations with his clanspeople. He saw himself forgiving them. Then he considered their ingratitude, his mood darkened and he constructed elaborate fantasies of revenge. He saw himself disrupting the genteel atmosphere of the conclave. Then it ended, as always, with a lucid depression, for he knew he would be forgotten unless he battled for remembrance, but he had neither weapons nor strength.

~

Then Mitradas visited and insisted on talking in the kitchen instead of the living room. 'I belong to this house.'

The ex-Minister sat beside him and asked, 'So. Who else are you all ignoring?'

Mitradas's voice was pleasant. 'Don't say that, Kuldeep-jiu. Everyone in CAS says you're not well and that you shouldn't be disturbed. But here you look healthier than most of us.'

The ex-Minister was mocking. 'My blood. It keeps me strong.'

Mitradas' voice turned pleading. 'You have to come to the conclave, Daju. How did you know, Kuldeep Daju, that TB was a snake? That it would all become like this?'

'Would you all have listened? You were all so happy. Tyau-tyau here, tyau-tyau there.'

Mitradas pressed his hands together. 'I wish I had seen it as well. You know what they are doing? All our gods gone, all our customs gone. Everything will get a new name. We have to change our names. It's going to be Chadat now. No "n" in our names, they say.'

So Mitradas wanted him as an ally. Curiosity supplanted irritation. 'Many new changes, I heard.'

Mitradas was anguished. 'Too many, Daju, too many. You heard, the HCM is saying "No more Dasain now, we have to focus on Nehepau Doh instead."'

The ex-Minister shrugged, that he did not mind. Mitradas said, 'Daju, there's going to be a new all-India organization. Above CAS, above CHAPS. And TB will be the chairman. It'll be an elephant with a snake's head.'

The ex-Minister clicked his tongue. 'I've done what I could. You fight if you want to. But I'm on your side. I want to die with my gods over me.'

The conversation tired him. He had another, far more important matter pending with Mitradas, in his capacity as the cousin of Dr Kuldeep's father. When there was a lull in the conversation, the ex-Minister said, 'How's it with Riwaj?'

'Our families are close.'

'His son, the doctor...'

Mitradas caught his meaning immediately. 'Perfect for Yogita. Why didn't I think of it before? Give me some time.'

Before he left, Mitradas said, 'You have to become stronger Daju, healthier, for all of us.' He put the ex-Minister's hands to his eyes. It was an extraordinary gesture, one that had come after years of rupture, and the ex-Minister surprised Mitradas with his tears.

~

He received his invitation, but from an unexpected source. The *Sikkim Everyday* had covered the Multiple Award Winner closely; he was only a day away from Gangtok. He phoned the ex-Minister. 'Daju, many Chandanths in my procession. So many of them living near the Burma border. So you were right.'

This lifted the ex-Minister, who had heard of it for the first time. 'Of course, of course.'

The Multiple Award Winner asked, 'So I will see you there?'

The ex-Minister was deliberately sad. 'If only everyone thought like you.'

The Multiple Award Winner enquired, the ex-Minister explained, and his explanation inspired outrage. 'Nonsense. This is more important than politics. I'll send you a card and, when you enter the hall, throw it at the face of your number-one enemy. I'll enter on the second day.'

The ex-Minister was surprised by the Multiple Award Winner's clout, for a card was delivered to him that afternoon, on the last day before Libhanaya Bhod.

When he heard Yograj come into the house and go to his room, he waited for a while. Then he walked up the staircase, assisted by Pemba. He saw Yograj trying out a kanchnaki. It was the first time he had seen his son in their ancestral attire and his heart swelled. 'You've chosen the right colour.'

Yograj pretended not to hear him; he fumbled with the strings that held the top together. The ex-Minister sat on his son's bed. He said, 'I'm coming to the conclave.'

'Who sent you the card?'

The ex-Minister waved the card. 'See, it has my name. Your father's name. It came in this afternoon.'

Yograj turned away and returned his attention to his kanchnakis. He had had two sets tailored, one for each day. He began to try the other one on. The ex-Minister went down, assisted by the boy. A while later, he heard Yograj leave, and he settled himself, waiting for the calls he knew would come.

There were none. They had all tired of his threats. The ex-Minister placed another round of calls to the Core Committee to announce his receipt of an invitation, but none of them answered their phones, except for the Vice President, whose wife said he was still very weak. The ex-Minister cursed his own decrepitude, which made it impossible to simply take a taxi and go to each member's house and challenge them to settle it if they were children of their fathers.

On the morning of the conclave he took care to get dressed. Yograj had left early. The ex-Minister wore his kanchnaki and wrapped the thread six times around his waist. He placed his seytupi on his head and, formally attired, ate his morning meal. He walked to the main door but it would not open. He swung his walking stick at it when he realized that Yograj had locked him in.

Officially Backward 2: Libhanaya Bhod

DAY 1

He gave the metal grill a few limp shakes. The lock was new and large and its metallic glitter mocked him. He called out to Pemba, who arrived and did the same. He considered shouting from the window of the living room but realized that it would bring local ridicule. He phoned Yograj and Pradeep SE, their phones were switched off; it was a coordinated effort. Pemba looked up at him. 'I can go over to Ani's house.'

Pemba led the way to the ex-Minister's room and pointed to the new window, it was close enough for him to jump over to the momo-seller's flat. He watched as Pemba surmounted the sill and walked delicately on the mossy ledge, jumped over onto the ledge of her building, equally green with effulgence. Pemba rapped on the windows, they weren't open. He hit a pane lightly, broke it, opened the window, clambered in, disappeared for a moment and opened the window from the inside. Pemba's head looked out. 'She's not in. Should I get someone else?'

He nodded. Pemba returned to the ledge which, at one end, connected with the concrete porch of a lower building. The ex-Minister watched in horror as Pemba vanished around the corner, and then, after a while, emerged on the street below, scampering in the wrong direction.

The ex-Minister's humiliation was tempered by longing. At the Sikkim Conference Centre, it would be time for the conclave. He saw the bustle of the gathered organizers and the invitees, exchanging news and ailments. They would soon be shushed, and the day's programme would commence with all eyes on the stage, ready for the roster of rituals and speeches. He thought about the food. Tea and biscuits in the first break, a heavy lunch, then refreshments in the evening.

He heard a child, perhaps a Tiny Genius, bawl in the next building. It reminded the ex-Minister of a pig being poked, one of the sounds of his childhood. The urgency of his situation struck him. He thought of people who could come and help him. He was reluctant to phone the momo-seller for he would have to confess Pemba's entry into her flat. Nima Thendup's phone was unreachable. He refused to call any of the CAS traitors. How small his world was! He settled on Shambhunath, and the glazier answered his phone at the first ring.

'Saar!'

The ex-Minister explained his situation. 'Come with a hacksaw.'

'My daily wages Saar. Five hundred and fifty rupees.'

'I'll pay it.'

'Taxi-fare saar. One hundred and twenty rupees.'

'I'll pay it.'

'And money for the hacksaw blade, Saar. Twenty rupees.'

The ex-Minister exhaled. 'I'll pay it.'

Shambhunath took two hours to arrive. By then, the ex-Minister's resolve had broken. He only felt weak, and in need of rest. He asked for some food, before the lock was cut. Shambhunath brought a packet of biscuits from a nearby shop and passed it through the grill. The ex-Minister loosened his kanchnaki, sat on a stool and munched as Shambhunath cut through the lock. Pemba returned and stood beside Shambhunath. 'Couldn't find anyone.'

An arm of the lock gave way, the gate was opened. The ex-Minister paid Shambhunath and offered him some tea. Shambhunath drank his tea in silence but made no effort to leave. The ex-Minister said, 'Don't have any more money.'

Shambhunath looked at the ex-Minister as if he had made a painful insinuation. 'Please talk to Agya Nima, Saar.'

'About what?'

'It's my son, Saar.' Badri had worked with his father for a few months. But a friend of his had seen him walking in Deorali with a saw and had taunted him. Badri had refused to work after that and nothing, neither threats nor beatings, would change his mind. Then he had visited Nima Thendup and taken the payment due to them for himself. Shambhunath's features, triumphant only a few minutes ago as he had cut through the lock, turned abject.

It was an appropriate subject to discuss with the ex-Minister—the nourishment of ungrateful children. The glazier learned what to expect from Badri in the future, if Yograj's behaviour was the usual path.

The ex-Minister tried Nima Thendup's number. 'His number's not reachable. And no crying here.'

And, a scheme forming in his mind, the ex-Minister asked Shambhunath to come by later in the evening with a hacksaw blade. He would make another attempt to phone Nima Thendup and recover what he could of his payment.

Shambhunath left, the ex-Minister phoned the Vice President, who answered. The ex-Minister said, 'I was thinking of visiting you. From one sick man to another.'

The Vice President said, 'It's your house, President Saab. Anytime you want to come.'

The ex-Minister got Pemba to lock the house from the outside and help him down to the road and hail a taxi to the Vice President's house, near Deorali Girls' School. A set of steep staircases accessed his house and Pemba helped him up.

The house was filled with noises of domesticity: voices carried through from other rooms, and it was full of people—his third wife, his sons and daughters-in-law—who fussed over the Vice President. They welcomed the ex-Minister, seeing in him some company for their patriarch. The Vice President was in bed, a light cast over his left leg. A month earlier, he had slipped on an algae slick, the result of four months of incessant rain. He loosened his trousers and showed the ex-Minister a swelling on his thigh. He asked, 'They didn't invite you?'

The ex-Minister sat on a chair beside the bed. 'They wanted me to attend but I said no. We must give charge to the younger generation. They'll never learn otherwise.'

The Vice President scratched his unshaven chin. 'If only everyone had your wisdom.'

The ex-Minister said, 'If only.'

The Vice President's wife entered with medicines and a cup of warm water. She took the ex-Minister's hands to her eyes and said, 'He scolded me for talking rudely to you.'

They had married two years earlier and the scandal of the thirty-year age gap between them had been softened by his status as a widower. The ex-Minister envied the Vice President's companionship and wished that Yograj's mother had not left him so early. How comforting it would have been to have grown old together in the traditional way, as enemies who have exhausted their weapons and hostilities, and to whom the only way out is to negotiate a treaty of friendship.

The food arrived instantly. The Vice President's wife had made pork. The Vice President was served in bed but he ignored his lunch and instead talked longingly of the food they would be serving at that moment at Sikkim Conference Centre.

The ex-Minister said, 'I heard they are serving chicken this year.'

The Vice President was indignant. 'Chicken, never! The HCM will never allow it.'

'She did. One of the reasons I didn't go,' the ex-Minister said and continued, 'Dasain is nearly here.'

The Vice President adjusted his false teeth in preparation for his meal. 'Let's hope we live to see it.'

The ex-Minister raised his voice a fraction. 'But others will not leave Dasain, there will be a lot of chicken sold. What is the use of a Chandanth Chief Minister if she can't even ban a simple meat?'

The Vice President took a handful of rice and shoved it into his mouth. Some gravy dribbled out. He said, 'It is an insult to us. They still insist on selling our sacred meat, despite the Chief Minister's promise.'

It was well known in Chandanth circles that the Hon'ble Chief Minister had, upon first assuming power, promised to ban chicken in Sikkim. She had proclaimed it as a sacred duty then but had since stayed silent on the matter.

They completed the meal in silence. The ex-Minister returned to the subject. 'You've always been the voice of CAS.'

The Vice President sucked contentedly on a bone. He paused, and nodded with distant pride, as if remembering a youthful valour. 'I still have very good relations with the press people.'

The ex-Minister rose to wash his hands. He returned and said, 'But think about it. And do it only if you have the strength. Not like me, I'm good for nothing.' Here, the ex-Minister's voice cracked, 'I have arrived at a great understanding. My life's efforts has been a waste.'

The Vice President knew the ex-Minister had come to be heard, but it was time for his afternoon nap. He looked at his feet within his blankets and yawned. 'Don't cry. I'm the one who's sick here.'

The ex-Minister's voice broke. 'What is the use of knowledge if you cannot make other people understand?'

He heard a soft whistle. The Vice President was dozing. The ex-Minister's chair was comfortable and he too felt the effects of the meal. He was woken up a little later by the smiling wife of the Vice President who helped him to the cot at the far end of the room. He slept again and when he woke up, he saw the Vice President sipping tea, and instructing his son about a village matter. They resumed their conversation. The Vice President reiterated, 'They don't deserve you, President Saab.'

The ex-Minister left with Pemba when he was sure the conclave had ended for the day. The Vice President's son dropped the ex-Minister and Pemba to Tibet Road. On the way, he examined his feelings, and found that he did not feel tormented. His time was over, he conceded, and he felt a dim gratitude towards his children for making him see it; better these things came from within the family.

~

At Tibet Road, there was no time for reflection. The momo-seller visited almost immediately to shout at him. 'Are you training Pemba to become a thief? And who will repair the glass?'

'I'll call Shambhunath.'

In an unguarded moment, she reached for Pemba and slapped him. 'You do that again and I'll break your legs.' When she left, he overheard the murmurs of a detailed list of instructions to Pemba in the kitchen, and he could make out the words, 'you will be responsible if his light goes off'.

Pemba brought in his food and set it down with force, to register his displeasure. The ex-Minister gave him five rupees, he was appeased. Then Shambhunath arrived with his lock-cutting tools, ready to spead the night in the ex-Minister's house. Immediately, he said, 'Saar. You'll talk to Nima Thendup Saar please.'

The ex-Minister phoned Nima Thendup, who was now reachable. He had been away on a day's trip to Phagcha, and mobile phones did not work there. The ex-Minister narrated the day's events, and described his injury, his bitterness increasing as he saw his position more clearly, until he was sobbing. His sobs provoked Nima Thendup to hysteria. 'I'll come down and fix both of them. Just tell me.'

The ex-Minister, desiring only outrage from his nephew, counselled restraint. He could take care of himself; he was their father, they could not teach him anything. Still, Nima Thendup offered, 'If they do anything, call me first.'

He then brought up Shambhunath. 'The glass carpenter's sad as well. He says that you cheated him.'

'His son cheated him. The next time he comes here, I'll show him how people actually cheat.'

Despite his bluster, Nima Thendup was easily pacified. He agreed to give the carpenter a nominal sum. He also agreed to accompany the ex-Minister to the second day of the conclave. After the phone call, Shambhunath, after displays of gratitude, wanted to leave to look for his son. The ex-Minister said, 'Stay here tonight or no money for you.' He instructed Pemba to lock the main gate from the inside, and kept the key with him.

When Yograj came home, he rang the bell. Pemba told him, 'Key is with the old man.'

Yograj rang the bell again. The ex-Minister emerged from the kitchen and said, 'You lock me in. I'll lock you out.'

His son pleaded with him. 'At least let me take my second kanchnaki. For tomorrow.'

'Wear the one you wore today. We would wear the same one for months when we were young.'

They bickered across the locked gate. Yograj threatened to cut open the lock. The ex-Minister told him that the police had been warned. Yograj's shouts grew louder, but the ex-Minister knew they would not exceed a certain volume, lest he attract attention from the street. The ex-Minister sat serenely in the kitchen with Pemba and the glazier nervously cowering beside him. In the end, Yograj gave up. As he left, the ex-Minister said, in a voice which did not carry, 'I'm coming to the conclave tomorrow. Inform your new parents.'

Half an hour later, he received a call from Pradeep SE, to whose house Yograj had gone. 'What's happening, Appa? Why are you treating your son like an outcaste?'

'You are his coach,' the ex-Minister said, 'you take care of him. And if either of you try to stop me tomorrow, I'll come to the hall with Nima Thendup. He's my son now.'

~

DAY 2

The next morning, the ex-Minister checked the gate. Yograj had not inserted a new lock. The glazier was in the kitchen drinking tea. Immediately, he said, 'Nima Thendup coming, Saar? He'll have my money with him?'

The ex-Minister thought about the birdling who suffered under the weight of its feathers. He said, 'Yes. I've told him.'

Nima Thendup arrived. The glazier offered him a namaste with the urgency of a salute. Nima Thendup's face soured. 'Your face. So early in the morning.'

'What to do, Saar?' Shambhunath began to recount his troubles. Nima Thendup said, 'But I didn't know I would meet you here. I didn't get your money.'

Shambhunath looked tearful, as if he had been swindled. The ex-Minister asked him. 'How much?'

'Seven thousand, Saar.'

'Five,' Nima Thendup said.

The ex-Minister went to his room and emerged with the money. The glazier took it and tried to touch the ex-Minister's feet but he pushed him away. 'I'll call you soon to repair a window. You better come them.'

Shambhunath said, 'Of course Saar. You're like my father,' and left the house.

Nima Thendup said, 'He won't come back.'

'I know,' the ex-Minister said and requested Nima Thendup to help him get dressed.

As Nima Thendup assisted the ex-Minister, he asked, 'Are you sure they have invited you?'

The ex-Minister showed his invitation card. Nima Thendup said, 'Still a big man!'

The entrance to the Sikkim Conference Centre was decorated with banana leaves and poinsettias. Nima Thendup said, 'You'll have to go from here. I'll be in the bazaar. Call me when you want me to come.' The ex-Minister nodded. The first CAS member he met was the Press Secretary. 'You've come?'

The ex-Minister assessed the Press Secretary's surprise. 'Tell all the CAS people and my sons that I'm here. I will not say anything. I just want to be here.'

The Press Secretary paled. 'It wasn't my idea. I said no till the very end. I wanted to bring the card myself, President Saab, but they didn't let me.'

The ex-Minister walked past him and took a seat in the second row. He picked up a copy of the programme schedule from a neighbouring seat. There had been dances on the previous day, performances by actors from Nepal, and a play by tribal activists from Bhopal. There had been a German filmmaker who showed his film on animism amongst the Himalayan tribes, and two short papers had been read out: on 'Upper Caste Hegemony in Cultural Readings' and on 'Subalternatives: New Histories for an Ancient People'. There had been speeches and he was pleased to see that neither TB Chandath nor Mitradas Chandith were amongst the speakers. He scanned the whole programme, the excerpts of papers and the abstracts of talks for mentions of Chandith or Chandanth, silver or sandalwood. There were none.

He observed that the setting was better designed than in other years; the organizer would have had much more money. The stage and the auditorium were excessively decorated with flowers. The lighting seemed to be stronger, the stage was back-dropped by a banner that took up its breadth and height. It said 'Diversity and Unity—A Conclave for the Chandari Speaking Peoples'. The banner showed a girl child and an old man, wearing traditional clothes, her grandparent perhaps, in a soft-focus photograph. The child was wearing a pindhara, a thin gold chain that looped over the base of the ear and culminated in a small pendant. Again, the ex-Minister thought, again they had got it wrong, for the pindhara was worn by girls between puberty and marriage.

The seating had changed. There were four modestly comfortable sofas on the stage on which the Hon'ble Chief Minister, TB Chandath, DB Chandath, Pitu Kej Chandeth and the conclave's chief guest, the Union Minister of State for Tribal Affairs, were seated. On their right was a lectern, lit up by a focused light, and on their left, a portable screen for computer presentations. The effect was bitterly impressive.

He wanted to be approached by the Core Committee but they disappointed him. The Treasurer gave him a friendly wave from a corner, but the Joint Secretary and the new President stared at the stage. He guessed the stories of his efforts to prise the invitation from the Steering Committee would be known by now. He felt no shame. The discomfort of his rivals was recompense enough for the ex-Minister. He looked around for his sons but they could not be seen.

The Press Secretary took a seat beside him. The ex-Minister leaned towards him and said, 'Past is past.'

The first event of the day was also its noisiest. It saw the entry of the

Multiple Award Winner. He had camped overnight at Ranipool, at the base of Gangtok, and had resumed his walk in the morning, with a police escort and flanked by motorbikes. He entered the hall in his running clothes, and concluded his run in the hall, his final step taken in the presence of the Hon'ble Chief Minister. He took her hands to his eyes, bowed to receive a medal from her, and turned around to wave at the gathering.

The ex-Minister found that he was tired and could not pay much attention to the talks and presentations. They were all by people he had never seen or heard of. It pinched him that he knew nothing of them and he was gladdened that his people were being studied seriously by scholars.

One talk in particular stood out. It was called 'Sacred Trees in a Spiritual Landscape' and was presented by Professor Robert Black. He was introduced as a worthy successor to Thomas Burney-Thrale. The ex-Minister remembered him from the time of Pamphaa's possession. The professor spoke in a mixture of English and Nepali and listed all the trees that were worshipped in the Chyalu Valley by the Chandiths, showing individual trees and giving detailed histories. The ex-Minister was gratified to find that four out of the fifteen trees studied were sandalwood.

The ex-Minister leaned towards the Press Secretary. 'Very intelligent man.'

The Press Secretary, eager to compensate, nodded fervently. 'Very sensitive also.'

There were many questions for Professor Black, including one from the Press Secretary, which was lost on many because it was in Chandari. But there was applause from the audience after Robert Black answered in Chandari, in a tone devoid of accent or affectation.

~

When the gathering broke up for lunch, the ex-Minister stayed in his seat. The rest should know that it was not for the food that he had wanted an invitation. He saw his sons exit through the furthest door, Pradeep SE was in close conversation with the Treasurer. It was the

Press Secretary, still anxious to make amends, who brought him some food on a plate. The ex-Minister sent it back. 'I'm here to feed my soul, not my body.'

Professor Robert Black came to greet him. 'I heard you were not well. You should not have come today.'

The ex-Minister said in a deliberately firm voice, 'This is my life, Mr Robert.'

The Professor bowed lightly. The ex-Minster said, 'What you said was good. So four out of fourteen trees are sandalwood.' The Professor said, 'Yes. I knew that part would interest you. You know I've followed your sandalwood theory with interest.'

'It's not a theory. It's the truth,' the ex-Minister said and patted his arm. 'Mr Robert, you should have been born amongst us.'

The Professor acknowledged this compliment and asked, 'So how is the lady? The one who experienced the spirit.'

The ex-Minister composed himself and said, 'Too much spiritual business. I gave her a holiday.'

~

The end of the lunch break was announced. He dozed slightly in the second half. The only talk he heard was by someone he did not know. She was a young woman and her name was Kavita Chandath. She had just completed her PhD on Chandath culture. She gave profuse thanks to TB Chandath, who had nurtured her first steps in Chandath anthropological studies, and to Robert Black, her thesis supervisor. She was working towards a double doctorate, and her next thesis was tentatively titled 'Aspects of Identity amongst the Chandiths in India'.

The ex-Minister was offended that the girl had completed her PhD without once dropping by his place for guidance. He turned to the Press Secretary and said, 'Lot of big English words coming up.' But he also felt a pang of regret and wished Yograj would find someone like her to bring home.

She had a slideshow, the first speaker after Robert Black to do so. She had investigated ways in which aspects of the mother culture had survived amongst the Chandiths in India. She had spent the previous four years travelling amongst the various Chandiths located in Dehradun, West Bengal, Sikkim, Meghalaya, Assam, Manipur and Nagaland, and she had collated data on their similarities and differences. She would not bore the distinguished crowd with all the details, but her final conclusion was that the Chandiths were fundamentally a tribe, and still displayed aspects of tribal cohesion despite having ramified into so many unconnected branches.

She concluded by reciting a prayer in Chandari. Hers was the only speech which did not refer to the Chief Minister.

~

There was a short break for tea. He saw Yograj from a distance, following Kavita Chandath around, eager with his words and gestures. He saw her treat him with respect and then irritation. He saw his son skulk away.

The Multiple Award Winner broke away from a crowd seeking his attention and greeted the ex-Minister. 'So you came, Baraa. You look so weak.' He looked around the hall, 'Who didn't want to let you come? Tell me, I'll fix them.'

The ex-Minister patted his hand and said, 'It doesn't matter.'

He was pleased to be given attention in this way. The Multiple Award Winner was called away. Someone else greeted him during the short break. Mitradas Chandith came, put his eyes on the ex-Minister's hands and said, 'All this would have been nothing without you.'

The ex-Minister patted his hands. 'It'll be my last one.'

Mitradas disagreed. 'The first of many.'

After the tea break there was the vote of thanks and this year too it was delivered by the Hon'ble Chief Minister. The ex-Minister did not find out what she said, for he chose this moment—this too was thought out—to leave the hall. He stood up and started to move with his walking stick. He doddered and the Press Secretary steadied him. Then, in full view of the audience, he walked out slowly, assisted by no one, while the Hon'ble Chief Minister gave her address.

The Multiple Award Winner was seated nearby. He called out to him. 'Baraa, where are you going?'

The ex-Minister drew his breath in and said loudly, in a voice meant to be heard across the rows, 'World tour.'

Outside, it was early evening and the setting sun was nearly infringed by a single large gilt-edged cloud. He asked Nima Thendup to drop him home; his presence had achieved its purpose. His nephew stayed with him for dinner. The ex-Minister gave him a list of detailed procedural instructions if he should die. He then concluded, 'You'll have to finish the temple.'

His nephew covered his eyes with a hand. 'Don't leave me with that headache. You couldn't handle those people, how will I manage? As it is, there is tension upon tension.'

'You're half-Chandanth. The full ones are useless, so we have to rely on the half ones now.'

Nima Thendup uncovered his eyes and sighed. 'Okay, but only for you.' The ex-Minister knew that his nephew would not do it, but he did not protest, for even a cosmetic agreement was assuagement enough.

The exertions of the previous day had tired him. After Nima Thendup left, the ex-Minister made Pemba massage his back with oil heated with fenugreek. The boy's hands were callused and their roughness made him recall Pamphaa's firm yet supple touch. He took his medicines in slightly increased doses. Despite this precaution, he was restless and spent much of the night marking boundaries between the aspirations of his youth and the realities of his achievements. When the awaited blankness came, he seized it gratefully and his sleep outlasted his dreams.

Reconciliation

For a week after the conclave, Yograj and Pradeep SE stayed away from Tibet Road. The phone calls resumed, but the ex-Minister did not take any of them. Then Yograj returned home and found the gate locked. His father appeared at the gate and said, 'Go stay with your step-brother. Learn all you can from him.'

Yograj shook his head. 'Let me take my clothes at least.'

But the ex-Minister had resolved to deny him that comfort. 'Ask your new fathers to buy you new ones.'

Yogita phoned, but the ex-Minister, assuming she was being made to plead for Yograj and Pradeep SE, ignored her. Then Nima Thendup visited, on behalf of all of them, and he could not be denied entry. 'You shouldn't be alone at this age.'

Nima Thendup offered to keep him at Mountain View Resort. The ex-Minister declined. Before leaving, Nima Thendup said, 'They are your children. Talk to them or they will do the same to their children.'

His visit prompted the ex-Minister to make concessions. He phoned Pradeep SE, who received the call eagerly. 'We've been so busy, all of us. Been meaning to come to Tibet Road. For blessings.'

'If my blessings came true, you wouldn't be alive. Tell your brother to take his things from my house or I'll burn them.'

Later in the evening Yograj came, rang the bell, and was let in. He packed his clothes and, under instructions from Pradeep SE, left without confronting his father.

~

His world contracted. It became his room, his bed, the bathroom to which every visit was a struggle and the new window with its view of the window with the broken pane, which the momo-seller no longer opened to greet him. It became the drone of passing vehicles on Tibet Road, the songs and playtime shrieks of the Tiny Geniuses, or the screeches of their tired teachers, of Pemba's battles with the utensils in the kitchen. And it became, increasingly, the world of memories, the succession of wives, the bloodless revolution against the king, his fulfilling term as a minister, and then, at the door of old age, his emergence as the deliverer of his people. His mind took refuge in the past. It could be ordered; its successes magnified, its failures compressed, its distresses resized. The present defied control, and offered only disgrace. It deserved to be shut out.

But he could not do it endlessly. Lurking worries needled him, calling for redressal. Estranged as he was from his children, he feared that his removal from CAS was complete, that there was an unspoken directive to cease all work with him. He waited to be contacted. If the Vice President visited, it would signal reconciliation, and if the Treasurer came, it would mean exile.

It was the Treasurer who came. 'I have no fault in this,' he said, looking at the floor. The General Secretary had invited them for a meeting to her house. There she had made it known that she was to be the new President of CAS, on 'orders from above'.

The ex-Minister said, 'It doesn't matter. I am done with my people, done with CAS, done with all of you. I have my resignation letter all ready. Tell the General Secretary she can become President. You can do what you want with that building. There won't be objections from my side.'

'You have?' The Treasurer exhaled. He had expected a more difficult encounter. And, just to be sure, he asked, 'And you don't want anything?'

The ex-Minister had prepared for this. 'Ten lakh. I know the money is there in CAS's account. I don't care what you do with the rest. I'll build it in my village.'

The Treasurer stared at him, 'A temple with ten lakh rupees! You won't even have enough to excavate the foundation.'

'A shrine. I'll build a shrine. Our gods deserve a shrine at least, no?'

The Treasurer looked hurt. 'We didn't expect this from you.'

'I have no time to fight with you and the rest. If they don't agree, tell them that I'll file police complaints against the whole organization.'

The Treasurer jerked up in his seat. 'Who will you complain about?'

'Anyone I feel like. And I'll say anything in the complaint. That they threatened me not to come to the seminar. That they beat me. That they stole the cups I had offered them tea in.'

'But they didn't do that. No one said anything.'

'Let them prove it,' said the ex-Minister. He then spoke at length. He only wanted to finish the temple before he died. He would hand over his duties, but only after his conditions were met, and if they tried to remove him without his consent, he would go public with his grievances. And then the consequences would not be his responsibility. All of them: his children, his CAS colleagues, his servants, had all chosen for themselves. It was only he who had remained unselfish until now. It was shameful, he knew, what he was asking, but he felt no shame. It was one of the advantages of his age, the extinction of shame.

~

He did not tell his sons what he had done for them. They would find out soon enough. When Yogita phoned, he answered the call. She said quickly, 'What's this I'm hearing? You're asking your own organization for money to quit. Have you gone mad?'

The ex-Minister was curt. 'Don't lecture from Delhi. It's my money. It's my temple.'

She did not question him too closely on his project. On the acquisition of land, on the hassles of material and men. She only saw an occupation for him, something that would keep him busy and help ease his sourness until she returned to Gangtok.

When the Treasurer visited him after four days, he found the ex-Minister calm and unaffected by all that he had caused. 'We had a meeting yesterday,' he said, 'and we can spare eight lakh.'

The ex-Minister agreed. He had expected them to bargain. He made another demand. 'The estimate for CAS House will be prepared by the Technical Secretary and the contract will be given to Yograj.'

The Treasurer scowled. 'That may not be easy. It's Chadat Bhavan now. The site is central, convenient for a good office building, not just for CAS but for all Chadats, for AICPC and for WCC. But we will be in charge of building it, HCM has given her word.'

These were new names. The Treasurer explained. A five-point resolution had been passed at the end of Libhanaya Bhod. He could remember some. The children of Chyalu in Sikkim would have a single name from now on. The name henceforth to be adopted by all Chandaths, Chandiths and Chandanths was Chadat.

An umbrella organization was to be formed: the All India Chadat People's Congress (AICPC), to work towards getting the Centre to Constitutionally recognize the Chadats as a tribe. Its Chairperson was the Hon'ble Chief Minister, its President was TB Chadat and its Vice President was Buddhadas Chadat.

Along with AICPC, another worldwide organization would be formed, a World Chadat Congress (WCC) and Professor Robert Black was to be its first President. An encyclopaedia of all aspects of Chadat animist culture was going to be the first task of the WCC.

'Everybody knows,' the Treasurer said, 'you would have known, if you had not walked out in the middle of the CM's speech.'

The ex-Minister had expected all this. 'You people work it out and then come to me. The land deeds are still with me.'

The Treasurer said, 'I'll take it up with the High Command.' Then he was envious. 'You're fortunate, Daju, you can give it all up. It's not like the old days, Daju. Then we were revolutionaries, and now, now street dogs have to worry less about their food.'

The ex-Minister probed. 'You always had a large heart. Easy to get hurt.'

The Treasurer yielded. 'That's what. The General Secretary—you haven't resigned yet and she's already calling herself President. HCM this, HCM that. She's trying to run the organization like her kitchen. She wants to start preparing for next year.'

'Another conclave.'

'No more conclaves. It'll be a symposium and she wants to be in charge.'

The ex-Minister affected wisdom. 'There must be reasons. But she should respect the senior members.'

The Treasurer's shoulders fell. 'Who's going to tell her that? Even I'm thinking of resting.' He paused and said, 'Something for me also, Daju? I spoke for you, you know, the rest wanted to go to court.'

The ex-Minister stood up unsteadily, the audience had ended. The Treasurer offered his shoulder for support. The ex-Minister held it till the main door and then patted it. 'Of course, Bhai, of course. You above all else.'

~

The ex-Minister's leadership of CAS ended the week before Dasain. He had requested cash but the Treasurer had a cheque sent. The ex-Minister went with Pemba to deposit the cheque and collected the cash a week later. The Treasurer phoned every day—he was worried if the check was valid—until he was informed that the transaction was successful.

He dropped by in the afternoon. He sat in the living room and looked out of the window. 'The rains have gone. The Dasain sun is out.' And then he stuck his tongue out, for mentioning the festival which they were no longer supposed to acknowledge.

The ex-Minister put up a fist. 'In this house, Dasain will be celebrated as long as I'm alive.'

The ex-Minister had an envelope ready. It had thirty thousand rupees in it. The Treasurer accepted it and put the ex-Minister's hand to his eyes. Before he left he said, 'I wanted to bring the papers with me but the Press Secretary insisted on delivering it himself.' He winked. 'I don't know why.'

The next day the Press Secretary came to visit him, bearing a formal document. It was the minutes of the most recent CAS meeting, conducted a week earlier, in which he had been shown to be in attendance. In it, he had offered to resign, and donate the half-built structure and the land to CAS. The Core Committee had accepted. 'Who wrote this?'

'Came from the General Secretary. Must be one of the people in her office.'

'I won't sign it. Not until it says the design and estimate will be made by the Technical Secretary. And that the tender will be given to my son.'

The Press Secretary said, 'The General Secretary is talking about an open tender.'

'I'll open her tender for her. Tell her I want the appointments made.'

The Press Secretary returned the next day with the necessary amendments—a formal order authorizing Pradeep Chadat, the Technical Secretary, to make an estimate and oversee future construction of Chadat Bhavan, and a post-dated order appointing Yograj Chadat as the contractor for the works. He knew their names had been spelled in the new way to mock him. Even in this, he thought, even in this he had lost. He signed the order for his sons, the order that he had wrangled for them, in their new names, names he could not bring himself to speak. These were his final directives as President of CAS.

The Press Secretary had a final set of documents, forms to initiate the transfer of the land's ownership. The ex-Minister signed these. 'So, all well at CAS?'

The Press Secretary dropped his chin to his chest, shook his head and said, 'What to say now, Daju? It hasn't been the same since you left.'

'I heard.'

'She's acting like a queen. Doesn't know about the documents I have with me about the time when she was in the Food Department.'

'Must be explosive,' the ex-Minister said. The Press Secretary, chin still on chest, nodded. 'Exactly.'

An envelope for him too. The Press Secretary received it with both hands and said, 'You were always the one with the biggest heart.'

The ex-Minister acknowledged this. 'To have a big a heart is a problem in its own way. Anyone can hit it.'

The Vice President visited with a letter. It was the ex-Minister's resignation letter as President of CAS, for health reasons. The Vice President was untouched by the recent changes at CAS. 'Then Vice President. Now also Vice President.'

The ex-Minister had an envelope for him too but the Vice President would not take it. 'I didn't come for that.'

The ex-Minister placed his hand on the Vice President's knee and said, 'What about me? Do you think I did wrong?'

A faint disapproval crept into the Vice President's voice. 'You went through a lot. More than any man could bear.'

He did not expect, and he did not receive, any visits from the General Secretary and the Joint Secretary. He phoned TB Chandath and, with grace, congratulated him on his appointments. With equal grace, he accepted, and acknowledged the ex-Minister's service to the larger cause.

He phoned Mitradas who said, 'You really showed everyone that day at the conclave. That is called courage.' The ex-Minister accepted his compliments. Then Mitradas asked, 'About Riwaj, about his son, Dr Kuldeep. He told me Daju…' But Mitradas did not get to complete his statement. The ex-Minister interrupted him, 'So Vice President of all-India organization now.'

Mitradas apologized. 'What could I do, Daju, we have to move with the times.' The ex-Minister resisted a retort. It did not matter anymore. It was his last Dasain and everything in his life seemed to be nearing a resolution. He did not want to begin any new feuds. Claiming urgent work, he ended the call.

~

After he left, the ex-Minister initiated the next step—a reconciliation with his sons. He phoned Pradeep SE first. 'It's done. I've resigned. As for the office, you will make the design and estimate and Yograj will do the contract.'

Pradeep SE had heard, and he had more immediate concerns. 'And the money? They paid the money?'

The ex-Minister mocked, 'You should know. You're the Technical Secretary. Or are they hiding things from you?'

Pradeep SE was defensive. 'Anything is possible.'

The ex-Minister did not mock him further. 'The money has come through. The Treasurer sent the cheque last week.'

Pradeep SE's voice lifted. 'He did?

As the ex-Minister expected, Pradeep SE visited him the same day. He said, 'Welcome Pradeep Chadat.'

His son was instantly pained. 'The name change is not permanent. The HCM said she would do it and then everyone followed her. She planned it all.'

Pradeep SE looked prepared for more rebukes. The ex-Minister gave him an envelope instead. 'Fifty thousand in here for you.'

Pradeep SE could not, despite years of practice, mask his disappointment. 'Only?'

'Later. Stay for dinner and talk with me.'

Pradeep SE needed minimal persuasion. He phoned his Mrs and said, 'I'll be eating outside.' The ex-Minister heard a cackle of rapid invective from Pradeep SE's phone, and then he shouted, 'Where am I going to eat? I am going to eat at my own father's house.' He disconnected the call with a flourish.

The ex-Minister said, 'You're too harsh with her.'

'Women need a firm hand.'

'Get her here next time. I'll talk to her.'

Pradeep SE planned to do no such thing; he knew the only outcome of such a meeting would be a united strategy against him. He said, 'What about Yograj?'

'Send him back. There's something for him too.'

Yograj returned with two bags and went to his room without greeting his father. The ex-Minister, assisted by Pemba, went up to his room.

'Don't unpack your bags. Who knows when you decide to leave again?'

Yograj continued to unpack. After a while, the ex-Minister probed. 'So you all Chadat now?'

'Not me. Too many affidavits to file. But it's only a name.'

'Only a name,' the ex-Minister said. Later he gave him his share and said, 'I've decided. We'll celebrate Dasain this year in our house.'

They had not observed Dasain for a while now. He had tried, after the year's mourning for Sumitra had ended, but it seemed to be an affair without any depth, for it reminded him of his dead wife and his exiled sister. When he had been involved with the woman who was now the President of CAS, she had tried to celebrate it with him, but he had resisted, finding in her attempt a violation of his status as a widower. It was one of the episodes that had contributed to her departure. Then Yogita and Yograj went to cities outside Sikkim for their college degrees, and Yogita had not returned. Pradeep got married and showed up for the first few years, after which he began celebrating Dasain with his wife's family. The last attempt had been five years earlier, when Nima Thendup came, but left angrily after bringing up his mother's exile.

Yograj agreed, it would do them all good. But Pradeep SE was guarded in his response. 'We're not celebrating Dasain from now on. Everyone promised at the conclave. We have to wait for Nehepau Doh.'

The ex-Minister appealed to the bureaucrat in his son. 'Was there a resolution?'

'No. The HCM said it was too controversial for a resolution. Best for everyone to make up his own mind.'

He sensed his son was expecting a rebuke. 'So if it is not in writing, then it is not official.'

Pradeep SE said. 'Point noted.'

'Unless you have to go to Namchi.' The ex-Minister referred to Pradeep SE's Mrs. His habit of visiting his wife's house was contrary to social expectation, and was cited as one of the marks of his Mrs' control over him. But his promotion had made him assertive. 'I'm coming here. If she says anything, I'll take care of it.'

The ex-Minister asked Yogita, who promised to apply for leave from her office, and if they didn't give her leave, she would quit. Either way, she would be home.

Festival

The ex-Minister was wrong about the glazier. Two days before Dasain, Shambhunath reappeared at Tibet Road and startled the ex-Minister with his appearance. He was unshaven, thin, and his clothes were straggly. The ex-Minister looked closely to see if his destitution was calculated. 'Look at you. What do you want?'

'Saar, what do I tell you? Life has been mocking me. Saar,' he yelped, dived at the floor and held the ex-Minister's feet. The ex-Minister shook his feet free. The glazier gripped them again.

It was his son, Badri. After the incident with Agya Nima, he had located and punished his son but he remained unreformed. He had since fallen in with local miscreants. They had taken to petty thievery. They climbed into people's houses at night—it was easy with the buildings stacked so closely together—stole, and fondled sleeping women. They were caught, all the others had family members who knew someone or the other at the police station. Shambhunath alone was an outsider, without influence or familiarity. In the police station, they had slapped him and told him that bail had been set at five thousand rupees.

'Saar, he's my son. Where do I send him, what do I do?'

The ex-Minister could not say how much was true, for Dasain was a time when tradesmen expected a bonus. He went in and emerged with an envelope. 'Two thousand rupees here. How you get the rest is not my problem.'

Shambhunath held the envelope closely. He then dropped a large tear to show that the alleviation of his troubles was beyond monetary soothing. The ex-Minister said, 'Return after Dasain. I need you to fix the momo-seller's window.'

The glazier agreed and left. The ex-Minister's day had not begun frugally. 'Early in the morning and money's already gone.'

He made Pemba call out to Ai Doma from the window of his room. She appeared and said, 'What?'

'The glass carpenter will come after Dasain to repair your window.'

Ai Doma was unconvinced. 'He better come or I'll throw stones at your house. Minister or not, I don't care.'

He followed Pemba around the house throughout the day, supervising everything he did. Everyone he called had agreed to come home for Dasain. Yogita had negotiated her leave. She said, 'This time I want to discuss my future.' Nima Thendup confirmed his attendance. His festivals were months away and even though the hotel was swarming with tourists, he would be there. Pradeep SE promised he would go to Namchi only after the ceremonies at Tibet Road.

Yograj's enthusiasm surprised his father. He shopped for the ceremonies and for the food. He purchased ten kilos of mutton, along with a bowl of goat's blood needed for the primary rituals. He bought other items central to the ceremonies: the vermilion, the pumpkin seeds, and a kilo of red maize. The sandalwood shavings, he got from the store in the lowest floor. The ex-Minister's own enthusiasm was muted. The festivals of the previous years, which he had endured alone, had left him with no memories of convivial gatherings. He scowled when Yograj told him that the alcohol alone had cost twelve thousand rupees. 'Vultures!'

~

In the afternoon, Nima Thendup phoned the ex-Minister; he was being held up by a group of tourists. The ex-Minister was curt. 'Stay in your hotel and make your money. Don't ever call me Appa again.' An hour later, true to the ex-Minister's calculations, Nima Thendup arrived with Thinley Machi, his daughter and the young monk, Karma, who had come to deliver a package from the Head Lama from the monastery at Phagcha and who, with no one to watch over him at Mountain View Resort, had been brought to Tibet Road.

Yogita arrived in a taxi. When Nima Thendup saw her, his first words disappointed her. He said, 'You're in advertising, no?' He then questioned her closely on branding, logos and marketing strategies. He was getting a complete package done for his hotel. She said, 'Let me unpack at least.'

Nima Thendup's excitement soured when Pradeep SE entered with his Mrs and daughters, who were on vacation, and who wore new frocks. It was a loud entry, for his Mrs was conscious that it was her first

Dasain at her Mr's house in many years. Her daughters considered the gathering with frank boredom.

Nima Thendup sought his wife out and tapped her arm. 'Remember him?'

Thinley Machi remembered clearly but was in a benign mood. 'Never mind. Not in your Appa's house.'

Thinley Machi was preoccupied with another matter, something she had come determined to resolve. She tried to seek out Yograj but he was busy in the kitchen, having taken over the cooking from Pemba. He said, 'Machi, we'll talk later. Too busy now.'

Pradeep SE's daughters and Nima Thendup's daughter were left in the living room, where they played warily with each other, aware of the distaste that existed between their parents.

They gathered in the kitchen and the ex-Minister's room, where he stayed in bed, too weak to move, Yogita at the end of the bed, his feet in her lap. When it was time to eat, they assisted him to the dining table, but denied him mutton. They appreciated Yograj's cooking and Yogita promised to take over the next day. The conversation was marred briefly by Nima Thendup. 'So all well with CAS? Not coming much in the newspaper nowadays.'

Pradeep SE covered up any awkwardness. 'More action, less talk.' Before he could reply with a barb of his own, his Mrs, alert for any signs of an altercation, asked Nima Thendup, 'How's the hotel?'

'Resort,' he corrected her. His complaints occupied some time. The guests were not worth calling guests, they swarmed in like flies, the staff was unreliable. Thinley Machi had a few things to say here. 'Even the receptionist! I have a feeling she'll leave soon.'

Nima Thendup picked up from there. 'She's been having fights with her husband. We think she's having an affair. She has been telling friends she'll leave him and go with the other man.'

Thinley Machi turned to her daughter and played with her hair. 'What was she saying?'

Her daughter stood up and, with the solemnity of a school recital, said, 'She said her boyfriend is handsome and kind and speaks English very well. She said her husband is too rowdy and is wanted by West Bengal Police for murder case.'

Yograj stopped chewing. Thinley Machi said, 'What else did she say?'

'She said that her husband had found out about her boyfriend but she had deleted his number from the phone just in time.'

'Interesting,' Yogita said. Thinley Machi's daughter sat down. Yograj stood up, his appetite gone. He was in regular touch with the receptionist from Mountain View Resort. Progress was slow; she had proved difficult for someone who was otherwise feisty. The possibility had not dimmed completely, until now.

For Yogita, this was the homecoming she had always wished for. 'We should do this every year.' Everyone agreed; it was what they had said to each other through the evening. They pestered the ex-Minister until he testily agreed to henceforth observe Dasain every year. 'Unless someone dies.' They scolded him for his pessimism.

After dinner, Nima Thendup and Thinley Machi, and Pradeep SE and his Mrs departed; they would return again in the morning for the tika ceremonies. Yogita lingered on in his room, but the ex-Minister said, 'After tomorrow. We'll talk after tomorrow. You're here for a while, no?' After she left, and when he was sure that everyone was asleep, the ex-Minister walked with difficulty to the kitchen, heated a bowl full of cooked mutton and ate it.

~

Yogita woke up at dawn to initiate the busy day. She found her father in bed with a slight fever. He was insensate, but when she felt inside his quilt, she found that he had not soiled himself. 'How are you feeling?'

'I would have been better if my son-in-law was a doctor,' he said, and raised his eyebrows to show he wasn't serious.

She spoke softly to him, smoothing the stray hairs on his head. A little later, he said, 'So have you decided to get married to that Punjabi?'

He had delayed it for too long, a wait would not change the outcome. Yogita was relieved that the preliminaries, more fearful than the actual exposition, had been avoided. 'He wants to meet you. You'll like him when you meet him.'

The ex-Minister nodded weakly. 'Maybe I will. Call him after Tihar.'

Yogita bit her lip and released it. 'I will return and look after you until you are well again.'

'We'll see. Now it's time for other things.' She offered him food, but he would eat only after the prayers and the ceremony. He had her fetch Yograj, who helped his father put on a kanchnaki and a seytupi. They assisted him to the sacred room on the terrace, its entrance framed by severed banana trunks. As the family's head, the ex-Minister performed the preliminary ceremonies alone, praying for the last time to the gods of his ancestors and those of his childhood. Where he forgot, he improvised. It was enough that he was trying. Kumbura was not a petty god.

By the time the prayers were done, Nima Thendup had arrived, and along with Yograj they carried the ex-Minister downstairs for the tika ceremonies. Pradeep SE and his Mrs fretted in the kitchen; they had to leave for Namchi immediately. Yogita had cleared the living room and laid blankets folded sideways on the floor. They sat in a line, eldest to youngest, with Nima Thendup's daughter in-between Pradeep SE's daughters. She knew money was distributed after the tika and she had sat against her mother's wishes, and with her father's encouragement. The only ones absent from the line were Thinley Machi, who was in the kitchen, and Nima Thendup, who stood at the doorway, commenting on the proceedings. 'All animists from next year, eh! No gods, only trees and mountains.'

Yograj was resolute. 'We won't forget Dasain, no matter what happens.'

Pradeep SE said, 'Two holidays instead of one.'

The ex-Minister fought the impulse to lie down. He began with Pradeep SE: applying the curd, rice and sandalwood paste to his forehead, sprinkling pumpkin seeds on his hair and delivering received wisdom in a voice audible only to himself and his son. At the end of it, he pressed some money into his hands along with poinsettia petals and a maize seed. Pradeep SE put his father's hands to his eyes, then he bent over and applied his eyes to his father's feet, right to left.

After he was done with Pradeep SE and his Mrs, the ex-Minister turned to Nima Thendup and said, 'Come and sit down.' His nephew was unwilling. 'I get your blessings everyday, whether I want to or not.'

As Yograj received the tika from his father, Pradeep SE's Mrs said, 'Next year there will be two of you, no?'

When it was Yogita's turn, she said, 'It's high time for you as well.'

The last one to receive tika from him were his grand-niece and granddaughters. They were vocally disappointed with the money given to them by their grandfather—fifty rupees. The ex-Minister refused to supplement it; to his mind, it was a lot of money. Yograj and Yogita called them aside and added a hundred rupees each, Nima Thendup outdid them by giving five hundred rupees each. Yogita also gave a hundred rupees each to Karma and Pemba.

They ate lunch in batches; Pradeep SE and his family, due to depart for Namchi, ate first and left soon after lunch. The rest ate in a second batch. The ex-Minister felt his fever rise but did not request any help. He asked to lie down after the meal. He heard the conversations from the kitchen. Nima Thendup was instructing Yogita on advertising and marketing, and Yogita was protesting at everything he said. He heard Yograj tell Thinley Machi, 'It was she who kept calling me.' He was aware of Nima Thendup's daughter at his bedside, watching him. He drifted.

~

He heard Ai Doma call out to him from her window and demand that samples from all the dishes be sent to her as well. It was the first time she had reached out after Pemba had broken in through her window, which remained unrepaired. The ex-Minister instructed his grand-niece to carry the message to the kitchen, and have some food delivered to her. 'Send the monk.'

Karma went to the momo-seller's house, a casserole in hand. 'Ay, you're from the house upstairs? You know Pemba?' The monk nodded and she let him in.

The flat seemed to have three rooms and smelt overpoweringly of steamed flour and boiled onions. She showed him into a room that was neither the kitchen nor her room but something intermediate. It had a bed, a cupboard with a mirror on one panel, and two chairs. She motioned him to one of the chairs.

'How old are you?'

'Eighteen. They say I'm eighteen but I don't really know.' He spoke in Sikkimese and Ai Doma, who had almost forgotten the language of her childhood, scrambled to find the adequate words.

'You have a girlfriend? Lots of monks your age have girlfriends.'

Karma shook his head. 'No, Ani.'

A sad panic rose inside Ai Doma when he said this. Just until a few months ago, boys his age were calling her Ai, elder sister, and now they called her Ani, aunt. What had happened in between?

She made tea for him and sat on the other chair. It was the first time the monk had been so close to a woman who was neither his mother nor sister. He pressed his thighs together. She brought a biscuit to his lips but he did not open them to accept it. He finished his tea in large gulps and left.

~

The monk returned to the ex-Minister's house and leaned against the door of his room. He saw the ex-Minister on the bed and Nima Thendup sitting beside him. The ex-Minister said, 'You are the elder brother to them, not Pradeep. He'll sell them if he gets a chance.'

He reached for his nephew's hands. 'And if anything happens to me, remember my instructions. Use the sandalwood in the godown.'

Nima Thendup turned to Karma and asked for some warm water. He said, 'Plenty of time left for talk. You need rest right now.'

The ex-Minister was soon asleep. Nima Thendup told Yogita, 'He's weak. Not serious but quite weak. Call me if anything happens.'

The house emptied of its guests. When Yogita went in to talk to her father, she found him asleep. She phoned friends and made plans for the evening, as did Yograj. Before they left, they exchanged the names of their respective venues, so that mutual avoidance was possible. At night, the ex-Minister dragged himself out of bed and ate a few more pieces of mutton.

~

He was woken up by a body ache so severe that he feared he had miscalculated. He felt himself shrink; the pain seemed simultaneously localized and engulfing. As long as he did not soil himself, he thought, he could withstand the pain. He blacked out near dawn, or it might have been the resumption of sleep, he could not say. Yogita was alarmed when she came to greet her father in the morning and found him with his mouth open, his pillow soaked with saliva. She shook him, he revived and said, 'I'll be all right after my medicines.'

Froth appeared at the edges of his mouth after he took his medicines. In a panic, Yogita woke up Yograj and phoned Dr Kuldeep. He was not celebrating Dasain that year; an uncle had passed away. He came immediately and when the ex-Minister came around, the doctor was checking his pulse.

He felt no joy at seeing the doctor, nothing of his former affection remained. 'You only visit my house when I'm about to die.'

The doctor remained serious. 'Did you eat anything?'

'Nothing, son. Just my normal food.'

Yogita came around the bed and put her hand on his head. The ex-Minister sensed the tension between his daughter and the doctor. He felt responsible and tried to speak to ease the air. But the words stayed trapped inside him. Then the world went black again, and he felt an injection in his vein. He did not know what it was but it gave him strength and they sat him up. He wanted them to make him some promises, on their marriages and the children that they would have, but he restrained himself. It was not noble, he thought, to end his life by binding them to vows.

Before the doctor left, the ex-Minister heard him tell his children, 'He should be fine. If he hasn't improved by tomorrow we'll take him to the hospital.'

She ate her food beside him at night and before sleeping she took his temperature. It was high but not alarming. She made Pemba sleep on the floor beside him, in case he wanted something at night. After she left, the ex-Minister poked Pemba and showed him fifty rupees. 'Get some mutton. It will give me strength. A few pieces.'

Pemba accepted the money and brought him four pieces of mutton, washed of their curry. The ex-Minister calculated that it would raise his fever just enough to give him a few days more to live. He wanted to allocate the money in his bank accounts. He thought about the deeds to the land and the half-finished building. The final transfer documents requiring his signature were yet to come. Let them work it out, he thought, they are the government, they will find a way.

The ex-Minister had misjudged the depths of his body's enervation. He was discovered cold in the morning by Pemba, who informed Ai Doma by shouting into her flat. The momo-seller came and, after inspecting the body, woke up Yogita and Yograj. She then placed a call to Nima Thendup, with whom she had developed an acquaintance. Pemba did not speak of the mutton that the ex-Minister had asked for and consumed, and was relieved that nobody questioned him too closely.

Beside the River

Nima Thendup arrived at Tibet Road unsurprised. He had expected an emergency; it followed from his observations. But he wished it had happened after the season had ended. His hotel was full, and he received the call from the momo-seller as he was arguing with a guest from Bangalore who wanted a discount because the hot water in the bathroom was available only through the tap and not the shower-head. Instead of settling the dispute with his fists, as his instincts recommended, Nima Thendup gave the tourist his discount. 'You don't know how lucky you are.'

He informed Thinley Machi, who told him to leave immediately; she would follow after settling the guests in. At Tibet Road, he found Yogita in the kitchen with stunned eyes, held by the momo-seller, with Dr Kuldeep standing beside her. Yograj wept by his father's body inside; Nima Thendup had a hundred words for him but he held his tongue, it was too late now. Nima Thendup conferred with Dr Kuldeep who told him a post-mortem was unnecessary, everyone knew of the ex-Minister's ailing state.

Nima Thendup had practical words for Yogita. 'There's nobody in the kitchen. Make a shopping list and send the boy out.' It worked, he overheard her giving orders to Pemba. The two hiphops arrived. Their shirts were still loose, their trousers still hung precariously from their hips.

The spatial arrangements followed the precedents set by Pemba's death a year and a half earlier. Nima Thendup and the hiphops laid out the body in the living room, on a white sheet spread on the floor. Nima Thendup posted a hiphop there and took the other one with him to the terrace. This was where the people who came to pay their respects over the next nine days would be fed. The kitchen below would be used only for tea and light snacks. On the terrace he made a mental estimate for a tent—it was October but there were still chances of occasional showers—and phoned a caterer who specialized in mourning houses. He turned to the hiphop beside him and gave him his vehicle's keys. 'Go to the caterer's house in Sichey, next to the District Court. Tell him Nima Thendup sent you. Ask him to hurry up and help him pack the utensils.'

Ai Doma offered to feed the people who had gathered until the caterer completed his set-up. She took Pemba with her, and from her flat began to send in freshly made momos and phalays. As he helped her, she told Pemba, 'See, I told you to look after the old man well. Now Buddha Bhagwaan will give you a bike.' There was a poster of the Buddha meditating under a tree. She made Pemba touch the poster with his forehead.

Pemba prayed intensely for a few moments. Then he asked, 'When will the bike come?'

'Three years. He's asked me to begin saving it for you. So you have to stay with me if you want it.'

~

The same priest who had officiated over Pemba's death arrived with a hajuju, who worked in these circumstances as an understudy. It was the hajuju's job to clean up the corpse while the priest went to the sacred room and recited prayers. Visitors arrived; word was going around the locality. They waited in the kitchen, and their inconsequential claims—when they had last seen him, his last words to them, how it just seemed like a minor fever—made the house less morose.

The hajuju finished his work in the living room and opened it up to the mourners. They went in and saw the ex-Minister with cotton in his nostrils, his corpse wrapped in a white sheet which had leaves pinned to it. There was a cluster of lit incense on either side, with three maize seeds beside each cluster.

Nima Thendup took the largest photograph of the ex-Minister from the trophy cabinet. It was just after he had met the Vice President of India. He stood against a draped background, in a kanchnaki and a seytupi, holding a framed copy of his certificate. It was an appropriate choice. He placed it near the hajuju, who corrected his slouch.

The momo-seller came in to check. She saw the visitors and grunted, regretting her earlier commitment to provide for everyone. She was relieved by Thinley Machi, who arrived with her daughter and took over the kitchen.

~

There was a brief commotion when Pradeep SE came in with his Mrs. He had been in Namchi, four hours away, when he had heard, and had left immediately. He rushed into the sitting room, wailed loudly, and caught the corpse's feet. 'I want a few moments alone with him.'

They moved outside and shut the door behind them. A little later, Pradeep SE emerged from the living room in sunglasses—he did not want to exhibit his grief. He then peeked into different rooms and embraced anyone who was crying. His first beneficiary was Pemba, who had acquired a special status because he was the last person to see the ex-Minister alive. He saw Yograj hunched over the dining table, sobbing. Yograj accepted his hugs; he had not known that his father was so weak, he had seen him only through his own vitality.

He found Yogita discussing purchases with Nima Thendup in the ex-Minister's room. She resisted his embrace. He tried again. She bit his forearm and said in a low voice, 'Murderer.' Nima Thendup held her head in his hands and said, 'No one did anything like that. He was ill for a long time but he asked me not to tell you because you would worry. And there'll be people coming, so you'll have to handle the kitchen with Machi.' Pradeep SE removed his sunglasses, wiped his tears, and put them on again.

Elsewhere in the house, there was a steady bustle. Feet shuffled in the passages; people ordered each other around; a large plastic-wrapped appliance was carried to the terrace, it scraped the floor and men called out adjustments; doors opened and closed; there was a clang from the kitchen and a raised voice carried through.

The house stilled, then the caterer arrived in the early afternoon, and the noise revived. With the hiphops' help, he set up his kitchen in the terrace. A canvas marquee was rigged, chairs were arranged beneath it. The priest, distracted from his unsupervised recitations in the sacred room, came out wearing a garland of poinsettias and conversed with the caterer.

Then the caterer and his assistant prepared a list of supplies they would need. Nima Thendup sent a hiphop to the market with some money. Downstairs, the room with the new window was converted into an additional seating area. The priest announced that the funeral could be held the following day.

~

Some members of the Core Committee—the Treasurer, the Joint Secretary and the Press Secretary—arrived and space was made for them in the living room. The Treasurer stood up. 'Just last week I met him and he said, you know what he said.' The others did not know. 'He said, our work will never finish.' With this he broke down and had to be comforted by Pradeep SE's Mrs, who had come to deliver tea. He embraced her and she held his head as he sobbed. Then Yogita entered, and the Treasurer abandoned Pradeep SE's Mrs and walked towards Yogita with open arms. 'My daughter!' She turned around and walked back to the kitchen. The Treasurer's arms fell.

The Press Secretary counselled a muting of their grief. 'A man who has died in such a fortunate manner should not be mourned like this.' The ex-Minister's good fortune in dying in his sleep would often be cited over the period of mourning.

They became reflective. Pradeep SE entered; his sunglasses lent his grief sophistication. The Press Secretary said, 'You're handling it very well. True head of the family.' They all agreed. The former General

Secretary and new President of CAS arrived and dabbed a handkerchief inside her spectacles. She didn't fool anyone, and the Press Secretary, in pointed fealty, referred to the ex-Minister as the President. She outflanked them by referring to him in the same way.

The Vice President arrived and his grief was loud. 'I should have gone instead of him.' The Core Committee ignored him. The Joint Secretary said, 'Another controversy, Vice President Saab.'

They referred to an article which had appeared in *Sikkim Everyday* the previous day, authored by the Vice President, in which he had called upon the Chief Minister to ban chicken and eggs, for they offended the sensibilities of the 'most important people in Sikkim'.

The Joint Secretary said, 'We cannot ask such things. You know how the others will protest.'

The Press Secretary said, 'If we ban all the meats sacred to everyone in Sikkim, we'll run out of vegetables.'

The Vice President looked with tear-filled eyes at the ex-Minister's garlanded photograph. 'If he had been alive, he would have understood me.'

The President admonished them. 'Not here. This is not the time.' Then Pradeep SE's entry halted further talk. He removed his sunglasses, displaying his red eyes, and greeted the President who said, 'It's all in your hands, SE Saab. You are the head of the family.' He put his sunglasses back on, walked up to the corpse and wiped away a blemish on its cheek. He blew his nose into a handkerchief and his sunglasses wobbled.

~

At night, the pick-up truck arrived, carrying three labourers. It was the same one from Pemba's funeral and the driver's cough had not improved. He parked it close to the building. Nima Thendup opened the room in the lowest floor and had the labourers take out the wood and load it on to the truck. The labourers were suspicious. 'Smells like sandalwood.'

Nima Thendup reassured them. 'It's scented. New technology, can make sandalwood out of any wood.'

One of them was the group's wit. 'My father had technology like that. If he pissed on iron, it became gold.'

Nima Thendup pulled the labourer towards him and slapped his scalp. 'Joke after you get your money, on your own time. This is for a great man who has just died.'

The labourers giggled and loaded the twenty-seven beams of wood. Nima Thendup boarded the truck and went to Ranipool in it. There he met the caretaker of the cremation ground and gave him five hundred rupees. 'Mix this with the other wood. It's scented. The old man's last wish. And make sure all of it goes, I'll count in the morning.' The caretaker agreed without surprise or protests. Nima Thendup returned to Tibet Road for the night. There were rumours that the Hon'ble Chief Minister would attend the funeral, and it made the preparations for the funeral more elaborate. Nima Thendup had to mollify Thinley Machi, who had taken charge of the snacks at the cremation ground, and who did not appreciate this development.

~

The funeral procession left early next morning. There were many vehicles and the cortege took some time to negotiate its way out of Tibet Road. As was consistent with custom, no one was left behind, in order to give the spirit of the departed a last run of the house. Yogita and Ai Doma went with Nima Thendup, and Yograj and Pemba followed in Pradeep SE's car. His Mrs went home for she had been afraid of funerals since childhood. Dr Kuldeep took the priest and the hajuju in his car. The Core Committee and other mourners followed them. The traffic policeman at Amdo Golai saluted when the pick-up truck, draped with khadas, drove past.

At the cremation ground, they found members from CHAPS waiting for the cortege. Mitradas Chadat and TB Chadat both wore sunglasses and took turns to pat Pradeep SE on his back. Beside the river the preparations went on, with the hajuju dabbing the body with sandalwood paste and the priest chanting his prayers beside him. Yogita and Yograj sat in the concrete pavilion where they were comforted by strangers. A little further off, Nima Thendup, also wearing sunglasses, spoke on the phone while Thinley Machi awaited the arrival of the Chief Minister so that she could begin to distribute the food packets.

Hills rose up around the narrow valley in which the cremation ground was located. They were still green after the recent season of rain. They were dotted with buildings in settlements linked by roads. A road led to Pakyong further to the east; across the river, another road skirted the hill's base. It was busy with constant traffic, and it led to Siliguri, the mouth of mainland India. And interspersed in no particular pattern, houses and small clusters dotted the hills, half hidden by the green cover.

More people arrived. There were seven vehicles of relatives from Suikeybung, and except for the nephew with the birthmark, none of them had spoken to the ex-Minister since his defeat in the elections of 1992. There were Yograj's friends, and some of Nima Thendup's immediate family. Pradeep SE was responsible for a majority of the crowd. Almost the entire Gangtok office of the Urban Infrastructure Department was in attendance. A large contingent also represented the Department of Village Roads. The public servants were restrained but their surprised cheer at being granted a holiday could not be suppressed completely—a constant murmur, and an occasional laugh, escaped from these groups.

Heera Babuni was dressed in black trousers and a black silken top. She had covered her head with a black scarf. She had heard the news the day before from the pony-tailed peon. Her heart swelled again for Pradeep SE. She turned to the pony-tailed peon. 'The SE has no one left now.'

Heera Babuni had also phoned Sarata Babuni the previous day. She had cried on hearing the news but had phoned again in the evening. 'Don't mind, Didi, I can't go tomorrow. Two fathers lost in a year.' Heera Babuni commiserated and Sarata Babuni explained further. 'And if I go, they'll all look at me with sharp eyes. I can't bear that.' Heera Babuni had congratulated Sarata Babuni on her maturity.

Julie Babuni declined. She was with child; it would be inauspicious to attend a funeral in her state. And there was another reason. 'My Mr is very possessive.'

Heera Babuni had also phoned Sumati AE but was unsurprised when her call was neither acknowledged nor returned.

Interspersed in the crowd were former politicians, some as old as the ex-Minister, and a few older. There were some members from other community organizations; it was a fraternity of a kind, whose members were bound together by ambition, noble uncertainties and, occasionally, the possibility of lucre. They alone understood each other's hopes and constraints, and the ex-Minister was amongst the first of their kind. He had shown that there was life after defeat in politics, and that a living could be made pursuing the best interests of one's ancestry.

They checked the day's edition of *Sikkim Everyday* and found that it did not carry an obituary of the ex-Minister. They chatted amongst themselves, mostly about the ex-Minister and his fortunate death, for a cremation ground was no place to conduct politics. They had all heard that the Hon'ble Chief Minister would visit. It was countered by another rumour, the Hon'ble Chief Minister was not going to come because of the controversy generated by the Vice President's statement on chicken and eggs. They also noted the scent of sandalwood in the air, and this too was counted as one of the reasons why the Hon'ble Chief Minister would stay away.

Occasionally, some of the more distant mourners strayed to the pavilion, where the sadness was concentrated. There, Yogita, Dr Kuldeep, Pemba, Ai Doma and Yograj sat in a circle and anyone who approached them did so with an appropriately mournful expression, offering hugs and words of comfort.

A siren wailed, which they recognized as the Hon'ble Chief Minister's pilot car. The mourners waited for the flurry of security personnel who accompanied her but the entry to the cremation ground remained undisturbed. Then the siren echoed through the valley again, and they saw the Hon'ble Chief Minister's cavalcade on the opposing hill, travelling swiftly on the road that led to Siliguri, flicking in and out of the foliage left by the recently departed monsoon. At the same time, a van entered the compound. Its sole passenger was the Multiple Award Winner and he, too, wore sunglasses. It was the first time anyone had seen him in a vehicle.

Thinley Machi looked at the distant line of vehicles and held her tongue for she was on sacred ground. She called the hiphops in and instructed them to begin distributing the food packets. 'Start with the men, not with the girls.'

~

Yograj and Pradeep SE were called by the priest for the final ceremonies. The body was laid out beside the river. The pyre stood a few feet away and it looked unusual, with planed sandalwood beams stacked along with rough-cut wood.

A little while later, Pradeep SE, Yograj, Nima Thendup and the hiphops lifted the corpse and put it atop the pyre. Pradeep SE lit it. The flames crackled and the smell of sandalwood spread. Nima Thendup was the last person to remain convinced that it was ordinary timber which had been scented. His conviction was dispelled only after Pradeep SE took a small piece off the pyre and put it to his nose.

Pradeep SE panicked. He caught Nima Thendup's sleeve. 'It is illegal.'

Nima Thendup shrugged. 'Let them catch the culprit. He should be reincarnating soon.' He caught Pradeep SE's arm and drew him close. 'If anyone asks, say it is scented wood. And you would have been in bigger trouble if it had remained in the godown.'

Pradeep SE, still alarmed, looked around but the scent, mixed with the scents of butter, flowers and burning wood, blended and affected no one. As the flames gathered strength, the smell of concentrated acridity grew more intense and people close to the pyre, overcome by nausea, moved further back.

The few politicians and members of various organizations, disappointed by the Chief Minister's absence, waited until the flame caught the corpse's shroud and left. The Core Committee stayed for a little longer along with Mitradas Chadat and TB Chadat. They took turns comforting the children, and the Treasurer was disappointed when Yogita said sharply, 'Comfort but don't touch. Please.'

Yograj saw Heera Babuni come up to him. 'At moments like these, you think nothing matters very much.' She moved to give Yograj a hug and, when she had her arms around him, Yograj pressed against her and squeezed her left breast. He let his hand linger. He waited for a reaction and when he heard an intake of breath, he squeezed it again. She shuddered and disengaged from the embrace.

The officers and clerks from the Department of Village Roads began to leave. The pony-tailed peon was heard asking the babunis if they wanted a ride with him. Before she left, Heera Babuni stood close to Pradeep SE and said, 'You should not let this affect your work. I'm there if you need me. Just like how you were there for me.' Then she stopped by the pavilion again to bid Yograj goodbye. She said, 'You will get very lonely now. I will call you for dinner and you must not refuse me then.'

The sickly sweet smell from the pyre spread to the neighbouring settlements, it would later be remembered as a pleasant one. The remaining people left after they heard the corpse's cranium burst. Yogita was led away by Dr Kuldeep, Yograj and Thinley Machi left with Pradeep SE. Nima Thendup and the hiphops stayed behind. When the corpse was nearly burnt through, there was a sudden shower, a remnant of the rainy season, and it extinguished the pyre. The shower passed; the caretaker moved to relight the pyre but Nima Thendup stopped him. He paid the caretaker and left with the hiphops, the hajuju and the priest. After their departure, the caretaker picked through the sizzling embers for the ashes that would be collected the following day to be scattered in the forest. He picked the unburned pieces of sandalwood from the remnants and kept them aside carefully.

AUTHOR'S NOTE

The names of characters in this novel were chosen at random. It is likely that there will be people, including those in the employment of the Government of Sikkim, who may bear the same names. I assure them that any such sameness is a coincidence. Similarly, the politicians and leaders depicted in the book do not reference real people.

This novel emerged from six short stories which were published in *Talk Sikkim* between 2008 and 2010. I am grateful to its editor, Mita Zulca, for the opportunity and wish the magazine, necessary to Sikkim, the long life it deserves.

I thank Tashi Chopel and Prajwal Parajuly for commenting on an early draft, and Hilda Peacock, Ravi Singh and Anurag Basnet for their close readings and precise suggestions.